AFFINITY FOR PAIN

R. E. JOHNSON

Author's Note: All characters in the book are 18 years or older, and this work is intended for mature audiences.
For a full list of triggers, please see:
rejohnsonbooks.com/trigger-warnings

ACKNOWLEDGMENTS

This book may have come from my imagination, but it exists because of so many others. I wouldn't have pursued writing as a career if it weren't for my fifth grade teacher, Sue Topping. Her guidance and love of words, even those written by an eleven-year-old, solidified my obsession with creating worlds through stories.

My parents have always been book lovers, particularly fantasy, and that love seemed to be genetic in my case. I've certainly got the gene.

To my first editor, Gram. She was always there to look at my early scribblings and correct my terrible spelling. I know somewhere she's thrilled that I've finally published something.

To my incredible beta readers, especially you Grey, your words and appreciation for Hope and Ciaran kept me going when I wanted to give up. Allison and Rachel in particular, my best friends, you listened to me rant about the characters so much and never complained.

To the professionals who helped me whip this book into shape and ensure it was ready to be seen by the world.

To my wonderful family who supported my dream every step of the way.

And especially to Ryan. You've been my rubber duck, my anchor, and my support system. For every late night brainstorming session and hours-long conversation about plotting and pacing, I thank you. For standing behind me as I take this leap into publishing, I thank you. For never giving up on me or my story, I thank you. For everything you do, I thank you from the bottom of my heart.

PLAYLIST

Listen along as you read. The songs are presented in chronological order. If you have a favorite, be sure the let me know.

1. My Name is Human- Highly Suspect
2. Revolution Begins- Arch Enemy
3. Blood in the Cut- K.Flay
4. Assassin- Au/Ra
5. Hold Me Down- Halsey
6. Nightmare- Halsey
7. Wicked Game- Lydia Ainsworth
8. The Promise- In This Moment
9. Keep It Simple- Tove Lo
10. Straight Shooter- Skylar Grey
11. Issues- Julia Michaels
12. Close- Nick Jonas (feat. Tove Lo)
13. Little Do You Know- Alex & Sierra
14. Like Real People Do- Hozier
15. Jambi- TOOL
16. Tempt My Trouble- Bishop Briggs
17. Love Is Gone (Acoustic)- SLANDER
18. I Want You- Elvis Costello
19. The Great Below- Nine Inch Nails
20. Open Your Eyes- Snow Patrol
21. Hurt- Nine Inch Nails
22. Say Something- A Great Big World
23. Lay Your Gun Down- In This Moment
24. Don't Give Up- Peter Gabriel
25. A Warm Place- Nine Inch Nails
26. Everything Changes- Sara Bareilles
27. Forever- In This Moment

ONE

"And now I'm late. Ugh. This guy better die quick."

Hope secured her Beretta back inside her jacket, but her arm dripped with blood thanks to the brief detour from her evening's plans. *Really? Of all the nights to get randomly mugged. I have shit to do.* She wiped off the blood and shook her head. This was her favorite jacket. Why did muggers insist on interrupting her? Sure, they couldn't tell she was a demon by looking at her, but they learned real quick. Not flinching when she got shot tended to do that.

As she climbed the textile mill's escape ladder, her heart thumped in her chest, hard and quick. *Wait. This is new.* Hope looked down at her arm. Nope, no change. Still bleeding a bit, but that was it. This other sensation in her chest was completely alien. Her palms were slippery, her breath short; her skin was tight.

The hundreds of other hits had been easy and utterly unmemorable. How did she suddenly feel like her chest was going to explode? How did she feel at all? Perma-numb was her every day. What the hell was this?

On the roof, Hope pressed her back against the brick wall. *Seriously, you need to focus. Snap out of it.*

She could hear dripping from a pipe at the end of the alley, and the streetlamp at the corner flickered and buzzed.

"Nope."

She reached into another pocket and pulled out a small dart gun. Hope fired a small probe at the lamp post. It blinked for a moment and fell to the ground. The light flicked off. One less distraction.

She sunk to her knees and lay on her stomach. She reached out and found the large, thin case she'd placed there the night before. She pressed her thumb to the fingerprint scanner to open things up and smiled down at her favorite toy. Switching on the sight for the Savage 110 BA rifle, Hope coiled her hand around the custom grip. The thing was a work of art and cost just as much. She had to hunt it down during a trip to an arms dealer in NYC. As Hope peered inside the scope, she lined up her target and adjusted the focus.

Hope was just able to see in the dark alley, but she needed audio. Good thing she always packed a headset. With it in place, she could hear inside the mark's small office.

Hope glanced around, checking that her gear was ready. Gods, why did she take a job in this shitty part of town? She double-checked the file marked "O'Connor, Ciaran Patrick" for a refreshed visual on the target. The room was free of witnesses, and she was seconds from a go. One issue, however. The mark was sitting, feet up on his desk, reading an old book, and the dumb old thing blocked a view of his face.

She couldn't fire until she could confirm his identity. Body shape and hair said yes, but Hope was nothing if not a professional. As he turned a page, the one behind it tumbled to the floor. Hope could hear him mumbling something, and normally she couldn't care less, but that voice. It echoed in her headset and brain like a shot of whiskey.

Her finger tightened near the trigger, and she swallowed hard.

"Hope, focus, please."

She glanced at the black-and-white photo. Whoever took this must have been fighting the shakes. Hope readjusted her gaze as he sat back up.

She still heard his voice in her head. It was eating at her like she was some rookie. The air smelled different, and her ears weren't working right, all ringing and muffled sound.

She shook her head and caught a glimpse of the Celtic sword tattoo on the mark's shoulder. It snuck out from under his Hanes tee. *Makes sense, he is Irish.* As he returned to his original position, he lowered his book to the desk. *Finally, a clear shot of his face.* His eyes were dark and distracting. And that goatee in person was more appealing. He was really . . . beautiful.

"Picture doesn't do you justice," Hope said, surprised. She stared into his eyes, and her grip on the rifle loosened. She couldn't look away, barely blinked. A pounding in her chest finally got her attention. She looked down and put a hand over her heart. She could feel the thumping inside her ribcage. *Omaeriku? Ciaran? Oh, gods no. This can't be happening.*

Panic rang in Hope's head. She heard her heart thump and the loud cracking of her ribs, or was that something else? Everything was all spinning and strobe lights. With one final surge, her heartbeat slowed.

Hope looked around. The cracking she'd heard was, in fact, her rifle tipping off the bipod. It was hanging precariously on the ledge, and Hope groped for the stock of the gun.

Across the alley, Ciaran stood up as a voice in the other room called him. Distracted by the noise, Hope watched as he hit his knee on the underside of his desk.

"Son of a bitch," Ciaran's voice was like a knife in her headset.

Hope hugged her knee close to her chest as she watched Ciaran rub his. Her knee was suddenly hot and loud and sharp. She collapsed from surprise, bumping her rifle, yet again. Hope strained to reach it, but still in the grips of *omaeriku*, she missed the stock, and it launched off the edge of the roof. As the rifle fell, it landed with a shattering crash in a metal dumpster. *Dammit.*

Of course the sound was loud enough to draw Ciaran to his window, and he scanned the street.

"What the hell was that?" Ciaran yelled. When he couldn't see the source on the ground, he looked across at the textile mill. He looked right at her.

Hope ran across the roof and out the gray door, her rifle case bouncing on her leg as she dashed down the stairs.

"Fuck, fuck, fuck! This is so not good! Fuck!" Hope grabbed the door frame and swung herself around the side, "Why? Why now? After all this time, all the work? Ugh!" She ran down to the alley, sticking close to the wall. Thank Maker her black clothes blended into the darkness, this escape was just a bit messier than she'd planned.

The street smelled of urine and decaying food, and Hope tried to take shallow breaths to avoid retching. She whipped off the headset, desperately worked to untangle it from her hair, and threw it into her bag.

She bent over, scanning the ground for her rifle. After finding the most expensive piece of weaponry she had in a puddle, she cursed and put it back inside the safety of its case. *Omaeriku, omae-fucking-riku. I can't believe this.*

It was too late. The bond had formed. Nothing except death would break the connection, and death she was good at. She just had to hit her mark before the bond had a chance to fully develop, and problem solved. But how? She couldn't just barge in, guns blazing.

How could this be happening? One look and I'm fucked? That's total bullshit. I don't even believe in this crap, and here I am fighting against it. And it had to be my fucking mark?! I . . . really? I mean I do spend all my time at work, so, of course, I'd find my "one and only" on the job. Well, fuck this! Fuck all of this. I'm getting my hit.

Hope kicked the wall behind her and looked down at her case, now parked under the ledge of the building where it was dry. She reached inside and pulled out the profile folder. Ciaran's life spilled open.

```
Subject: Ciaran Patrick O'Connor. Born: October
18, 1984. Location: Newborn City,
NY. Summary: O'Connor relocated to NBC from NYC.
Underground fighter for NYC's
Inferno Club. O'Connor is aggressive, strong,
well-trained, and well-funded.
```

"Oh yeah, that's why I wanted to shoot him from a distance. Damn it." She put the file back in her case and stared down at the ground. Direct approach was a no since this location was totally blown, and his house was a fucking fortress, which left her with . . .

"Seduction. Maker, I hope I can act." Hope scoffed. It was always weird using her name in a sentence. *Yeah. I get the joke, Mom. Hope in one and shit in the other. Ha.*

Hope grabbed the case and walked the three blocks to her car.

The 1969 Aston Martin DBS was a thing of beauty, and on a night like tonight, the luxury was extra appreciated. Though it was less than subtle, especially painted fire engine red, the car was her special way of saying 'fuck you' to her old life.

She placed the case gently in the back seat and patted it softly, "Sorry for dropping ya. Fucking genes, you know?" She turned around in her chair and started the ignition. The engine purred for her, and she took off, grateful for the speed.

"Like lightning" hardly described how fast Hope sped away. She was running on autopilot and flew down to the turn for CR-33 without really thinking about it. The trip home took around an hour and a half on a normal day, but today Hope made it in fifty-five minutes.

She never ran into cops either, thanks to the scanner, and knew the trip like the back of her handgun. She was smack dab in the middle of Seventy-sixth and Bradley Creek Road. There wasn't a soul for miles. Before the Dawning, there had been farms and families, but the increased demon population had taken care of that. It was perfect.

The house wasn't a mansion, by any means, but it was off the beaten path and served its purpose. The small cottage looked unimpressive from the outside and did well hiding the high-tech gadgetry inside. Most passersby would think some old lady and her cats lived there, not a well-funded assassin.

Hope pulled the car into her garage and ran her hand across the underside of the driver's seat. Pressing the hidden button to deactivate the security system, the garage door slowly opened. She bounced her leg as she waited.

Inside the structure, Hope watched in her rear-view as the door lowered, and she didn't get out until it finished. She pressed the security button under again and heard the reassuring chirp of the alarm coming back online. Before going inside, Hope hooked the garage door to a ring bolted to the floor. Not accepting visitors, no soliciting.

With her fingers curled around the house's doorknob, Hope paused, waiting for the fingerprint recognition to realize it was her. The door finally unlocked, and with a sigh, she stepped inside.

The space was large, the massive kitchen giving way to a vast expanse of hardwood floors in an open plan that truly shunned the idea of walls. There was a couch in the living area and a couple of chairs. They were all low-slung and leather.

A glass coffee table sat in the center with only the remote to her colossal TV on it. In the corner, a tall, wooden bar sat expectantly. Hope walked over and pulled out a glass, plus her favorite whiskey, Glen Garioch. She poured a couple of fingers and swung it back. As the glass clinked against her lip rings, the chestnut liquid caressed her throat. She could taste smoke and chocolate.

"Ahh." Hope set her glass on the coffee table and plopped down onto the couch, kicking off her boots and resting them on the table. After a second, Hope realized she could hear her breath move in and out of her lungs.

"Well, that's enough of that," Hope said as she reached for the remote. "Come on, clicker. Find me something good." The news flashed on the screen.

"Next, next, next, oh god next." Hope flipped through CNN, sports, some sitcom, and a televangelist. "Crap, crap, and more crap. So much for TV." Hope switched off the giant let down and padded to her bedroom.

She waited another long five seconds as the second security knob read her prints. She flipped on the lights and closed the door. Hope stood just inside the door for a moment and waited for the sound of the knob relocking. As the click-click sounded, she walked over to her bed.

Empty, Hope put her whiskey glass on the nightstand. As she reached her hands up to take off her jacket, the leather pulled as it broke free from Hope's dried blood. She'd forgotten all about the bullet graze. It was probably a good idea to take a shower. She slid her jacket off the rest of the way and tossed it on the bed; the fabric barely stood out from the black satin sheets. As she took off her tank top, her skin glowed in the soft lamplight.

As with everything in her life, the room was purposeful, and yet, it was the one place she let a little of her personality shine. The silky sheets, deep red walls, hardwood flooring gently softened by a Chinese rug—all so warm and decadent. But the room was also triple-bolted, protected by a dual alarm system, and held a small panic chamber in the closet.

Hope shrugged out of her tight pants and let them fall. She pushed off her socks and stepped out of the pile she'd created. Her fingers must've been cold because she could see the tips were red. Hope briefly wondered what goosebumps felt like but dismissed the thought. She slipped her bra off and tossed the garment aside. As she slid her panties off, her back cracked loudly, and she was even more excited for the shower.

Hope stared down at her body and took note of the lack of scarring. After all the scrapes, bullet wounds, and broken bones, she still looked pristine, unchanged, minus the piercings and tattoos, of course. The metal all over her shone in the lamplight. It created a constellation of her form, a glint alighting on each shoulder, all over her face, the tips of her breasts, the center of her stomach, and on each hip.

The master bathroom was enormous with a stand-alone shower and a massive Jacuzzi tub, his and hers sinks, even though there was just her, and beautiful tile work everywhere. The floor was unchanging under her feet, thanks to the heated coils, and the air was sort of warm. The thermostat read eighty-seven degrees Fahrenheit, but it was nothing to her. Hope stepped in through the glass door of her shower.

The black marble and stainless-steel fixtures gleamed in the overhead light. As Hope pushed the square button in the center, the shower program was initiated, and hot water burst through eight different spouts in the wall.

After only a few seconds, Hope could see that the heat was raising her blood pressure enough to make her wound bleed again. As she cursed softly to herself, she stepped to the corner out of the warm spray. She knew she had to get any shrapnel out now before the wound started closing. *Shot? Omaeriku? Can't really decide which is worse. Oh, wait, yes, I can. Omaeriku hands down. If this Maker-forbidden bond fully forms, I'll feel this shit.*

Hope pushed her fingers deep inside the wound. She could sort of feel the pressure but nothing else. So, no, there wasn't any pain. What plagued her was the sensation she got on the roof. That strange, sharp feeling in her knee. The change in texture inside the wound brought her back to what she was doing. She pinched the hard fragment in between her fingers and pulled it out.

It was so small, but left in her arm, it would continue to cause damage, creating horrible scar tissue that could hinder her movements. No fucking doubt, that baby was definitely powerful. She had learned that lesson before.

Hope stepped back into the hot water. She rinsed off the wound and began to sense her accelerated healing like a hum of energy. Once she was thoroughly rinsed, she pressed the square button again, and the water switched to a handheld sprayer. Hope took the nozzle and ran the stream all across her skin. She watched the hot beads run down her body, falling from her shoulders, across her butt and thighs, around her legs.

She could sort of feel the extreme heat, but the path of each droplet was lost on her. Often, she'd get dressed before she was completely dry because she couldn't tell if she was wet, or she'd drop a freshly opened beer because she couldn't feel the condensation. That one was a bitch.

And Hope wasn't an idiot. She watched the world, and she knew what she was missing. The sensation of a hair tickling your back, of a breeze, of someone's fingers. She couldn't feel any of it. Extremes were a little easier, but never complete. Boiling water felt barely warm, freezing cold felt maybe cool, excruciating pressure felt like something must be touching her, and that one, she almost . . . liked.

Hope angled the nozzle at herself, sprayed her breasts, hips, and then she let her arm relax and the warm water went between her legs. She could sort of feel something and could almost discern it as pleasurable, but as soon as the sensation was there, it was gone. Hope sighed and hung the sprayer back up. She pressed the square button twice, and the water turned off.

Walking to the sink, Hope opened the cupboard and pulled out a medical kit. She patched up her arm quickly enough, sticking a large bandage over the wound. It was already closing up.

Hope examined herself in the mirror. The wound was covered nicely, and all the blood washed clean. She didn't look that bad. Sure, she'd towel dried her hair so that she looked like a mad scientist and the white streak in the front looked especially funny against the brown like that, but otherwise not terrible.

As she turned to leave, Hope caught a glimpse of red on her shoulder. Had she missed some blood? She angled her back toward the mirror. Nope, not blood. She'd burned herself, again. *Whatever. It'll heal.*

Flopping down on the bed, she stretched out, trying to get her body to relax. Hope barely slept, usually only a few hours a night, and that was when she wasn't dealing with a biological fly in her craw. She kept running the seduction plan through her head. If she was going to pull it off, she needed to rest. She needed to look rested, at least. Getting into Ciaran's office was going to be a challenge, and if she looked like a sleep-deprived junkie, making him comfortable with her was a no-go. *Ugh, enough already. Just sleep.*

Hope closed her eyes and tried to stop the endless checklist in her head. As time dragged on, she was left with one lingering thought. What would being touched feel like?

She dragged her fingers across her skin, pushing hard on her flesh. Hope could imagine the pressure. Her nerves guessed at what must be there. She pulled back, pushing lightly. The faintest echo of sensation skittered across her skin. She let her fingers drift across the bare flesh at her core, silently begging to feel something, anything. She wanted that thing humans and demons talked about.

As her fingers brushed the soft skin, Hope's brain kicked up a haunting image. The bright blackness of Ciaran's eyes. As she saw his stare, a tiny jolt of electricity rippled under Hope's fingers, right at the very core of her.

Hope shot up in her bed, sweating and gasping.

"Oh, fuck no! I'm not letting myself be manipulated by fucking omaeriku. . . . Shen-fucking-dara! No! No. It's so not worth it." As Hope lay back down and fought against the vision, an unrecognizable sensation quickly passed through her thigh. It was almost similar to the feeling she had in her knee on the rooftop, but as soon as she started to zero in on it, she fell asleep.

TWO

It was official, the whole world knew of the existence of demons. At least, that's what the humans called them. For centuries, the "demon" clans had agreed to keep their existence a secret. Humans could be violent, after all. "Finally." Hope sighed and clicked off the TV.

Demons had pretty much all known each other. There were some clans that weren't on the map. They were like uncharted continents or something—the Shin D'ri, the Daemos, and the Bimfishy Bobs. Okay, the point was that she didn't fucking know. There could still be demons that no one had seen, especially if they were pureblood. That was all changing, now. Some jerks are going to come looking for us. They're not all gonna like what they find.

Certain clans wouldn't appreciate this newest development. A lot of them weren't comfortable being seen on an off chance, let alone on the 5 o'clock news. It was a good possibility that this would not only interfere with their quiet lives but fucking tear them to pieces. Hope was alright with being seen; she had desperately wanted to get out of Ontario and New York State wasn't too far. She just hoped her POS car would make it.

Hope had been waiting for this moment since the rumors had started. It was hilarious that of all the days, it was on Halloween. Though, All Saints' Day was always more like "All Demons' Day." The one time of the year purebred demons could go out in public, even if it was just kids.

Sure, she never left her home, but that was her clan's doing, not her skin's. Everything was her clan's doing, and she'd been pretending to be the doting daughter for too long. After all this, plus the braednas ceremony, she was done.

Hope thought of the demon-whatever on her TV. He looked human, too.

"We're constructing a new settlement in upstate New York. Over the foundations of Endwell, a haven for demons will be created," he'd said.

Free-to-be-you-and-me land was just a drive away. No father, no clan laws, no ceremonies. A blank slate called Newborn City.

Hope walked down the small hallway from the living area to her bedroom. The door displayed a giant "Do Not Enter" sign and padlock. She fished in her jeans for the key, opening the door with a loud bang. But even over that racket, Hope could hear her father's voice outside the trailer. He was talking with Jonathon, another priest of Shendara. *They were panicking about the CNN report. She just laughed.*

She grabbed the brown backpack she'd had since she was four and set it down on her bed. The twin was covered in cheap, kitten sheets. Hope rolled her eyes. The matted purple carpet, the posters of Devon Sawa and David Boreanaz, Buffy the Vampire Slayer *and* Xena. *Gods, she'd been obsessed with that shit, convinced demons made them.*

Her father had put a stop to that quick. "Humans are to be avoided at all times. They fear and hate us, and they let that fear and hate control them. They are murderers who persecute our clans. Better we hide away from them and stay in the shadows."

Hope could remember the stories like all the others told to the yanyas. The horrific tales told to children of how humans had hunted demons. Maker, after the tales of vampires, it was no wonder demons chose to stay under the radar. I mean coffins? Garlic? Vamps are always evil creatures that burst into flames at daybreak. Please, nothing could be further from the truth. And don't get me started on the devil. . . . Sure, he didn't like people very much, but he was just a flame demon, not the commander of an army of unclean hell spawn.

Now, that was over. No shadows anymore. She grabbed the few clothes she owned and her notebook. Hope was done with this shit hole, and she'd never look back. But something deep inside her would always hold onto that night.

For hours, she'd sat outside of the braednas temple waiting, watching the males exit out the front and the females sneak out the back. She could see some of their white robes stained red. The females looked skittish; the males looked satisfied. Hope had waited her turn like the others, sitting totally still. The twenty or so girls who were deemed ready were lined up outside the temple to do their duties, and then in the following few months, their bellies would grow and grow until they were sequestered away and a new young was a part of the tribe. The madrus were never seen again, shuffled off to make their lives somewhere else.

"Yup, I think twenty-five years here is enough."

Hope turned off the light, the bile rising in her throat. All this time spent waiting . . . for the braednas, for the Dawning, for something, anything to get her the fuck out of here. She reached for the brassy knob and closed her door, leaving the padlock open.

Surveying the trailer, Hope took in the frayed couch, the mustard yellow fridge, the sink spitting brown water. Peeling laminate partially covered with a shag carpet, a giant wooden fork and knife on the wall, a Formica countertop. Never again.

Hope stepped out of the puke green trailer. Outside the air was fallen leaves, wet earth, and rain, instead of mac and cheese and Dawn dish soap. Her steps rattled the tin steps, and she started for her car.

Jonathon glared, shaking his head. He bowed deeply to her father, and they clasped arms before he walked away. She'd been his son's partner for the braednas *ceremony.* Whoops.

"If you leave us, leave the safety and love of your clan, you will be alone, and you will fail." Her father's voice was deep, proud. He wasn't looking at her.

The high priest stood in the yard with his arms crossed over his chest. His dark hair was pulled back, making his pale skin tight. The long, blue robe, his symbol as a spiritual guide to Shendara their Maker, was tattered and the hem fell open. His brown moccasins poked out, dusty from the gravel drive.

"Love? What the fuck is that? You know, as well as I do, that love isn't how this clan works. And Madru isn't the only mother to leave and you're not the only father forcing their yanyas into braednas." Hope walked past the statue-like figure and over to her blue Geo Metro.

She threw her bag into the trunk and grabbed her CDs. She had to pick the appropriate tuneage for such a momentous occasion. Hope pulled out Arch Enemy, Tool, A Perfect Circle, *and some mystery CDs. She slammed the trunk shut, rattling the entire car.* What a piece of shit. I'm hocking you for parts as soon as I hit town.

"And what do you plan on doing? Beating your way into the human world? Not even they would appreciate your violence. . . . The race must go on, Hope. I won't force you to stay, I won't. By leaving, you avoid the risk of omaeriku, *and we all know to fear araj, even you." Her father's eyes were tired, his wrinkles standing out like cracks.*

Hope thought of the bond, her madru's words echoing in her head.

"I'm leaving, Hope. You know how our people are. Women, mothers, do not

stay. You know the pain you've already felt. You're better off alone, remember that. As soon as you learn to live without me, without anyone, you'll be free. Don't get attached. The pain will kill you," her mother's soft voice burned.

Hope could see her leaving, her soft blonde curls and amber eyes glowing in the sunlight.

Hope thought of the toothache. At least, what her mother told her about it. For all she knew, it never happened. But it had worked. Madru made her good and scared, for a while.

"I fear nothing. Omaeriku *is a dying magickal impulse. I'm not controlled by sensations, by emotions. It's nothing but hormones and a dose of superstition. Learn to live without fear and your own avoidance. I have. You already said you won't stop me from leaving, so find a place or be left behind. . . . Ontario isn't safe. Not after the announcement. If you're really concerned, leave. Go where the Dawning hasn't touched."*

Hope turned away. The road out of this Shendara forsaken "community" was in the opposite direction. Hope tossed the CDs on the passenger seat and adjusted the mirror. She could see her father, the wind blowing dead leaves into piles at his feet. He was just staring.

After a minute, she pulled the car out of their driveway, kicking up gravel toward his legs.

The drive down their private road took forever. Hope waited to see the highway and the Territory Property sign that marked their lands. They had stolen it, and it was falling apart. It was useless now, but it would stay. Bravery and a good sense of "fuck it" didn't run in the family.

As she reached the end of the five-mile drive, Hope could finally see the sign. A chain in equally shitty condition held it in place. She rolled down the window. It was quiet except for a few crows and some semis. Hope cranked up the volume on Arch Enemy and skipped to 'Revolution Begins.' She looked back in the rearview and gunned it for the chain.

A satisfying snap echoed around her, and she actually smiled. As she sped off, she held her hand up and flashed a one-finger screw you.

A few miles out, she noticed a black SUV parked in the main intersection. She couldn't veer around it, so she pulled alongside. As Hope stepped out of the Geo, she tried to peer through the windows, but they were super tinted.

"Alright, so you got me to stop, now what?" Hope swung the hair out of her face and her ear piercings shone in the sun. A long vertical bar ran from top to

bottom, and the rings running down the side of the other ear lay in a perfect line. There were barely any spots on her ears that she hadn't poked a hole through. They masked her powerful hearing, and they always got looks. Like now.

Hope had trained herself to hear outsiders. So now, she steadied herself to listen and heard car doors unlocking and guns being cocked. Hope stilled and pulled the tension up inside her muscles. Bring it on, fuckers.

"Now, we talk." The male voice was low.

The tall, dark-blond human was unlike any Hope had ever seen. He was so calm; serene, despite being surrounded by serious hardware. Two rather large men came out of the car and stood to either side of him.

"I have been watching you. And yes, I know you must think I am a demented stalker. But trust me, you are not my type. I have been watching you because I could use a woman of your talents, to be clichéd, and I would like to offer you a position in my employ." He certainly got to the point.

Hope quirked an eyebrow, but she wasn't leaving.

"What did you have in mind, mister. . .?" Hope raised her eyebrows and smiled, playing with the curved barbell in the center of her bottom lip. It was a nice partner for the simple ring she had on the right. Hope could see Blue Eyes staring. "I believe I asked you for your name. So, maybe, you could stop staring at my lip and speak the fuck up."

"Always so direct, I like that. I happen to be CEO of The Company; you may call me Dante. Like I said, I have a desire for your skills. After all, it is not every day that you meet someone who cannot feel pain. Or is it? I suppose in your 'clan,' it happens all the time, but for a mere human like me? To that end, I," Dante waved at one of his thugs and the stout man handed him a manila envelope, "have an important investment, which I need to protect. I believe that your talents, along with some careful training, will help to ensure the safety of my project."

Dante stepped forward. "You see, recently, there has been some damage to a property of mine, and I wish to eradicate all those responsible for the loss."

"Yeah, well, Dante, was it? I see your predicament and if you have been watching me, you creepy fuck, I assume you know my predilection for violence, developed as it is, happens to be geared to a specific type." Hope stared coldly into Dante's eyes.

"Yes, my name is Dante, and I am aware. They are demon killers, thugs, and scrap. These people have stopped me at every turn. I am trying to make a life for demons and men, alike, within Newborn City and these pathetic, myopic fools insist on playing into a fear that old men in robes created centuries ago. Do you

not see, Hope? I must use the power I have collected to destroy those that would stand in the way of our cultures coming together. Their prejudice must not be tolerated."

"And you just showed up, randomly, on the day I chose to leave, and the Dawning just happened to take place?" Hope put her hands on her hips.

"Yes, as I said I have been watching you. I have numerous demons in my employ, and I enjoy their talents, such as locating a particular demon and keeping tabs on her."

Hope was silent as she thought about what he was offering.

"I understand your apprehension, truly, but I am a busy man. I should also mention that the position includes an extensive retainer, benefits, and a beautiful house with state-of-the-art amenities and absolutely no smell of," he paused, but then smiled and said, "macaroni and cheese."

How'd he know that? *Yeah, mind-reading demons existed, but this guy was human. She looked around and saw a dark figure still seated inside the car.*

"Understand also, that I will spare no expense in your training. With my help, you will be able to realize the full potential of your gift and, if I can be so bold as to say, you shall learn how to survive and eliminate all threats . . . without any other person's help."

The bastard has his pitch down, that's for sure.

"Well, Dante, it appears as though you've got yourself a new employee. When do I get to start killing these fucks?"

"Soon, my dear, so very soon."

*

Ciaran rolled over on the small mat and listened for the guards. The cell was slab cement and smelled like sweat and piss. The back of his Hanes tee was stained with blood. Ciaran was wearing sweatpants that were stiff with dried sweat and his feet were bare. Best of all, it was fucking freezing and his teeth chattered.

Ciaran couldn't hear the sounds of fighting, and Dimitri wasn't there either. This cell was new and way better fortified. He was sore and the floor mat did fuckall to keep his arse bones from pressing into the concrete. First things, first. How the fuck do I get out of here?

As he stood, Ciaran gasped. The pain in his bruised ribs burned like a roaring fire and almost matched the pain in his back and stomach. He'd been worked over pretty good in the ring by Rook. That had been over quickly. Marcus had not been so generous.

The aches were a not-so-friendly reminder of what had gone down before he wound up in this cell. Ciaran remembered impressing Marcus by managing to stay standing, chained by his wrists to the ceiling and ankles to the floor. That only made the fucker bored, and he'd resorted to more creative techniques. The memory of the braided leather strips biting the flesh on his stomach and back was alive and well. Thankfully, a fight had broken out, and Marcus had to excuse himself.

Ciaran had taken advantage of the fragility of the chains. He bent his knees and jumped in place. It hurt like a bitch, but it was worth it. Freed, Ciaran was just barely able to reach the key on the table and left bloody fingerprints as he grabbed it. He couldn't risk sitting, so he'd bent over to unlock his legs and nearly passed out.

And he'd paid for it all. Marcus had sent guards, and they weren't thrilled with his departure. The bigger one had punched his misshapen fist into Ciaran's gut, and he'd fallen to the floor. They both got in a couple of kicks, which sent Ciaran to a wonderland where he had the overwhelming desire to puke his lungs out. Then, they shuffled him to this cell, and he'd passed out.

All of which brought him to this locked room. Ciaran had no fucking clue how he was supposed to escape. He peered around the cell and examined the door. The side had two hinges, top and bottom. They were big, thick pieces of metal and supported the weight evenly. If he could manage to dislodge one of them, the weight of the door would break the lock, crushing the tumblers, and the door would fall sideways.

But what do I use to push up the hinge? *Ciaran didn't have many options, but he might have one, the toilet. He walked over to the john and took off the lid. The various pieces looked entirely unhelpful: the pump was a no; plastic handle arm was a no; but the metal float arm held promise. Ciaran pried the arm out; it was just the size of the pins inside the hinges.* And whoever said being a handyman was useless? If only I had a hammer.

He looked at the toilet again and tried to think. What could he use to hit the metal float arm hard enough to dislodge the pin? The only thing that was solid enough to give him the force needed was the tank lid, but that was made from porcelain, and he'd have one chance to make it work. Ciaran took the lid off and set it down on the mat. He wadded up the shirt he was wearing, which sucked ass since dried blood stuck to the wounds on his back and tied the bloody fabric around the lid. Ciaran went to the door and forced the float arm into the hinge. The sharp edge scratched his palm, but it stuck.

The door was in the corner and there wasn't a lot of swinging room. He got as close to the wall as he could with the modified tank lid in hand. Lifting the lid had been a small treat of pain to his ribs, and Ciaran stiffened at the thought of how swinging it would feel. He took a deep but shaky breath. This is gonna suck.

Each muscle fiber in his torso pinched down on his ribs like a vice. There was a loud crack as the lid hit the float arm, and the hinge pin popped out like the cork in a champagne bottle. Ciaran sagged against the cold cement wall. You're not supposed to let that happen. God, weird fucking thought. Ugh, I'm going to pass out. No, no time for that.

Ciaran somehow managed to stand up and lift his head. The door hadn't moved much, about an inch. Damn it.

As Ciaran considered some serious wall punching, he heard the lower hinge start to creak, and the metal made the most horrible grinding noise. In one clean swoop, the hinge broke off the wall and the door fell to the ground.

"Fuck me, that was loud. Better get Dimitri," Ciaran whispered.

He struggled to lean down and get his tee from the lid. The lower his head got, the more he felt like a wobbly noodle.

"Fine, no shirt, it's not like I have shoes," he mumbled. Blood was dripping down his sides and he was sweating up a storm. Ciaran really couldn't let anyone see him, so he checked to see if there were any visitors in the hallway. With it clear, Ciaran left his cell and headed for a miraculous beacon, the glowing exit sign.

Ciaran followed the sounds of fighting down to the ring and walked to the fighter's "locker room." He seriously considered slamming his fist into the cheap plastic. Locker rooms, right. *He shook his head and pushed through the doors.* Now, where's that black key box?

Just visible from his corner cell, the pin pad protected box held the key to unlock the cells. His cell was now empty, since he'd killed his roommate Rook, and thanks to the fight going on, there wasn't a guard in sight. Ciaran held his arm around his ribs as he entered in the memorized code. There were three rows of three, and he pushed the bottom middle, middle left, top left, and bottom right. He'd never seen the numbers from his angle and saw that it made two, four, seven, three. The metal door swung open, and Ciaran pulled out the circle shaped key with a smile.

"You fucking did it. I can't believe it!" Dimitri slapped the bars of his cell.

Ciaran's neighbor had front-row seats to their escape. With a laugh, Dimitri reached out for Ciaran. He wore the same prisoner's uniform, but his pants dusted the floor. At a whopping five foot ten, Dimitri was a shortish, dirty-minded Russian-American from Brooklyn, and his bright green eyes were filled with the joy of expectant freedom.

Ciaran couldn't help but be thrilled he'd found the guy. The shifty fucker always came out of the ring alive, and it always surprised him. But, there was a helluva lot of muscles plastered onto that small frame. Plus, he was a demon.

"Fuck, man. What happened to you? D'you lose a fight with a weed whacker?" Dimitri asked.

"Well, have you seen the elephant?"

"What elephant?"

"The one who jumped on me ribs." Ciaran chuckled as he spoke, but his ribs kicked up another fuck-you-stop-that.

"You fuck. Get me outta here." Dimitri slapped the top of his head as Ciaran pushed the round key into the main lock. A satisfying click echoed down the line and all the doors slid open.

"Exit is through that door, don't stop for anything. No one is going after Marcus. Not even me. We just need to leave." As Ciaran's voice rang, a wave of prisoners brushed past him and ran out the swinging doors. One of them who never listened to anyone, Red, stopped in front of Ciaran.

"Explain to me why we aren't killing Dentry?" Red's yellow eyes stared angrily at him and her blood red skin glowed.

"'Cause you're gonna help me do something better." Ciaran smirked, and Red rolled her eyes.

With her hands on her hips, her muscular physique was staggering. Ciaran couldn't help but stare sometimes. This godforsaken place was his first exposure to demons, and she certainly looked the part.

Red was fucking red—her skin, her nails, and her hair faded from a deep, black red to yellow, a blaze personified. The fucking fire-demon was exactly what he pictured when he heard the word. A towering inferno of fire and brimstone, minus the horns and tail.

"Oh yeah, what?" Red faced off at Ciaran.

"Burn the place down. Something I've heard you do well." Ciaran watched as Red's face changed from horrifyingly pissed to happy beyond reason.

Dimitri had been playing escort to other escapees, but as she started to laugh, he came running over. "What's so funny? Oh, wait, Red's laughing that means something's about to blow up." Dimitri smiled and Red chuckled openly as she nodded.

"You fucking know it. Now, what do I have to do?" Red focused on Ciaran, and it was like her stare was burning a hole in his face.

Ciaran saw her skin start to glow, and he took a step back. "Easy there, tiger. I have no intention of being a crispy critter. I need you to follow me outside and then around back. I figured out this place must run off a generator. The security systems, heat, lighting, it's too much to tap from the public lines. I need you to make it blow."

Ciaran looked at Red and then Dimitri, who was staring at her intently.

"Explosions are a little harder. Straight-up flame, no problem. Do you think heat alone will make it blow?" she asked.

"Last week, when I was in Marcus's office, I managed to get a peek at his accounts. The generator runs on gas."

Red blazed, her deep red skin shining and a bubble of heat forming around her.

"Fuck, yes! You certainly know how to get a girl hot." Red laughed and gestured toward the exit.

Ciaran shook his head and ran out the swinging doors, Dimitri and Red tight on his heels.

"You know, ah, how do I say this? Your back looks like ground beef." Dimitri's voice trailed off behind Ciaran.

Ciaran had been avoiding any thought of the damage. Pausing on it only made the cuts, gashes, and broken bones pull him closer to the la-la land of near coma.

The trip down the hall was fast and quiet; each of the escapees knew better than to risk being heard. As they reached the exterior wall, they followed along the brick until they found another blaring exit sign. Ciaran slammed into the push lever and the heavy steel door swung open. The light from the sun was bright and even Red squinted. It had been months, hell years, since any of them had been outside. He hadn't been out since his plane touched down in New York. Fuck, he'd been out of Ireland for like three months when Marcus grabbed him, literally.

He'd been such a young, optimistic idiot. Fresh-faced off the plane from Dublin and ready to take on the world. He knew the basics of the maintenance man trade and could easily learn the new systems of voltage and watts. He had it all planned and nowhere on the list was the job title: killer.

Sure, he'd been in some scrapes in Ireland. Hell, who hadn't? It was practically a pastime where he grew up. But life there had been peaceful. As boring as watching your Gram knit throw pillows, but peaceful. He went to work, came home, ate dinner, went to bed. Repeat. Later, he had added "visit Ebony" to the list. Ebony, Jesus Christ, I haven't thought of her in forever. Lovely lass Mother shoved at me. Life with her is looking better and better the longer I'm in this shit-hole. *As Ciaran's mind wandered, the task at hand finally reemerged from his likely-concussed brain.*

"Around back, it's the only safe place to position a generator." Ciaran nodded and jogged around the building.

"How the fuck does he know where to put a generator?" Red looked over at Dimitri as they trotted behind Ciaran.

"Oddly enough, he was a handyman in Ireland, fixing plumbing, basic electricity, and I don't know, pulling cats out of old lady's trees? Or is that firemen?"

"Yeah. Now, if you both could hurry the fuck up. I want out of here." Ciaran stopped just in front of a yellow, box-like device that hummed something fierce. "This is it. The generator is diesel powered. If you can burn through the metal tank, we should be good. I would try it at a distance."

"Yeah, duh. I'm not an idiot, human. Now, how about you do a lady a favor and hold her clothes?" Red looked back at Dimitri and winked.

"Say what?" Dimitri went pale as Red started to strip.

"Well, I can't really set fire to my clothes now, can I? Running around naked is frowned upon in the human world, I believe?" Red tossed her sweatpants and t-shirt at Dimitri and laughed.

"Just get on with it, Red." Ciaran grabbed Dimitri by his sleeve and backed away from Red, who started to glow. Behind a car would have to do.

Crouched behind a sedan, Ciaran and Dimitri could see Red's body begin to light up like a steadily heating torch. In a few moments, she was too bright to look at, and they ducked down behind the car.

"This is probably gonna be loud, buddy." Ciaran looked over at Dimitri who was clutching onto Red's clothes. "You alright?"

"Oh, yeah. Just, Red once told me that this wipes her out. We'll need to carry her to safety once she's finished." Dimitri's eyes were pinched in worry. It was a look Ciaran had never seen him wear.

"No problem. We can grab her. We're getting outta here."

As the heat from Red's flame grew stronger, the sound of cracking metal and steaming fluid filled the air. The massive blast from the explosion was almost anticlimactic. It was loud, but the surge of air Ciaran expected wasn't horrible. In fact, it was Dimitri who got up and ran to Red first. He lifted her and brought her back behind the car.

As they struggled to pull her clothes on, Red tried to speak, "It's not finished. . . . That was . . . the first blow . . . hasn't reached the tank . . . just gases. . . ." As soon as the words escaped her mouth, a huge blast of heat hit them, and they all huddled together. As the crackle and hiss reached epic proportions, Ciaran looked over at Dimitri and smiled. They were out. They were free.

Three

The sun setting past the office window threw beams of light across the linoleum floor. Ciaran sat in his office, feet resting on the top of his desk, reading one of his various, ancient books. It was quiet, and business was slow. The phone hadn't rung all day and as much as he needed the distraction, Ciaran enjoyed the peace. For now, anyway. Silence had a way of gnawing on him, and he'd eventually have to bust out some tunes so he wasn't alone in his head.

A loud adjusting of wood echoed through the office as the main door creaked open. Loud footfalls shattered the silence of the once serene office, and Ciaran's shoulders tightened.

Dimitri sauntered in, swinging the door so wide open that it hit the bookshelf behind it. His eyes were flaring with trouble. "Ciaran! What are you doing?"

Ciaran peered over the top of the book, his head barely moving. He sighed and put it down on his desk.

"Reading."

"Well, you're done. It's Friday night. We're going out."

"That's okay. I'll just stay here and watch the office."

"Watch the office. Are you fucking kidding me? It's not like it's going anywhere. Come on, aren't you Irish supposed to be fun?"

"I think I've had enough *fun* in my lifetime." Ciaran's pulse jumped as a memory threatened to surface, but he shrugged it off.

"Ciaran," Dimitri sat on the edge of the desk and let out a tired breath, "you can't keep doing this."

Ciaran frowned, glaring at Dimitri. "Doing what, exactly?" He leaned forward, putting his feet back on the ground. But it wasn't enough. Ciaran shifted uncomfortably and finally stood up, running a hand through his hair.

Dimitri had backed away from him. Ciaran could easily intimidate anyone, especially his small partner, but the retreat still made him feel like shit. He was angry, sure, and didn't want to go out, so he was being a dick, but he never wanted his only friend to fear him. But, rather than look like a pansy, Ciaran just leaned on the desk with both hands.

His hair fell slightly in front of his eyes. He should've gotten it cut more, but it was out of his way enough for fighting and the lady at the barber's said it was how he *should* be wearing it.

Ciaran absolutely dreaded the notion of going out, parading around like he had a right to enjoy himself. And the light and music and energy were things the living enjoyed, and he never thought himself worthy to hang with that bunch. After years of violence at the Inferno, he merely considered himself as useful as a gun. Point it at bad things and stand back. Don't let it around women and children. Joy, homes, families, that stuff was for people who were good and clean, not the broken, mess of blood and shit he was.

The memory of the only time he'd gone out after his escape popped in, and that only proved that he shouldn't try it again. People had died, not all of whom deserved it, but the thing that stung him the most was the way the little girl had looked at him.

As if he could see Ciaran running through all of this in his head, Dimitri smiled and leaned his back against the door frame.

"You know what? You never leave the office. Never. Just because you spent your previous employment in a less than peaceful manner, doesn't mean you can't have fun."

Dimitri stared at Ciaran waiting for a response; his small, wiry figure seemed exaggerated when he argued. He'd been in quite a few scrapes and his sneaky gift for words seemed to help him far more than his right hook did. Although it probably got him into as many fights as out.

"This is fun," Ciaran answered.

"It's not real fun. You have to leave the office. I repeat, 'leave the office,' once in a while."

"I leave," Ciaran said defensively.

"Not on a job. Need I remind you that you aren't supposed to fill your day with violence?"

"It's what I'm good at." Ciaran sat back down in his leather chair with a plop. At once, he changed from intimidating to pitiable. His shoulders slumped, and he began to fiddle with his book.

"Not the only thing. You're fabulous at brooding."

"I'm no brooding." Ciaran tossed his book down and leaned back in the chair.

"Fine, you're sulking."

"Okay, brooding it is." Ciaran looked across at Dimitri and shook his head. "I'm not going to win this, am I?"

"Nope."

Ciaran sighed and finally said, "Okay . . . where are we going?"

"Fever. New club that just opened downtown." Dimitri's smile was all teeth as he spoke.

"Umm, okay, just let me finish this chapter and get ready." Ciaran looked down at his book and began reading again.

"Fine, you've got twenty minutes, bro." Dimitri shot out of the office and left through the door like the room was on fire.

Ciaran put his feet on the desk and scanned the book to find his place. The thing was yellowed and weak with age, the pages crackling each time he touched them. But the familiar Gaelic words relaxed him and made him remember his father who taught him to read them.

His few books and the Celtic sword on his bicep were the only tangible reminder of his past before New York. But the scars everywhere else would never let him forget the Inferno.

Even as he tried to be gentle as he turned the pages of the *Morrigú*, one fell to the floor in a quiet sweep. "Every time I turn a page, one falls out." Ciaran leaned over to pick up the paper, setting it on his desk. Ciaran sighed as he stared at the floor. *Fever. Oh gods, please help me.*

Reading was okay, drinking alone was pretty damn okay, punch the crap out of his punching bag was fun, but nowhere on the list he had just made was watching drunk, pretty boys eye-fuck half-naked girls as said pretty boys tried to get as plastered as possible. In fact, nothing involving fucking was anywhere on his list. That shit was a total no-go. Any thought of it made his stomach turn to lead and his throat close, well, except for the dream but he couldn't really control his subconscious, now could he.

"Ciaran! Come on!" Dimitri yelled from the front office.

Ciaran pushed his chair back with his legs and stood up, smashing his knee into the lip of the desk.

"Son of a bitch!" Ciaran rubbed his knee and yelled back down. "Shit.

Dimitri hold on a second, alright!"

He shook out his leg and started toward his office door, dragging his feet at the idea of going to Fever. From behind him, he heard a loud crash echo down the street. *The fuck?* Ciaran jogged to his window and looked down to the street. Nothing.

"What the hell was that?" Ciaran shifted his gaze to the textile mill and scanned the roof. There was a dark figure running into the door facing his building, and it appeared to be limping.

He watched the door to the roof closed and swallowed hard. He was a target, but why? He hadn't been to the New York scene in years, and no one had followed him here. At least, he didn't think so. Wait, was he jumping to conclusions? But as he tried to put together everything he'd just seen, the image of a long case in the figure's hand stood out. It had been the perfect length for a rifle. Damn him, it was just too coincidental, and he wasn't that lucky.

Great tidal waves of pain and panic flooded through him. *They can't find me. They can't kill again—not Dimitri. I can't . . .*

Ciaran shook his head and watched the street below, but never saw the figure run away from his building. They must've taken a different route. It was smart. Never leave an obvious trail. That's what he thought he'd done, but here he was at the wrong end of a hit.

Who was he kidding? Of course, they tracked him down. They had a lot of resources at their disposal. He just didn't understand why their boss wanted him dead so badly. It wasn't like he was going to bring the Inferno to light. He was plenty guilty himself. No judge was going to buy the whole "I was forced to kill them" defense.

"What's the holdup?" Dimitri swaggered in. His usual cocky gait made Ciaran grind his teeth.

"You didn't hear that?" Ciaran gestured to the window with his thumb.

"Hear what?" Dimitri looked at Ciaran impatiently.

"Look, I'm no stalling. I heard a loud-ass crash." Ciaran slumped down onto the corner.

"Really? Well, we aren't in the nicest neighborhood."

"No shit, but it was close. I saw someone run across the textile roof when I looked to see what happened. I think he had a gun."

Dimitri's eyes grew wide. "They were after you? But why?"

"I don't know. But clearly, they are. Fuck, I really hoped they'd forgotten about me."

"Umm, no offense, Ciaran, but it would be near impossible to forget the exit you engineered." Dimitri smiled and shrugged. It was true, explosions and blood tended to stick with people.

"God, damn it. I so don't want to deal with this shit. Dimitri . . . you should go. I don't want you caught in the crossfire again."

"Trying to get me to leave? You're the reason I'm not still in the Inferno. No. I'm not fucking going anywhere." Dimitri crossed his arms over his chest.

Ciaran couldn't help but smile. The wiry, little fucker had been his "personal assistant" since they broke out. He could remember nailing him in the gut with a punch when they first fought. He'd convinced him to stop fighting and stay with him, promised him freedom and life back with his family.

Of course, that didn't work out. As soon as the guy got back to his clan's land, he discovered that Marcus had them all slaughtered. Ciaran figured he lucked out in that regard, no clan to murder since he was human, and his "loved ones" were already dead. His chest pinched.

"Ciaran? Ciaran?"

"Sorry. Distracted."

"Remembering something?"

"Yeah, and don't ask. I'm no in the mood to share."

"Are you ever?" Dimitri eyeballed him, but this was one thing Ciaran wouldn't compromise on. "Fine, but I'm still not leaving."

"I can see that, but I think Fever is out of the question."

"Ah, fuck. Those douchebags really know how to fuck up a party." Dimitri stepped further in and shut the door behind him. "So, my violent friend, what are we gonna do about this? I mean, we can't really go after them. We could find the shooter, but what do we do with 'em?"

"I don't know, but I don't really want to worry about being shot while I'm reading."

"Tell me about it, that'd be a fucking lame ass way to die."

"Shut up." Ciaran waved off Dimitri. "Ugh, I can't do anything tonight. I need light and tools. Besides, a drink and a soft bed sound real nice right now." Ciaran walked toward the door to the basement.

"Ciaran, just don't pound it too hard. I know where your head's at, and it wouldn't end well."

"Lay off." But Ciaran knew he was right.

"Fine, just promise me you won't spend the whole night thinking about that place." Dimitri stared him down like he knew the promise wouldn't stick, but he was still going to try.

"Yeah, well, you know me."

"Unfortunately, I do." Dimitri and Ciaran joined in a short burst of laughter, the inside joke making the sting in his chest subside slightly.

"Okay, I'm going home. Lock up, after you leave." Ciaran beelined for the door. He didn't want to watch Dimitri continue to pity him.

Outside the office, his car was waiting to take him home.

Ciaran drove his '92 Crown Vic into his brick-faced garage. The car was old and not well cared for, but the engine wouldn't quit. Plus, best of all, it had been cheap, and he paid in cash at a salvage yard. No paper trail. He shut off the engine and went inside.

The manse was isolated and quiet. He had a million rooms in the empty, old house with enough space for all of his needs, including safety.

Inside, it was cool and dark, and he turned one light on at a time. The brick facing was the only splotch of color in the whole building, the red giving way to dark blue and black marble. Black marble floors, counters, and all the appliances were stainless steel. The walls were deep plums and navies with antique black trim.

The houses in Ireland and England he saw in his youth inspired him. Ciaran figured making a bundle off beating people to death could go toward a home. But it ate at him. He bought his dream home with blood money he'd stolen from Marcus. The house was going to be condemned though, so he got the forgotten relic to be forgotten in. *So much for that.*

It had three levels. The main floor with a kitchen, office, security center, and the living and dining rooms. The upper floor with the master suite, twelve guest bedrooms, upper office, and a wraparound balcony. And downstairs with the training and med rooms, mudroom with garage access, a den, and another bedroom, which he used instead of the master. There were a few other rooms on each floor: closets, storage, and vacant areas that he couldn't find a use for. Plus, there was an attic.

In the center of the main floor was a massive, wrought iron staircase he had specially made. It connected all three levels and showed Celtic and gothic designs, the swirling metal similar to his tattoo.

Ciaran let his hand trace the railing of the stair as he practically ran down, his boots making the metal clang. He drank in the dark colors and shadows of his private space. Unlike the upstairs, down here all the walls were exposed brick and the floors were dark hickory. It was such a contrast to his office; everything there was cheap, economical, and utterly unimpressive.

All that time ago, he'd managed to hire a tech expert to steal the winnings from his fights at the Inferno. It was way more than expected. Apparently, he'd been one of the top three fighters. And the money was an unfortunate godsend. He'd have been piss poor otherwise. If it was out of the public eye and wouldn't draw attention, Ciaran was alright spending it, sort of. He donated a lot, and the rest was secured in an account somewhere; Dimitri had taken care of it. Ciaran didn't really want to know how.

Kicking off his shoes in his coat closet, he noted his collection. Converse, Doc Martens, and more Converse. *Classy*. He closed the door and went to the kitchen. As he went past his bedroom, he pulled off his black shirt and wife beater, tossing them on a leather chair. The air around his skin was cold and glorious. *God, I need a drink.*

Ciaran continued to the kitchen. With the checkerboard tiles and stainless appliances, the room was sleek, dark, and not fussy in the least.

He reached into a small cupboard under his sink and pulled out a dark brown bottle that looked older than his copy of the *Morrigú*. Pulling out the cork, there was immediately the overwhelming smell of strong ass alcohol. The poitín was about 95 percent alcohol, and as Ciaran took a huge swig, he could feel it burn away the cold as well as a layer of his esophagus.

As he choked down the liquid, he brought the bottle to his bedroom. Ciaran rolled his shoulders a couple of times and then let them slump down again. Renting himself out as a bodyguard, and occasionally to bounty hunters, was paying the bills, but it killed his body. But when the occasional case came around where he got to beat the shit out of some loser who couldn't take no for an answer, Ciaran almost enjoyed it. He didn't really need the money and he definitely didn't need the violence, but he couldn't find anything else to fill up his day.

Fuck, what am I supposed to do about this? If I could just find the hitter, I could get me hands around 'em and beat the truth out of 'em.

Ciaran sat on his bed, running his hands across the sheets. It wasn't the cement of the Inferno. He let himself fall backwards. Setting the bottle of poitín on his nightstand, Ciaran took off his watch and shoved it in the drawer. He started to lay on his side when his phone jabbed him in the thigh. So he plugged the thing into the charger. His alarm was set for 4:00 a.m.. *Ugh, well, I'm not about to sleep in me pants, and I'm no getting up.* Ciaran reached down, undid the button and zipper, and slid out of his jeans. The sound of them hitting the floor was loud.

Laying there, his muscles ached like were trying to rip themselves off his bones. The stiffness in his bad knee, the dull pain in his left side from an old knife wound, he could feel every inch of his body protest the slightest sensation. Breathing, stretching, moving, even his muscles relaxing. It was all painful. He would give anything to feel something other than pain. And just then, a familiar image surfaced. Ciaran stiffened beneath the sheets.

He sighed. His body and mind were never on the same page. It always wanted something from him and whenever he gave in, it just wanted more. Ciaran couldn't bring himself to find a partner. So, the job of keeping himself level always fell on his own shoulders. *It's no for pleasure. I just need to sleep.*

In his head, Ciaran could be the kind of lover a woman deserved. To the woman who filled his mind with a sense of longing and always wanted him, accepted him. As the fuzzy, watercolor swam up from the depths, Ciaran repeated the mantra. *No for pleasure. Just to sleep.*

Ciaran pushed off his boxers. He kicked them out from under the sheets, his body protesting the movement. His biceps squeezed tight, his abdominals tightened, and the muscles in his hips ached, almost as much as his erection. He slid his hand down to himself and gripped as hard as he could take.

As he stroked hard and fast, his body momentarily forget about all the aches and pains, focusing on the sensation in his groin. Tighter and tighter, he stroked himself fast, the tell-tale sensation of his balls pulling tight against his shaft riding up. The dream woman came to him. Never whole, clear pictures but hazy suggestions of curves and shadows. Since before he could remember, she'd stared out at him from his unconscious, soothing aches and burning into him. Deep brown eyes peered out from dark hair, eyes that wanted him. That *loved* him.

There was some semblance of pleasure as his orgasm drew nearer. As the delicious pressure grew, he white-knuckle gripped his shaft and let the orgasm rocket through him. The hot stream that shot out was the highlight of his day.

But as he came back to himself and the aches returned, he was empty. There wasn't a body beneath him. There was no face to look at as he fell asleep. And there was no way he could push past what had been done to him at the Inferno to actually give any of that a go. As his eyes began to close, the dream woman was a fuzzy image of dark hair with a silver streak in it.

FOUR

Hope woke up with the strangest sensation rippling through her skin. She imagined that if she could feel hundreds of tiny insects all over her skin biting her flesh, it would feel like this, but how was she really supposed to know? All she knew was that it made her want to move and run and kick her legs, and it was definitely worse when she held still.

As she stretched and finally got out of bed, the feeling slowly melted away and she was right in her own skin again—a return to that familiar numbness. But the oddness of the sensation stuck with her. Hope couldn't feel the quilt on top of her. Why would she feel a strange—God, she didn't even know how to describe it? *Tickling? I don't even know what that feels like.*

She stretched and shook the sleep out of her brain. As she went to the closet to pick something out for the day's "errands," she started running through her plans. First, of course, was to get to Ciaran's office and find a way into a quiet and undisturbed place. Second, remove any and all distractions that might cause her to be unable to kill Ciaran. Third, determine the best method to kill said mark, depending on the current surroundings and the number of possible witnesses in earshot.

Of course, that really could go only one of two ways, either she would be able to kill him up close and personal with her gun or hands, or she would have to outfight and outmaneuver him because he discovered her motives and that would be much messier. *What to bring? What to bring? Well, I'll need my gun, suppressor, back up rounds, cell, and . . . hmm, I guess I'll need my pentobarbital just in case. It'll give me about fifteen minutes to get the fuck out of dodge.*

She quickly changed into a tight, black dress with a very low-cut back. Hope wanted to seduce Ciaran after all, at least to a certain extent. Plus, the fabric was thick enough that her gun holster didn't show and the gun itself could be easily maneuvered to the inside of her thigh. Uncomfortable car ride and walking in general, but you have to expect a few discomforts when you're on a hit. Plus, this bitch was going to pay so well that she'd be able to take a break for a while. If she could pull it off.

The dress hugged her beautifully, showing off every curve and the demon tattoos marking her lineage. They ran along either side of her spine and connected at the base just above her butt. As much as she wanted to forget her clan, she really loved being a demon and the tattoos. But that was mostly because she had designed them herself, using the ancient language, and oh, the lecture she got about defacing her flesh from her father? Priceless.

She clipped up the top half of her hair. Her ear piercings gleamed in the light. After all the years spent acquiring more piercings and tattoos, she still enjoyed her ears. They never migrated and stayed with her all collected, like a visible timeline. She was up to so many now, covered in as much metal as skin. Two in her lip, her nose, her nipples, the dermal on either shoulder and each hip, her belly button top and bottom, and her eyebrow, horizontally just for funzies. Damn, she was certainly blinged out.

The demon tattoos weren't to be shoved off. They ran all over her body, now. She had been adding more with every paycheck. From a small, lower back piece to a solid, flowing trail of ink all over her. From her lower back, it split over her shoulders and went down the inside of her arms, then curved around her wrists and dripped down each finger. Another section ran around her sides and just under her breasts, where it joined again and went down the front of her stomach. Then it split again and ran across the bones on her hips to the sides of her legs all the way to her toes.

She put on a coat of bright red lipstick and tossed on her favorite black peep-toes. Popping a pair of black crystal earrings into her first hole, she paired the look with a large silver snake ring on her middle finger and a matching necklace that hung just to the top of her cleavage. "Hey Ciaran, stare here so I can distract you while I empty my chamber into your skull." With a quick spritz of some rose scented perfume, Hope was out the door.

The drive back to Ciaran's office was much slower than her previous trip. Hope listened to the sound of other cars flying by through her open window and hummed quietly to herself. Nothing like blaring her metal collection to draw attention to her car.

Hope could remember singing to pass the time but ever since the gunshot wound in her neck, she couldn't do anything but hum. A piece of the bullet near her voice box kept her from completely healing.

Damn that job. She was just starting out and wasn't completely prepared for all the things that could go wrong when you were trying to kill someone. The target had been a small-time businessman, who was, in actuality, an anti-demon radical planning an attack on a local demon-friendly homeless shelter. Talk about low.

The news must have gotten back to him that he was under a kill order because he'd been armed. Thankfully, she was faster and stronger than this particularly awful specimen of the weaker race. The tussle for the gun ending in her favor. It was lights out for that unlucky customer. The neck wound, however, was a reminder of why you should always do your homework, kids.

She considered having surgery to remove it, but that would require insurance and medical files, and personnel. yeah, *no*. She wished she could have managed to get it out when it happened, but she was half dead from the blood loss and more concerned with stopping the flow than maintaining her singing voice.

Yes, she sure was doing a fantastic job distracting herself. *Ugh*.

The air smelled like lilacs as she passed open fields of the country, but as she drove farther, the air changed to exhaust fumes, gasoline, and the stale metallic smell of wet building. She peeled through the rural district, the uptown hipster areas, and into the industrial area where Ciaran's office sat. It was way off to the west, a mostly empty area with a few parks and a baseball field.

The old, brick building was smack dab in the middle of it all. To Hope, it still looked like the packaging plant it once was despite the ivy growing on it. Adding a new door and some offices couldn't change that.

It waited quietly at the end of the street, ever so expectant for the business it desperately needed. By all accounts, the private security biz was not going well for Ciaran O'Connor, but he seemed to manage. *Probably, because he made so much fucking dough fighting. Dante said he used to be one of his top fighters before he went traitor.*

Hope's heart pounded in her chest. She could feel the pull of *omaeriku* as she drew closer to the office, closer to her *jabalv*, as her people called him. But, like hell, if she was going to let some pathetic, pseudo-magical bond control her. If she could learn to control emotions and muscles, she could certainly learn to control her fucking hormones, magickally induced or not.

As she drove closer, she could feel her sort of pulse. The sensations were overwhelming. Hope mentally groped for her training. How she felt nothing after her mother's departure. She'd made herself numb.

Every foot closer to the building, however, made it harder to fight the random images *omaeriku* was kicking up. Something about it made her want to be alone with Ciaran, but not to kill him. No, *omaeriku* wanted her alone with him in a different way and possibly without any clothes.

"Where the fuck did that come from?" Hope didn't think about sex, ever. The concept was so alien to her. Chakals didn't really sit their children down and talk about intimacy. Mostly, they waited until the female was ready for *braednas* and sent in a male to impregnate her as quickly as possible. Shut in the darkness so that they couldn't tell which female they were with, the males would use their bodies to create a child and then leave. The females were sequestered until they gave birth with no contact from the outside world to risk *omaeriku.*

The thought of being close to someone just seemed like an invitation for pain, real physical pain. Hope could remember the women of her clan coming out of the *braednas* temple, blood on their gowns. *How the fuck could something that left you bleeding be fun?*

But none of what she knew explained why her subconscious was showing her images of throwing Ciaran down on a desk and ripping his shirt open.

Shedara-damn, useless hormones! How did humans, and other demons, for that matter, deal with them? This muffled thought, one she'd never had before, was pushing against the stone-etched will she'd spent her entire life developing.

There was no time for that. Hope had to put on her game face and woman the fuck up. She checked her make-up in the mirror, wiping a pinky finger under her eyes and around her lips. Satisfied, she went up to the building's door. Her hands were shaky and sweat had apparently formed on her hands. *This is fucking stupid.*

Hope shook her head and relaxed her shoulders. With a practiced smile, she knocked firmly on the glass window. The signage rapped under her knuckles, and where Ciaran's name was printed, she imagined beating the shit out of him, punishing him for putting her through this ridiculous *omaeriku* crap.

"Just a minute, please." The voice she heard behind the door didn't sound like she expected. It was a little higher and there was no trace of an Irish accent. Didn't he have one last night?

As Hope straightened her dress, a shorter, red-haired man opened the door. She thought back to the first time she saw Ciaran, he was sitting at a desk, and maybe he was shorter than she thought? But his profile said he was six-foot-four and at her five-nine, the man approaching her just made it past her head.

"Hello. I'm Dimitri, how can I help you, ma'am?"

Hope released a breath she wasn't aware she'd been holding.

"Well, for starters, don't call me ma'am. And secondly, where can a parched girl like me get something to drink?" She smiled coyly and slinked her way inside. She let her hips sway more than normal and could practically feel the tiny, horndog's green stare all over her ass. *Piece of cake.*

"I'm sorry, force of habit. I can get you some coffee or water?" The thick Brooklyn accent was grumbly and well ingrained.

"Anything stronger, cutie?" Hope winked and bit her lip ever so slightly. She could read this little fuck like a picture book and guessed that he would respond rather well to the sweet damsel in distress meets total whore persona.

"Yeah, I can do that."

Dimitri walked to the main office and offered her a chair. She walked past it and sat on the edge of the desk instead. He sat behind it and pulled out a pair of glasses. She swiveled her legs in front of him and crossed one slowly over the other. Hope leaned back on one arm and watched Dimitri pour the brown liquor. Eat your heart out, *Basic Instinct.*

As Dimitri looked up and handed her a glass, she smiled and sipped. It was whiskey and not cheap stuff, either. Ciaran had good taste.

"Umm, so what can I help you with, other than the drink?" Dimitri sat in the boss's chair and looked ridiculous.

"Well, Dimitri, right?" Hope said, with a coy grin.

"Uh huh. That's right. Miss?" Hope could hear the desire in his voice, and he probably had the physical reaction to match.

"Turner. And, you see, Dimitri, I'm afraid that I'm being stalked. I'm so afraid to go outside alone, and I need your company's help protecting myself." Hope leaned down close to Dimitri's face and let the deep V in her dress stretch tightly around her breasts. As she got close enough to Dimitri's face to kiss him, she reached her hand around her leg to the small holster she had strapped to her thigh. Holding the small gun out of sight, Hope thought about how ridiculous she must look, throwing herself at this guy and practically falling out of her top.

Hope blinked and suddenly her mind was filled with the memory of one of the many men she'd killed. A contract kill for only him, his wife had jumped in the line of fire and died trying to protect him. She failed, not standing a chance against an automatic weapon, and both of them wound up shot to death in a manner of seconds.

Hope could picture leaving the scene and being dumbfounded by the woman's actions, she still was. Why would a person willingly die for another when the opportunity to escape had been right there? The smart killer could use that as leverage. Two birds, one stone equals lovely dead birds. People were fools, especially humans, hell, especially her own fucking clan. Getting sucked in by *omaeriku* and made a plaything to its whims. Or hiding in fear instead of controlling it, dominating it with your will. *Idiots.*

The sound of Dimitri's Brooklyn accent snapped Hope back to reality. "Oh, well, you see, my boss, Mr. O'Connor, usually handles that type of situation, personally. I mostly just file paperwork. He's the trained bodyguard, after all."

"I see. Do you know when he'll be available to speak with me?"

"He should be arriving any moment, actually. He had to drop off the electricity payment to the landlord."

"You two don't own the building?"

"Yeah, no. We rent. Mr. O'Connor and I live outside the city."

"Oh, really? Country boys, huh?" Hope leaned a little closer and cocked the gun quietly.

"O'Connor maybe, but not me. He's way out there. Off Route 33."

Hope smiled to herself. Pumping Dimitri for info certainly wasn't hard. And she had almost all the info she needed. "You're so helpful, Dimitri. Getting your boss to help me with my . . . problem. You boys must be doing quite well for yourselves. Helping scared women like me."

"Are you kidding? No, we're small beans here. Mr. O'Connor could buy this whole block if he wanted, but he says he just isn't that type. Likes to lay low, keep to himself. I, personally, like going out. I could probably show you the time of your life instead of sitting in the dark." Dimitri eyed her up and down.

She bit her lip, as she looked down at him and let her head fall back in a fake laugh. "I bet you could. And it's only you here, all alone in this big office?"

"Yeah, just me, no other employees to worry about." Dimitri grinned as the possibilities ran through his head.

"Wow, no one. Well . . . Dimitri, that leaves just one thing." Hope pulled Dimitri close and kissed him. It caught him off guard and as soon as he was fully invested, tongue roaming, she lifted her gun and pressed the barrel to his temple. His eyes shot open, and he went slack-jawed. Hope let herself smile wide and real. "Oh, what's the matter, Dimitri? Not what you had in mind? Oh, well. Goodbye, Dimitri."

FIVE

The sound of his fists hitting the punching bag echoed in the empty room. The pain in Ciaran's knuckles ran through his fists, into his wrists, and up his arms, resting in his shoulders. He'd been at this for about an hour, and it was beginning to get annoying. But his brain was churning away. He barely slept and woke up shortly after his self-medication to find that he was antsy as fuck. The restless leg syndrome was rearing its ugly head, and he wanted to kick everything off him and run a marathon. Not a fabulous idea when you have a reputation and a massive hard on.

So, when he heard his alarm at four, he figured it was okay to stop staring at the ceiling and go work out. He'd hobbled out in the dark to his homemade gym. It was nice to have a place to just focus on training.

Now, as he finished beating the shit out of his lifeless opponent, he checked his watch and saw that it was a little after five a.m.

"Shit, I should have left for the office." Ciaran ran down to his room, literally jumped into the shower and scrubbed himself down with soap. Not concentrating, he accidentally brushed himself and cursed as he got hard.

"Ahh, not fucking now. don't you ever get fucking tired?" As if in response, his mind flashed to the dream woman with the white streak in her hair. "No fucking way. I have to work." Ciaran rinsed off, threw on black pants, t-shirt, and boots, and was out the door.

"Sorry. Running late." Ciaran swung open the door to his office and found Dimitri sleeping in his chair. "Fucker."

Ciaran walked over, careful not to stomp in his Docs, and slammed his hands down on the desk.

"Holy fucking shit!" Dimitri shot up in his chair and Ciaran wondered if he'd pissed himself. "Fuck, bro. What'd you do that for?"

"'Cause, you have a house you can sleep at, not me fucking leather office chair."

"Lay off, you may get up at the crack of ass, but I need a little motivation. And you're just not that cute," Dimitri yawned.

"Dimitri, do you think you can manage to stay awake long enough to watch the office while I run this payment downtown?" Ciaran had a ton of errands, and he didn't really trust Dimitri with them. Well, trust that he wouldn't be recognized, anyway.

"Sure. But, if you don't start the coffee on your way out, my nap is your fucking fault." Dimitri leaned back in the chair and stretched his body out to its full length.

"Get out of me chair and consider filing those invoices from last month. I know it's not as fun as putting fifty-grand down on a horse named Rosie and losing, but do it." Ciaran smiled smugly and escorted Dimitri out of his office.

"I don't understand why you don't just buy this place. No more costly rent payments or drives to the landlord's ghetto ass house." Dimitri stared at Ciaran and shrugged his shoulders as he left.

Ciaran let his body fall into his chair and held his head in his hands. *Buy the office? Well, that would put me name on the lease. No, thank you. It's hard enough to stay under the radar, without adding me name to the bank's list of customers.*

Ciaran sighed and reached into the top drawer of his desk for the cash rent payment. God, it would be nice never having to see the landlord again, but times were hard, and this was the only suitable location for his business. Being in personal security was tricky. Most people didn't know they needed a bodyguard, and the people who did usually went to private firms.

"Ugh, I really don't want to see that bastard." Ciaran's entire body stiffened. The bloated, sunburnt man always seemed to look at him like a piece of meat, and even with the physical odds stacked against him, Ciaran couldn't really do much. Hilariously, Frankie had his own personal security.

Ciaran walked out to the main door. "I'm going to run this downtown. I'll be back in like an hour. Hopefully, I won't have to stay any longer than I have to."

Dimitri poured himself a cup of coffee, fresh from the twelve-dollar coffee maker, and sat down on the edge of the couch in the waiting area. "Okay, cool. I'll make sure the office doesn't scamper off like a bad little room."

"Ha. Look, just take care of any clients, and try not to burn the building down.'"

"I fall asleep with a smoke in my hands once, and now I can't be trusted?"

"No. Ugh, I'll be back as soon as I can. I fucking hate going, so I shouldn't be long." Ciaran rubbed the back of his neck like he could feel the bastard's halitosis crawling up his skin.

"Sure, boss, whatever you say. I think he just likes you." Dimitri winked.

"That's the problem."

"Are you serious? No fucking way that guy wants you. Right?" Dimitri's eyes were huge, like green saucers in his face.

"It's like the fucking Inferno all over again." Ciaran's shoulders pinched and a light sweat broke out on his forehead.

"Well, fuck that guy. You can take him, even with his so-called bodyguards. After all, you're the Laoch Dubh."

Ciaran glared. "Don't call me that."

"Sorry."

"I'm going to drop this off."

"Hopefully you return with your balls intact." Dimitri smiled and shrugged as if to say he couldn't help himself. And try as he might, Ciaran couldn't help but smile.

Frankie's "office" smelled like cat pee, pot, and a hint of spilled beer. Cheap-ass beer, too. Ciaran walked to the door and after knocking, heard the usual, "Yeah, what d'ya want?"

He told him he was there to pay rent.

Behind the closed door, Frankie perked up and yelled, "Oh, Ciaran, well, son, why don't ya come in?"

Inside the apartment, Ciaran tried not to touch anything and kept a watchful eye on the two thugs near the back. Burney was sloppily eating a sandwich and Roy was sitting in the corner picking at the underside of his nails with a butter knife. After peering around, he saw Frankie lounging on a pea soup green couch, his beer gut hanging out and a glass pipe in his hand.

"Frankie. Here's the payments. Electricity and rent. I'll be going, now."

Ciaran tossed the envelope down on the sticky coffee table and turned to leave. Frankie cleared his throat and before Ciaran could turn around, a sweat-slick grip was around his neck. Roy smiled at him and waited for orders like a good boy.

"Now, now, Ciaran, why don't you stay? Besides, I was just telling Roy here how you neglected to visit me and that your payment is a whole day late."

Roy pulled Ciaran's head around and his body followed. Roy's fat, dirty hands pointed his face at Frankie. The slovenly man walked in front of him.

"Mm. Electricity and rent, huh? Well, maybe, is not all I want. I've heard some rumors. Nasty deets that you were an employee of the bombed Inferno Club." Frankie planted his feet, waiting for a response.

Ciaran's first instinct was to say nothing, wait until he got bored and let him go, but Roy's hand squeezed tighter.

Ciaran grunted. "Ugh. yes. I got out of that business, and you know I'm in private security." Ciaran shifted his neck in Roy's grip and looked sidelong at Burney, still occupying himself with the sandwich. "Isn't something I discuss. So, there's your payment. I'll be on me way."

Frankie gripped the belt that held up his corduroy pants. Adjusting himself in front of Ciaran, he rolled his eyes and shook his head. "No fucking way. How lucky am I, Roy? I've got one of Dentry's whipping boys right here in my house. You know, Dentry and I, well, we have a few things in common. One of those things? We like our money on time."

The back of Ciaran's neck moistened with sweat and bile crept up this throat. He thought about his last night in the Inferno. He tried to forget that place but faced with a familiar threat, the memories bled into his consciousness.

*

Ciaran lay on the floor of his cell holding his ribs. The cement was cold on his skin, and it was amazing. His sweat dripped, creating the outline of his topless torso. His legs burned, and his bare feet touched the bars of his cell. He had won his life in the ring, again, but another man was dead, probably still lying in a motionless heap. The smell of sweat, blood, and grime was everywhere. Breathing through the pain of his bruised ribs was taking its toll, and Ciaran was moments from passing out.

"Ciaran, shit man, are you alive?" Dimitri reached his arm through the adjacent bars and patted on his head.

"Yeah, unfortunately."

"You're a fucking demon, man. I can't believe you lasted through Rook's

barrage. Not unscathed, I see." Dimitri nodded at the darkening spot on Ciaran's right side.

"Yes, well, he swung a mean fucking right. I don't think they're broken, just bruised. And no, I'm not a demon. Too bad, too, this probably wouldn't hurt so fucking much. Well, unless, of course, I wound up being some pissant demon like you." Ciaran smiled and laughed. "Ow. Remind me no to laugh."

"Whatever, you're on your own, fucker. I hope they're broken." Dimitri slapped at the top of Ciaran's head, and they both chuckled, "Marcus isn't going to be happy that you killed Rook. Weren't you supposed to take a dive in the ninth?"

"Yeah, but you know me."

"Yeah, unfortunately." Dimitri grinned, shaking his head. They were both aware it was a stupid move. And Ciaran was going to pay for it.

He tried to roll over but could only manage to move his head. "He can't be that pissed, right?"

"Well, actually he can," Marcus spoke calmly as he approached Ciaran's cell.

His glare was almost palpable, and the sound of his privileged voice grated in Ciaran's ears. "You cost me quite a lot of money, Ciaran, and I do not think too kindly about such actions."

Marcus's deep blue eyes blazed in his face. He was clean-shaven and showered, composed and professional, dark blond hair cut neatly. The taut stance he was famous for, held in place no matter his anger. His black suit was tailored silk, hardly the attire for a den of demons and murders, but he always liked to look his best and make the difference between himself and the prisoners as plain as day.

"Open the cell." Marcus's bodyguard stepped forward and unlocked the rusted metal door that kept Ciaran in his place. One bodyguard remained and pushed in tighter to Marcus in hopes of deterring any attempts of violence. Ciaran might have enjoyed pissing Marcus off, but he wasn't stupid. This was not the time or place. As Marcus stepped in, the door was shut behind him. Clearly, Ciaran wasn't a threat right now.

"What am I supposed to do with you? Hmm? You were supposed to take the fall in round nine and instead, you stood up with broken ribs and cracked Rook's neck." Marcus stood silent for what seemed like hours, peering down at Ciaran, who had pulled himself into a seat against the back wall. Ciaran waited for Marcus to do something, beat him, leave, ask him to stand, so he could punch him in the ribs, but nothing. He just stared down expectantly.

"Go fuck yourself, Marcus. I'm no dying for you. You know I'm just waiting

until I can break out of here." Ciaran struggled to his feet, the pressure increasing on his ribs. He didn't wince or flinch but pushed himself straighter, standing at his full height and towering over Marcus.

Marcus's eyes traveled down Ciaran's body. He could see them stop at his neck, his growing bruise, his groin. He stiffened unconsciously and the muscles around his ribs dug at the battered bone. A cold sweat started. If he stood much longer, he'd be doing a concrete nosedive.

"Take him to my office. We have important debts to settle." Marcus walked up to Ciaran and took his chin in his hands. "After all, Laoch Dubh, you have taken a great deal from me. It seems only right that I should return the favor."

Out of the past and back in the grungy apartment, the feeling of dread grew. Frankie's hand reached down for the belt buckle holding Ciaran's pants, and Roy began to chuckle in Ciaran's ear. His body turned to rock. Lifting his right leg, Ciaran used Frankie's groin for leverage, kicking back and sending Roy into the wall behind them. The sound of Roy's head smashing into the wall got Burney's attention, and the lard ass came running to help his boss.

Free from Roy's grip, Ciaran ducked under the wild haymaker Burney threw and swung out his leg to hit him at the ankles, knocking Burney to the ground. Once there, Ciaran leapt on top of Burney and drove his head into the floorboards, knocking the goon into the happy land of unconsciousness. Ciaran stood up and turned to see Roy lying limp against the wood paneling.

"You son of a bitch. You bastard, you're dead." Frankie's voice made Ciaran turn around to see him holding his balls.

"Shut up, Frankie, and listen." Ciaran knelt down and pulled him up by the neck of his stained wife beater. "You will never touch me again. You will never talk to me again. And you will never receive any payment from me again. I am now the unlisted owner of me building. Any and all payments and required expenditures will come out of your grease-stained wallet. I will never see or hear from you unless you have come to tell me that you plan to end your disgusting life. Are we clear?"

The black blooded fury in Ciaran's voice struck the heart of the slimy landlord, and fear beamed out of his face.

"Clear." The pathetic, shaky sound of Frankie's voice was barely a whisper. Ciaran had his former landlord scared shitless into believing that he was a reaper come to steal his twisted soul.

Ciaran let go of Frankie's shirt with a shove and turned to leave. The sound of his Doc Martens pounding on the floor rang throughout the silent apartment, and Ciaran fought back the desire to snap Frankie's neck.

"Laoch Dubh." Frankie's voice was so weak the sound barely made it across the room.

It made Ciaran stop with his hand squeezed around the rusted handle of the screen door. He froze for a second, then turned to look over his shoulder. "In the flesh."

*

Ciaran's body shook with leftover rage as he drove his Crown Vic to his office. Walking up to the ratty door, he gripped the handle and had to pause. The near-overwhelming desire to kill Frankie was still coursing through him. The adrenaline, the satisfaction of defeating someone, breaking them, and destroying them, he enjoyed that feeling even if he hated it, and his commitment to avoid such displays of violence was wavering.

He tried to breathe and focused on the face of the little girl from that club. The horror in her tiny features, the reflection of his kill-hungry gaze in her eyes, the blood on his hands, the empty joy that faded as soon as the blood dried. *Laoch Dubh*. The thought reverberated inside his skull. *Laoch Dubh*. His trademark, his title at the Inferno. *Laoch Dubh*. It meant dark warrior and the sound of the words, even in his mind, made Ciaran want to smash through the glass of his office door.

But he didn't. He breathed in and opened the door into the waiting area.

The room was empty and quiet. Ciaran was thrilled that Dimitri might have left to go do something, anything really; he didn't care. He wanted to sit in his office and stare into the darkness. He wanted to let his mind stop circling, to ponder anything but how good it would feel to watch the life leave Frankie's eyes. *Fuck, maybe, I'll even try to sleep. Apparently, me office chair is really comfy.* As the thought of receding into the blackness of slumber filled him, the memory of the dream woman floated to the surface.

His body surged at the thought of her. The alien desire for her was as uncontrollable as the desire for revenge, the adrenaline pumping through him for an entirely different reason. The muscles in his neck squeezed, and he tightened his fists. *What would it be like if she were real? I haven't felt anything good since Ebony, fuck, not even then. Not that I really deserve that shit.*

Ciaran walked to his private office, still tangled in his thoughts, when he heard people talking.

"Wow, no one. Well . . . Dimitri, that leaves just one thing." Ciaran realized it was a woman and frowned.

"He's got a fucking chick in me office. That's just great." Ciaran hesitated. The idea of walking in on Dimitri fucking someone wasn't really what he had in mind but letting them mark his desk was worse. He slowly pushed open the door to make sure Dimitri hadn't already started "entertaining" his guest.

"Oh, what's the matter, Dimitri? Not what you had in mind? Oh well, goodbye, Dimitri."

As he pulled the door further open, Ciaran heard a change in the woman's voice. She was plastered all over Dimitri and sitting on the corner of his desk. The tight, black dress she wore left little to the imagination, and as Ciaran pried his eyes away from the most perfect ass he'd ever seen, he saw the handgun pressed to Dimitri's temple.

"What the fuck?!" Ciaran plowed in.

When Dimitri saw him enter, relief washed over his face.

"Oh, thank god." Dimitri was shoved backward and onto the floor, and the dark-haired woman shifted around to face Ciaran.

They didn't even have enough time to make eye contact before she started shooting. Ciaran dove away from the woman's rapid gunfire. Rolling across the floor toward her, he popped up under her arm and grabbed her wrist. He dug his fingers into her tendons, and she automatically dropped the weapon. As it fell to the floor, Ciaran kicked it away and shoved the woman back against the desk, pinning her down using his body weight. Straddling her with his legs on either side of her so she couldn't roll away, he pushed down on her shoulders.

Ciaran shouted for Dimitri. "Are you alright?"

"Yeah, I'm fine. Ms. Turner went fucking crazy." Dimitri stood up behind the desk and rubbed the lump forming on the back of his head.

"Who's Ms. Turner?" Ciaran looked down at the dark-haired woman he had pinned to his desk. With time now to truly look at her, Ciaran was shocked. She was extraordinarily, absolutely, perfectly gorgeous. From her long, curly hair, to her glowing, cinnamon eyes, to her fucking knock out body. Hell, she looked like she was handcrafted by angels. And as if that wasn't enough, her sweet face was decked out with piercings galore, her body covered with what appeared to be one continuous tattoo. She was a dream; in fact, she had a white streak in her hair.

Ciaran lost his grip, and Ms. Turner knocked him back with a solid kick. As Ciaran stumbled backward, the woman tucked into a roll and seamlessly grabbed the gun off the floor, standing in front of the door with the muzzle leveled at his head. *There's no fucking way. The dream. . .*

"That would be me."

Dear god, her voice. It was deep and soft, fierce and clear. He could listen to her read the fucking phone book, but as he realized what she was answering, his gut dropped. Ciaran focused on the gun. Ms. Turner might be the most beautiful creature to walk the earth, but she clearly wasn't a client.

"You must be Mr. O'Connor. Well, I guess I can skip the middleman." A sadistic smile slid across her face, and she cocked the gun.

Dimitri started toward her, but she swiveled her arm to face the gun at him faster than he could reach her. "Fuck off, Dimitri. I'm willing to drop you where you stand or leave you be. It's up to you."

He stopped in his tracks and looked over at Ciaran. Ciaran shook his head. He couldn't let Dimitri get shot, not trying to save his worthless arse. Dimitri's eyes silently argued, but he eventually realized he'd be no help dead.

Ciaran stepped closer to Ms. Turner, and she switched her attention back to him. He held his hands out to his sides. "Just let Dimitri leave."

"Aww, how sweet. No. I think I'll have him stay," She looked over at Dimitri, who glared back, fists clenched. "Can't have you go run off and call the authorities, can we?"

Ciaran was fucked, and he had no idea why. *Something to do with Marcus no doubt. But who is this chick?* After all the time hiding from that fucker, he'd finally found him, and he was going to die in his shitty office, and then, Dimitri was next. She would do it. Her body was poised and tight. She was calm, tactical, and definitely not a newbie.

He could think of worse ways to die. A shot to the head would be fast, but not Dimitri. It was his fault Marcus was after him, and Dimitri was just in the wrong fucking place at the wrong fucking time. *Goddamnit. This isn't right. Fuck you, Marcus, you cock-sucking prick.*

The hammer of the gun was back, the safety was off, and the resident assassin's finger was squeezed around the trigger. Ms. Turner's brows pinched together, and her gaze was like a rifle sight. She looked down to the ground, then met his stare with her eyes. *Hi, Death. Nice to meet you.*

SIX

Hope was dying. No other explanation. The pounding in her chest had reached epic, your-body-is-slowly-losing-all-its-oxygen proportions. Holding the gun level and pointing it at Ciaran pulled on her arm. Pressure in her feet from standing in the heels squeezed. All of it, she could . . . feel.

Ever since that bastard had pinned her to the desk, Hope was aware of too many sensations. The weight of the gun in her hand, the dull unpleasant something in her shoulders, even the tightness of her dress, her brain was actually interpreting the information and experiencing it.

It was horrifying and incredible.

She was desperate to look calm. Poker face on lockdown. *I felt it, the desk, and this gun, whatever this is in my back. I . . . Dear god, what's happened?* Hope eyed Ciaran. Unless he was a better bluffer, Ciaran wasn't upset about potential dying.

But then it wasn't about his expression. It was his face. His deep, brown eyes, the smooth skin of his lips framed by a goatee, the healthy glow behind his flesh, the strong column of his shoulders. His body was sculpted and brutal, the cords of muscles pulled taught over his bones. He was ferocious, powerful.

She came back to his eyes. Ciaran wasn't glaring, wasn't strangling her with a look. And she wasn't either. Hope's finger relaxed around the trigger.

What would his velvety skin feel like under her fingertips? What would it be like to feel the power of his body underneath hers? They were still staring at each other, and Hope couldn't look away. She . . . didn't want to.

In all its pure essence, what she really wanted was . . . him, all of him.

It was completely fucking crazy. Everything in her brain was screaming at her to pull the goddamn trigger and avoid whatever was happening. Hope knew this was *omaeriku* at its fullest, and if she wanted to continue with her life, she needed to kill him, now.

But she couldn't.

If his eyes were actual pools, she'd just fallen in and was drowning. The hold she had on herself was failing, bleeding out of her.

Everything was too tight, suffocating. The gun in her hand, a struggle to hold up, the dress on her body, constricting, made of lead. Hope looked down at the floor and couldn't understand why she wasn't crumpled into a ball, forced down by the weight of the very air. Her chest couldn't expand to keep her breathing, but somehow, she struggled in a breath.

Something smelled different around Dimitri. Hope concentrated on what her nose was telling her. She didn't lift her head; afraid it would distract her.

For a few nanoseconds, Hope closed her eyes and breathed deep, scenting what Dimitri gave off. It was like old moss and earth, a wet crispness like the inside of a cave with burnt ozone backing it up. Hope had never smelled anything like it, but she knew what it meant. *But if he is. . . Dante lied.*

Hope looked back up at Ciaran. "He's not human."

"What?" Ciaran was surprised, his hands still raised up by his face.

"You know what. Dimitri's not human." Hope suppressed a growl. *All of this bullshit with* omaeriku *and now this. You've got to be fucking kidding me. Dante, you lying son of a bitch. You used me.*

The reaction on Ciaran's face changed, and it wasn't utter disbelief. He knew. He worked with a demon, and he knew. *So much for the demon-hating murderer line.*

"I know. What does that matter?" Ciaran began to put his arms down and shook his head.

"It matters because it means it's your fucking lucky day." Hope lowered her gun, and Ciaran's mouth fell open.

"Why? Why not kill me? Please, tell me You're not afraid of Dimitri?" Ciaran looked over at his partner and got a wicked scowl in return.

"No. Idiot. I don't kill demons." Hope rolled her eyes and something red flitted by.

"What now? Why are you staring at the wall?" Ciaran seemed less than amused.

"Didn't you see it? There was a red light or something." Hope searched frantically, and as the dot returned to the door Hope's heart dropped. "Fuck."

"What? Your crazy train come in early?" Dimitri spoke up from the corner and scoffed.

"Jackass, just get down, before—"

Dimitri stepped in front of the window and shots echoed from across the alley. Hope dropped and skittered back against a wall. Ciaran quickly dropped and rolled over to Dimitri who'd barely missed the bullet.

"What the fucking hell! Who'd you bring with you, crazy bitch?!" Dimitri screamed as the gunfire continued to make hole after hole in the drywall.

Ciaran held his arm across Dimitri's chest and tried to push the little prick back.

"Fuck you! I work alone, and I'm guessing it's just another of your various admirers." Hope tried to peer out the window to see how many were firing, but the stream of bullets was too continuous. She shifted around to stick her hand out the now demolished window and fired off a couple rounds. The barrage of bullets stopped long enough for Hope to see four men in protective gear and a black van parked in the alley.

"How many?" Ciaran looked over and shoved Dimitri back, keeping him from standing.

"Four, and they're in gear. Plus, there's a van." Hope ejected her magazine to check it, "Got anything in here? I'm almost out."

Ciaran nodded and crawled over to a bookcase. "Yeah, not much. And unfortunately, an RPG is not among my collection." Ciaran pushed up a false bottom to reveal a cache of weapons and extra money. He pulled out a pair of Walther PPQs. Hope was impressed by the mini arsenal.

Ciaran tossed over both a pistol and enough ammunition to last a while. He loaded up the other gun and slid it to Dimitri.

As Dimitri picked it up, he leaned in close to Ciaran. "You're seriously giving the chick that just tried to kill us a gun?"

"Clearly, she's not the biggest threat right now. I get the feeling they started shooting, 'cause she didn't. Hmm?"

Hope shoved a magazine into the PPQ and crouched closer to the window. "Yeah. And no, I didn't realize they were there. Yes, they got the drop on me. And no, I have no fucking idea what's going on. Bad information."

"You didn't think to ask about Ciaran or his friends?" Dimitri shifted onto the balls of his feet and squared off at the window.

"Don't ask many questions in my line of work. It gets you killed."

"Apparently, not asking does the same." Dimitri smirked, and Ciaran slapped his arm.

"Would you just shut up? Nothing about this situation adds up. How'd they find us? Why'd she stop? 'Cause you're a demon? Why'd they omit that little detail? Is this Marcus's people? I for one would just love to find out, but if you don't shut the fuck up and help us get out of here all we're gonna do is die."

The grip Ciaran had on the PPQ made the veins in his forearms stand out, and the air of benevolence Hope had seen was buried. This Ciaran was calculating, strategic. He was leaving this room with everyone in it and getting the answers he wanted. She had to appreciate the decisiveness.

"Sorry. What's the plan?" Dimitri shifted back into position.

"There are only four of 'em across the roof. All we have to do is take out the two in the middle, and we'll have enough time to stand up, get the fuck out here and—"

"Get over to the roof, take out one, and question the other. Get some of those answers we're all rather interested in." *Including why the fuck an ex-fighter seems to know so much about infiltration tactics.*

"Right." Ciaran frowned in that agreeing way.

She figured she'd have to take out both targets, but who knew.

Ciaran looked down at his gun. "Still the same formation?"

"Yeah, they're still lined up in a pretty fucking row," Dimitri grumbled.

Ciaran inched up and scanned the rooftop as the shooting mellowed out for a moment. "Ready?"

"You know me, buddy, always eager to please." Dimitri winked and kissed at Ciaran, who knocked him over with a hard shove.

"You two make a fabulous couple. Now, if you're done with the foreplay?" Hope smirked.

Dimitri laughed it off and got up to cover the right side. But Ciaran looked at her and clenched his jaw. But then he just shifted to the middle and got ready to return fire.

There was a second of silence and then in a collective exhale, the three of them emptied their clips into the opposing team. Hope adapted to the kick of the PPQ and landed three shots in the man farthest to the left. One shot ripped through the muscle of his left arm and forced the guy to lose control of his rifle, the next barreled through his right thigh and knocked him backward. The final bullet sliced through his neck, and the bastard lay bleeding on the gravel rooftop. *One down, one to go.*

Hope turned to see if the boys had any luck with their targets, and low and behold the rookies actually knew their way around a firearm. Ciaran's shots had punctured holes in the skulls of the middle two assailants, and Dimitri had noticed quickly enough to drop the last with a shot through the shoulder. As soon as the bullets cleared the last man's shoulder, Hope was running over to the rooftop.

"Wait! God fucking damn it! What the fuck does she think she's doing?!" Ciaran screamed across the now silent room.

Ciaran and Dimitri appeared near Hope on the roof. She had the last assassin pinned to the ground and had begun the interrogation.

"Why did you come here?!" Hope pressed her fingers into the bleeding wound on the man's shoulder. He screamed, and the sound echoed below them.

"We were told to follow you. . . . Make sure . . . you got the job done . . . or do it ourselves. . . ."

"Did Dante give the orders himself?" Hope squeezed again.

"Ahh! yes, he was practically freaking out about the job . . . like it was real important." The shithead's breath was coming in gasps and blood had dripped all over Hope's hand.

"Move." Ciaran snatched the shit out of Hope's grasp and held him up off the ground. "Who's this Dante?"

Hope shoved at Ciaran. "What the fuck?!"

"Look, Ms. Turner, You're not the only one who's getting some fucking answers." Ciaran looked back down at the man dangling in his hands. "Answer me!" Ciaran shook him hard, his head flopping around like a rag doll.

"The boss! Alright, the fucking boss. He runs . . . everything. . . . Ugh." The man's chest heaved, and then he began acting the role of a sack, going limp.

"Way to fucking go. Now, we get nothing." Hope glared at Ciaran.

"Yeah, 'cause me shaking him is what killed him. Dimitri probably hit an artery." Ciaran dropped the guy.

Dimitri held up his hands. "Do not bring me into this."

"You work for 'em, you have to have a way of—" Ciaran's voice stopped short as they all noticed the supposed corpse get up and reach for the gun in Ciaran's hand.

He tried to keep the gun, but the shit's hands were too quick. Hope rolled forward and went for the weapon she'd set down. As she spun around on her knee, she saw the muzzle flash of the PPQ. It fired just to the right of Ciaran's stomach. Hope squeezed the trigger, and the shots rang out one right after the other.

A sharp, hot sensation flared on her left side. Hope missed a breath and forgot where she was and what she was doing. Her heart kicked hard, and sure as shit, it stopped in her chest. It was like with her knee when she first saw Ciaran, but millions, trillions, of times worse. She instinctively grabbed her side and lowered her gun arm. The weight of her muscles was immense, and bile rose in the back of her throat.

It was pain, *araj*, alien to her since birth, and it fucking sucked. Every nerve ending screamed, thousands of tiny, white-hot receptors overloading. After the hours of listening to her *padru*, her clan, go on and on about the horrors of pain, she actually felt it. And nothing in their vocabulary or hers could describe it.

As it rocked her ribcage, Hope gasped and coughed. Her diaphragm yelled in protest. As soon as she got enough air to remain conscious, her body forced it out. *Araj* was taking over and pushing tiny squeaks and hisses out of her mouth.

As the seconds dragged on, the sensation dulled slightly. Hope breathed slowly, and it was better than the hyperventilating, making the sensation return in short waves of heat. And hey, she was still standing. That was good. She needed off this damn roof though. Hope fought against the pain, but it was like groping for a lighter in the dark. *Come on, just walk over there, find out what happened, and then get the fuck out of here.*

The assassin was down. She'd punctured a large hole where his eye socket once was. Dimitri ran to Ciaran.

"Fuck! Buddy, are you okay?" Dimitri knelt down next to his as he leaned over on one knee with his head down.

Hope walked over to assess the damage.

"Fine." Ciaran's throat sounded tight, and his teeth were gritted. *Fine? Really?*

Hope knew exactly what he was feeling, and it was anything but fine.

"I think the bullet just grazed me." Ciaran lifted his hand from his side, and his palm was covered in blood. The shirt he wore was slashed open through the side, exposing torn flesh underneath that steadily oozed blood, and Ciaran struggled to breathe.

Hope had seen dozens, maybe a hundred, dead bodies. Some killed by a simple bullet, others torn to pieces by massive gunfire, but the sight of Ciaran's side actually turned her stomach. He was so quiet, and Hope expected him to pass out, but he just shook his head and little droplets of sweat flicked off his brow.

"Really, I've dealt with worse. I'm golden." Ciaran pushed his body upright, but the moment his spine was straight, he wobbled like a cooked noodle.

"Sure, that's why you're hanging all over me like a drunken prom date." Dimitri hitched Ciaran up onto his shoulder, and Hope could feel the burning flare in his side. She tried to hide her response by coughing. Both of their eyes went to her.

"We need to get off this roof. At least I do. I'm out of here." Hope tucked the PPQ into her waistband and turned to leave, phantom jolts of pain shooting through her side.

"One fucking second. You're not just leaving. I have questions, and now that the fucker's actually dead, that leaves you." Ciaran managed to lift up his head and give Hope the stink eye.

She rolled her eyes. "And what makes you think I'm going to stick around?"

"You don't have anywhere to go. your boss knows you fucked up, and I'm betting that going back to your humble abode isn't an option. But mine?" Ciaran cracked a smirk and hissed in a bit of air.

"You want to do what?! You can't take her back to your place. You've clearly lost too much blood." Dimitri fought to keep Ciaran standing as his friend's blood seeped onto his shirt and pants. Ciaran was going to bleed out in a few minutes.

"Pretty sure, he couldn't take anyone anywhere, right now." But he had a point. Dante knew about her place, but not Ciaran's. That info was safely kept in Hope's cranium. After all, Dante enjoyed the plausible deniability. "Look, I'll go back with you on one condition. One night. You get your answers, and in the morning, I'm gone. And no looking for me, either. We pretend we never had the displeasure of meeting."

Wait. What am I thinking? I don't know who the fuck this guy is, and Dante's going to be fucking livid after tonight's little debacle. Hope's mind bubbled like a damn percolator, but something else vibrated inside her.

Not just the epic pain she tried to convince herself wasn't there, there was something else. She wanted something. She was fucking exhausted, but it wasn't sleep, eating sounded as fun as puking nails, and her skin was on fire. Hope definitely wanted to take her clothes off. But she also wanted to be physically close to Ciaran. Hope imagined being in a car with him. It made the pain lessen.

What the fuck, brain? Get a grip, Hope. The image of a very naked Ciaran popped into her head, and she literally had to shake it out. *No, no, no. I'm going because once he has his answers, this entire shit cluster of a night is just a bad memory. I get far away and* omaeriku *is an ignorable itch. Dante can find another patsy for his master plan.*

"Do we have a deal?" Hope stared coldly at Ciaran. He shot a glance at Dimitri, who shrugged.

"Yeah, one night. That's all. I don't really relish the thought of hanging out with an assassin, anyway." Ciaran pushed off Dimitri and forced himself straight, only to collapse on top of Hope.

As she held him off the ground, they both gasped. "Sorry to startle you. Didn't really plan on taking a nosedive. Maybe you better drive."

Ciaran smiled and the sound of the blood in her ears was deafening. "Fine. But your car's a no go. I'm not driving that POS. Besides, I doubt you have a triage kit in your death trap."

"Yeah, and yours has one because what, you like helping injured puppies?" Dimitri pressed in closer and resumed his place at Ciaran's side.

"Assassination's a messy job." Hope was getting really sick of Mr. Sarcastic's comments, "Also, we're going to need a distraction."

"What?" Hope could hear the pain in Ciaran's voice as he tried to straighten again.

"Look, would you quit doing that? You're going to pass out. If my car takes off somewhere, I guarantee it'll be followed. Dante always has back up. We're going to need something else for them to follow. For instance, your ride. They'll expect us to haul ass out of here in it, and once they're hot on your car's ass, we can get the fuck out of dodge."

"It's you, man."

"Fuck that noise." Dimitri's voice was almost a growl.

Hope glanced at his hands and could swear there was a blue whirl around them, like an aura. But as she blinked, it was gone.

"It has to be, I can't drive, and we can't trust her to come back." Ciaran pushed off Dimitri again and hobbled over to Hope.

Not so gracefully, he grabbed her arm and leaned on her. She could feel his heavy weight settle on her shoulder. The fact Dimitri could hold him up when he was unconscious was impressive and strange considering his size. *He is a demon, though.*

"Look, Dimitri, I trust you. Just get whoever is out there to follow you. Drive 'em out past 29 and dump 'em by Fredericks. The small back roads will confuse the shit out of these fuckers. We need to go, I need—" Ciaran gasped as the wound stretched and Hope almost let them both crash to the ground.

"To get patched up. Now, just do it. Please," Hope answered for Ciaran.

"Oh, with fucking sprinkles on top, too, I didn't really picture you as the please type. Well, fuck you, Turner." Dimitri stared into Hope like she was an ant under a magnifying glass. "You hurt him, and I won't use bullets to rip you apart."

"Just a patch up. He gets his answers, and I get gone. I never back out of my deals."

"Don't think I won't find you if you do."

"Alright, gentlemen, I would love to sit, now," Ciaran said in a gravelly voice.

In the silence between jousts, Hope could feel Ciaran's weight press down harder. She'd distracted herself from what she was feeling pretty good. Maybe there was a chance out of this *omaeriku* shit. Hope could feel something else, however, a warm sensation again, on her side and leg. There was something more too. As she looked down and saw the bright red on her thigh, it clicked. Wet, his blood on her leg was wet.

"Alright, time to go. Wait, did you just call me a dude?" Hope looked to Ciaran.

"Yeah." As he spoke Ciaran laughed, and Hope could feel the pain ricochet through them. "No more laughing, check."

Hope shook her head.

"Get out of here. Just meet me at my place tomorrow morning. I'll be waiting, not so patiently. Ciaran, just, um . . . watch your back." Dimitri nodded and ran to the door. He was so protective; they ought to be dating.

Ciaran was in Hope's arms, now. "You're strong."

"Demon." She didn't look at him.

"So, Ms. Turner, where'd you park?"

"You're gonna get blood all over my car."

SEVEN

The inside of Hope's car was warm and a perfect match for the Bond-style exterior. Clean, filled with all sorts of hidden goodies, and still the single most uncomfortable drive of all time. The forty-nine minutes and twenty-three seconds had been completely silent. After Hope patched his side with the triage kit, the bleeding slowed enough that they could leave, and that was that. No nervous banter, no casual hey-we-both-got-shot-at-how-are-you-doing. Nothing.

Ciaran just told Hope where to go. Occasionally, he would catch her stealing a glance at him, and he would get caught doing the same, but Not. A. Fucking. Word. He thought he saw her wince once, but she didn't do it again. Now, they were getting closer, and he needed to navigate. The idea of being the first to break the silence seemed about as fun as a hand job from a lobster.

The leather squeaked under him as he adjusted in the seat, and he could feel a hot sting of pain cut through his ribs. He needed stitches and was less than thrilled that portion of the night still lay ahead. *Shit, she's going to miss the turn if I don't say something.*

"Umm, you want to turn left up here."

"I got us all the way out here just fine. I think I can remember the last left turn."

It was true. She managed to navigate the nonexistent roads off 26 easily.

"I just want to get home, so you can stitch me up. Bleeding to death isn't my favorite past time." Ciaran looked over at Hope as she rounded the last turn and smirked.

"I highly doubt you're dying." As the car straightened out in his driveway, she smirked right back. Her eyes hit his, and he forgot to breathe. The dark coffee color of her stare was illuminated by the sun behind him and sparkled with flecks of gold. They looked like tigereye gemstones. *Wow, when the fuck did I become the world's biggest sap? I'm in trouble. Actually, strike that, she's in trouble. No one survives around me long.*

As they pulled onto his drive, gravel crunched under the tires. The bouncing made his wound bleed harder, pain pressing down and choking his lungs. But he was so close. As long as he could make it to his master bath without passing out, Hope wouldn't have to drag his heavy ass up the stairs.

"Holy fuck." Hope pulled up to his door and killed the engine.

Ciaran unbuckled and opened the door, the red stain growing on his shirt. "Oh, guess I'm bleeding a lot, huh?"

"Actually, I was talking about your house. It's fucking huge. Underground fighting really pays well."

Ciaran winced. "Yeah, well, I woulda earned it another way if I could."

"Aww, hooker with a heart."

"Let's just get inside. My bathroom has everything we'll need." The pain intensified at the thought of the Inferno.

"Laoch Dubh, Laoch Dubh, Laoch Dubh!" The echo of the crowd blazed in Ciaran's ears. The warmth of blood soaked through his sweatpants and dripped down his chest. The floor was cold and wet underneath his feet, and J'Zargo lay crumbled beneath him. Choked gurgles spilled out of his mouth.

"Laoch Dubh! Laoch Dubh! Laoch Dubh!" The momentum of the audience's cheers was growing, and among the voices, Ciaran could hear one shout out, "Finish him!"

J'Zargo wasn't going to make it much longer. He was drowning in his own blood; the demon's bottom ribs pushed through his lungs.

Ciaran had racked up quite the body count and the cash to go along with it. Marcus's latest attraction and prizefighter, the bastard had a special account set aside for his winnings, so he could gloat. Ciaran was worth millions to the sadistic proprietor of New York's underground sensation.

Marcus Dentry was the leading supplier of a new wave of demonic violence that the city all but devoured. Who could possibly have guessed that an entire race of beings lived in our cities pretending to be human? Not Ciaran, that's for damn sure. He was shocked the first time he saw them. Red, Rook . . . Blight had been a particularly ugly bastard. Then again, Dimitri, the little shit in the cell next to him, was a demon, and he just looked like a Russian goon for the mafia.

This demon was harder than most he'd fought. After the months locked up in the Inferno, Marcus was stepping up his game, sending more challenging opponents every match.

It was starting to take its toll.

Ciaran's body was being broken down and stitched back together each week. There wasn't any of the baby fat he had when he arrived, and his knuckles didn't look like a maintenance man's, but rather those of someone who'd broken them repeatedly on near-strangers' faces.

Still, no matter the training or the strength of these new demons, Ciaran managed to find a weakness, and even this demon needed to breathe. He almost felt bad, even now, even after all of the fights. But killing had become his bread and butter.

It was all old news now. They were just products, Marcus's property to do with what he pleased. And they really weren't that different, anyway. They all had homes and family, lives that sucked at times and were pretty okay at others. They all died; they all bled; sometimes they bled blue, but they all still needed it. J'Zargo may have had intimidating cat eyes and claws, but he required blood to function just like a human.

"Finish him!" The voice was shrill and strained.

As Ciaran reached down, grasped J'Zargo's head, and twisted until the bones of his neck snapped, all noise in the room stopped. The crunching pop echoed in the octagon, and the demon's body went limp in Ciaran's hands.

A mouthful of blood squeezed out of J'Zargo's lips and fell onto Ciaran's hands, the body hitting the floor with a slick slap. The dark, red-black liquid was sticky and warm. Ciaran wiped his hands on his white shirt, the new red stain adding to the faded ones already there. In the stillness between death and victory, he looked up to Marcus Dentry's cushy box. His dark blue eyes stared, his deceptive features twisting into a malicious grin. Ciaran's vision blurred, his stomach churned, and he watched his captor mouth, 'good boy.'

"Hey, Ciaran? Ciaran! Are you alright?" Hope's voice penetrated the blackout and Ciaran blinked up at her.

"What? Yeah. Sorry. I'm fine." Ciaran pushed off the ground, gravel cutting into his hand.

"Yeah, well let's not pass out on me again. You're heavy as fuck." Hope almost smiled, just almost. *What the fuck is her deal?*

"Well, I'm not planning on it. Let's just get up to my bathroom."

Ciaran tried his best to climb up the massive set of stairs, but he couldn't without Hope's help. Every step burned deep in his ribs, and by the end of it he was breathing hard. So was Hope. *Shit.* He couldn't get his fat ass up the stairs, so now Hope was forced to drag him up.

The slate floor was one of the most beautiful things Ciaran ever saw. The gray squares were almost as good as morphine. But the hard surface came up to meet him fast as Hope set him down to grab the lights. Ciaran didn't even have enough strength to slow his descent and his arse bones vibrated from the abrupt stop.

"Okay, where's the kit?" Hope faced him, the bright lights making her skin glow.

"Bottom left cupboard. I can—" Breath flew out of his lungs as he tried to go to the sink. *I will not be carried to my own damn toilet.* He pushed himself forward and slammed down onto the john.

"Yeah, well, I don't think you can. Whatever it was you wanted to do." Hope knelt down to grab the supplies. The hair covering her neck fell into a sleek blanket across her face. The curving wave revealed the image of . . . Well, horns were the only way to describe them.

Black tattooed lines poked out from under her shirt like curved bull's horns. Ciaran's eyes followed the lines down the back of her neck where they disappeared and then reappeared over the top of her shoulder, curving around the underside of her arm. But, they weren't just lines. They were intricate markings of curves and angles, more precise and interesting than most tribal shit.

"Is that a tattoo? I mean, I guess it is, but what is it?" Ciaran's voice sounded thready.

Hope pulled the kit out of the cupboard and set it down on the sink, opening the large backpack. She unzipped the first section and grabbed a pair of gloves. Sliding her thin hands inside, she tried to pull them tight, but they were too big.

Hope plugged the drain and poured in some rubbing alcohol. She placed the suture needle, a pair of tweezers, and EMT scissors into the disinfectant. Then, she grabbed the Quikclot pad and handed it to him.

"Yes, it's a tattoo. Lean back."

Not a request. *Man, being a patient is loads of fun.*

"Let's take a look." Hope tried to peel the blood dried shirt off his side, but it stuck to the wound. She retrieved the scissors. "I hope you don't like this shirt."

As she knelt again by his side, Ciaran froze. He prepared for the searing pain of Hope ripping the fabric from his skin, but she was surprisingly gentle. She lifted his shirt slowly and delicately slid the scissors under the cotton. The metal was cold, but as her knuckles brushed his side and were warm and soft. The long slit she created exposed his stomach and the loose flaps fell to his sides. The bandage Hope applied earlier was completely soaked through. Hope pulled the wet pad free. It didn't even hurt.

"Give me that." Hope held her hand out for the Quikclot. "This may feel warm."

"Okay."

Ciaran didn't know why she was telling him. *To warn me? Why would she care? Weren't we enemies an hour ago?* The pressure on his wound got his attention, and he grunted. Hope gritted her teeth.

"Squeamish?" he asked.

"No. I just imagine it hurts."

If anyone else had said it, Ciaran would have thought they were being sympathetic.

After a minute or two, the bleeding stopped, and Hope removed the pad. The area was still covered in blood, and there was no way Hope would be able to see enough to sew him up, which meant cleaning the area. *Oh goody.*

Ciaran realized Hope was finished when he saw her put the bloody tweezers to the side. The cleaning process pushed him to the edge of consciousness, and it was a godsend. At least this way, he didn't remember what just happened. Hope patted the wound dry with a clean swab and opened an iodine pouch. She swiped it around the wound, which looked far less terrifying now that it was clean.

Retrieving a sterile suture needle, Hope threaded it with the nylon from the kit. Ciaran was laid out as flat as he could get on the toilet with his head resting on the tank, but this was going to be tricky. After a quick spray of blood clotting aerosol and the resulting burn, the Lidocaine numbed his skin.

Hope stared up from her knees. "You ready?"

"Man, I really wish you were down there for another reason." Ciaran smirked.

"That's a yes."

Ciaran knew the spray numbed the top layers of skin, but that was it. Hope had to sew deeply enough so the stitches wouldn't just tear when he moved. Pierce through the skin, then down into the wound, and up through the other side. *This is gonna suck.*

To her credit, Hope went as quickly as she could. She didn't pussyfoot around. Every couple of stitches she would look up, a nonverbal are-you-gonna-pass-out? He didn't. Somehow the occasional glance helped, more like he didn't want to duck out in front of her and look like a pansy arse motherfucker who couldn't even take a bullet for her. *Well, not for her, just take one. I mean I wouldn't . . .*

"Well, I'm finished. I'll put a bandage on it, and you should be good." Hope peeled open an abdominal pad and held it to his wound.

The warmth of her skin leaked into him, and he felt a little fuzzy. Or was that the blood loss? She wound more bandages around his ribs and secured them with tape. Her face was inches from his chest. He could feel her breath on his pec make his skin tingle. God, she smelled fabulous. Some expensive perfume, but something else, too. Something that was purely her, like clean water, like rain.

As she finished wrapping his wound, Hope's eyes met his, and for a moment they just stared at each other. He had no idea what she was thinking, but one thought stood up and shouted in *his* mind. An image of her pale skin decorated in that tattoo with nothing covering it but air.

And then Ciaran was extremely hard.

He shot off the toilet and pushed past Hope to the door. Before he turned to face her, he pushed himself behind his belt, facing his erection up. His very eager friend reached past his jeans and fought for some airtime.

"STOMP, huh? Sure, do you know how to pack a med kit with everything you'll need." Ciaran struggled to smile as a number of naked thoughts infected his brain.

"The kit? Yeah, I've got the same one at home." She paused. "So, what do you plan on feeding me? I mean, I'm here all night."

*

The kitchen wasn't any better. Watching Hope bend in front of the fridge in search of options made Ciaran want to crawl out of his skin. Not like he'd even be capable of satisfying her, right now. It didn't stop him from thinking about it though, not even for a second.

But who was he kidding? He could never satisfy her. She was beyond out of his league, and he couldn't have anyone that close. He was damaged goods. Ciaran's thoughts scrambled.

She *had* been that close. She'd practically been in his lap, and he didn't feel the same instinct to flee as he normally did. Going out with Dimitri was terrible. Those women trying to grind on him made Ciaran nauseous. But somehow, when it was Hope . . .

"Don't entertain much, do you?" Hope leaned her head out of the fridge and laughed. As she ducked back in, he could hear some clanking and the meat drawer open and close. "Cheese and beer it is."

"Don't have anybody to bring over, so no. Toss one here." Ciaran lifted his arm, and the beer landed soundly in his palm. He cracked it open.

"Guinness boy, huh?"

"I am Irish," Ciaran rolled his eyes, "and that's the last question I'll answer until you tell me what the fuck just happened?"

Hope stood across from him, leaning against the counter. She shifted her weight, clearly not excited about this conversation. Ciaran was glad he was sitting at his island. Something told him this was going to be like pulling a conscious rhino's teeth.

Hope folded her arms across her chest. "Fine. What do you want to know?"

"Well, for starters, your name."

"Hope Cerridwen Turner. Didn't lie about the name. Born in a demon settlement in Canada. Assassin. Anything else?"

"Well, I'm curious why you became an assassin? Was the settlement really that bad?" Ciaran remembered the close-knit community he was from and, though, it was far from nice, it wouldn't make him turn to murder. Well, probably not. But Hope's face said it all. It really was that bad. Her teeth were tight together and he thought she might be sick.

"Sorry, I didn't—"

"Yeah, well, whatever. It was shitty. End of story. I met Dante my first day out."

Change the subject. Got it. "Dante, that's the guy yet mentioned before. What's his deal?"

"He owns the hit company. Targets demon haters. At least that's what I thought. So far, everyone I've ever killed has been human and to my knowledge, a prejudicial prick."

"Obviously, that's not actually the case." Ciaran paused. "Why are you being so forth coming? It's not like you couldn't just kill me and leave."

"I may still be playing with that idea. But the truth is, you're not the only one who got set up. I'm not one to let betrayal slide, and everything I know about Dante could be used to hurt him. Whether or not I do it alone remains to be seen."

"So, I'm your patsy. Kill him with my help, and then leave the cleanup to me." Ciaran could admit when he saw a good plan. He just didn't care for the side of the table he was on. Plus, none of this explained why he was a target. How did this Dante know who he was, and why did he care?

"Maybe. The plan has its pros and cons. But, I'd rather not risk my life for revenge, at least not this revenge. So, Dante screwed me; it's common in my line of work." Hope pulled one of her heels off and then the other. She placed them under the island and slid up a stool across from him.

"This still doesn't tell me why. Why arrange the hit? What could I have possibly done to piss this guy off?"

"Like I said, I don't ask; I just kill." Hope unclipped her hair and the top half fell forward. The dark waves rippled. As she grinned, the piercings in her lip caught the light, and Ciaran found himself wondering what it would feel like to have those glistening silver balls drag alongside his cock. *Holy shit, man. Pull yourself together.*

Ciaran took a huge pull from his Guinness and thought it was about time for another. "Need another beer?"

"Sure." She sighed. "Look, I guess I'm, well, sorry. I never questioned the hits before. Guess, I should have." Hope stared down at the table and bit her tongue. The idea of her believing she'd made a mistake, let alone vocalizing it, seemed impossible.

"But you woulda killed me if it was true. If I actually did attack and kill demons."

"Yes."

Hope handed him another beer and in truth, he was okay with her response. He liked the idea that she was a fighter. It made her well, fuck, it made her hotter. "Tell me something, this company, what's its deal?"

"Well, as far as I know, it was started in New York. It arranges hits on, well, I guess anyone it wants. Dante is in charge, but I mostly deal with his second in command, Roger. I don't have a last name. He's tall and thin, long black ponytail, wire-rim glasses."

"What. Did. You. Say."

"Roger, he's always breathing on them and wiping them off with his—"

"Handkerchief. Hope, what does Dante look like?" Ciaran leaned forward and resisted the urge to grab her arms.

"Tallish, dirty-blond hair, dark blue eyes, and despite all that, a straight-up evil-looking fuck bag. Why?"

Ciaran's heart stopped. After all this time, he'd found him, and this woman was helping him. But she didn't know who he was, and that prick had somehow convinced her he was helping demons. How did he find him? *Ugh. I'm gonna break that bastard's neck.*

Letting out a breath, he asked, "Hope, did you ever hear of the Inferno?"

"What, like the book? Dante's *Inferno*?"

"Ha, and there's the joke. No, the club. Did he say anything about a club? That fucking cock-sucking bastard!"

"Whoa, whoa, slow your roll, Rex. The only thing he ever mentioned about this hit was that the guy, you, had it coming. Destroyed one of his investments or something. I wasn't really listening. Why are you freaking out?"

"Cause that prick is the one that . . . He lied to you, Hope! He kills demons; he kills humans. Well, mostly he likes to watch 'em kill each other. At least he did. His name's not Dante, it's Marcus, Marcus Dentry. I just . . . I'll let you leave right now and never look for you if you can answer me one thing. Where is he?"

EIGHT

For some Shedara-forsaken reason, Ciaran was pissed, completely livid, and it had everything to do with her ex-boss. What was so exciting about some dick that pranced around in a tailored suit and never lifted a finger? But Ciaran was practically attacking her for an answer. The rage coming off him was palpable. Maybe she should knock him out before he did something stupid?

Not like Ciaran would actually hurt her. Not like he could, what with the bullet graze on his side, but even if he was fit as a fucking fiddle, he wouldn't attack her. Hope swallowed. *Pretty sure of that, aren't you, Hope?*

As for the douchebag's location, hell if she knew, but she was so tempted to lie. Dante, or Marcus whatever, could be anywhere. But if Ciaran was going to let her go? Hope didn't want to feel Ciaran's every stretch and rip of that wound, hiding her reactions, watching him spill beer all over his shirtless chest. Well, maybe, that last part.

The thing was that as much as her brain was saddled up with that plan, something else wanted to stay. And besides that, she was kind of curious about Ciaran's past. If she was restrained and tight-lipped, Ciaran was the human equivalent of Homeland Security or the NSA.

During the entire patch-up process, he hadn't said a word. No moans, barely any grunts, and Hope knew exactly how bad it hurt. She would've screamed if it weren't for the concentration she had to maintain, but Ciaran had no excuse for being so controlled, he just was.

Normally, she could read anybody, determine motives, but when it came to Ciaran, she was at a loss. So, she'd stay, purely out of curiosity. At least, that's what she told herself.

"I don't know. He moves around constantly."

"No, you have to fucking know. You can't be serious."

"Well, I am."

"God fucking damn it!"

The air in the kitchen seemed to drop twenty degrees around Ciaran. He could kill something right now. Sure, defending your office was one thing, but Ciaran was capable of walking up behind this man and slitting his throat.

The burn in her side was back, and she knew if Ciaran kept up this show of anger they were headed back to the bathroom, and that room was too tight, too small. She remembered being close to him and the cold air of the kitchen was suddenly a godsend.

"Stop. Ciaran, just stop. You're going to rip open your stitches." Hope pointed to the small stream of red that escaped Ciaran's side.

He looked down. Suddenly, this bank vault was breaking. The frame of the two-foot thick, steel-walled cage was warping under tremendous internal pressure.

"You . . . You just have to tell me everything you know. Even if it seems small. This man, this thing, needs to be put down." Ciaran gripped his fists tight and then relaxed them with a sigh.

But his eyes told more than his body ever would. They burned. She thought it was rage or passion, but no. Far beneath the surface, in a small corner of his impenetrable labyrinth, was pain.

Why am I thinking about this? Sure, physical pain held its reasons, but mental baggage was not connected to *omaeriku.*

It was true, she was curious about his past and truthfully, about his everything. Hope wondered what it was like to have such strong feelings about a friend. To fear for your own safety. She could remember reading a comic as a child and seeing, "A man without hope, is a man without fear." Yeah that was her. She never dreamed of a beautiful house with a white picket fence and 2.5 kids . . . and she never feared losing it. Can't miss what you don't know. *Or can you?*

"Hope. Oh, my god, could you at least pretend to listen?" *Shit. Had he been talking this whole time?*

"I'm sorry. My brain's a little fried." Hope sighed and tried to force a laugh.

She was actually exhausted. All the times she would stare at the ceiling racked with insomnia, turns out all she needed to sleep was one-part *omaeriku* and one-part shooting. She hit a wall here, though. Hope could either divulge all her acquired info and team up with the root of all pain, or she could lie, book-ass out of this place.

"Fuck . . ." Hope breathed out.

"What? You're not suffering from some moral dilemma, are you? Ha, that's a laugh."

"To be honest, Ciaran, yeah, something like that. I could kill myself with what I'm telling you. If he ever figured out I'm the leak, there's no end to what he'd do. I just fucking met you and you're asking me to put my life on the line. I don't do that shit. I don't trust others to stand by their word. Can't imagine you do either. And you're asking me to go against everything and trust you?"

"I get it. But I need what's in your head . . . Does it help to know that you're sticking it to him? The guy did betray you."

"Slightly." *Why are you doing this? Oh, my god, you're really doing this.* "I met him about three years ago. I was leaving my clan's land. They didn't really offer much. I, umm . . ." Hope knew that if she stopped talking her vocal cords would lose the momentum, but memories of that night flashed to the surface. Images of threats, empty words, and supposed freedom.

"I had gotten out of a shitty situation, and I wanted to be free of them. Dante—Marcus offered a way to make that happen. He said he had just the position for a woman of my talents. See, in my race, women can't feel pain. Unless this *omaeriku* thing happens, it's not really important. The point is that I was good at it, violence and all. It seemed like the perfect fit, and it was until I met you. I guess I was naïve. I bought into every lie he fed me. I wanted to punish the world for their shit. I was younger. I did the teenager thing, all angst and I-don't-need-you, even if I wasn't even close to a teen at that point. I've changed so much. Killing makes you grow up, I guess. Anyway, I was told that someone had destroyed a very profitable office of his, and I was to exterminate any and all threats. All leading up to you. Every job was preparing me for this one. This was to be my main show. After this, I could choose my targets. Ambition, kind of a bitch, huh?"

Wow, she just opened that can up. A load of past imperfect to the face. She was even suffering some mild eye-glazing. Maker, she was pathetic, but that night had a way of getting in her head. And Ciaran was a deer-in-the-headlights. He kind of laughed and coughed, adjusting in his seat. Hope could feel the quick, hot stab of pain in her side. Ciaran winced with an echoed expression.

"Okay, now what was that? You've been doing that all day. You're balls deep in that face at the same moment I am. What about the no pain?"

"Oh, you see, that's because of a hormone change, that is it, umm . . ." *Oh, god, I can't lie. Wait. No, no, no. Stop this. This is* omaeriku. *You do this. You lie your ass off.* "It's a demon thing. That *omaeriku* I was talking about. It'll pass."

"Okay . . . I still don't get it. What's the deal? Can't you just tell me? Or are you afraid that my inferior human mind will implode with such information?"

Well, there was the rub, Hope couldn't just tell him without dragging him into this whole mess.

"It's just hard to explain, Ciaran. Summary, female Chakal demons, my clan, don't feel pain, unless they experience *omaeriku*, the ability to feel the physical pain of people near to them. It's a tactical advantage. We can understand an enemy's weakness. Know when we've wounded them and so on." *Hell, that sounded pretty good.*

"But if you feel the pain of your enemies, doesn't that, well, you know, hurt?"

"Well, now, yes. I'm just developing it. At first, we can't separate the actual pain from the ability to just feel that it was caused. I mean how fast did you learn to walk?" She hoped the nonchalant pose was convincing.

Ciaran quirked a brow and then just shrugged. He bought it. For now.

"So, until you get a hold on it, every time I'm in pain, you're in pain? That kinda sucks." Ciaran shuffled and sat up straighter on the stool. "Anywho . . . thank you for telling me about Marcus. He's a bigger dick than you know, and we have a history as you've probably guessed. I just want him stopped. I don't want to just wonder where to go next, how to survive, it's exhausting."

He was blathering as much as she was. It was sort of comforting.

"I know this will sound bad, but what the hell, right? You're an assassin. I'm sure you're not all sunshine and rainbows." Ciaran laughed, and his side burned.

"No, not really." Hope stared at her beer and downed the rest of the bottle.

"I was, umm, an unlicensed fighter. That sounds weird out loud. He had people fight and took bets. The fighters never really lasted long, not unless they got good at it. People would start building a serious rep if they made it past a month. Past three or four, and you were golden. It really only got worse the longer you were there. If you were attracting people, you'd fight more. If you fought more, you got your arse beat more. And the weaker, more tenderized you got, the easier it was to die. Plus, if you were getting too good, the audience got bored. Marcus would order you to take a dive, which was basically suicide. I was there a while."

"How long?"

"Over a year."

"Damn." A strange pull in her chest got her attention. It was like Hope's heart had migrated to her stomach.

"Yeah." Ciaran looked at his forgotten beer and drank the rest in one solid gulp.

Hope stared at white bandages around Ciaran's abdomen. The longer she stared the more her mind decided to do things without permission. "I should really check that."

"What? Oh, yeah, you're probably right." Ciaran pushed his chair back.

The large expanse of his chest moved up and down as he breathed. The tension in his muscles looked like it might rip them off his bones.

Hope rounded the counter and rubbed her hands together. Apparently, holding a cold beer made your hands cold. Who knew? She tried to offer a friendly glance, but never having tried one before wasn't sure how it looked. He smiled back. It was sort of lopsided and easy. The dimple in his cheek stood out. *Is it really hot?*

Hope wondered if it was the pain she sensed from Ciaran, but it wasn't entirely unpleasant, just uncontrollable. *Bodies should listen to their owners.*

"Sorry, if my fingers are cold." Hope knelt in front of him and sat back on her feet.

"It's fine. I'm a little warm, anyway."

So, it was him. But the moment she touched his skin, the fire amped up. It was so smooth. The bandage came off him in a sweeping circle. The graze was healing well, no doubt a side effect of being extremely healthy and in phenomenal shape. He was like a sculpture. Every curve and ridge of muscle etched to perfection and covered in velvety, tan flesh. He was decorated, too. Not nearly as much as she was, but still. There was the Celtic tattoo and a few on the insides of his arms.

They were numbers on each arm, seven digits, but fuck if she knew why they were there. As her eyes traveled the muscles of his forearms up to his biceps, Hope was overwhelmingly hot. Touching Ciaran was doing it, but she couldn't let go. Did she like it? *I guess I do. It feels . . . nice. Ahh, this is so weird.*

Hope began to wind the bandage back around Ciaran's torso and her head brushed his chest. *Dear Maker, he smells fabulous like leather and firewood and cinnamon and something else. I don't know.* Strange thoughts whispered into her mind, and they were so very physical. *Touch him, touch him more. Put your fingers against his flesh and drag them across his skin.* What was she thinking? Why was it so loud? *If he smelled this good, surely, he would taste like heaven too.* Shendara, *I want to . . . kiss him. Holy Maker, I want to kiss and touch and . . . oh fuck.*

Without the presence of mind to understand what she was doing, Hope laid her hand on Ciaran's chest, directly over his heart.

"It's pounding." Shit on a stick, did she say that out loud?

"Yeah, how about that?" Ciaran's skin prickled under her fingers and his pecs tensed.

"Am I hurting you?"

"You'd be the first to know." Ciaran chuckled softly, and the sound made Hope feel drunk. "No, I'm fine. . . . Just warm."

Hope was still staring at his chest. She faced him and pretended she wasn't imagining him like a piece of something yummy. But Ciaran was looking down at her, and as soon as she could pull her eyes from his chest, they met his stare. Their faces were inches apart, and his eyes were on her mouth.

Ciaran's breath brushed her lips, and she cursed that everything about him was so fucking warm and that she could now feel it. *Omaeriku means you can feel pain; when did everything else get added in?* The bandage had fallen into his lap, and her hands were on his shoulders as she knelt in front of him. *When did I do that?*

She released quiet, heaving gasps. She couldn't stop her eyes from visiting his lips, and they were so red. Her blood was loud in her ears and neither one of them had spoken in a while.

"It's really warm." Her voice barely broke the air.

"Yeah. Warm." Ciaran was on the edge of his chair, and he started to move his arms.

"Umm."

His hands went to his knees, mere centimeters from grazing her breasts. Brain function ceased. Her only thought was of Ciaran's shirtless chest.

"Hope."

Just her name, and it still made her heart pound, and the juncture of her legs burn. *Shendara*, she was aroused. Truly, for the first time, Hope was aroused.

She'd spent ages wondering what it would be like, and it was nothing, if not all-consuming. Deep inside her, she knew the ripple this would cause would echo through everything. Not just tonight, but forever. Like being struck by a bus and equally destructive. Internal warning bells screamed at full volume.

A rational side of her brain tried to protest. "I don't think—"

But she stopped.

Her fingers gripped Ciaran's shoulders, and she trembled. The room was suddenly small with every part of them mere inches apart. Hope hovered in that space.

His flesh was painfully close, and her core burned, wept with invitation. The Maker had seen fit to grant her with a will etched in steel, but it also seemed that *Shendara* implanted the complete and utter inability to resist Ciaran. Something in her roared to seize him, surrender to his touch. *Omaeriku*, the bond, had sealed the two of them inexorably together.

The strained gasp that escaped Ciaran pulled her out of her head. She enjoyed hearing him make that noise, and her arousal only peaked at the thought of hours of it. Hope smiled, and this time it was real. She met Ciaran's eyes, those impressively dark, chocolaty eyes, and apparently, that smile sealed the deal.

In seconds, his hands left his knees and grabbed the sides of her face. He cradled her jaw so delicately, but Hope could see the pained control he was forcing, hanging by a thread. Ciaran was on the edge of his chair like he was at the edge of a deliciously inviting cliff. His powerful legs surrounded her. She was trapped between them and truly didn't care. He could have rushed, pushed, but he didn't. He waited. He waited for her.

Ciaran was breathing as hard as Hope and staring at her with a lidded gaze. Hope watched as his eyes traveled along her neck down to her breasts and back to her lips. She was devoured by it, consumed by his hungry eyes. The center of her flared, and Hope wondered if she would actually burst into flames.

Ciaran shifted further to the edge of his chair. *He wants to be closer, so much closer. Really?*

And then he was kneeling in front of her. The pain in his side barely registered, and his hands never left her face. Ciaran loomed above her on his knees, moving to touch his body to hers. Flat against each other, the contact was still so light. Hope gripped Ciaran's hips, holding him close. *Gods, why am I doing this? I just . . . Gods, I want him to devour me.*

"Hope."

There it was again, her name from his lips. Every time she heard it, she was enveloped by the hot sensation blooming from inside her even more. She was nearly bursting, and the feel of his fingers entwining in her hair was incredible.

His hands were rough, used, but they weren't demanding, fingertips touching her skin so lightly. He lowered his forehead to hers; a light layer of sweat had formed. Hope breathed in. So many sensations, hot and tight and desperate, and she was intoxicated by them. And then her lips touched Ciaran's.

NINE

Ciaran's eyes were wide. He was frozen as Hope's lips pressed against his. Nothing in all his life could've prepared him for the sensation that ricocheted through his body. He was sure he'd been electrocuted. The sharp, warm snap inside him breathed fire through his veins and pumped it back into the core of his heart. Something, although he didn't know exactly what, had changed in him forever, and the light, breathy touches from Hope weren't even close to enough.

He knew this was going to happen. Ever since the bathroom, Ciaran's brain tried to tell him that if he got close to Hope, he would lose it. He'd been alright, for like a second. But then she touched him, pressed herself to him, and it was all over.

It was just too weird, though. He was never aroused, not for so long, not after Marcus. God, he couldn't think of that.

But how did this happen? He barely let Dimitri in, and here he was letting a woman he met less than a day ago make him feel . . . He didn't know. Alive? Yeah, and for the first time in a long while. Hope definitely got under his skin, but how? The only thing that ever stole his attention was the dream. *God, that's it. White streak and all. She's real and here. Oh, Jesus, do not let me wake up.*

His erection strained inside his jeans and demanded to be inside of Hope, heart thundering like he was running a marathon, and his grip tightened.

Ciaran cursed to himself. "Hope, I want . . . need to be inside you."

He pulled her closer, the feeling of her soft breasts against his chest sending shock waves down his groin. He kissed Hope more, and she let his tongue dart inside of her. He stroked her tongue with his own and on every withdrawal nibbled at her plump bottom lip. Damn, he needed her so bad. It was nothing he'd ever felt before, and his head swam as image after image flooded his lust-crazed brain. The moan that escaped her lips between frantic kisses made him shiver as she dug her fingers into his shoulders.

Ciaran all but tackled her. He tried to cushion her fall to the floor with one arm and held his weight with the other. The graze in his side burned. Was he hurting her? Fear tickled at Ciaran's spine.

Hope reached up, pulling him down to her mouth. The sweet taste and smell of her overwhelmed his senses. She let his hips push her legs apart and the hard length trapped in his pants pressed against her. *So much for hurting her.*

"Ciaran . . ." Hope's voice was barely a whisper as they continued to explore each other's mouths. She held him tight against her body, breathing hard, and the sight of her breasts moving up and down made his hand move on its own. He pressed his fingers lightly, dragging them down the side of her neck to take her seductive breast and squeeze. Hope arched and ground her hips against his. He pushed away the fabric caging her and tore the flimsy bra free.

"Fuck . . ." Ciaran groaned.

With the lace gone, more of Hope's perfect body was revealed, and it shot his arousal through the goddamn roof. The rosy pink of her nipples would have been enough, but the icing on this particularly delicious cake was the gleaming metal beads that danced on either side of them. He'd never thought about pierced nipples, and now, he was obsessed. Ciaran had to have them in his mouth. To touch and play with the sinful, little pieces that hugged the tips of her full breasts.

"Oh, Hope, please, please let me kiss you here." Ciaran squeezed again, and Hope's released a moan. "Please, Hope, say it."

He had to hear her, had to know she wanted this. He couldn't force her. *No one should do shit they don't want. . . . Oh, god, get out of your head.*

"Oh, god, yessss."

Good.

Ciaran wanted to entice those sounds out of her over and over. He looked up at Hope as he licked one gloriously hard nipple. She was arched up off the floor, eyes closed tight, and gasping. It was the most sensual thing he'd ever seen. *More.*

The dress was off with barely an effort, and when he saw Hope's skin in all its tattooed, pale glory, Ciaran nearly came.

The artwork, which was one continuous tattoo, weaved all across her breathtaking body. It curved around the top of her shoulders to the inside of her arms and down to her fingers. He'd seen those, but the sweeping section that curved around her ribcage and down her flat stomach was new.

The tattoo accentuated the sensuous curve of her breasts, scooping under them and meeting at her sternum, then jutting down to her navel. The black lines traveled straight down to the front of her stomach to the top of her pelvis only to teasingly split again and run down the outside of her legs. And she sparkled everywhere, a jewel encrusted in each shoulder and hip.

Did he dare venture where that tattoo feared to go? Fuck, yes, he did. With a hand still grabbing one of Hope's full breasts, he kissed his way down to her hips. Her alabaster flesh was framed in dark hair. Hope's sweet, intoxicating smell was all around him, and he hungered to taste the honeyed flesh of her core.

"Hope. I have to."

"Wha—"

The question deserted her as the tip of his tongue licked gently at her clit and holy lord, the taste of her. Ciaran would never get enough. She was sweet, rich, and blazingly hot. He welcomed the scratches of her nails in his shoulders as he sucked and pulled her into his mouth like he was drinking molten gold.

"I should . . ."

Hope tried to speak, but Ciaran was enjoying himself far too much. He flicked his tongue across that magick place and began to drag his hand up toward his mouth. With one long lick across her, Ciaran let his fingers join the fun. Her core was weeping and so ready for the orgasm lingering just around the corner. She was tight around his fingers and blissfully warm.

As Ciaran pushed in and out of her, Hope bucked off the floor. She clawed at his shoulders and grabbed his hair. Hope was so close, so ready to release all that built-up tension. Ciaran was beside himself, the joy of making her orgasm lit him up from the inside. When she cried out his name, he nearly lost it. But Ciaran had to be inside her when he came.

The surge of her muscles around his hand was incredible. Ciaran watched awestruck as he pushed her over the edge and made her come over and over. When he finally released her, she was drenched and gasping. The erotic taste of her slid down his throat and stirred his hunger. In all of two seconds, his pants and boxers were off and left under the counter. In the brief moment Ciaran wasn't closed in around Hope, she sat up.

"Ciaran, holy fuck . . . I really should . . . tell you . . ." Hope struggled to speak between breaths, and he pulled her close.

"What? What is it?" He kissed her neck as he spoke.

"I've, oh god, I've never . . . I've never done this."

"Neither have I. I promise I don't make a habit of taking girls back to my place." Ciaran continued kissing and nibbling at the side of Hope's neck and let his hand run down her body to her breast. He gently pinched her nipple ring and breathed her in.

"Ugh. I . . . No, Ciaran that's not what I mean. I've never, well, I've never, umm, had sex." Hope stilled in his arms.

Ciaran shook his head. He must have heard wrong. How could someone as utterly sexual and stunning as Hope have never done this? But she was still frozen in his arms and staring at the ground.

"What? Oh, my god, I'm so sorry, I didn't—"

"No, don't be sorry. I still want to. I really, really do. I just wanted you to know. And I guess, I wanted to . . . know what this was going to be like." She looked up at him, her fierce eyes showing a hint of embarrassment. "Never really had a sex talk."

Ciaran was speechless. What the hell was the right thing to say? God, should he even be doing this? But at the thought of someone else, some other man, being the one to do this with her made him think seriously of finding said man and driving his head through a wall.

"Hope, we don't have to do this. I can't lie to you. I really want to. Sitting here next to you, so very naked and not devouring you, is taking some serious strength of will. But, you have to want to."

Hope's eyes seemed to search him, looking for something to make her decision, and Ciaran tried to show everything his words couldn't. Unfortunately, his thoughts started to swirl in his head again, and a game of chicken with the past started. Ciaran could almost feel himself fracture down the middle.

Half of him wanted Hope so bad he'd be willing to chop off his leg to get close to her, but another half wanted to shake with all the cool of a fucking "fraidy cat" child in the dark. To panic with someone close enough to see all of him and take what they wanted.

But Hope wasn't taking. She looked at him and gave him control over how this would work. *This could be good. I'm in control. I can stop or go, whenever I want.*

"I want this." Hope leaned in, offering herself to him.

Ciaran pulled her close and the hard tips of her breasts touched his bare chest. The screaming desire took its rightful place at the front of his mind. This beautiful demon was the single sexiest woman on the planet, in the whole fucking universe, and she wanted him. *How'd I get this lucky?*

"Alright. I do feel I should tell you, it can hurt at first if we go too fast. I'll be slow."

"Okay. Now, please, Ciaran." Hope's voice burned.

He could listen to her say his name over and over.

But the moment she touched him again, his skin set on fire. With surprising strength, she pulled him down to her mouth and on top of her. Her knees fell easily to the side, and Hope nibbled and kissed his neck. Ciaran was hard enough to cut a diamond.

He couldn't be aggressive though, so he focused on the feel of her lips. As he looked down at Hope, the tension inside reached epic proportions, again. Her wavy hair with its white streak was tousled and wild. Her lips were swollen and red, her pale flesh bathed in a euphoric glow. He slid a hand down to the hot, wet center waiting for him.

Hope moaned, and Ciaran worked his fingers. She panted again and pressed herself against his hard-working hand. Groaning and cursing, Hope pulled his arm close to her face. She turned and bit into his forearm, the release poised at her core finally bursting free. He strained against the unbelievable desire to slam into her, but as she angled closer, the tip of his erection slid teasingly across her.

Ciaran shuddered at the heat between Hope's legs, and he gave in. He gripped Hope's hip with one hand as she continued to bite his other arm, and slowly began to sheathe himself. Together, they created an incredible friction.

Hope's grip tightened around his forearm. "Are you okay?"

"Yes. Don't stop." Hope grumbled the words as she bit her lip.

Ciaran continued to move back and forth inside her. She squeezed around him.

Hope let out a shattering cry and ripped into Ciaran's skin with her nails. The sensation was tremendous, an elixir of pleasure and slight pain. Hope stared up at him, and as their eyes met, Ciaran found his favorite look in the world. She was completely blissed out.

Her long, graceful legs fell further open, and she took every thrust of him. Ciaran squeezed her hip tight, anchoring himself as he pushed deeper and deeper. Hope arched back, orgasm after orgasm rocketing through her. Each one made the fierce muscles inside her clench his shaft and brought him closer to his own release. Every inch of Ciaran's body burned. The magnificent, crushing pressure poised in his erection transformed him, the weights beneath it pulling up tight and exciting the animal in him.

The roar that rumbled out of his chest was unadulterated, primal lust—a demand to possess Hope and give her everything he had in return. Hope screamed out through smiles. Her voice covered Ciaran in another sweet layer of desire, the ecstasy bursting from her called for more and more of him, and he would give it to her.

Ciaran grabbed Hope's hips with both hands and flipped her to her stomach. The floor pressed her luscious breasts up to her chin, and she lifted her hips up to greet him. The softest skin of her body was luminescent as the fading light kissed the wet flesh. It was beautiful, and Ciaran dove into her with passionate force. The rhythm they created was a divine dance of possession and submission, giving and taking. He reached a hand to her throat and pulled her tighter against him. Hope's hand covered his, her nails digging into his fingers, but she was pressing it harder to the tender skin of her neck, gasping and sighing, as she opened herself up for still more.

She was his. She had given her body over, and the act was enough to make the fearsome tension inside of him finally boil over. The orgasm that had been out of reach his entire life split him open and burst with such force it left Ciaran breathless. Hope's core embraced the release and squeezed down all around him, coming right along with him. Ciaran couldn't stop. Every thrust pulling out more, until she'd milked every last drop.

The final growl of pleasure from Ciaran harmonized with Hope's and echoed in the quiet house. Both of their arms gave out, the sweet feeling of completion taking over. Ciaran laid on the floor beside her and pulled Hope to his chest. The skin of her back was moist against him, and her heart pounded. She was quiet aside from hard breaths rushing in and out.

"Are you alright?" Ciaran whispered into her hair.

Hope's eyes were closed, her cheeks rosy. She was so beautiful and sort of fragile, he'd never noticed before. She probably hadn't let him, but now with her cradled against him, she was small. Marcus could never get his hands on her.

She stirred beside him and rolled onto her back. When she looked up into his eyes and smiled, Ciaran nearly melted.

"I'm great. I'm kinda sore, but great."

She wasn't lying; she was great. But reality rushed back in. There was still so much going on. For now, Ciaran rolled onto his back and pulled Hope into the crook of his arm. She fit perfectly, and as she closed her eyes, Ciaran let himself drift off to the best sleep he'd had in ages.

TEN

The floor under her was cool, but kind to her hip it was not. Consciousness ran up, and Hope flicked her lids open. Ciaran lay next to her on the kitchen floor, holding her in one arm. He smelled good, and Hope took a deep breath against his tan skin.

She pushed up onto an elbow and looked down at the sleeping figure of her *jabalv*, barely able to see in the fading light. His chest rose and fell slowly, his thick, black eyelashes rested gently on his face, and his lips were slightly parted. He was so . . . beautiful. Fierce and masculine of course, but right now peaceful. The memories from the hours before spun. The amazing touch of his skin and power in his body. *What just happened?*

She laid her head down on his chest and heard the solid beat of his heart. The steady rhythm was slow. As she studied him, a twinge of warmth radiated out between Hope's legs. She was so sore. Ciaran had completely overwhelmed her body. At first, she didn't think she could stand it. Coupled with the burn from Ciaran's wound, it was so intense. But he'd gone slow, and her body slowly opened to him. She'd become completely overcome by the pure sensation of it all. Ciaran's strong hand around her throat, his powerful hips barreling into her. She was marked by it. It was . . . addicting. Even now, she wanted more.

Gods. What did I do?

She had completely bonded with Ciaran. The physical act, an animalistic ritual of submission to *omaeriku*. There was no out now. No escape. She was Ciaran's until an unbelievable distance or death separated them. A cold rock formed in the pit of her stomach. Hope had just damned herself. She knew the power of *omaeriku* from afar, but now, it was all around her like a straightjacket. The madness she'd let herself fall into, sinking in. *Oh gods, oh gods.* Hope's heart pounded in her ears. She was dizzy and chilled and hot.

No, this wasn't right. Hope never gave anyone anything. And here she was lying naked in Ciaran's arms. She'd know she'd never have sex, never. But now? She had just given in. But who the fuck could argue when six feet of hot-as-hell was staring at you like a desperate, hungry wolf.

Ciaran stirred and turned his head toward her, his arm curving around her and squeezing. That arm she'd bitten in her desperate attempt to release pent-up desire. She could see the marks. It had hurt them both, but not in a bad way.

He'd let her bite him.

Of course, she'd let him taste her. Let him touch every inch of her. She'd offered up everything she had and then some. Ciaran had pushed inside her and pulled something out, unleashing a sensation from deep inside and throwing her over the edge over and over. As if he wanted to become a part of her. And he was. He was fused to her in that moment of . . . she didn't know what.

He was falling into a similar trap. He could have killed her as easily as she could him. They had opportunities all day and yet here they were. *He could've, he could've bolted, he could right now, but instead . . .* As if in response, Ciaran's arm squeezed again and pulled her body closer. He held her so tightly; it was like he was afraid she might disappear.

Hope stared down at him. Ciaran's tan skin glimmered in the dying light. But even he got uncomfortable and turned over, and then she saw them. Huge, pale slashes covered his back so that barely any unmarred flesh was left.

Ciaran's voice echoed in her mind. *Over a year.* What had they done to him? What had Marcus done to him?

Acid rose in Hope's throat, and she clenched her fists. Someone had torn into his flesh over and over. She imagined the heat of the lash. Hope's stomach dropped. If she'd met him then, she *would* have felt it. His pain was hers. Hope tried to think of something, anything, else, but the grotesque image of his ragged flesh being torn from his back burned.

Marcus would pay. She wasn't a person to fuck with and Marcus had. Royally. Maker, she had to talk to Ciaran. Hope had to know what had happened even if it was only to determine the particular type of implement to use to peel that bastard's flesh off. Of course, he'd probably want to know about her. About *omaeriku*, her past, and what happened with her clan. *Oh, Ciaran, by the way, I'm bound to you forever, and I can feel your pain, just yours, and now you're stuck with me. Sound good? Ugh. How exactly can I both want something and not at the same time?*

"Hey. You're awake."

Hope jumped.

"Ha, sorry." Ciaran shuffled under her and shifted to sit up. His broad shoulders were covered in small nicks from her nails and his bandage was twisted. But as he leaned back against the cupboards, Hope didn't feel much pain, just a small twinge.

"Hi. Apparently, you are, too." Hope curled her legs under her and sat next to Ciaran, pulling her hair in front to shield her breasts.

"Don't." Ciaran pushed her hair back and gave her cheek a stroke. "I like to look at you."

As Ciaran's eyes traced the flesh of her breasts, Hope could feel her cheeks flush. The juncture of her legs moistened, and her skin was too small.

She was so exposed. The women of the *braednas* ceremony wore robes. And the thought accidentally pulled forward the horror of the past.

The hand around her arm squeezed tightly. Hope noticed nothing. The braednas *temple waited, and two males shoved her inside and locked the huge doors behind her. There was another female waiting there too. Hope furrowed her brow.*

"Kneel." The woman pointed at a small piece of wood with a white cushion on top in the center of the room.

Hope walked over and did as told. The small cushion was barely big enough to fit her knees comfortably.

"Lean forward." The woman spoke again, her words a threat.

Hope leaned her hips awkwardly on the higher cushion. She didn't know what to do with her hands and as she wondered, the other woman took her wrists and placed them one on top of the other at the small of her back.

"You will stay like this until it is finished. You will not speak or make any noise. Nod to show you understand."

Hope nodded.

"Good. I will send in the impraenata. *Be still. Be silent. Then, leave through there."*

With that, Hope was left to kneel in silence. Face down, all she could see was the white stone floor. It was the same shade as the walls, the curtains, the robe she wore; it represented the holy nature of the braednas *ceremony. Hope hated white. The hem of her dress was turning brown from dust, and the curtains showed wear from years of brushing the floor. If she looked closely, Hope could see every trace of dirt and grime all of the space.*

Hope clenched her teeth, squeezing her hands into fists.

The front door creaked open. The impraenata *must have entered. A rush of air flew in, and Hope watched the dress around her feet flutter. She knew she wouldn't feel when the* impraenata *touched her and performed the mating act, so she didn't know how to tell when he was done.* Perhaps, I'll wait until he leaves and then, know to leave myself. *His voice sounded just behind her.*

"I did get a pretty one."

Hope saw the edge of her robe leave the floor and sensed a slight change around her legs and bottom. He must have lifted the robing.

"You are so pale of flesh, except here. Here you are rosy."

Hope didn't know what he was referring to.

"I think I shall ensure the completion of this ceremony many, many times."

Hope remained silent and waited.

"You say nothing, as you were told, but perhaps you have nothing to say. After all, you are merely here for my use. Doing your duty, lying there as an empty-headed sack to be filled."

Hope couldn't have spoken if she was allowed, but his words made her mouth fall open. Was she not as important in this ceremony? She was told this was a sacred task for all female Chakal. She was to usher in a new generation. But this man was comparing her to the women she knew they used for pleasure alone. A whore, the humans called them. As he chuckled and apparently continued to enjoy the sound of his own degrading voice, Hope's mind recoiled from the onslaught.

Had all of the women faced such words in this sacred temple? And in truth, Hope had not seen the need for this ceremony, the number of her clan was numerous, and there were many others who seemed more aligned to the task. She didn't want this and faced with the raining torment of his words, she filled with an emotion she had not experienced much.

"Yes, you lie before me as nothing but a cup. I shall fill you with my pleasure, and when I am through, you shall clean, and I will never have to deal with you again. You cannot even tell that I lay hands upon you, can you, whonadana?*"*

Hope chewed her lip, squeezing her fists tighter. He'd called her a whore.

"Such a useless gift. Such a useless gender. Your body acts without your knowledge. Even as you hold firm on your cushioned board, your untouched flesh

weeps. A pathetic waste. Do your duty and move not as I steal pleasure from your pink flesh."

The taste of blood seeped into her mouth; her lip torn open unknowingly. To this man, this creature, she was not a vessel for the race; she was a sexual tool to be used, cleaned, and tossed aside. Until he saw fit to use it again. Hope could not remain still.

A familiar, nagging thought argued against the teachings of the book of Shendara. *Should she not press on as the daughter of the shaman should? No, no longer. This assault was the last. As the thought of carrying an unwanted* yanyas *in her womb crept along her spine, and the vision of ostracized women in her clan swirled around her, something broke free.*

A great anger broke down the wall of the "good daughter," and Hope stood up to face the impraenata. *His eyes grew wide, and he began to speak.*

"Wha—"

"Say nothing, if you want to keep your teeth." Hope took a deep breath, remembering how the human male who brought supplies spoke. "You are a son of a bitch, and you won't touch me. I'm done playing this bullshit role of the perfect, little girl. Get the . . . the fuck out of this room. You . . . you bastard."

The male was shaking and sweating profusely. Now, who was pathetic? *But as strong as she felt, she would pay for this affront to* Shendara. *As he scrambled and fell, running for the back door, Hope lifted her chin and walked out the front.*

"Hope? Hope, are you okay?" Ciaran was leaning toward her, holding a hand to her face.

"I'm sorry. I was thinking about something . . . Well, something shitty." Hope shook her head and started to stand.

Ciaran's hand around her wrist held her, and she sat down beside him. For seconds, there was nothing but silence.

"What is it? You look like you want to say something." Ciaran sat back against the cupboards.

He was giving her space, but it was still so strange. She wanted to tell him, but something made the words form a lump in her throat. Her pulse throbbed in her temples, the pit of her stomach heavy and achy. After all the time fighting her clan's traditions, *omaeriku* was slapping her in the face. She could still run, go back to her normal life. If she stayed far away, she could ignore the pain, but something about the thought made her chest ache, sinking and deflating.

How was this supposed to work? She was an assassin and a demon, and he was in private security and a human. This couldn't last, and tomorrow morning she was going to drop Ciaran off with Dimitri. They'd never see each other again. *Shendara that makes me feel gross. What is this?*

"If you don't want to talk about it, that's fine. I'm not gonna push." Ciaran smiled awkwardly and tucked a stray hair behind her ear.

"Sorry. I'm just too in my head, right now." Hope sort of laughed. Man, was that an understatement.

"Well, how about this? We go upstairs to the bathroom and get some awesome shower love?" Ciaran stood up and the pinch in his side had improved even though it'd only been a few hours. He reached a hand down and held it open, waiting.

It was so stupid, but Hope knew that if she took his hand, that was it. If she took what was offered, there was no going back. Her pulse thundered in her ears. She could barely hear herself think. Hope started to sweat and too many sensations flooded her. The memory of the bullet graze, the ache coming from Ciaran's knee buzzed in her own, the cold air made her skin ripple, the hardwood pushed against her ankle bones, the pressure in her knees from sitting on them. It all pressed down harder and harder.

Then, she took Ciaran's hand and followed him upstairs.

*

The shower was amazing. The heat, the water running down her skin, it was more perfect than she could've imagined. Sex was still Hope's favorite, but this was a close second. She'd been standing under the spray when Ciaran grabbed a bottle from the wire rack hanging from the shower head. She went to face him, but he smiled and twirled his finger, telling her to turn around.

Hope heard the bottle open with a funny squishing noise. Ciaran was so quiet, and Hope just watched water droplets fall.

Ciaran's hands on her head made Hope jump a little. He chuckled, and she bit back the desire to slap him. Ciaran's fingers pressed gently into her scalp, moving in small circles. He was washing her hair. The scent of shampoo wafted through the steam, and Hope sighed, her shoulders relaxing.

"That feels, just . . . wow." Hope couldn't help but smile.

"Never had someone wash your hair, huh?"

"No, and besides, I wouldn't have felt it, anyway." As the words left her mouth, Hope's stomach dropped. *Oops.*

"What?"

Ciaran stopped, and he turned her around. Hope admired his naked body. His muscles were wet and glistening. And now that she could look closely at him, she realized Ciaran was huge. Hope's eyes widened and a tinge of blush crept up. Ciaran's face was hard, however, and it snapped her back into focus.

"Did I not mention that?"

"You know you didn't. Now, spill." Ciaran frowned and rinsed his hands. She couldn't keep looking at him, so she turned and watched soap bubbles go down the drain.

"Before *omaeriku*, I couldn't feel anything. I mean there were some vague sensations, but mostly nothing." Hope met Ciaran's brown eyes and waited.

"Nothing? Really?"

"Really."

"Is that a Chakal thing?"

"For the women, yes."

Ciaran was silent and the sound of the water hitting the shower floor grew deafening. Hope looked from his face to the floor and back. Had the shower gotten a lot smaller?

Ciaran lifted a hand and dragged them lightly down Hope's arm. When his fingers reached hers, he laced them together.

"When I got shot, 'cause of this *omaeriku* thing, you felt it. Was that the first time you felt pain?" Ciaran's grip was tight, his eyes locked on hers.

"Yes. One of the first things I felt at all actually."

He looked to their hands, and the shower was quiet again. Then, he stared at her face for what seemed like centuries.

"I'm so sorry. I'm so sorry you had to feel that pain, 'cause of me." He was shaking his head.

Hope's mouth fell open. He was apologizing. He was fucking apologizing for something he had no control over. Hope lost her voice. It left a be-back-in-ten-minutes sign on her vocal cords. She just stared at him, feeling the squeeze of his hand on hers.

The shower stayed quiet. Ciaran slowly let go and trailed his fingers back up Hope's arm. With his other hand, he reached to the wire rack again and pulled down a bottle of White Rain body wash. As he squeezed a large handful into his palm, he made sure to still be touching her. He replaced the bottle and dipped his free fingers into the soap.

He rubbed the bubbling suds over Hope's arms and down her collarbones. He continued down her breasts and onto her stomach. Ciaran turned her around and washed the skin of her back and neck. All through it, his fingers were light, feather soft. As he turned her back, he went to his knees in front of her. Ciaran rubbed the remaining soap together in his hands and smoothed it down her legs. Hope couldn't stop staring.

As his hand swept across her thighs and butt, the burning in her core returned. Even compared to the water, his touch was so warm. Ciaran stood again and rinsed his hands behind her. As he looked down at her, a small smile brushed his lips. Locked into his stare, Hope let Ciaran get her under the spray. The warm rivulets rinsed her clean.

Ciaran's hands returned to her shoulders and smoothed the water off her skin. His hands repeated their journey and caressed the soap off her back, then butt, and thighs. Hope was on fire, and the steaming water wasn't helping. Ciaran knelt down again, running his hands down the inside of her thighs. His was firmer as he moved her feet farther apart.

Ciaran's hands slid up her thighs and brushed her sensitive skin. Hope was shaking. *We did this. . . . Why does this feel so much . . . more.*

The rasp of his goatee against her bare flesh sent shockwaves down her spine, and Hope arched despite herself. Ciaran's hands drifted softly across her tender flesh. The peaceful kisses were both calming and exhilarating. As he looked up, Ciaran smiled, and Hope leaned down to kiss him. Her hands found the side of his face and pulled him off his knees until he stood before her, powerful and aroused.

"I'm not finished with you," Ciaran said against her mouth and fumbled to turn the shower off.

Hope ignored it and continued to enjoy his lips and tongue. Without warning, Ciaran whipped open the shower curtain and lifted Hope into his arms. He gracefully stepped out, and Hope playfully squirmed. Ciaran's strong arms kept her in place easily.

Ciaran walked out of the bathroom and went down the hall as quickly as he could with Hope in his arms. He kicked open a dark wood door. The room was pitch black with night in full bloom. Ciaran nodded toward the left, and Hope flipped on light.

The room was huge and extremely well done, but it didn't seem lived in.

"Is this your room?" Hope looked up as he held her just inside the doorway.

"Well, no actually. This is the master bedroom, but I sleep downstairs."

"Then, I want to go there." Hope smiled. Ciaran was going to take her down the stairs, and she'd be damned if he was putting her down.

"Fine. Just had to make me do more work." Ciaran shook his head.

"Yup."

As Hope laughed, Ciaran tossed her up slightly and threw her over his shoulder. She grunted as his shoulder pushed into her stomach and pounded lightly on his back.

"Ciaran! My ass is totally up for grabs like this!"

A sharp slap landed right on her left cheek. "That's how I like it."

Hope could hear him laugh, and the sound melted her. Thank the Maker that he couldn't see how big she was smiling.

"Put me down!"

"Oh, I will, but not here." Ciaran walked over to the huge, wrought iron staircase and went down the winding steps making sure Hope bounced slightly as he went.

As she heard Ciaran open another door and saw there was another kitchen downstairs, Hope wondered why everything he used was in the basement. Ciaran carried her into his room, and it was much more like him. The dark blue walls ate up the light, but the exposed bricks offset the darkness with their rusty color. There was a large bed with a nightstand and that was pretty much it. *Just the essentials*, she thought.

Ciaran set Hope down at the foot of the bed, and she glared at him.

"Lay down," Ciaran commanded and put his hands on his naked hips. His tight muscles were gleaming in the soft illumination of the small lamp. His dark hair slick and his goatee sensually menacing.

"You know, I don't like taking orders."

"You will from me."

"Oh, really?" Hope dragged out the words and matched Ciaran's stance. The posture made her breasts push forward, and she could see Ciaran's eyes eat her up.

"Yes. Now, lay down."

Hope moved backward and onto the bed. She pushed herself across the soft, cotton duvet and leaned back on her elbows. Hope watched Ciaran smile naughtily. He was right. She did like this. The satisfaction of arousing him was a powerful drug.

"Good, but I want you all the way down."

Hope rested her head on his pillow.

"Much better." Ciaran stalked across the bed and held himself over her.

Hope got an eyeful of his vicious form. The muscles of his forearms were rock solid. His abs pulled taut. And below, his straining erection was glorious. He was almost as big as her forearm.

"Stay."

A lick of fear at the familiar command prickled Hope's skin, but Ciaran's eyes were excited, not the demanding, angry glare she remembered.

Ciaran swept the hair back from her neck and lowered his full lips to her collarbone. He nipped and kissed. The small pinches of pain were fascinating. She was so aroused that the sensation only seemed to heighten her desire. They mingled together to form a new feeling. It was hard to understand what danced across her skin, but she marveled, nonetheless. She felt everything so clearly, but it wasn't overwhelming. It was Ciaran. His lips and teeth. His hands. Hope relaxed into them.

Ciaran's lips on the top of her core forced her out of her head. He slowly licked the top of her cleft and started to push her legs apart. The wet sensation grew between her legs, and she tried to look down.

"Hey. Lay back down. I'm gonna be here a while."

Hope gave up and laid back with a smile.

She trusted him. That was new. Hope gave him free rein to do whatever he wanted. She should've been terrified. It was insane, giving in to him like that, but she did. Hope just laid back and relished the feelings.

As Ciaran pushed her to the edge, the wetness skyrocketed. The feel of his soft tongue rocking her and making her arch against his mouth. He moaned, and the vibrating of his lips pushed her closer and closer. But as soon as the sound escaped him, Ciaran lifted his mouth. She looked down at him.

"Are you close?" he asked.

Hope stared at Ciaran's thrilled, possessive gaze. "Fuck, yes."

"Do you want to come?" Ciaran pulled farther away, and Hope started to sit. He gently pushed her back down and smiled, "Do you, Hope?"

"Yes. I do."

"You what? Tell me, Hope." Ciaran loomed over Hope, his arms on either side of her face.

"I want to come."

"Ask me permission. Say it. Say, 'May I come, Ciaran?'"

"May I come?"

Ciaran pulled Hope's hair into his fingers. The pain was slight but sudden, and it threw her off. It didn't, however, stop the pressure building inside her womb, in fact, it amped it up.

"Ask correctly."

"May I come, Ciaran?"

"Yes."

Ciaran snaked down her body and licked her weeping core in one long motion. The sensation was a bolt of electricity that slammed her nervous system into overdrive and every part of her body released the built-up tension. The orgasm seemed to last hours. Ciaran's tongue and fingers pulling everything out of her. As the aftershocks receded, she realized the bed was wet from her. Hope was gasping and totally unable to move.

"That's my girl."

Ciaran was absolutely glowing with pride. He smiled down at her and pressed a deep kiss to her mouth. Hope could taste his efforts, and it revved her right back up.

"I have to be inside you. You're so beautiful and delicious, and oh, fuck . . ."

Ciaran pushed deep, and Hope lost all concentration on his words. This time his entry was swift and forceful, and Hope closed her eyes tightly. She stretched at the sudden invasion, but it was perfect. He locked into her, fitting like they were crafted to be together, and slowly began to pump. The force of his powerful hips moved her up the bed, and Ciaran wrapped an arm around her shoulders to keep her in place.

As he pushed deeper and deeper into Hope, she burned, but the pleasure it was mixed with was intoxicating. Hope opened her eyes, staring up at Ciaran as he worked his erection inside her. With impressive speed, Ciaran rocked his hips back and forth, each thrust forward ending with a delicious swivel of his hips. Hope could feel the blunt head of him rub inside her and every time it caressed a specific spot, she was sent ever closer to another orgasm.

"Come again for me."

At Ciaran's request and sudden surge of motion, Hope let herself fall. Her quivering seemed to push Ciaran closer to his own release. She was gasping and throbbing and smiling.

Ciaran moaned, and Hope could feel him grow even harder inside her. She pulled his face close and kissed his reddened lips. As Ciaran's tongue darted in and out of her mouth, mimicking his hips, he grabbed a handful of Hope's hair. He used the hold to pull her on top of him as he leaned back. Hope wrapped her legs around his hips and the new position pushed Ciaran deeper. Hope let out a happy scream, and he pulled her head back by her hair.

Hope couldn't move her head or body thanks to Ciaran's firm grasp, and she loved it. As tightly as he held her, she was responsible for the pace and enjoyed controlling the friction between them. With Hope's neck exposed, Ciaran bit the side of her throat. Again, the mixture of pleasure and pain sent Hope to the brink. She was so close.

"Ciaran, please. Oh, Maker, please!"

Ciaran pulled her down hard onto his erection and lifted her up again. Taking control, he let her crash over the invisible canyon and gave her the release she so desperately craved. As it took her over, Hope cursed loudly.

"Again, Hope. Do it again." Ciaran's commands were hotwired to her core, and as he spoke, she came again and again. Hope could feel her muscles grip him as he moved inside her, and Ciaran pulled her head to his, kissing her fiercely. Their lips met in a desperate attempt to push each other over the edge, and Ciaran hissed.

The orgasm gave him more strength, and he plowed into her even harder. Ciaran pushed her hips down onto him with all his might, and they shattered. Ciaran let out a growl as he came, and the pleasure she gave him made Hope's own climax reach epic proportions. As Ciaran released, the warmth pooled inside her. Hope's orgasm milked him until they were both so spent, they collapsed sideways on his bed.

For a few minutes, they just breathed.

"Holy fuck, I don't know if I can move." The complete happiness in Ciaran's voice made Hope beam.

"Please do. You're crushing my leg."

Ciaran laughed as he pulled her out from under him and tucked her against him.

For a few moments, they both just lay there, still catching their breath. When she finally felt like she could, Hope leaned up on her elbow and looked over at Ciaran.

"What?" Ciaran smiled.

Hope returned the grin. "You know you're going to have to pay for that, right?"

ELEVEN

Ciaran smiled so massively that his cheeks hurt. Hope was flushed, her hair scattered all around her, the long mahogany waves pooling on his bed. Her mesmerizing, cinnamon stare was glazed, and her pierced lips were bright red from kissing. The shower had washed away her makeup and any product that was controlling her hair. She looked well and thoroughly satisfied. *God, You're beautiful. I could stare at you for hours like this.*

Jesus, the shower . . . He'd tried so hard to soothe her and had completely intended to leave it at that, but that was not what happened. The moment Ciaran had gotten close to her, on his knees, all he wanted to do was taste her again. But the closeness of the shower had set off something else, and he wanted to show her he cared. He hated that he'd caused her pain. It seemed right to make up for it.

Now, after the most amazing sex of his life, Hope's smile floored him. She was immaculate. Even the way she fought against his control was amazing. Hope let him have it, eventually, but he had to earn it. She didn't take his crap at face value. She was just amazing.

Whoa, what's happening? Ciaran's heartbeat was suddenly very loud in his ears. His hands were clammy. *Why's my heart beating so fast?* He never acted like this.

As Ciaran stared at Hope's smiling face, she flopped down on the bed. Ciaran shook his head and grinned.

She lay on her back, eyes closed and breathing deeply. Her pale skin looked creamy, and breath puffed out of her rosy lips. She seemed so happy, and it was because of him. A weird pride beamed in his chest. *Served my woman right.*

And then he remembered why she was there. *Marcus.* Ciaran saw the Inferno again. One of the first so-called employees.

Ciaran was sick to his stomach. Hope was going to leave. Tomorrow morning. They had mere hours left. A choking joined the nausea.

His eyes stung, and he had to force himself to breathe. Who was he kidding? Of course, she had to leave. He wasn't exactly a stable guy, and she didn't seem like the type to settle down, especially now that she knew how great sex was. She could have anyone she wanted.

As images of Hope entwined with other, many other, men, ran through his brain, the nausea peaked. He imagined just how long someone who touched Hope would last. Dimitri's phrase of choice was "New York minute," and Ciaran decided on half that.

If only she could stay, he could protect her from Marcus. Not that she needed protecting. Hope could definitely take care of herself. She deserved a hell of a lot better than his sorry ass too, but he'd trade his left nut to ensure her safety.

Only a few hours left. She's going to want a hand in taking care of Marcus. God, if we worked together, she could get killed. I want that prick dead, but if she fights with me . . . Fuck.

"Are you okay? You look like you're going to be sick. Did the stitches tear?"

Hope stared up at him.

I'm a total jerk. Ciaran nodded.

"Yeah. I'm fine. Go to sleep."

Ciaran knew she needed the rest, but, god help him, he wanted her up, wanted to hold her, talk with her, be with her.

Hope was still staring. For a moment, he thought they were on the same page, but she laid down and closed her eyes.

"Hope."

"Hmmm?" She looked positively adorable with the question on her face, eyes closed.

"Come here."

He lifted her up, and they shuffled to the head of the bed. Ciaran stretched out onto his back, and Hope laid her head right over his heart, snuggling close. She tapped her finger on his arm in time with his pulse. *Still ticking, huh?* She was leaving in the morning. This was the last he'd get of her.

"Ciaran?"

"Yeah." His voice sounded shaky, even to him.

"Umm . . . never mind."

"Come on. What is it?"

When their eyes met, Ciaran latched on, begging the universe to do something, but when had the universe helped? That would be a big and fat never. *Goddamnit. Maybe, I should just say something.*

Ciaran started to speak. "Hope, I don't think—"

"I want to work with you, to stop Marcus."

Ciaran's heart nearly exploded and without thinking, he squeezed Hope's arm.

Hope squirmed. "Ciaran, ow."

He quickly let go. "Sorry. I want your help, but he's dangerous. I don't want anything . . . You should probably just go."

She eyed him. "Ciaran, I'm not some wilting flower. Besides, from everything I know and you've told me, someone needs to take that fucker down. And who better than his best assassin?"

Ciaran let out a short laugh. He should fight this; tell her she wasn't safe. Nothing came out though

Hope laid back down on his chest. "You know you're gonna have to tell me a little bit more about yourself."

That would be a helluva conversation. "Can we do that tomorrow? I'm really tired."

"Sure." Hope breathed deep, relaxing.

"We both need the rest, I guess." Ciaran smiled. He'd seen this woman so many times in his dreams. Fuck, maybe a guy like him could get lucky once in a while.

Everything went quiet, and he listened to Hope breathe. The sound filled the room. It filled him. Hope was so warm, and Ciaran brushed her hair off her shoulder. As he watched her sleep, the Inferno, Ireland, and his life before and after Marcus, swirled in his head. He'd never been able to get past it, but with her body cradled against him, the possibility didn't seem unthinkable. He actually had some hope.

Ciaran laughed to himself. *God, that's fucking cheesy. I should start writing for Hallmark.* From decades ago, and unprovoked, his father's voice popped into his head, the name he'd call his mother. Ciaran pressed his lips to the top of Hope's head and whispered, "Anam cara."

*

Ciaran slipped into unconsciousness, the other dream penetrating him. He'd almost let himself forget. About the blood. About where he lived for over a year. About the ring. About Marcus. He almost forgot . . . almost.

The familiar nightmare was grainy and choppy, a bad home movie of his darkest, dirtiest nights. Ciaran could see intricate, damask wallpaper, steel cuffs chaining him, golden goblets filled with wine, a bloody riding crop on a white tablecloth. And they were real. The sharp metal cut Ciaran's skin, the pulsing through the skin of his back, the ache from kneeling, the sticky, bitter substance running down his throat, the smell of sweat, and the sound of Marcus's laugh.

The sound grated, each ecstatic burst carving out chunks of who he was, leaving a bleeding, brutalized husk. The crescendo expanded until it took over everything and pushed at the confines of his memory. The images all smashed together in a spin cycle, creating a blurry slideshow. They twisted and melded and randomly lashed out in a never-ending attempt to abduct what was left of him. In the swirling madness, the only thing that stood out was Ciaran's choked gasps as the back of his throat was relentlessly assaulted.

Like always, he woke up gagging. In the black of his room, Ciaran didn't know if he was awake. He couldn't see, just like the dream. He was alone, just like the dream. . . . *Was I even dreaming?* Ciaran's pulse thundered. Could he still be in the Inferno? Was his escape the dream? Did Marcus still control his entire existence? Sweat poured down his brow, and he gripped the sheets hard enough to make his fists howl.

"Ciaran? Whoa, Ciaran, are you okay?"

Who was there?! *Hope.* He'd been in bed with Hope.

No. "Yeah."

Hope sat next to him. As his pupils dilated, Ciaran could see her. He could see her wavy hair, her dark eyes; he could see her.

"You don't lie well." Hope stared, her concern biting.

"Ugh. I just . . . if it's alright, I'd rather not talk about it, right now? Later?"

She studied him. "Sure."

Hope lay back down and curled around his arm, pulling it close to her and resting her chin on his shoulder. Ciaran stared at the ceiling.

*

The morning light fought its way through his drapes. The crack in between the black curtain and the glass of the window let the sun pour in and land directly on Ciaran's face. The warmth was nice and all, but it was impossible to keep pretending he was asleep that way. Ciaran started to roll over to face away from the dreaded window and met Hope's face.

She was real. The dark contrast of shadow lay upon her face, and she breathed evenly, still very much asleep. Her full lips were slightly parted, her hair a mess. She was still there; the sun's rays hadn't chased her off. After the nightmare, something about Hope's hold on Ciaran's arm grounded him. It reminded him where he was, not where he'd been. His mental hurricane blew his shitty boat around at 60 mph, but Hope was a human anchor. *And there I go with the fucking Hallmark, again.*

Ciaran smiled and ran a finger down the side of her face. In return, she nuzzled into it and sighed. Her cheek was soft against his rough hand, and Ciaran shuffled closer. He could feel how warm she was. She radiated heat like a furnace, but she looked happy, so he'd dealt with it. As he laid a kiss gently on her lips, Hope jumped wildly.

Ciaran smoothed his hands down her arms. "Hope! It's just me."

"Oh, Maker, sorry. You scared the shit out of me. Ow, what were you doing?" Hope rubbed her forehead.

"I was going for a kiss, but then you head-butted me." Ciaran rubbed at the bridge of his nose and considered licking his lips to see if he was bleeding.

"I sort of forgot where I was." Hope shuffled in the covers and pulled them up under her arms.

She seemed off, her armor back on tight. Hope stared at her hands, and the silence thickened.

Shit, this isn't going to work. Hell, that's my fucking fault. Had to be a joy to spend the night with. Can't imagine she'd want to put up with my baggage. Ciaran tried to swallow, but his throat was made of old felt and pipe cleaners.

That same, raspy voice echoed between his ears. *'Laoch Dubh. Laoch Dubh. Laoch Dubh will destroy.'* Destroy was right. That's all he was ever good at. God, how could he have touched Hope? She'd be tainted by all his filth. His mouth had been on her, all over her, to the very core of her. How could he do that? That mouth had been other places. Bile rose in Ciaran's throat, remembering the taste Marcus had forced into him.

"Are you alright? No offense, but you're kind of green," she asked.

Verification of his new tint only made it worse. The god-awful sensations were there. Ciaran could feel Marcus's hands on the back of his neck, the sweaty but firm grip forcing him still. The tell-tale half cough as his gag reflex screamed, yet again. *I'd still choke.* It was all too real.

It was all happening, the relentless pounding of a fleshy sword into his throat. As Ciaran's eyes began to water, his throat shortened, and his stomach got ready for an in-flight ejection. It was too much, and god forbid Hope watch this.

He struggled up. This was happening, right fucking now.

"Don't follow me." His words sounded garbled around the rising bile.

The bathroom's smell made his nausea worse, and Ciaran flung himself at the toilet. The cold tile was amazing. As the sweat started, Ciaran's stomach clenched and tried to force itself inside out. Barely anything came out. He was clammy and shaking when he heard footsteps behind him.

"You don't listen very well, do you?"

"No. Not really." Hope sat on the floor next to him, putting a hand on his shoulder. He flinched.

"You alright?"

Hope's concern jabbed into him harder than the floor on his arse. *Ahh, fuck. don't look at me like that.*

"Yeah, just weird stomach stuff."

"You're a bad liar. . . . 'Member how I can feel your pain? Well, *my* side hurts because you tore your stitches."

Ciaran looked down and sure enough, there was fresh blood on his side. He stood up shakily, but Hope stopped him, pushing him back down.

"Easy there, cowboy." Hope grabbed a towel and plopped down in front of him, blocking any exit.

"It's fine, Hope," Ciaran shoved at her hands, she shouldn't have to touch him, "Stop."

"Ciaran, just let me clean it."

"No, really. Just stop."

"Ciaran!"

"Stop! You'll get it all over you! It can't touch you!" Ciaran screamed at Hope and had her back against the cupboards.

Her eyes were wide, and she was tense all over, ready to attack.

"Oh, god, Hope . . . I . . . fuck."

His hands and arms were shaking like a little boy. *I'm such a useless piece of shit. I can't even keep it together for a whole fucking day.*

"Ciaran, what's wrong? I mean, you don't have to tell me, but something's clearly up."

"I really don't want to talk about it. Don't want to puke on you." He tried to make like he wasn't about to tear up.

"Ciaran."

"Ugh, fuck. It's a long story. Hope, I . . . Damn it." Ciaran could taste the bile again and hear Marcus laughing at successfully driving a grown man to his knees. Again. "I never talk about this. Never."

"Look, we both agreed to open up. I . . . care. I want to understand you, your story." Hope squeezed his hand and looked him right in the eye.

His smile was halfhearted. Even now, he was causing her pain. What kind of good for nothing hurt an innocent person? He knew exactly who did that, and Ciaran wouldn't be like him, not as long as he could help it.

"The Inferno really screwed me up. Sometimes, I dream I'm there."

"But why did you freak out when I tried to clean your side?"

Ciaran couldn't say it. He couldn't get the words out. Hope stared at him, but he just froze. Vocalizing the shit that went on down there was impossible. He tried, he really did, but aside from his mouth opening, he didn't move. Deer in the headlights.

She sighed. "It's alright. Let's just get you cleaned up."

She helped him up and reached over to turn on the faucet. The sound of the water gushing into the basin was impossibly loud. They stood there in silence as Hope wiped the dried blood off Ciaran's skin, both of them flinching as she touched freshly exposed nerves. *Yup. Just one giant, raw nerve.*

The silence continued. Ciaran focused on the warmth of Hope's hands. He watched her face as she went back and forth from him to the sink, the white towel rinsed clean again and again. Bloody, clean, bloody, clean. If only souls were that easy to disinfect.

Hope seemed so still, completely unfazed by the lay that spewed molten crazy all over.

"Thank you."

Hope looked up and nodded. "You're welcome."

"I'll get there. I just need some time and a better mood."

"Would killing him help?"

"Immensely."

"Well, lucky for you, that's what I do best."

"No." The pull inside Ciaran blocked everything out. After all the shit from this morning, she still did something to him, something *new*.

"Let's eat, huh? I know I'm empty." Ciaran tried for a nonchalant smile, but even he knew he failed.

"Okay, but please nothing soupy." Hope winked at him.

Ciaran couldn't help smiling. "Oh, shut up."

*

"This is so yummy!" Hope smiled in her chair and did a little dance. Who knew waffles would turn the hardened assassin into a kid? It didn't help that she wore one of his shirts like a dress.

Ciaran grinned. "Haven't you ever had waffles?"

"Well, yeah, but I couldn't tell how hot they were. Hot food is way better." Hope offered him a bite.

The waffle hung on the end of her fork, and she cupped her hand underneath the precariously dangling morsel. Ciaran ate it and actually felt better. Hope was sharing her food, and the gesture seemed so natural. All of this did: feeding her, standing in the kitchen getting ready, making coffee, planning their day.

He was on the brink; he could tell. He didn't know how to stop it. It was coming like a big, fucking freight train, and all Ciaran could do was let himself get flattened like a bug. *Yeah, I'm a real tough guy. Can't even win a fight with my own brain.*

Ciaran blinked and realized he'd been standing there without talking. "Sorry, I'm a little in my head right now."

"Yeah, I know. I'm trying to distract you. Obviously, I need to up my game." Hope smirked so subtly Ciaran could barely see it. When she stood and pushed in her chair, she swayed her hips.

Ciaran stiffened. If he freaked again, he might as well declare his dick officially for show. As she walked up toward him, Hope was so graceful, so sexual. He wanted her so badly. He *needed* to get out of his head, even for a second, but the nausea crept up. Marcus scratched and clawed to get in his head, to send Ciaran right back to the toilet.

"Hope, I just . . . Damn it."

"Shh, you gave me something yesterday that meant, well, a lot. Now, I get to give something to you," Hope put her hand on the side of Ciaran's face and all of the mad ramblings left his mind. Something about her touch was magical. Wow, that sounded ridiculous, but she was a demon; maybe she was magic.

"Ciaran, look at me." Apparently, he'd been staring at the floor. "It's just me. No one else here. Just focus on me."

Ciaran looked up and saw Hope's marvelous brown eyes. She was so beautiful, and she was real. After all the dreams and insomnia-filled months, this fabulous woman with her Rogue-like white streak was here, trying to help him.

"Okay." Ciaran let his shoulders relax. For once, he'd let someone take care of him. Let someone else take control. Who knew, maybe, he'd like it, though he highly doubted that one.

Hope smiled and took his hand. They went to his bedroom, and she gently pushed him to sit on the end of the large bed. She lifted herself up and perched on top of him. Hope was predatory. She was straight up deadly, and it was hot as hell. Her every move was animal and fierce, powerful, and yet, she was being so gentle. He fucking hated it, but god did he need it.

As she straddled his lap, the smell of her hair all around him went straight to his cock.

"God, Hope. I want you so much, but—"

"No buts, I need you inside me."

That certainly motivated him. Ciaran's blood rushed directly between his legs, and he got harder with every second. He reached up to Hope's shirt, but she stopped him.

"Why are you stopping me?"

"I'm treating you this time. Just lay back and enjoy."

Ciaran couldn't help but laugh. He wasn't a good passenger, but Hope took control of this ride so firmly that he'd have to learn. And fast.

Hope leaned in, kissing him deeply, not hard, just deep. Every bit of his mouth was involved, not to mention the sensations further down. As he tried to push closer, Hope's hands brushed his sides, and his shirt came over his head. A joint hiss echoed as Ciaran's wound stretched.

"Well, at least I'll know if I'm hurting you."

"I hate that," Ciaran said.

"Well, don't sweat it. Not now. I didn't feel anything before you. You've given me . . . so much."

And now he wanted to write poetry, or sing, or do something to make her smile and laugh and hell, right now, he wanted to make her moan. Not really being familiar with romance, he'd have to settle for moaning. Then, killing Marcus.

"Ciaran."

He shook his head, focusing. Hope placed a hand on his chest and that magick connection knocked him out again. *Goddamn.* She truly floored him, her beauty, her no-bullshit attitude, her strength, yeah, especially that. She was so much stronger than him. Just as a mood-ruining distraction was about to hit, Hope's warm hand slid to Ciaran's pants and popped open the button.

Like a diamond couldn't describe just how hard he was. As Hope freed him from his jeans, a desperate tear coated the tip of his erection. Ciaran felt slightly exposed, but he was dying to get inside her. She stripped off her shirt. Hope sparkled in the beams of daylight that broke into his room. Each piercing flashing and reflecting.

She bent over him, and her rosy lips kissed their way down his pecs and stomach. As Hope's warm tongue began to caress his erection, a curse slipped out of him. She swirled and dragged her tongue all over him, and it drove Ciaran absolutely mad. Every bit of tension and reserve flew out the window. He finally began to feel like himself, and it was all because of Hope. She truly was a savior, one who'd tried to kill him, sure, but how wonderfully the tides had turned.

"Holy god, Hope." Ciaran nearly came as Hope sucked him in and took all of him in her mouth. She was hot all around him, and as Hope moved her head up and down, she created the perfect rhythm. His skin tightened and an amazing pressure grew in his hips and groin. Just as it started to become too much to handle, Hope released him. The cool air was a shock, and she smiled up, her lips glossy and red.

"Close your eyes," she said.

Ciaran was in no state to fight, so he lay back. Every inch of him was ultrasensitive and with his eyes closed, all of his remaining senses screamed out for input. Hope's fingers obliged. As they slowly traced the curves of his muscles, the bed shifted and Hope's knees touched either side of his legs. She hovered over him, and he reached up to touch her face. She found his hand and guided it to her cheek. Ciaran could feel her smile and smiled back.

Hope moved his hand to her breast. The full, soft flesh filled his palm and sent rockets of pleasure down his shaft. They were works of art; the tight buds of her nipples constantly erect from her sinful jewelry. Ciaran wanted to taste the pink flesh and as if mind reading was another of her numerous talents, Hope lowered the delicious skin to his mouth.

As he took his time enjoying the taste of skin surrounded by metal, Hope lowered herself onto Ciaran. Their gasps ricocheted around the still room.

"Fuck, Hope. You're so warm."

"Mmm, so are you."

Ciaran gripped Hope's hips tightly, and she swiveled around his cock. He was so close, the orgasm poised at the tip of his erection. It was almost painful. His desire, his need to come made his head swim and blood pound. Hope moaned low in her throat. It brought out the animal in Ciaran, and he began to thrust hard. The furious pace didn't seem to bother her. Hope only moaned louder and yelled his name. Moments later, Hope tightened around Ciaran.

He loved making her come and as he did, the core of her became wetter and warmer. The sheer fact that Ciaran could make Hope do that made him so achingly close to exploding he almost wanted to cry. So, when she arched back and pushed down hard on his cock, it was too much to handle.

Ciaran growled as the orgasm shot through him like a bullet out of a 50 cal. Hot jets soared out of him and into Hope, and they wouldn't stop. His body was in overdrive and wasn't quitting until Hope had completely emptied him.

He came twice more, immediately after the first time. Both of them were panting and red like they ran a marathon. As the sound of their breaths filled the room, Ciaran's thoughts started up again. Everything had been so perfect; he didn't want to go back into battle with his demons.

This particular demon he'd love to spend time with, but not Marcus. He'd have to, however. He had to kill him before he stole anymore of his life, or someone else's. Especially Hope's. Ciaran held her on top of him. Her breath flowed over his chest and the silky weight of her hair fell on his arm, her heartbeat matching his.

"I'm going get my act together. I swear to you. I just need time." Ciaran waited for a response. And waited.

"I'm not going to lie to you and say I don't have baggage, too. Or that I understand what kind of pain you're in because I don't. But I do want to tell you that I feel as lost in this as you. Maybe more. I don't know how we ended up in this crazy-ass situation, aside from Marcus screwing us both, but I know I want to figure it out, preferably soon and preferably . . . with you."

Hope sighed and muffled a laugh against his pec. "Wow, I can't believe I said all that. I sound ridiculous."

"It wasn't bad."

"I'm just not used to this. Normally, it's just point and shoot."

"Ha. That shouldn't be funny, but it is."

Hope wiggled off him and punched him in the arm. They both flinched.

"Damn it! I can't even take out my frustration without being in pain!"

Even though her voice was angry, a grin spread across her cheeks. Ciaran rubbed the side of Hope's face and smiled back. Maybe, if she was around, he could keep from losing his marbles. Maybe.

"We should go meet Dimitri. He's probably shitting himself."

"What? Why?"

"Well, Hope, you seem to have made us an hour late."

"Whoops."

TWELVE

How the hell? I mean, seriously. How the hell did I get myself in this situation? Fucking omaeriku.

Hope was utterly burnt out. After the past thirty-some hours, she'd managed to get herself shot at, had sex for the first time, and second, and third, learned some crazy shit about her ex-boss, and to top it off, was feeling some serious emotional . . . stuff about Ciaran.

She was still on the fence about that one.

"Alright, I apologize in advance." It was the fourth time Ciaran had done so during their ride to Dimitri's.

"Quit it. It'll be fine."

"You don't know him like I do. Dimitri might actually try to shoot you."

"Good thing I've already proven that I can handle myself just fine."

"I'm not worried about you getting hurt, not really. I would just prefer it if I didn't have to break up a fight."

Hope couldn't help but laugh. The possibility wasn't entirely unbelievable. Dimitri could be an ass, and Hope enjoyed kicking asses.

"Can't promise anything, babe."

Suddenly, the car was very quiet.

Hope looked over at Ciaran. He was staring at her like someone had told him money really did grow on trees. Hope couldn't see anything, no sirens, no gunshots.

"What?"

"Nothing." Ciaran shook his head and faced forward in his seat. Maybe, he was just thinking too much again.

The car remained silent, and instead of facing another twenty minutes of that, Hope switched on the radio. The station blared out pop music. They both looked at the device with disgust. Ciaran reached forward and started to play with the dials in a desperate attempt to find anything that didn't sound like cats in heat. When it looked like all was lost, he finally stumbled onto an In This Moment song.

The song that played seemed to get them both thinking. Lyrics screaming "I'm dangerous for you" made Hope swallow hard. She could practically see the wheels in Ciaran's head spinning, and hers weren't far behind.

I'll get him killed. I'm a fucking hit woman for Maker's sake. Dangerous? That's an understatement. Hope had no idea what she'd gotten herself into, and she didn't think Ciaran was any better. She was driving this damn car to see his best friend and then what? They were supposed to pull off an elaborate assassination of a well-to-do murderer and ride off into the sunset? *Sure.*

She'd get him killed and maybe, Dimitri and herself, too. Death and destruction lay in their future. *Dangerous. Yup. Maybe Mom had it right?*

But, she couldn't turn the car around or pull over. As hard as she fought against what she was doing, it didn't work. Her brain screamed at her to stop, but something else kept her foot on the gas.

She didn't want Ciaran hurt in all this insanity, but he wouldn't sit back and let her take care of it. Screaming sounded really great. This car was too damn small and too damn quiet, even with all the music. She silently begged for the next turn to show up, and sure enough, the road parted to reveal a nice, long driveway.

Please, Maker, let this end. Dear Shendara, *are you fucking kidding me? This damn driveway is like a hundred miles long!*

"Hope, it's right there. Hope. Hope!"

She saw the house pop out from behind a small hill and skidded to a stop right in front of the steps.

"Shall we?" She smiled over at Ciaran and all but leapt out of the car.

"Yeah." Ciaran dragged out the word and his shoulders bunched under his t-shirt. *Let the fun begin.*

He didn't so much as look at the house as he did the sidewalk. Ciaran's brows were down and together. Something was clearly brewing behind those lovely, dark eyes, but Hope was at a loss. After this morning, or more specifically, after that nightmare, Hope could see a storm in there waiting to break. He'd been so scared. Not freaked out, not startled, terrified. The dream was enough to break him and step on the pieces. And unfortunately, asking didn't seem to help. Hope saw that look on his face, and her chest ached. He'd been horrified, disgusted. Why? Something about the Inferno and surviving gladiatorial combat sure, but what?

Her lack of social knowledge sucked. Her experience was so limited. She'd gone from clan to hit woman practically overnight, and neither of those places was great for emotional growth. Maker, she'd kill for a little insight.

As they approached Dimitri's, Hope looked over at Ciaran. He looked normal enough, but something was behind his eyes and more than yesterday. Was she making things worse? He'd been dealing with all this shit, and he wasn't cracking—not yet at least. But now she was here, poking around at his unmentionables.

"What the fuck took you guys so long?" Dimitri stood on the crumbling porch of the brick house.

They went well together, both a little rough around the edges with a vaguely old-world twist.

The building had definitely been around a while. The ivy crawling up along the outside walls was thick and bushy, the suckers firmly attached to the building's mortar, slowly eating Dimitri's house alive. The rusty brick matched Dimitri's hair. Hope thought of the trailer. Why would Dimitri let himself live here? For that matter, why did Dimitri do half the things he did?

The steam rising out of his mug hung around his face, and Hope wondered, for the billionth time, what kind of demon he was.

"Traffic was bad!" Ciaran shouted.

Dimitri folded his arms around his cup and glared. "You suck at lying, bro. Too late for traffic."

"You know, I was just saying what a bad liar he was this morning." Hope couldn't help herself. He was too easy a mark. Ciaran shot her a look, and she just laughed.

"Well, we're here now," Ciaran said.

They walked up to the stairs next to each other.

"Did I miss something?" Dimitri nodded down to them from his porch.

"What? No." Ciaran's cheeks turned a subtle red, and Dimitri burst out laughing.

Hope could kill him. It was much more fun when their flirting annoyed him, not made him bust a gut. The little punk was just yucking it up, and it was working her last nerve. "Can we just get inside? I'd really like to start working on how we're going to catch this bastard."

Dimitri sneered at her. "Says the assassin he hired to kill us."

"Actually, just Ciaran. You didn't make the cut."

"Seriously, could you have worse taste?"

"I could be dating you." Ciaran smirked.

"In your dreams."

Hope walked up the steps, pushed past Dimitri, and into his living room. She was done dealing with people judging her, and men, and everything else this crappy town kept throwing at her.

The shabby house was about as orderly as a war zone. There were clothes everywhere. Hope assumed they were dirty, but something told her Dimitri would have more designations than just clean or not. The coffee table (at least, she thought it was a table, she couldn't really see it) was butted up to the bottom of the couch and a large air mattress filled the floor.

"You sleep on that?" Hope knew Ciaran's "business" wasn't rolling in the dough, but Dimitri could surely afford a bed.

"Yeah, it's comfortable."

"Sure."

Ciaran picked up a pile of newspapers and made a spot on the small sofa. "Dude, you need a maid?"

"No, I don't. No one's ever here, besides you, and I don't have to impress you."

"Clearly." Hope swallowed as she attempted to sit on the couch near Ciaran.

"Remind me why you're here?" Dimitri assumed his natural position, arms crossed, leaning on the door jam.

"Which one of us has actually seen Dante, or Marcus, or whatever his name is, in the past month?"

The room was silent.

"That's what I thought." Hope caught Ciaran's smile out of the corner of her eye. Goddamn, he was cute.

"Ugh. Guys keep the googly eyes to a minimum, please, and did she just say Marcus?"

Ciaran frowned so hard Hope though his face would crack. "Yes."

"Nice taste, toots," Dimitri said, shaking his head.

"Dimitri, one more crack from you, and I'm beating your sorry ass back to your clan like the whiny, little baby you are." Hope walked up to Dimitri, and they stood nose to nose, seconds from throwing punches.

Dimitri fumed. His shoulders pushed back, the veins in his neck standing out. Something changed about him, his inner demon bubbling to the surface, but Hope didn't back down. It didn't add up, though. She'd said and done worse, and he took that in stride.

As Hope continued to stare, Dimitri relaxed.

"You're lucky I don't hit girls. And that I like anyone with the stones to talk to me like that."

"Not a girl." Hope turned away and walked toward what she guessed was the kitchen, "You better have coffee left."

Hope sauntered into the cold, echoey room, each step squeaking and slightly sticking to the linoleum floor. Somewhere garbage stunk fiercely, and there were brown crumbs, well, everywhere. *Shendara, he needs to clean.* Hope searched the countertop for a coffee maker, no luck. She couldn't imagine Dimitri would be willing to speak, let alone, work in the morning without coffee, so where was it? On the greasy stovetop was a pot, just a pot, with hot water. *The trailer was like this.*

Hope was nauseated. The dirty towel that draped over the metal faucet, the cheap can of Folger's next to the sink, the grimy fridge nearly ransacked of all its contents. It was way too similar to the singlewide. She grabbed the can of imitation coffee and dropped a couple spoonfuls into a mug she found on the counter. She turned the stove knob to high and waited for boiling water.

She could just make out the sounds of the boys talking. Ciaran's voice was low and chocolaty, a bitter temptation to do something wholly inappropriate in front of Dimitri. The dark, even timbre of his words was like listening to a tragic, yet beautiful composition on a cello. A tune definitely composed in a minor key.

"Okay, apparently *omaeriku* has made me a sap for classical music. What's next? Poetry? Uck."

The rattling sound of the pot brought her back to the kitchen. As she poured the hot water into her cup, she tried to hear what the guys were saying.

"Ciaran, you're serious?" Dimitri's Brooklyn accent blended into the sounds coming from outside. Ciaran's, however, cut through like a blade, the Irish brogue standing out in the sea of sounds.

"As a fucking heart attack. We get this bastard, now."

"Don't you think you're being a little, oh, I don't know, insane?"

"Dimitri, with Hope's help, we can actually take this douche out."

"Yeah, about that . . ."

"What." Not a question.

"You need me to say it? Ahh, god man. She fucking tried to kill us. And really, I get it. She didn't. But I don't want to go risking my neck, 'cause you're being led around by the short hairs."

Hope heard a loud thud and ran toward the living room. She stopped short at the corner of the hallway, hiding just out of sight. She saw Ciaran pinning Dimitri against the wall.

Ciaran's knuckles squeezed Dimitri's throat, as he spoke. "Shut. The. Fuck. Up."

"Whatever, Ciaran. You can't tell me you don't have any doubts. And I'd think after what he did—"

"Dimitri! What the hell did I just say?"

"Don't even try that shit with me. I'm your best fucking friend, and I'm trying to be straight with you. Ugh, get the fuck off me!" Dimitri shoved Ciaran back, but he didn't go far.

"Be straight! You just don't like that she's here!"

"Oh, my god, Ciaran! It has nothing to do with that! And yeah sure, I'm a little resentful 'cause of the shit you pulled in the past, but this is not about Red. I just don't want to see you get killed, not for anybody, and not because we barged into something like our balls were on fire!"

"I'm not barging! And I'm not fucking sitting here while Marcus finds another assassin to kill us both!"

Dimitri stepped back. "Fine!"

They were both quiet.

"For the record," Dimitri cleared his throat, "I know how badly you want him dead. I do, too. And I know what's going on with Hope, so don't lie to me."

"Yeah."

"I'm not kidding. I get it. You're totally gone for her. I can see it all over your face. I just pray you know what you're getting yourself into."

"Me, too."

With their bromance moment over, Hope went in. She leaned back against the door jam, mirroring Dimitri's position and met him eye to eye.

Ciaran frowned at the floor. "We were discussing our plans."

"Oh, I know what you were saying. I have excellent hearing."

"Demons." Dimitri smirked.

Hope cracked an angry smile right back at him. "You gentlemen done with your pissing contest?"

"I take it back. Ciaran could do a lot worse than you."

"Gee, thanks." Hope forced herself to drink the sludge; she needed the caffeine. The acidic and chalky taste was absolute torture. "No one should have to suffer this much for a little pick me up."

"I'm cheap, so drink it or chuck it, but it's all I've got."

Hope choked down another gulp. She couldn't help but make a face. Ciaran smiled and Dimitri just shook his head.

"So, where we at? Personally, I want to get this done fast. I don't relish the idea of Marcus being out there running free." Hope set the mug down, half a cup would have to do.

"Well, we know that your Dante is actually Marcus from the Inferno, that he hired you to kill Ciaran because he was imprisoned there, as was I, and now, after all this time, he wants Ciaran dead and apparently, you, too. Probably, because you didn't kill Ciaran, and he most likely assumed that you found out about me, and that's against everything he told you he was about."

"Damn, exposition much?" Ciaran laughed at Dimitri's less than concise explanation.

The thing was, hearing it all laid out like that was kind of insane. There was no way that was actually her life. It was ridiculous. Straight out of the movies.

"Yeah, I remember that, actually. I *meant* what do we know about him. Where does he live, hang out? How can we find him? Who can we get info from? The bastard into anything illicit? Can we use it to our advantage? I've only had like two meetings with the guy; you know him better than I do. What should I know?" she asked.

Both men stared at Hope like she was on drugs.

"Hope, I just beat the shit out of people. I don't know how to set up a sting." Ciaran's crooked smile faded as he sat back.

"Well, then, we start simple. We ask the guys who shot at us."

"Hate to burst your bubble, but all those dudes are dead," Dimitri said.

"No shit, Dimitri. But, they're also probably right where we left them, complete with a hit list and a cell phone in their pockets. I'm not sure where the local HQ is, but you always have the number in your phone. Unfortunately, mine is at your office in pieces, courtesy of their bullets. Their phones, however, are most likely just fine." Hope eyed her mug but decided to leave it unfinished.

"Okay, gotta say, life as a hit woman comes with some pretty bad-ass skill sets." Dimitri's mouth turned down as he nodded. Ciaran stood up and marched toward the door.

"Whoa, dude. Where's the fire?" Dimitri tried to catch Ciaran by the arm.

"Those bodies are going to be found, eventually. We get our arses there, now." Ciaran pulled his arm out of Dimitri's grip with a quick twist and headed out the door. Hope followed, and Dimitri wasn't far behind.

*

Bright yellow tape surrounded the entire block and Ciaran's office was smack dab in the middle of the cordoned off area.

"Apparently, the local response is fast. Surprising, right?" Ciaran sighed and put his clunker in park.

Hope scoffed. Why they couldn't take her car was beyond her. Too conspicuous, right. At least she got shotgun.

"I was afraid this might happen. Heavy gunfire tends to draw attention. No prob, I'll get inside and grab the phones." Hope rummaged in her bag and started to get out. Thank Maker, she was able to grab it from her car and that it had a change of clothes.

"Are you crazy?! They're not just going to let you waltz through the crime scene." Dimitri had shot forward in his seat, his head shoved between Hope and Ciaran.

"Hope, you'll get yourself arrested." She almost missed Ciaran's worried stare, but he shoved Dimitri's head out of the way so he could effectively glare at her.

Hope laughed and held up the gleaming badge and stolen CSU vest. She slipped the crime scene personnel uniform over her jacket and put the badge around her neck. Her hair in a ponytail and a black baseball cap completed the illusion. She swung open the creaky door, slid out, and sidestepped behind the tape.

Hope swiped a set of gloves and some small tools from an open kit and walked up to the door of Ciaran's office. It was swarming with cops, investigators, the press, and someone whose brand-new Armani loafers did not fit in. Hope could hear him talking with one of the beat cops.

"On the roof. Alright, well, I'll take a preliminary look at the scene and photograph any obvious trace or prints."

The man sounded generic, easygoing, and he was most definitely lying. *Preliminary work would have been done hours ago, amateur.* As an assassin,

Hope knew human law pretty damn well, if only to break it safely. She waited for Armani to go into the building and then approached the door. The blue at the entrance turned to her.

"Another one." The cop was already annoyed by the circus, and clearly, in no mood to deal with people mucking up the crime scene, Hope could work with that.

"He might want these." Hope held up the gloves and smirked.

"God, I could just tell that guy was a noob. What an ass."

"You have no idea. I'm going to make sure he doesn't fuck anything up. It's certainly not *my* first day."

"First day! Just my luck. Get up there before the rookie touches anything."

Hope nodded and jogged up the stairs. Thank Maker, her boots were quiet. Armani probably worked for Marcus, and he'd be her only lead. She reached to the waistband of her pants. The small gun Ciaran gave her wasn't anything special, but it worked, and it would leave a mark if he was less than cooperative. As Hope rounded the door, she saw him digging through the pockets of their former co-workers. *Definitely one of Marcus's.* He was the right type, boorish, big, terrible manners.

Hope slinked behind him, holding the gun level with his head. With the safety off, Hope spoke up when Armani grabbed one of the deceased's phones.

"Thanks for grabbing that for me, it's always such a pain rooting around in a stiff's pockets. Hard on the back, you know?"

Armani turned around on his knee and slowly got to his feet. At his full height, he must have been pushing six-six. The bastard knew how he came off, too. Well, he could take that posturing and shove it.

"Yeah, such a hassle. Who the hell are you?"

"Now, now, such manners. Dante didn't tell you?" Hope smirked. "He just sent you out here to clean up his mess, and he didn't even tell you what to expect? How thoughtless of him."

"Grab the phones, all I need to know."

"Well, obviously not, seeing as there's a woman with a gun leveled at your head." Hope held her hand out. "Phones, please."

"No way. Not handing over nothing. You probably can't even aim that pissant excuse for a gun."

Hope's fingers moved so fast there was no way Armani would have been able to maneuver out of the way. As she squeezed the trigger, Hope actually noticed the weapon fire, the kick in her hand, the vibration from the noise being muffled by the suppressor. It was weird. She was so much closer to the action, and it was hard to distance herself.

The bullet ripped through Armani's thigh and flew out the back, lodging itself in a brick wall. The suppressor managed to keep the boom down to a wine. As the thug fell, Hope ran over and smashed her knee into his face. The crack that rang out confirmed his nose was broken. The bummer was with him unconscious, it was going to be a pain in the ass to lift him. Thankfully, there was a fire escape away from the circus out front.

Hope shoved her gun back in her pants and stripped off the CSU vest. She wrapped it around Armani's leg as a tourniquet and the bleeding slowed. Perfect shot, if she said so herself. *Femoral artery completely unharmed.* Hope took the three phones and the gun tucked in Armani's waistband. With a shot to his leg, he certainly wouldn't be fast, but he could hobble his fat ass down the fire escape.

"Wakey, wakey." Hope pushed the heel of her boot against Armani's wound.

"Ahh! You fucking bitch!"

"Oh, poor baby. Did someone get an owie?" Hope pulled him to his feet and started toward the escape ladder.

"Let go of me, whore!"

Hope smacked Armani across the face, paying particular attention to his nose. "Move it. I'm not finished with you."

She shoved him down the first couple of stairs, and Armani went ass-over-teakettle down to the first landing. It continued that way for the next two sections until he realized that he was causing himself a lot more pain by resisting. At the bottom of the escape, Hope forced her hostage to Ciaran's car. It was a good thing he'd moved around back. When Ciaran and Dimitri saw her coming, they both shot out of the car.

"Pop the trunk, will ya?"

Ciaran opened it up, the rusted metal creaking loudly.

"Holy shit, Hope!" Dimitri came around the side of the car and watched her shove in her "package."

"He definitely works for Marcus. We can question him back at Ciaran's."

Hope slammed the lid down on Armani's head.

"Duck," she said in a sing-song voice.

Then, all of them were inside the car. But Ciaran was being really quiet, and Hope couldn't help but feel like he was pissed at her. When they'd been on the road for a bit, she finally spoke up.

"What's eating you?"

Ciaran exhaled deeply, "You were gone a while. I couldn't go in. I . . ."

"I'm fine. I had it under control."

"You didn't tell me what was going on. I had to sit here, on my arse, and wait."

"Sorry, but I knew how to get in, and it was easier alone."

"Yeah." He exhaled. "Look, I get that you're good at this shit, but clue us in next time. There are other people involved now, and we need to know what you know and what you're doing."

The car was silent, but Dimitri took care of that. "Dude, Ciaran, you sound like a chick."

"Fuck off." Ciaran slammed on the brakes and Dimitri, who was leaning forward and not wearing a seatbelt, whacked his skull against the back of Ciaran's seat. The thud in the back reminded them of the unconscious guy in the trunk.

"Ciaran, sorry. You're right. I should have told you, but maybe, you could try not to kill the only lead we have. Dimitri?"

"Ow. And yeeess." His accent was exaggerated.

"Next time you feel like butting in, don't."

This time Dimitri stayed quiet.

THIRTEEN

"She's just gonna walk in there?!" Dimitri was being way too loud, and their parking spot by the alley wasn't completely hidden.

"Would you shut it! No going to help her by getting us caught."

But Ciaran was equally shocked. Hope just suited up and left without a word. Damn, he knew she was her own person and all, but he kind of wanted to be clued in. God, that sounded pathetic. At least, she was good at this. She was prepared with all her badges and outfits; she knew about the law, and how CSU worked; and Ciaran was learning it was very possible to be impressed and annoyed at the same time.

Hope didn't need him at all, and he was wholly inadequate when it came to sleuthing. He barged in. He was violent and deadly. Stealth was not in his repertoire. Aside from suggesting the stop to get her stash from her car, he'd contributed nada.

And yes, she was a great assassin, but a great communicator she was not. Though team sports didn't seem to be part of Hope's repertoire. What the fuck was he going to do?

And then, there was Marcus. The closer he got to him, or one of his flunkies, the more his skin seemed to set fire, the more he wanted to bash that prick's head against a wall.

Rage kicked up images of all the depraved things that Marcus had done. Ciaran could never push them back for long, and after all this time, he seemed to be more bad memories and anger than anything else.

"She's in." Dimitri's voice was quiet, and he stared at Ciaran like he was waiting for a response. Dimitri knew where his head was at. *Fantastic.*

"Good." Ciaran's blood pounded. Hope was already making her way onto the roof and fingers-crossed she'd be able to get the phones and get out.

Time dragged forward like crawling across a desert of rusty nails. At least Dimitri knew better than to try and talk. Lord knew anyone could see it. His knuckles were white as he gripped the steering wheel. His brow was down over his eyes, and his teeth were gritted, making his jaw ache. For chrissakes, he was even bouncing his leg up and down.

The car was so damn quiet, aside from some breathing and the occasional crack of Dimitri's knuckles. Ciaran always hated that nervous habit of his, but right now, it was keeping him from thinking about all the numerous things that could go wrong and had gone wrong in the past. *God, that night . . .* Ciaran's mind opened to the last day at the Inferno. When Dimitri and Red had helped him escape. *Jesus, I'm such a shit.* Ciaran could see Red's hair blowing behind her in the wind as she left.

*

The smell of smoke and gas was all over his clothes, and Red positively reeked of char. The motel room was stuffy and small and smelly and way too similar to his cell. The bathroom had cracked tiles, no tank lid on the toilet, water damage everywhere; it was a plumber's nightmare.

Something in him still wanted to fix it. Standing there in the tiny room with the cold air barely suppressing his nausea, all Ciaran could think about was how much he wanted to fix it. Fix everything. Sure, they were out, but what now? With every breath, he could smell the mold growing. Eventually, Ciaran would have to leave the bathroom and face his former cellmates.

But how? After all the time there, all the lives, the blood, how could he face them or anyone, for that matter? God, it was killing him. As Ciaran looked at himself in the mirror, he didn't recognize his own body. The muscles stood out from his bones in stark curves. His skin was so pale, and his eyes looked dull. Aside from the fact that he was cut, he didn't look so hot. Plus, he was scruffy from months without a proper razor, and his hair was shaggy like a dog's.

Ciaran desperately wanted to clean himself up, but it would have to wait. The three of them needed to find a safer place than this motel. Time to face the music.

Ciaran opened the door. Dimitri was kneeling on the ground beside the bed, and Red was still passed out. He must've seen her shivering because there was more covering her.

"She still shaking?"

"Yeah. She said it's normal," Dimitri's voice lowered to a whisper, "but it doesn't look like it."

"She'll be fine. She's done it before, obviously."

"Yeah."

Ciaran sat in the small, dingy chair by the window and stared at them. Red was curled into a ball under the sheet, blankets, a weird looking comforter thing that smelled like mold, two towels from the bathroom, and now, two curtains from each window. She even had her clothes and shoes on under all that stuff. It was odd thinking of Red cold, but apparently, it was a side effect of throwing that much flame. Something about "using her own body heat," Dimitri had said. Whatever. Honestly, this demon thing was still pretty new to him, and the Inferno wasn't the best learning environment.

Ciaran listened to their breathing in the quiet, and it made his brain churn. Swirling and landing on thoughts of Marcus's office. He had to break the silence before he fled to the bathroom again.

"You know we have to clear out of here ASAP."

"Yeah, I know. She's just not ready." Dimitri grabbed Red's hand.

Ciaran's stomach turned; he could barely sit through the car ride with Dimitri so close and the idea of actual physical contact? Yeah, no.

"Dimitri, we can't stay here. This is way too close to the site, and they're gonna be looking for us."

"I know, but she's not ready. For fuck sakes, she's still unconscious." Dimitri wasn't looking at him while he spoke. He just stared at Red, and all Ciaran could think was how gross it would be to have someone touch him.

"Look, I'm willing to travel with you, get somewhere safe, but I'm no hanging around here while you pine over some chick."

Dimitri's head flew around, and he glared. Man, pissing the guy off didn't feel great, but he was just too fucking terrified to stay in this place, and seeing Dimitri enjoy someone made Ciaran hate him a little. He couldn't be around for all that crap, not now.

"You've got to be fucking kidding me! She got us out of there!"

"Yeah, I know. And I'm grateful. But we're safer if we split up, and she probably wants to go back to her clan or something. Why keep her from that?"

Dimitri set Red's hand down and stomped over. His bunched shoulders and tight jaw gave away how he felt about her. "First off, fuck you. Second, I'm not leaving until I know she's okay. Third, I don't want to keep her from anything; that's why she can go wherever she wants. I'm coming with you. Because you have some serious issues, and I'd be an idiot if I let you out into the world alone. You need me way more than she does."

"I don't need shit, and you clearly want to stay with her."

Ciaran shrugged. "Well, then your eyes must be as broken as your head."

He wasn't the greatest person to ask about anything involving relationships. Marcus had been the longest—Great, the bile was invading his throat again.

"Fine. We wait." Ciaran sat down on the other twin bed and leaned back against the headboard. He shuffled to get comfy against the wood. The mattress was strange underneath him, squishy and soft and not concrete. Eventually, he just got up and lay on the floor. Before he closed his eyes, he said, "We leave as soon as it's dark."

Rustling woke up Ciaran. He rubbed his eyes and waited for them to adjust to the dark. As the forms started to make sense, he heard Dimitri and Red talking.

"I'm not a child. I can take care of myself," Red insisted.

"You're still shaking. And where are you gonna go?"

"That's none of your business, is it? Thanks for helping me get out, Ciaran, too, but I need to figure things out on my own."

Red had the right idea. Get out of here and don't look back, but something about it made him feel off. Dimitri wanted her to stay but wasn't saying anything. I'm staying out of this. I'm not his goddamn cupid.

Ciaran watched Red leave. It was windy, and her hair blew around wildly. He saw Dimitri's face for just a second. He looked like someone kicked him in the nuts. Ciaran rolled back over and went to sleep for a few more hours. They'd leave soon, and a bit more sleep would be nice.

The car was still quiet, and Ciaran's head ached. He hadn't lifted a finger to help Dimitri with Red, mostly because he was way too caught up in his own bullshit, but it was no excuse. And now here he was, waiting for Hope. He really didn't deserve her. Not after what he'd done to Dimitri and so many other things. He'd been fucking cruel and so completely repulsed by the idea of connection that he just watched her break his heart.

And yet, he still wanted Dimitri to be okay with Hope. He still wanted her even if he had no idea how that was supposed to work. Ciaran looked over at Dimitri. His auburn hair was bright in the sun and dust motes floated around. After years of violence, bad decisions, and general jackassery, Dimitri still sat next to him, waiting for an assassin to come back to their car.

"I'm sorry about Red."

"I know."

Silence. Dimitri definitely slammed the door on that convo. So, they just sat there, waiting for the other to change the subject.

Ciaran said, "I can't believe she just walked in there without a second thought. She could get arrested. Or killed."

"She's a pro. I don't think there's anything in there she can't handle." Dimitri had a point.

That wasn't what Ciaran was really upset about though, was it? Even in his head, he could barely admit the real reason. *That fucker's supposed to be mine. After everything, I want my revenge.*

The silence stretched like even it was uncomfortable. It'd been around fifteen minutes since she went inside. Ciaran thought of the gun he gave Hope and prayed she didn't have to use it. The cops were starting to break up and head back to the station. The TV channels didn't get a good enough story, so they were packing up. All in all, it was getting quiet everywhere.

Off in the distance, Ciaran could hear something heavy landing on metal. There were clanging bursts every now and then. At the fire escape, Ciaran saw Hope shoving a person down. The guy had obviously seen better days, and there was a makeshift tourniquet wrapped around his leg and blood dried under his nose.

Handle herself. Right. As Hope escorted her guest to the car, Ciaran had to fight back the urge to attack the goon himself.

"Dude, not to piss you off, but she does look hot as hell handling that piece of shit."

Ciaran snapped out of his thoughts. "Watch it, Dimitri, you get too close, and I'll rip your balls off with me bare hands."

Ciaran couldn't control his temper on a good day, and when it came to Hope, it was a million times worse.

"Territorial much?" Dimitri scoffed.

"Yes."

Dimitri backed down. But unfortunately, he was right. Hope looked fucking amazing. She was in complete control of the hunk of meat, and the smile she flashed was priceless. *Look what I caught! Aren't I just the best?* Yes, she most certainly was. It infuriated him. That should be his prize. His ticket to Marcus. He was damn proud of her skills, but god, he wanted to lay into someone. The headache got worse behind Ciaran's eyes. And, he had to get out to open the trunk. The latch was broken, and for the first time since he bought it, Ciaran hated the damn Crown Vic.

"Pop the trunk, will ya?"

"I wasn't planning for company." His voice barely left his mouth.

Ciaran jammed the key in the lock, and Dimitri walked to the back a few seconds after, leaning against one of the doors to the backseat.

"Holy shit, Hope." The grin on Dimitri's face was going to get slapped off if it didn't vanish, soon.

Hope shoved the man inside the trunk and slammed the door. "He definitely works for Marcus. We can question him back at Ciaran's."

Ciaran stayed quiet and bit his teeth together. He tried to focus on getting the car started. He couldn't look at Hope, not yet. They all got in, and Dimitri took his place in the back. Ciaran could feel Hope's presence next to him.

He flew around the corner and headed for his house. He needed to get home ASAP. Ciaran wanted that thug in his trunk strapped to the chair in his cement room. He thought about all the questions he'd ask and the instruments to use and the time he'd need when Hope finally said something. "What's eating you?"

"You were gone a while. I couldn't go in. I . . ."

"I'm fine. I had it under control."

She sure did, and he just got benched. He wanted to peel the skin off Marcus, and since he couldn't, he needed another target. And there'd been one up on that roof.

"You didn't tell me what was going on. I had to sit here on me arse and wait."

"Sorry, but I knew how to get in, and it was easier alone."

Alone. Ciaran clenched his fists around the steering wheel.

"Yeah." He exhaled. "Look, I get that you're good at this shit, but clue us in next time. There are other people involved now, and we need to know what you're doing."

Silence again. Ciaran was getting real good at quieting a room.

"Dude, Ciaran, you sound like a chick."

"Fuck off." The brake under his foot pushed down of its own accord, and Dimitri's skull whacked into the back of his chair. The thud in the back was Hope's hostage, and he enjoyed the added perk of fucking with him, too.

"Ciaran, sorry. You're right. I should have told you, but maybe, you could try not to kill the only lead we have. Dimitri?"

"Ow. And yeeess." His mouth elongated the word, and honest to god he sounded like he was flirting with her. That was the very definition of insanity, though, and Dimitri, though a world class idiot on occasion, couldn't have been that crazy.

"Next time you feel like butting in, don't."

They'd gotten some of their frustration out, but none of the conversation had quenched his desire for violence. That nasty fuck in his trunk was going to have the joy of filling that need. Ciaran had the tools necessary for breaking open his tight lips, among other things.

*

Ciaran took the liberty of getting Mr. Lackey out of the trunk. As he grabbed the front of his shirt and pulled, his skull cracked loudly against the heavy door. Ciaran "accidentally" lost his grip and dropped the thug on his face in the gravel.

"Oops. Clumsy bastard, aren't I?" His accent was thick, a symptom of being so fired up. He shoved the guy over with his foot and smiled at the now bloody face beneath him. "We're gonna have a conversation."

Ciaran yanked on his jacket and hauled him to the house. The trip down the stairs was a comedy of purposeful errors, shoves, and one extremely bloody nose. The lump was a pathetic waste. *He better be worth it.* He took the man to the room at the end of the hall. When Ciaran swung open the door, the creep gasped.

"Oh, come now. Show a little spine." Ciaran kicked him into the room.

There was a light hanging naked from the ceiling. The walls were unfinished brick, and the concrete floor was covered in clear plastic sheeting. In the center of the far wall sat a large metal table, like one from a butcher's shop, and a lone metal chair waited patiently under the dim light.

Ciaran forced the thug onto the chair and grabbed two pairs of cuffs from the table. He linked the rings around each wrist and connected them to the back of the chair. The view from the seat must have been impressive because the prisoner shifted in his fancy suit. You couldn't blame him, the knives, pliers, mallets, and leather strips with nails certainly weren't child's play.

"Like the toys, do you?" Ciaran leaned down in front of him as he tried to avoid eye contact. "Oh, come on now. You gonna let yourself die looking at the floor?"

"Ciaran, you can't just kill him. We need the information first." Hope's voice was a shock.

He'd completely forgotten anyone else was there. God, he loved this way too much, and he didn't want her around to see it. *Goddamn, not good . . . But that fuck has to talk. He has to.*

"Oh, he'll spill. We'll get everything we need and more from this piece of shit."

Ciaran only partly registered Hope's step back and Dimitri's crossed arms. They both stood against the far wall. He saw them out of the corner of his eye. After that, he shut them out. He needed to focus.

Ciaran walked to the table. The set of pliers caught his eye. They always did, a tool of choice for Marcus. It seemed right to use them on one of his lackeys. They were cold in his hand.

"I'm not telling you dick. You think I'm going to spill to some pansy-ass Mick?!" the guy asked.

Ciaran could see the spit fly out of his mouth as he spoke.

"Not only do I think you'll talk, I think you'll beg," Ciaran turned the pliers in his hand, "but let's not get ahead of ourselves." He tossed them in his hand, holding the arms of the pliers.

"Now, where is he?" Ciaran was quiet.

"He who?"

Ciaran swung the head of the pliers down across the guy's right knee. A loud crack echoed, and the lackey screamed.

"Where is he?"

"Don't know what you're talking about."

Ciaran swung the pliers across both kneecaps, making sure to land the blows just to the side of the guy's patella to move the bone and pull at the ligaments. He yelled again.

"Where?"

"Fuck you!"

"Well, that didn't take long. Two hits and you're already fuming. This is gonna be easier than I thought." Ciaran tossed down the pliers and went for some of his more creative tools. There was a small knife, barely sharp enough to cut through paper, and salt waiting on the table.

Ciaran grabbed them and walked back to his guest. He went around to his back. With his wrists cuffed to the chair, the lackey's underarms were vulnerable. Ciaran slowly dug the dull blade into the man's flesh. The cuts were shallow, but they bled. Ciaran fisted a handful of the Morton's and rubbed it into the fresh gouges. The room filled with the sounds of the man's shrieks and curses.

"Where." Ciaran would repeat the word over and over until this hunk of meat gave him what we wanted.

"No!"

Ciaran traced more cuts into the back of his prisoner's arms. He curved the blade as he sliced through the man's epidermis and into the muscle. After a few minutes, the lackey was covered in C-shaped slices. Ciaran took a moment to breathe and wipe the blood off the knife. When the only sounds in the room were tired, ragged breaths, Ciaran rubbed more salt into the man's bloody arms.

After the screams died out again, Ciaran put the knife and salt back. He scanned the remaining items and picked up the leather strip.

"Marcus wouldn't just live anywhere." Ciaran walked to the man's back again. "He would have a decent place to conduct his affairs."

Ciaran raised his arm. The nails punched through the leather made soft plinking sounds as they hit the floor. "Where did you report to?"

In one solid swing, Ciaran whipped the man's back. Each of the rusty nails cut into his skin and left long trails of scored flesh.

"Ahh! Ain't . . . no fancy . . . place that . . . I've s-s-seen." The man could barely speak, but he was finding enough strength to avoid the question.

Ciaran was getting impatient, but he had to take his time if he wanted the truth. "Where."

Ciaran slashed the nails across from the other direction, the patterns making large Xs. Ciaran flopped the leather strip on top of the prisoner's shoulder between strikes.

Aside from screaming, the man wasn't talking much. *Time to switch things up a bit.* Ciaran dragged the nails across the fucker's back and listened to the strained hollers echo in the concrete room. When the leather strip fell to the floor, the guy was panting and sweating.

"Don't . . . know . . ."

Blood dripped down the man's back in pulsing streams. A few more cuts and a bit more time and the guy would bleed out. Couldn't have that, could he? Ciaran walked around again. The leather hung loosely in his hand, and the nails bounced off the concrete, making a symphony of dragging sounds, gasps, and pounding thuds from his boots.

The man's face was pale, and his eyes were unfocused. Beads of sweat dripped down his forehead, and his neck was having trouble supporting his head. Ciaran punched his captive as hard as he could in the face. His knuckles landed square on the man's broken nose. The sound of the impact bounced off the walls, and Ciaran heard his friends shift positions behind him.

They needed to leave, but Ciaran knew they wouldn't. They were going to make sure Ciaran didn't kill their best lead.

"As much as I enjoy this, and I do, I would prefer to have a different guest in that chair. So, I will say it again. Where."

"I was in a van! I didn't see!"

Ciaran was getting tired of this man's seemingly endless amount of crap. This was wasting time, and Ciaran had been honest. He loved ripping apart anyone connected to Marcus, but he wouldn't be satisfied until he had that bastard at his mercy.

Ciaran punched the man again. His blood splattered on Ciaran's fist. He grabbed the man's collar and shook the limp mess until the man's eyes rattled in his head. "Now, now. No naps."

The captive was barely conscious and the blood from his nose ran down his face. The newly turned snitch was choking on his words as he tried to speak.

"Don't . . . kn—"

Before the guy could finish his lie, Ciaran knocked over the chair and landed the man on his back. His head bounced off the floor, and he yelped like a dog. Ciaran leaned in and put a boot on the guy's groin. He pushed down hard with the toe of his Doc, and the fucker started screaming again.

"Hard to talk around all that blood in your mouth? Let me rinse you out."

Ciaran was gone for two minutes and returned to the room with a pot of hot water. Dimitri made eye contact for a split second, and then dragged Hope out of the room. Ciaran stepped inside and locked the door.

The captive still lay on his back and was obviously about to pass out. Ciaran kicked him in the ribs to bring him around. The pain shot his detainee up off the floor for a moment.

"You look like you could use a drink." Ciaran knelt down and lifted his head to swallow. His eyes were wide with desire for the water, and he opened his bloody mouth.

Ciaran poured the hot liquid into the man's mouth until it was filled. Putting a hand around his mouth and nose, he forced the lackey to drown or swallow. Ciaran could smell the blood in the man's mouth. He tried to scream against his palm, but the scorching fluid burned his esophagus. Ciaran let go and watched as the captive coughed blood onto the floor.

"Where."

The gasping and flapping slaps made a grim sort of music. The beats were almost rhythmic. As the thug struggled to breathe, Ciaran sat the chair back up and waited a few moments.

Ciaran couldn't believe he was letting the man up, but Hope and Dimitri were right. They needed the information. At least Dimitri had been smart enough to take Hope out. He didn't need her to see him like this. Ciaran swallowed hard. *Just a little longer*. This lump knew about the closest safehouse, so he just folded his arms over his chest. When the fuck finally spoke, Ciaran could barely understand him.

"I can . . . sssh . . . show . . . you."

"There now. Was that so hard?"

Ciaran turned and walked out of the room. Hope and Dimitri waited outside.

"Get him ready to leave." And then he was walking past them, forcing himself to stay calm and not break into a run.

He went down to his room and straight to the large bathroom off the side. Ciaran threw up nothing. He was a sweaty mess and his heart pounded in his ears. Then, he stood up, washed his face off in the sink, and went to his closet for a blood-free shirt.

"What the fuck did you think you were doing?" Hope was in his doorway blocking the way out. "I mean it. What the fuck, Ciaran?" She boxed him in his closet, and Ciaran was pressed against his many black t-shirts.

"What the fuck do you care? He's a fucking lackey. Who gives a shit if he's dead?!" Ciaran couldn't bring himself to say the real reason he'd torn into the guy.

He couldn't talk about Marcus. He just couldn't. He couldn't open that door to Hope. *Screw all of this.* He turned to his shirts and started tossing a pile together on the bed.

Hope snatched one of the flying tees out of the air and threw it at his face. Ciaran was ready to snap. All the crap from the Inferno was suffocating, Dimitri and Red riding shotgun in that car, and now Hope was ready to kick his sorry arse to the curb. And he deserved it.

"You son of a bitch. You know that's not the point. I have no problem killing people. I'm an assassin for fuck's sake. But we can't kill someone who we still *need* something from. That's just fucking stupid. Are you stupid?"

Hope wasn't nearly as tall as Ciaran, but he felt dwarfed by her. The whole situation was fucked, and a vice-like hold wrapped around his chest.

"No. I just couldn't . . . ugh!" Ciaran screamed into the shirt in his hands. "There's some shit from the past creeping up. I want answers out of that guy, maybe as much as you do, but you're nowhere near as angry as I am. I just can't let go. It's always in my head. And no, I don't want to talk about it."

He dropped the shirt and leaned against the door jam. The floor seemed good enough to stare at. Hope apparently disagreed because she put a finger under his chin and lifted his face up.

"Ciaran, you don't have to say anything if you don't want, but . . . Just like when I handled the guy on my own, this is causing problems. It's risking our safety. You have to keep it under wraps. This shit is so messed up to me. It was point and shoot before. I've never played on a team. I've lived this entire time thinking I was killing anti-demon sympathizers, when really, they were most likely all demons. I'm feeling things for you I never have before. Feeling at all, which is a helluva thing. I want to run like hell, but I decided to give this a shot. So, work with me, okay?"

Ciaran was floored. For not being a team player, she coached pretty damn well.

"Didn't know what you were getting into, did you?" Ciaran smiled out of exhaustion.

"I didn't exactly have a choice in the matter. And I learn fast."

"Didn't have a choice? You could've bolted at any time."

"I didn't." Hope's stare was very matter of fact. She put a finger on his mouth, quieting his remaining words. As she leaned forward, a wavy strand of her hair slipped over her shoulder. The white sections gleamed in the light. They drew the light to them and found a way to bathe in it.

After torturing Marcus's errand boy for what felt like days, Ciaran was disconnected and raw. He could still feel blood on his hands. Screams were the only distinct sound he could hear in his head. The rest of the world was a humming mess. He wanted to feel Hope. He wanted to tie himself to her and let her pull him back into the world.

Hope kissed him, surrounding his bottom lip with hers. She ate him up, stilling his thoughts with the warmth of her touch. Ciaran forced himself to focus on the sensations, the slight tickle as she ran her fingertips down his arm, the warm, wet caress of her lips, the weight of her chest against his.

In seconds they were a naked tangle of limbs on his bed. As they kissed their way across the mattress, her gloriously tattooed skin was a feast for his eyes. Not long after the covers had been kicked off the bed, Hope decorated his chest with embraces from her lips and hands. Her touch grounded him. He was here. He was with her.

Hope was a roaring fire that burned its way deep into the core of his bones. She was everything he wanted to feel. Alive, whole, worthy. It was greedy. He was using this connection to make himself feel better. He wasn't enough for her, and he couldn't keep using sex as a distraction. But just as he was falling into his thoughts, Hope's fingers dragging across his skin demanded his attention. She traced the curves of the muscles at his hips. It almost tickled, but she kept moving dangerously close to his erection.

The building pressure drove him mad. He was dancing a very thin line. Hope had control right now, and even though he could look up and see it was her, Ciaran's heart thudded in his chest. With everything that happened upstairs and where they were headed, Ciaran was perched on the edge of a knife, one wrong move and he'd be sliced open from navel to nose.

He tried to take deep breaths. The smell of clean, fresh flowers overwhelmed his senses. It wasn't the horrible herbal smell he half expected. It was Hope and only Hope. Ciaran exhaled. The focus had to be a thousand percent on what Hope was doing, and holy fuck did she deliver.

Wet, warm lips surrounded the head of his shaft, and he nearly came. The smooth, fluid strokes were heaven, and he wanted to be inside Hope too desperately to let her continue. Ciaran grabbed her by the hips and flipped her over onto her back. Using his own hips to spread her legs apart, he teased at her glistening core. Hope released the sexiest moan.

With one hand, he held her hands above her head. She playfully pulled against him, smiling. She was impressively strong.

Ciaran couldn't look away from her face, something pulling in his chest. *Come on, focus.*

With his free hand, Ciaran stroked the side of Hope's face and let the motion carry his hand to her perfect breasts. He cupped each one in turn and rubbed the rosy, pierced nubs with his thumb. As they hardened under his touch, Ciaran slowly let himself enter Hope. She curled up toward him, touching her head to his. Locked together, he moved in and out, creating a hypnotic dance between them. Hope squeezed all around him, and Ciaran's body begged for more, enough to make him burst.

Everything built up, and Hope pushed and rocked against Ciaran making him move into her faster and harder. They were breathing hard, but Ciaran wasn't even close to done with her. He released her arms and scooped her up against his chest, her nails digging into his back and ass and covering him with small scratches. They didn't hurt in the slightest; his adrenaline pumped too strong.

The intoxicating sensations had no limit. The pressure and desire heightened with each thrust. Ciaran wanted to be deeper, more a part of Hope. He released her back to the bed and smiled. Moaning, she bit her lip, and goddamn he loved that. Ciaran grabbed her legs and lifted them onto his shoulders. In one switch motion, he sheathed his entire length in warmth.

Hope gasped and cursed at the intrusion, and Ciaran began to withdraw. She pulled him closer and for a moment didn't let him leave.

"Harder, please . . . as hard as you can." Hope's voice was breathy and dazed.

"I don't want to hurt you." Ciaran waited for her response.

"It's good, please. All of it . . . it's amazing even when it's too much."

They locked eyes, and Hope's stare was striking. She was drunk on the sensations, aching for more. Ciaran saw his reflection in her eyes. Hope was really there with him, and as much as the sex was about the hard, rough passion, it was also about them. The two of them colliding in a great wave, nothing but the two of them.

Ciaran completely let go. If even just for now, the past didn't matter. It was amazing and painful. The heartbreak over being so broken, so naked, was fracturing all around him.

He couldn't close his eyes. He needed to know where he was, who he was with. Ciaran's head was down, and he was admiring Hope's beautiful body when she squeezed his shoulders. Ciaran could feel the tension in her fingers as she ran her hands up to his face. He heard her breaths fly in and out sharply, and she put her forehead to his, closing her eyes. For all the rough and tumbles they'd had in this exciting honeymoon stage of whatever it was they were doing, this was different. They both slowed down. Ciaran released her legs and surrounded Hope with his body. They both focused on the sensations, on each other.

"Ciaran."

His name wasn't a scream or a fleeting construction of consonants and vowels. It left Hope's lips and hit him like an electric jolt. She was calling out for the source of her happiness. It nearly brought him to tears. She was perfect and whole and untainted, and she wanted him.

The kiss she placed on his lips truly sealed the deal. Every ounce of desire was multiplied a thousand times, a million, a billion. Hope clung to his face, their mouths embracing as they both exploded. Ciaran's orgasm seemed to go on for hours, and Hope rode out the thunderous waves with him. At the end, she looked up at him, meeting his eyes and holding them. In the small universe they'd created between them, she was there staring up at him, something powerful glowing behind her eyes. Everything and nothing had changed.

Ciaran laid on top of Hope, surrounded by her hair.

"Hope," he whispered into the glossy waves.

She turned her face to him and touched her nose to his. The room was silent for a long time. Then there was a knock at the door.

Ciaran struggled to sit up, the intrusion coming too soon and too loud. "What!"

Dimitri's voice rang out, "Well, in case you forgot, we have a house to raid. Now, get a move on, Sir Shags-a-lot!"

*

The brownstone would've turned most people away, and this part of town wasn't the greatest. Ciaran parked on the corner of Carol Court and White Birch Lane. Such cheery names for the once homey streets. They were covered in garbage and expired newspapers now. Rich arseholes didn't want to live too close to their "cloven" neighbors. *Self-righteous bastards. They're all the same no matter where you go. Yeah, thinking about all this is totally helping.*

Ciaran knew he was distracting himself. If he stopped and let his brain focus on where they were, he would snap again. He was so close to getting some revenge. Marcus would finally be in his grasp after all these years.

Ciaran noticed his clenched fists. *Oops.* The memories were coming back hard and fast, stronger and more frequently. Then there was Hope. He couldn't stop thinking about her and everything she'd seen in the past forty-eight hours. *Wow, has it only been two days?* After his session with Mr. Lackey, she'd been an anchor. How was she even here?

Ciaran turned his head slightly so he could see her walking just behind him. She was quiet, her jaw clenching and fists squeezing and releasing. He was asking so much of her. Ciaran should let Hope know where he was at, and she'd asked him to be more honest. yeah, *how?* He'd just made up with her. He wasn't about to kill it with the tale of his days at Camp Inferno. He couldn't bear to have Hope look at him that way.

"There could be sensors. I'll take a peek." Hope jogged up to the main window of the house.

"So?" Dimitri was handling their snitch, who was cleaned up and looking less like a tenderized piece of meat and starting to get feisty again.

Ciaran buzzed with energy. When it came to Marcus & Friends, he couldn't keep it together. He was trying, and he'd been good for so long, but the past put him in the mother of all choke holds.

"Looks like we'll need one of my favorites." Hope rooted around in the black bag on her shoulder.

She pulled out a small, round device. Pressing some buttons on its top in some sort of pattern, Hope cracked open a window just barely and rolled the metal ball through.

"We should back up."

"It's not going to explode, is it?" Dimitri started backing away, holding the lackey in front of him like a shield.

"No, Dimitri. It's an EMP. So, unless you want an Android paperweight in your pocket, you should take a few steps back."

All of them retreated to an electronically safe distance. It was wet and cloudy outside, and the interior of that house looked a lot warmer. As the EMP did its thing, it certainly put the word pulse to good use. The air kind of thickened and dried out for a second, and the device made the weirdest noise, a cross between metal bending and static discharging.

Hope started for the house and Dimitri followed, shoving the lackey in front of him. Ciaran didn't move. His brain told his feet to step, but he just stood there, his chest aching from his heart pumping blood too hard. His hands were clammy and shaking, his head hurt, his shoulders squeezed down, and even his ears rang. Worst, he thought he smelled. . . . *Fuck, fuck, fuck* . . .

Marcus had been there. Ciaran knew it, and his body screamed, begged not to go in.

"You okay?" He heard the concern in Hope's voice.

"Yeah, just thought I heard something. Let's head in." Ciaran's sheer stubborn attitude got him moving. Being pigheaded had its benefits, sometimes.

Gravel crunched under his boots until he hit the brownstone steps. As abandoned as it looked, it was a fricking palace on the inside, and Ciaran was on guard as he entered. It was by no means a Parade Home, but it was way more than just functional. There were extra chairs, a dining room table, several couches. Everything was old and sun-faded, but it wasn't as dusty as it should've been.

It was very open too, almost one big room, and heavy curtains hung from every window. Secure as a fortress, but not without some unnecessary flourishes. Definitely, a Marcus safehouse. No one else would take the time to do, well, anything to it. Even if he was here for the grand total of two minutes, he expected perfection.

"This place is nicer than mine!" Dimitri shoved his human package on a couch. "You're treated pretty good, aren't ya? Fucker." He glared at the man and kicked him down with his boot.

Ciaran scanned the safe house and shook his head. Marcus didn't deserve the things he stuffed in this place. He deserved bars and filth and pain and a hell-on-earth sundae complete with a railroad spike up his arse.

"Where's your equipment? You must have a stash somewhere." Ciaran scanned the space.

He watched Hope lift cushions, check behind books, open cabinets, searching for guns, computers, hit versions of interoffice memos. She didn't find anything. *They wouldn't keep it just anywhere. We both know that. He would need a special place to . . . conduct his affairs.*

Ciaran looked toward the back of the house. Anything important would be out of the way, somewhere hidden and unexpected.

"Keep an eye on him." Ciaran pointed down to the human lump.

The tension was getting to him. The soft, crunch of his steps on the matted carpet screamed. The narrow corridor trapped him. The beige walls swam and swirled in the air, but there was a small room at the far back corner he wanted to check out.

Ciaran knew his feet were moving, getting closer to the wood-paneled door, but everything seemed to go backward like those weird camera tricks.

Bile rose and sweat formed on his brow and palms. As the movie effect died, Ciaran finally reached the door and was greeted by a not so friendly smell. It was familiar and crept out of the room's dark closet like a wraith trying to choke the life out of him.

He nearly threw up. The medicinal, herbal smell was too much of a reminder. The disgusting stench had been all over him most nights at the Inferno. Marcus never let him wash it off. *Don't puke, don't puke.*

Ciaran heard someone behind him, but he wasn't listening. He was too busy trying to keep his stomach under lockdown.

"Find a store yet?" It was Hope.

"'Bout to check the closet." He could just whisper.

"What's that smell? It's like tea mixed with tiger balm." Hope sniffed the air, her superior senses picking out ingredients.

"Yeah, I noticed that. I'm not sure." Ugh, his skin crawled.

Ciaran opened the cheap sliding door and the rollers creaked. It made his skin prickle. Lots of black suits hung inside. A shelf above the rack was mostly empty aside from a black box that sat perfectly centered on the wire. It was nearly identical to one he'd seen, the pristine black finish hiding depraved contents. Ciaran stifled a flinch.

He pushed aside the hanging Armanis and knelt down, knocking on the wood beams.

"Didn't you see the big, black box?" Hope reached out for the container. Ciaran had to stop her.

"Not big enough to hold guns, or files, it's probably just a pair of fucking shoes to go with all these stupid suits." He continued to knock on the floor.

"Could be phones or something."

It was too late. She was already opening the godforsaken kit.

"What the—" Hope held the thing away from her like she might catch something. Ciaran didn't want her to touch it; he couldn't take it from her.

"Is it—"

Hope cut off his question with her own. "What the hell kind of guy is this? I knew Marcus was a prick, but seriously? I mean, what is this stuff?"

The smell in the room was nearly unbearable now that the kit was open, and Hope pointed to the tube laying the box.

"I don't know."

The knot in his throat was the size of a grapefruit. Ciaran could taste sour on the back of his tongue, and just as the world decided to get wavy on him, he let his knees hit the floor and heard the hollow whack he was searching for.

"There are shackles in here for fuck's sake!" Hope was still reeling, but Ciaran desperately concentrated on the fact he'd found something.

"Hope, there's something under here. Help me open this."

Ciaran pried at the loose floorboards, and Hope tossed the box aside, the innards clanging loudly as they hit the floor.

As Hope knelt down, the clean smell of soap wafted around her. It was miles away from the herbal cream, and Ciaran's fingers steadied a bit. With them both gripping the scratched wood, the trap door opened. Inside, a set of stairs led down into the darkness. A long pull-chain hung from a fluorescent bulb.

Ciaran didn't know if he could go down. But he knew Marcus. That's exactly where he would keep his files. He'd want to be near the paper power while he was working someone over. Hope stepped down and pulled on the light. Her dark hair ate up the illumination and was the only thing he could look at.

A sting of guilt hit Ciaran, using her again. She was unknowingly his safety net. He felt like a fucking five-year-old. *Mommy, can you hold my hand?* He shook his head. The sounds around him tunneled in.

The creak of the wood stairs, the whoosh of their breaths, it was all more intense with each step he took. The walls were cement and cold and hung around them. There were pipes along the ceiling, and they dripped rusty water. The echoed plink of each drop was torturous, and not surprising, in the least. "Sometimes older really is better," Marcus would say. The most gruesome was the setup of a table and a section of wall.

The table was covered in a burgundy cloth and twin goblets sat on top. Each pewter cup was shaped into a hideous face. One the classic portrayal of the devil and one a cross between a man's face and a squid. An empty bottle of wine and a small white cloth were next to them.

"What's up with the fancy table and . . . that?" Hope pointed to the wall.

It was brick and at four points metal rings had been drilled into the mortar. Unfortunately for the people who would be chained there, the rings had been installed properly, anchored to withstand weight and force.

"One person gets to be nice and comfy. The other . . ." He pointed to the chains. "Poetic, huh?"

Hope was quiet. Ciaran let a little more out than planned. He did that a lot around her.

She took steps toward him but didn't touch him or say anything. She was just physically closer. The weight of her presence crushed him. If only she could un-hear everything, but it was too late. This was all so wrong.

"So, aside from . . . this, what do you think is down here?" Hope looked around the room.

Hope was so calm, so focused, it was comforting. Damn him for doing it, but Ciaran's mind wandered back to his room before they left. Hope hadn't pushed. She knew there was something under his skin, making him itchy and defensive, but she didn't *make* him talk.

"There should be a file cache. Somewhere hidden, but also kinda displayed. you might have noticed that Marcus really wants everyone to know how powerful he is."

"Yes, indeed I have." Hope crouched down and inspected the floor while Ciaran checked the walls.

He didn't know if he actually wanted to find something. Revenge was there, but the rest of it was too. Then, on the wall by the door, Ciaran saw a change in cement color. There was a lighter patch about the size of, well, a bread box, at eye level.

"Hope, come here." Ciaran waved her over and prodded at the wall.

Hope stood at his side. "Find something?"

He made a fist and punched through.

"Holy shit! What are you doing?"

Ciaran stepped to the side and let Hope see into the hole.

"That." He smirked at her. *Damn that felt good.*

"Wow. Look at that. How could you tell?"

"The lighter color, and when you look close, the texture isn't right."

"Handyman, indeed." Hope winked at him, and for a moment, his heart leapt out of his ribcage and into his throat.

"Time to empty this bad boy." Ciaran took out a largish, metal box.

It was pretty heavy and extremely dusty. As he popped open the rusty lid, Ciaran turned over the container and let it rain papers on the table. There was every type of form you could imagine. Medical forms, personal genealogy, as well as his closest associates' histories, daily agendas, order inventories from the Inferno, bet logs, but it was all for only the past three years and every form was signed or referred to Dante.

"Damn it." Ciaran tossed a recent order form for industrial strength cleaner on the table.

"What? We hit the jackpot."

"None of these say Marcus Dentry. I know he has files under his real name."

"True, but these go back three years, right? What happened, then, that could explain this?" Hope dug to the bottom of the pile and held up two forms, a birth certificate for one Dante Alighieri and a death certificate for Marcus Dentry.

Ciaran snatched them out of Hope's hands.

"What the fuck? The explosion?"

"Say what, now? What explosion?"

"When I escaped the Inferno, I used an explosion. One of the demons I met there was a fire demon. She helped me blow up the generator and get the others out, that's including Dimitri. Marcus musta faked his death. There was no way that fire was going unnoticed, and he wouldn't have been able to continue business if the police found out what he'd been doing. I figured he just bought 'em off but look—" Ciaran flipped over the death certificate and on the back was a clipping. The headline read, "Local man killed in gas fire at home."

"Killed at home my arse. The Inferno died, but Dentry sure as hell didn't. You'd think that the people at the birth office would realize this is a fake name. It's the author of the fucking book."

"Not everyone reads as much as you, Ciaran. My god, an explosion?

You'd think it would stop him. But he just started picking demons off, one by one. You must've hated him."

"Hate. Present tense." Ciaran let the documents fall. He knew his escape wouldn't stop Marcus, but it didn't even slow him down.

Marcus had once confessed to him that he absolutely despised demons. He loved that he could pit them against each other and sell some off to please his High Rollers. It was another reason he kept Ciaran around. If Marcus sold him, he'd have no one to play with, since he didn't lower himself to sleep with demons. Their gifts were "hideous flukes of nature," "slime to be cleaned up." Ciaran once said Marcus was jealous. He couldn't remember much after that. He'd passed out when Dentry ripped off one of his nails.

"Ciaran? What's up?" Hope had a hand on his cheek and was staring at him with wide eyes. He didn't even feel her touch him.

"Distracted."

"I can see that. . .. Look, I know I said that you don't have to say anything, and you don't, but I think it might help. Like I know anything about feelings, I know. But it looks like it hurts to keep it in. I've seen that face you make. Yeah, that one. I know this all makes you sick, and I can tell it was something serious, but I don't care about the past. I think it's fucked up for everyone. I was in a clan that just wanted me to get pregnant and keep the race alive. It was shitty, but I got out. I didn't want that choice made for me, and now, it won't be. I can't get pregnant if I'm not with them doing some fancy ritual. So now, I'm free to live my life. Maybe, if you can get it out, you can be done with it, too."

Ciaran stood there like an idiot. He didn't know what to say. She just laid stuff out like all the crap either of them experienced could be swept up into a tiny pile and thrown out. Damn, Hope was supposed to be a baby-making nothing in her old life. No wonder she left. And she could just talk about it.

"I . . . goddamn, Hope. That's not right."

"It's over, but thanks." Hope smiled gently.

It was a new face for her. She seemed different by lightyears, but also more who she truly was. *And to come clean like that* . . . Ciaran was protective of her, but she could clearly take care of herself, and he should be able to do the same. Shouldn't he?

"I just—Ugh," Ciaran exhaled hard and before he knew what he was doing, he was on the floor. His butt bones hit the concrete, and he let his head fall back against the wall. God, he was exhausted.

"Goddamn. Just god-fuckin'-damn, Hope. I'm so tired. Tired of fighting, of losing, of never being able to let it go. I'm just really tired. I didn't think surviving like this would take such a toll. I swear, I wasn't always like this.

"I think I used to be boring. Ha. Yeah, boring. Lived alone until my mam introduced me to this girl, Ebony, pushed us together like a bulldozer. Just wanted to make her happy. Didn't really like her, but she shouldn't have died. Nobody had ever died around me before, but when Marcus scoops ya up to fight, he makes sure no one will miss you. Dimitri lost his whole clan.

"I do really despise him, Hope. He ruined so many people. He ruined me, repeatedly. Not sure why he chose me. Guess I'm his type, not a demon. Now? I'm not a boy anymore. I've seen and done too much, but I can't be a man. He took that from me. I wish you were first. I wish you were the only taste I knew. I don't want to dirty you, and every time we're together, I get it all over you. I thought I stopped him. I thought it would just be me. But he probably has another room, just like this, in his new house with some other lad chained face-first to the wall.

"God, the smell down here! That fucking cream! 'Can't have you soft,' he'd say. Ahh, I can't get him out. Out of my life, out of my head. He's always there, laughing at me. I want to fucking kill him so bad, and I hate that. I hate what I know how to do 'cause of that place. I killed so many people 'cause he told me to, and I've done other things 'cause he said to. I can't stop it, this spinning. It comes back, over and over. I see him and feel him. I fight it. I swear I do, but it just keeps coming back, faster and more. And every time, I choke. It won't stop. I can't get away. I want to. I really do, but I can't make it stop. I just want it to stop. You have to know I want it to stop. I want it to stop. . . . Please . . . please, stop."

Ciaran's voice was small. He was hot and clammy. The sound of the blood in his ears was deafening. Ciaran gripped Hope's hands hard, and he couldn't even remember taking them. What was stranger was how his face was wet. Had he started crying? Ciaran was blown apart and didn't have any idea where the pieces went. The soundless space pressed in on him, and he couldn't stop the air from rushing in and out of his lungs. Everything was a dark mass that spun and twisted.

Where was he? That's right. He was in Marcus's safe house. The table and wall shone like they were under a fucking spotlight. The same laughter that always surrounded him, ricocheted in his skull. *You useless shit. How could you cry? I have to get out of here.*

Ciaran awkwardly pushed off the floor and flew toward the door.

"Ciaran, wait."

"Really, what? I can't—" He was going to lose what control he had left, and there'd be no going back. God, Hope couldn't look at him like that, anymore.

"We can't forget the files. If we're going to kill him, we need the files." Hope's voice was a straight edge in the dark.

Ciaran walked down a few stairs and stared at her face. "You keep doing that."

"What?"

"Never mind."

Ciaran walked up to her, and she didn't retreat. She didn't take an apprehensive step back. She wasn't scowling. Together, they gathered up the files and put them in the box. That was it. Hope heard it all, and her only reaction was to make sure Marcus would die.

"So, where—" The sound of glass breaking upstairs stopped Hope midsentence.

"Dimitri. Grab that shit and load up." Ciaran pulled the .45 out of his waistband and loaded a magazine from his pocket. When he heard a thud above his head, the safety came off.

Hope ran up the stairs behind him, and Ciaran could see her stuff the box in her bag as he rounded the corner. *Good. Safe and sound.* When they stormed into the living room, the place was a disaster. The couch was tipped over, and the window in front was shattered. There were blood stains on the floor and pieces of someone's shirt stuck in the broken glass.

The sound of punches landing outside grabbed Ciaran's attention. He ran out the front door and saw a blurred mass of limbs by his car. He could hear both men grunting and as Dimitri flipped over their prisoner, Ciaran saw a red blotch on his friend's side. Ciaran drew his gun, but they wouldn't stop moving. He needed a cleaner shot and after the "share time" in the basement, it needed to be a sure thing. As he tracked them with his gun, he saw Hope mimicking his actions.

"I've got this."

"I'm just your back up." Hope's finger was to the side of her gun, away from the trigger, but she watched the pair with trained eyes.

Ciaran eyed the lackey who'd jumped Dimitri as his friend landed a solid kick in the guy's sternum and the dick fell back. Ciaran fired and nailed the bastard in his right arm. He grabbed at the wound, blood seeping through his fingers. Ciaran ran over to Dimitri and tried to help him up. With his hand outstretched, he finally realized what Dimitri was saying.

"Watch out. . . . Glass . . ."

Ciaran could barely make it out through his groans, so he didn't move fast enough. The lackey clutched a large shard of glass. It scratched down Ciaran's back, tearing open his shirt and skin. Thankfully, the crafty arsehole couldn't get a solid grip on his weapon without hurting himself, and Ciaran made it to Dimitri, shoving him to Hope.

With a swift kick, Ciaran took the lackey out at the knees and heard his head hit the ground, ringing out in the empty area. Ciaran held him down and searched him again. No more hidden treasures. The guy got lucky with the glass.

"Ow. That sort of hurt. I imagine your arm hurts a bit more, though." Ciaran's words came out in a grunt as he pushed the toe of his boot into the guy's wound.

"Nice back . . . I've seen that M before. You're just another piece of property, aren't you? Just one of Marcus's playthings that's looking for some payback."

"Shit." Dimitri's voice was quiet behind Ciaran.

The gun went off before Ciaran realized he'd moved his arm. The lackey went limp, and a large chunk of his skull went missing. In the silence that followed, a weird beeping sound cut through and the smell of gunpowder wafted around him. Hope was in front of him and talking, but all Ciaran could hear was a wa-wa sound like an adult on the *Peanuts*.

The beeping was incessant, and Ciaran realized it was coming from the dead guy's ankle. *Is that what Hope said? Something about the sound, yeah, that was it.*

Ciaran knelt down and lifted up the corpse's pant leg. It was a grey ankle strap. In the center a red light flashed in time with the beeps. The device almost looked like a home arrest monitor but clearly, the prick wasn't at home.

"What the hell is that?" Dimitri had a hand on his side, and Hope helped him hobble forward.

"Ugh, quit it. Unfortunately, that's a heart rate monitor spliced together with a home arrest anklet. When there's no pulse, the device goes off with coordinates. Prepare for company, guys." Hope struggled with Dimitri, and he tried to break free and walk without her.

"You've got to be kidding me. That shit only happens in the movies."

Dimitri probably would've kept ranting but the crunching of gravel cut him off.

"Fuck. Get inside, now!" Ciaran shouted.

"We can't take on that many," Hope said.

"We have to." Ciaran helped Hope carry Dimitri back to the brownstone.

FOURTEEN

Shendara in Shiahla, her back hurt! Ciaran seemed barely affected by the slash, but Hope could feel it, and her whole mind-over-matter thing wasn't as developed. Thank Maker, she didn't have to deal with Dimitri's discomfort, too.

As they waited for the storm to hit, the house was oddly quiet. Once they were surrounded, backup would pour into the brownstone and kill anything in their path. Hope looked over at Ciaran; he was at the front loading his gun. She examined his back more closely. Beneath new and old scars, plus what she had to assume were burn marks, was the distinct outline of the letter M carved into his flesh. The edges were jagged and rough, but it looked as if it was done in one long cut. Hope could follow the old, gruesome capital M across his entire back.

Something dripped on her hand, a clear, fat droplet. Hope wiped her face. This was not a feeling she enjoyed. She shook her head and checked the ammo in her gun for a second time.

Hope closed her eyes and focused on the sounds outside the house. She heard at least six sets of boots on gravel. They were moving in a circular pattern and surrounding each wall. Two pairs went quiet, stopped on the grass outside the back door and side window to her left. Window-boy would have to be taken out first.

"You alright? Your side hurt?" Hope jumped at Ciaran's words and swung her head around.

"What?"

"Your side? 'Cause of Dimitri?" Ciaran nodded at her waist.

"Oh, I'll be fine. I was listening to our guests. Should be quite the party."

"How many?"

"I can hear six. Could still be some by the cars."

"Six? That's all?" Dimitri came into the living room from checking the back.

"Dimitri, how'd it look?" Hope had asked him to make sure the only points of entry were in the living room.

"Basement, room thing, is good. No doors down there. I jammed the doors to the other bedrooms, so they'd just get stuck in there. Only issue now is the back door and upstairs. Door is locked, but it also has a glass panel they might be able to shoot through. Upstairs rooms are jammed, but there's a window in the hall a person could fit through if they managed to climb up."

"Jammed how?" Hope asked.

"Broke some stuff off in the locks. They'll have to break the doors down if they want in." Dimitri swallowed hard. What could Dimitri have found to shove in the locks? But Hope didn't have time to question it.

"Does anybody else think they got here really fast?" Ciaran gestured at the door.

"They were probably on their way to the safe house. Weekly budget meeting or something." Dimitri had a good point. They were already coming here, which meant their luck royally sucked.

"He's right. Now, get into position." Hope nodded at the entry points.

"Yes, sir." Dimitri faked a salute and waddled off toward the back of the room. Ciaran hid a chuckle under a cough.

"When we're out of this, I'm kicking your ass. Both of you." Hope rolled her eyes at Ciaran, only to end up smiling.

Guns cocked outside and snapped Hope to attention. She raised her weapon and steadied herself with a deep breath. Nothing but near perfect was going to get them out of this.

"Ciaran, two at the front door. I'll take the window. Dimitri, try not to get shot," Hope whispered with force.

"You're no fun." Dimitri aimed his .35 at the door and crouched low.

Inside the brownstone, everything became silent and still. Outside, everyone paused. It was the deep breath before all hell broke loose. Hope mentally wished for Ciaran to remain unharmed. She didn't want him dying, and she wasn't sure if she could focus through any wounds he might get.

The sucking noise from someone inhaling outside the front door meant the party had just started. A thud against the backdoor meant Dimitri's "jam" had worked. Unfortunately, at the same moment, the window Hope had her gun leveled at broke, and a body leapt through. She fired a couple rounds killing the unlucky bastard who got stuck as the first wave.

As his body collapsed, it formed a small barrier. Ciaran's gun sounded off next to her. He put a few bullets in the two men who made a play at the front door. One went down hard and wouldn't be getting up, but the other managed to rush Ciaran.

Ciaran shot the gunman in the arm, but they were fighting for control over his .45. Hope aimed at the invader, but before she could get off a clean shot, the thug from the back door ran to the open window. Hope squeezed the trigger landing a round right between the asshole's eyes. He tightened his hand as he fell, sending a shot straight across Hope's left thigh. The burn ripped across her leg.

The pain was blinding, literally. Hope's vision went blurry and suddenly, she was sweating profusely. She shook her head and wiped her hands on her sleeves to get a better grip on her gun. Hope was queasy, and before she could react, her leg gave out. The jolt of pain in her thigh radiated up from the point of impact and seemed to wake her up.

"Fuck, you're bleeding a lot." Ciaran's voice sounded like it was passing through water. No thicker than water, oatmeal or Jell-O was more accurate.

Hope realized that pressure was being applied to her leg, and it really fucking hurt.

"Damn, I didn't need this today. You're already distracting enough." Hope forced herself up and stood like a baby deer, but the pain kept her conscious.

"You really shouldn't be standing." Ciaran held his gun tight in his hands, both of them bloody from tying a piece of his shirt around her leg and fired at the door. It kept the three men remaining, wait, now there were two, at bay.

"When there's no one left, and we're in the car, I'll sit down." Hope pushed off Ciaran. "Go get Dimitri. We need to take out the few remaining. Then, make a break for it."

Ciaran was nice enough to take the hint and not mention Hope's leg, anymore. She was well aware of how bad it was, and this pain she didn't like at all. The odd tightening sensation of Hope's stomach bunching helped her put together the connection between it and nausea. It was nearly as bad as the GSW.

Out of the corner of her eye, Hope saw Ciaran helping Dimitri to his feet and the skin on his back pulled. It stung in a quick jab but faded. If only her thigh would do the same. Hope heard the last two gunmen run to the front. She knocked over a couch, creating an impromptu barricade.

The men shoved at the blocked door. They grunted and huffed like pigs. Hope fired at the crack in the door, causing them to flinch and dart away.

"Hurry up, guys! We need to move!" Hope reloaded her gun having used the last six bullets to keep the douchebags by the door at bay.

"How much do you have left? Dimitri's got a full clip. I have about half." Ciaran held Dimitri draped across his shoulder and came up to the door as quickly as the noisy load would allow.

"This is my last one." Hope loaded the ammo and pulled back the hammer to chamber a bullet. She looked at the door and dragged her leg around under herself. How she was supposed to run was beyond her.

"So, how are we doing this? I can't run, and I don't see you running, either." Dimitri held his arm tight to his side. He had a gun in his hand, but it was shaky.

Hope visualized the trip. With the remaining bullets, they'd have to take out the last men standing between them and desperately needed medical care. A well-placed shot in the open crack could take out at least one, but whoever did it would have to be fast, because they'd be an open target. That left her and Dimitri out. That meant, for a second, Hope would have to hold Dimitri's weight while Ciaran got killing. *This is gonna suck.*

"Ciaran, take care of the one at the door. Then we're blasting our way out of here."

Ciaran nodded. Obviously, he'd come up with the same plan. Dimitri tried to stand and walk to Hope, but the side wound was too much for him. He collapsed, and Hope made the mistake of catching him.

"Fuck!" The muscles around the bullet-hole tore further, and Hope almost lost her breakfast.

"Sorry. But, I seriously feel your pain. Also, sporting the hole-look." Dimitri tried to adjust his weight, but it only made things worse.

"Just stop. Really." Dimitri's smell was so strong up close. The woody, moss scent made her think of ancient trees and clean, cold earth.

"What kind of demon are you, anyway?"

"The best kind, duh."

"Seriously, you're crushing my leg. You owe me."

"Not really polite to ask, chica. You should know that, being a demon and all."

Hope rolled her eyes. "One, I had a pretty sheltered life. Two, I left pretty young. And three; of all the people to give a damn, I can't believe you're one of them."

"Believe it or not, I keep things private about myself, demon things, anyway. I'll just say, my clan is one of the oldest in existence."

"Nice and vague. So, why's it so rude to ask?" Hope was really feeling the strain of holding Dimitri, but she could hear Ciaran getting into position at the door. *Not much longer.*

"Well, if you know what type of demon someone is, you know their weaknesses."

"Oh. Yet another downside of being trapped in my clan presents itself." Hope tried to adjust Dimitri further upon her shoulder, but between the pain in her leg, her back from Ciaran, and the sweaty mess she'd become, he just wouldn't stay in a comfortable spot.

"Maybe, you shouldn't bash your clan so much. You're the one who left." Dimitri was staring at the ground and his face made her stop the tirade she was about to launch. Something about his face, the look he had. *Marcus murdered his clan.*

Hope never really understood guilt. If she wanted to do something, she did it. Dimitri seemed the same, but right now, there was no air of his usual bravado. He was off, and it made her extremely uncomfortable. Apparently, she'd opened a can of worms she didn't know existed.

"Sorry." Hope looked from his face to the floor.

"It's fine."

They were both so quiet. Thankfully, the pop, thud, and slam of Ciaran shooting and hitting his target broke the tension. Ciaran braced a shoulder against the door and put his empty hand on the table to the side of the entryway. Hope shuffled over with Dimitri in tow. They both tensed from the idea of running, but there was no other way out. By all things holy, demon and human, she was not looking forward to this.

"You guys ready?" Ciaran was breathing hard, and as Hope focused on him, she realized how badly his back hurt.

"Oh, yeah, buddy." Dimitri shoved off Hope. "Let's see if I can get to the car before I bleed out."

Ciaran laughed slightly, but they all knew the shape they were in. "I open the door, you two get to the car, ASAP. I'll cover your backs. Hope, can you still shoot?"

"I've got bullets, don't I?"

Ciaran smiled and Dimitri stood, bracing some weight on the wall. *Just get to the car. That's all.* Ciaran nodded. His bangs swung into his eyes, and Hope wanted to touch his hair. Her thoughts were scattered. Hope had lost a lot of blood.

Hope tightened her grip on her gun. The metal dug into her palm. With every ounce of strength she had left, she focused on her hand and the running she was about to do. Metal on her palm, air in her lungs, feet in her boots. She gripped harder and harder, until, after a quick peek through the crack, Ciaran threw open the door.

Hope shoved Dimitri through. He ran surprisingly fast for a guy who'd been stabbed in the side, and he went straight to the car. Hope followed and couldn't begin to explain the trauma her leg was experiencing. Each step caused a shock wave that traveled up through her heel bone and landed right at the hole in her muscle. It burned, it ached, it throbbed, it was almost too much. If she stood on her leg much longer, she would've passed out, but they were so close.

Hope forced her body to continue and, thank Shendara, Dimitri made it to the car. His side was bleeding all over, however, and he struggled to get inside and start it. The rumble of the engine was one of the most beautiful sounds in the world. Though the gunshots were not a good sign. Hope glanced back and saw Ciaran fighting off the only remaining obstacle. Ciaran almost caught up with her, but the fucking guy leapt at him and tackled him to the ground.

Hope stumbled like she'd been hit and slowly limped her way to the open car door. She collapsed into the back seat. She couldn't see anything laying on her face, and when she turned around there was a red stripe on the rough fabric of the car floor where her leg dragged across. Hope looked around. Her vision was blurry again.

Dimitri was a fuzzy blob in the driver seat, but she could make out a red smear that stretched out from his side down the edge of the seat. Hope reached out and grabbed the handle above the door. She pulled herself upright.

"You're bleeding, like . . . a lot." Hope's voice sounded drunk.

"Yeah, you're one to talk. It's a good thing this car was already a piece of shit." Dimitri wadded up a shirt he must have found and pressed it to his side.

"Ciaran?" Dimitri lifted a brow as he asked.

"He's fighting off that guy. My hands are too shaky, can you take him out?" A pang jabbed in her chest. *I should be doing it. He's mine to protect.* The thought was strange. Shendara, Hope was freezing and sweating. Shock was starting to set in.

Dimitri's rustling brought Hope out of her head.

"Hold still, you bastard!" Dimitri yelled, aiming his gun with one hand.

Hope looked through her open door. Ciaran was only a few steps away, and the douche that chased him wasn't thrown. He ran up to Ciaran like a freaking crack-powered bloodhound.

They began to grapple for Ciaran's gun, and Hope fought for control over her eyelids, which desperately wanted to close. Ciaran was impressive, but his opponent had seen the injury on his back and was landing blow after blow on the tender flesh. Each time Hope hissed in pain and bunched her shoulders. Dimitri didn't seem to notice.

Just as Hope's eyes started closing, Ciaran lost the struggle for his gun. The blurry form that wasn't him held the .45 up and pointed it at her *jabalv.*

The next few moments went too fast. She heard what she believed to be two shots. Dimitri and Marcus's mercenary both fired. The man went down, Ciaran fell to his side, Hope's arm blazed with hot, searing pokers, and then, Dimitri was putting Ciaran in the car next to her.

All Hope could do was bounce between the two points of fresh pain. Her thigh pulled her toward unconsciousness, but her arm was burning so badly, it woke her back up. Everything spun, and she had this horrible fear racing through her veins. Was Ciaran really in the car? No, he couldn't be. With the amount of pain she was in, Ciaran was certainly dead.

Hope breathed faster and faster. Her heart screamed like an angry child in her head. There was something wet on her face, but she was almost positive she wasn't bleeding there. And what was that horrible noise? It was a gasping, scratchy moan, and it was so loud her eyes hurt. The noise got louder and louder. It echoed her breaths and started to choke her. As her breathing grew shallow, the noise got quieter.

"Dimitri, hurry. We're losing her."

The sound of Ciaran's voice was a pleasant hallucination, but it made the noise come back. *Damn the person making that sound.* It faded out. Hope's brain started to churn. She hurt all over, her chest was heavy, and she wasn't sure if she was lying down or sitting up. She was strangely unable to do or process anything. Was this dying?

"Ciaran . . ." Her thin voice barely passed through the air.

"I'm right here. Hold on." The voice sounded strong and healthy, but that made sense. People are always healthy again when they go to the Otherland. Everything went really quiet, and Hope was glad for it. She was so tired, and sleep sounded beyond amazing. Just for a second. She'd rest for just a second. Way off in the distance, someone was yelling.

"No! No! No! Stay with me!"

What? She wasn't going anywhere, was she? It didn't matter, really. Hope was falling asleep whether she wanted to or not. The last thing she heard before she passed out was the slam of many doors shutting.

*

In the name of all things good and great in this world, why is it so cold in here? Hope came back into her body and found it shaking. She never kept her house cold. Come to think of it, she was never cold at all. Why, or more importantly how, did she feel freezing? The blanket should be around her, so Hope reached around to find it. She found something soft and blanket-like, so she pulled it up around her shoulders. She was still so exhausted, and she didn't have any assignments, right now. Dammit, she was sleeping in.

Hope flipped over on to her side, and just as she was realizing that the bed was smaller, the horrific burn in her thigh brought her screaming back to reality.

"What the fuck! Ahh!" Hope shot up in the tiny bed and grabbed the air around her thigh since she couldn't grab her actual leg. Suddenly, she was very aware that she was wearing a hospital johnny in an all-white room.

"Whoa. Hope, it's me. Calm down." Ciaran's voice. That was Ciaran's voice.

Hope searched the white expanse and waited impatiently while her eyes adjusted to the light change and finally focused. As the blurry mass settled, Hope could see a tall, masculine figure sitting next to her bed.

She tried to speak again, but this time all she heard was that awful noise from before. *From before I . . . Oh, Maker. Before, in the car, when I . . .* Hope finally realized what the awful noise was. She was crying. To be more specific, she was sobbing, like a big, fucking baby.

"Hey. It's okay. You're at my house. Nearly lost you in the car. Your leg was really bleeding, but you're gonna be fine, love." The Irish in Ciaran's voice was coming out strong. Hearing it was weirdly good.

Hope swallowed and tried to regroup. After her breathing returned to normal, and she wiped the leaky mess off her face, she could see the worried look on Ciaran's face.

"Well, let's not do that, again." Hope sighed and tried to lean back in the stiff bed. It was as comfortable as a table.

"I'd prefer not to find my girl bleeding to death, too." Ciaran's arm was wrapped in white gauze and his shirt was off. There was an Ace bandage around his torso. His normal tan glow seemed much paler.

"It's not as bad as it looks. Stop looking at me like that."

"Sorry." Hope looked down at herself. She probably didn't look any better. Thank the sweet Maker, there wasn't a mirror in eyeshot. There was, however, what seemed like a giant IV bag and some guy with scrubs on in the corner.

"Thanks for letting me know we had an audience." Hope nodded at the corner and pulled the blanket up higher to cover the vast expanse of skin that the johnny left exposed.

"Trust me, wasn't looking. I was preoccupied with the massive hole in your femoral artery." The man's voice sounded different. He certainly wasn't from America originally, and he was a demon. Hope couldn't tell which clan, but he too had an ancient smell. His scent was clean and fresh like the air in a great field.

"Thanks, I guess. And you are?"

"At ease, Hope. This is Alexander Gallo. He's an EMT," Ciaran said.

"Felt more like a field surgeon, today. I would like to check your sutures if you don't mind." Gallo walked over and pulled a metal tray up to the edge.

"This is in your house?" Hope asked.

Ciaran seemed to have every type of room possible in his giant mansion. Torture chamber, hospital, training room, and bedrooms aplenty, what was next?

"Independent security, remember? I get hurt a lot. Usually, it's not necessary, but you needed more than stitches."

Gloves snapped at her side, and Hope jumped.

"Yeah, that was really loud. I apologize. I'm going to roll this down, alright?" Gallo's gloves were purple and smelled terrible.

"Sure."

"I'll try to be as gentle as I can." Gallo rolled down the thin hospital blanket and folded it across her feet with precision. He was so smooth and confident with his movements. It was strange, but she could picture him running with deer through the forest, majestic and gentle.

Hope laid back and let him examine her wound. Gallo pulled back the dressing in one swift motion. His fingers were too sure to just be an EMT. Hope looked down at the sutures in her thigh, and she was thoroughly impressed. They were tiny, perfect xs that closed the gaping hole in her leg, like it was nothing.

"You sure you're just an EMT? These look better than most surgeons in Newborn."

"I'm trained as an emergency surgeon, but I like being out in the thick of it."

There was a small bottle of red liquid on the metal tray, and Alexander dipped a long, wooden, cotton swab inside. The liquid was cold, at first, but as it sunk into her wound, her whole body got warm and the ache eased everywhere.

He swabbed a few more times, and Hope thought she saw some of her skin knit itself back together. She was probably just tired.

"What is that stuff?" Hope's voice came easier, and her eyes didn't feel as heavy.

"Magick." Alexander smiled. "It's a secret serum I made. Don't tell anyone." Through that smile, he was completely serious. Whatever he made, it was definitely not public information, and he wanted to keep it that way. *What is it with demons and secrets?*

"Well, thank you. You don't even know me. You didn't have to do this."

"I like to help people; it's in my nature. Besides, Ciaran and I have gotten pretty close, after all the scrapes he's gotten in, and I've never seen him so worried about anyone. If you saw his face, you would've done the same. He looked like someone shot his puppy."

"Alex! Arsehole! I was nowhere near that pathetic. . . .Was I?" Ciaran's crooked grin was positively dashing, and for whatever reason, Hope liked that he worried about her.

"Ha! Oh, calm down. There's no use denying it. Anyone with working eyes could see how much she means to you." Alex turned to Hope. "He was very protective of you. You're in good hands. Now, rest. I'm going to leave you some of the serum. Just apply a few drops every couple of hours. At the end of the night, Ciaran is going to remove your stitches."

"Already?"

"Yes, you'll be all healed. Like I said, magick. Speaking of stitches, I'm going to check on Dimitri."

Hope's mind flashed to an image of Dimitri in the driver seat with his side drenched in blood.

"Oh shit, his stab wound. Is he okay?" Hope felt horrible for forgetting, which was fucking weird. This physical pain trick seemed to come with a host of new, unpleasant emotions.

"He'll be okay. He thinks on his feet and used the seatbelt and an old shirt to stop the bleeding. Very clever." Alex started to pack up his kit, and Hope looked over at Ciaran.

"Yeah, that crafty fuck is doing fine. There's no way one stab wound could take him out." Ciaran reached out with his good arm and took her hand. It was better than Gallo's serum.

"I'm so sorry you got hurt. You really scared me." His voice was quiet, and thankfully, Gallo knew to excuse himself.

Hope gestured at the door. "How did you meet him?"

"I was hurt. On my way to the car, I lost my strength. I ended up in an alley behind a restaurant, and Alex came out the back to . . . Well, I don't know what, but he found me bleeding up a storm. I don't remember much after that, but he brought me to the hospital and patched me up. Asked about what had happened, and I spilled about the security job. At that moment, I knew I needed something closer to home. I had the money, so I hired him on and built this." Ciaran seemed glad to talk about anything but the previous day, but Hope needed to.

"I thought you died."

"What?" Ciaran nearly fell out of his chair.

"I did. I couldn't see anything, really. It was all blurry, and I heard the gun go off. I thought you were hit. . .. I was in so much pain." The gaping hole in her leg had somehow relocated to her chest. Hope shifted uncomfortably. She'd gone from assassin to injured woman in a hospital bed. *How the mighty have fallen.*

"Hope." Ciaran stood and pushed her feet over gently. She tried to create as much room on the tiny bed as possible and rolled onto her uninjured side. Ciaran lay down next to her. With his head all the way at the top of the bed, his feet still hung off. He faced her and pulled Hope into his arms.

Against his chest, she could feel the Ace bandage rub on her cheek and hear his heart pound. Hope reached around him and rested her hand right above the slash on his back. He was warm, so very warm, next to her cold skin. Today, or last night, she supposed, had thoroughly sucked but, right now, this lying in Ciaran's arms was fucking amazing. He was okay. Their limbs tangled perfectly together, wrapping each other and holding tight. She couldn't think of anywhere else she'd want to be, not even back at her home. If she let herself admit it, this was more home than that house ever was.

Maybe, this is the trade? Agony for . . . him.

"There's so much I want to say. All this crap with Marcus and my own shit." Hope started to shiver.

"But later, you need to rest."

"I don't think I can. My head won't turn off." Hope shoved her face in Ciaran's chest.

"Shh, close your eyes." Ciaran's arms tightened around her.

"I don't want to feel like this; it's pathetic. I'm an assassin, for Shendara's sake. I just . . . thought I lost you and that almost . . . I don't know. This is so fucking weird to me. I don't understand how I'm feeling or what I'm thinking. Damn it, Ciaran. What did you do to me?"

"It's mutual. I can't explain what's going on, but I promise you, I won't ever let you get hurt again. I'm sorry I let you down. It'll never happen again. Never."

"I trust you." Hope didn't feel like herself; the things she was saying were completely unlike her.

It was like every bit of common sense and self-preservation flew out the window. She wasn't sure if she missed them. And it was true, she did trust this man. Against all her training and logic, she completely trusted Ciaran. Hope couldn't bring herself to be happy about it, though. The last time trust was involved in her life, it didn't end well, and she couldn't just change everything about her life to be with Ciaran. She was an assassin, and she liked her job. She was strong and independent and willful, and she wouldn't, she couldn't, change that.

"The thing is I—"

Ciaran stopped her. "Shh, sleep, love." He rubbed her back and started singing softly.

Hope couldn't understand the words. It must've been Gaelic. Ciaran's voice, even when quiet, seemed to pierce the stillness of the empty room, deep and gravelly and painting the room with the foreign syllables. It dripped down the walls and covered her skin, blanketing her. Her brain emptied. The song there, too. It waded into the chaos of her brain like the sun on a cloudy day and brought a life back to her. Not her own, a piece of Ciaran's, given to her to heal.

It was harder and harder to open her eyes. As much as Hope wanted to watch the rise and fall of Ciaran's chest, she couldn't stay awake. Deep pains, some she'd forgotten about, faded, and Hope practically melted. As she fell further down the well of sleep, Ciaran's voice haunted her heart, and she let it soothe her. When she had to give in to sleep, Ciaran would keep singing, if she needed him to.

There was movement next to her. Hope tried to ignore it and fall back asleep, but in moments her stomach decided she was awake and starving. When she cracked an eyelid against the harsh light of the mini-hospital, she saw Ciaran gripping the top of the bed and planting a foot at the bottom. She couldn't help but laugh.

"You look ridiculous. Like a bear trying to ride a tricycle." Hope smirked as he scowled at her.

"You little shit." Ciaran furrowed his brow, but there was no mistaking the smile hidden underneath. "I need a bigger bed in here."

He picked her up, completely giving up on trying to lie next to her and set her down on his lap. She sat side-saddle and brushed the hair out of his eyes.

"I'm really hungry."

"Yeah, well, guess you'd better get cooking, eh?" Ciaran winked at her, and she punched him solidly in the arm. They both flinched.

"Jerk. Making the cripple stand and shit."

"Oh, fine. Big baby." Ciaran lifted her again and set her back on the bed with a plop. "We should remove your sutures first. Yeah?"

"Probably a good idea, I guess." Hope stretched out on her side and lifted up the hospital johnny. The GSW didn't look nearly as bad as she remembered. That serum was extraordinary. There was probably something demonic about it.

The skin around the wound was bruised, but the hole had sealed up already. It'd only been a few hours, and her flesh had knitted back together. Hope was powerful and advanced healing was a common demon trait, but this was extremely potent stuff. Whatever Gallo made was impressive, and it was no wonder he wanted to keep it a secret. People would kill for it.

Ciaran rolled over the metal tray which held all the necessary supplies. A spray stung for a moment before her skin numbed. Hope's thigh was tingly and exposed, but Ciaran made quick work of cutting the sutures and using a small pair of tweezers to remove them. She couldn't feel pain, but there was an echo of sensation, of something pulling in her skin. It felt gross.

The stitches slid out easily enough, but the tiny holes bled slightly, and she was glad for the numbing agent. It was almost like before, before Ciaran, when she couldn't feel anything. He cleaned up the blood, and after a moment or two of pressure, they clotted. Ciaran swiped on more of Gallo's bottled magick.

As it sunk in, Ciaran covered her wound with gauze. He taped down the edges, and then snapped off his gloves. Hope was a little sore, but all in all, she was millions of times better, and that brought her back to her stomach, which chose that particular moment to growl audibly.

"Do you have anything I can wear? I don't think Dimitri would appreciate it if I ran around the kitchen naked."

"I washed your leggings and sweater. They're right there on the chair." Ciaran moved the tray out of the way and stared at her. His eyes practically glowed, and Hope didn't think he was focused on food. "However, I'm not sure I want you to have 'em."

"Ciaran, if I don't eat something, I'm going to die." Hope had to hold her hands out to keep him at bay.

"If I can't have you, I might go mad. I need to feel you. To reassure myself, you're here and alive."

"If you feed me, I guarantee I'll reward you." Hope's voice was husky and full of promise.

She pulled her knees together. The flimsy fabric she wore bunched between her legs, and it was high around her hips. Hope knew the bottom curves of her ass were completely visible.

Ciaran tried to suck in a breath, and Hope smiled with half her mouth. He leaned close, an arm on either side of her bracing his weight. Hope did, in fact, want to eat, but teasing Ciaran was deliciously fun. It was addictive too, and Ciaran looming over her like a hungry wolf was not helping her focus on the desperately needed meal.

"Fuuuck. You better eat fast. I don't think I can keep myself off you for long." Ciaran kissed and nibbled her neck. He smelled clean but musky, and Hope could feel his erection push against her hip.

The bed started to creak, and Ciaran gripped the sheets making his knuckles turn white. His hips began rocking against her, and he reached up, grabbing Hope's breast, nuzzling it.

"Ciaran. Food. Please." Hope smiled while she struggled to push Ciaran off her. The weakness in her muscles was infuriating. *Stupid gunshot wound.* Ciaran was absolutely not helping. He was drunk on what he wanted and had pulled up her gown to her neck.

Hope was basically naked, the small amount of fabric a bunched mass around her throat. Ciaran groped her breast hard and licked her nipple. It hardened instantly, making Hope moan as her body set on fire.

"Ciaran." Hope's eyes rolled to the back of her head as she arched her spine. The rumbling of her stomach cut through the haze, however.

"Oh, okay. Goddamn though." Ciaran slowly forced himself to stand. His thin pants did nothing to hide how hard and impressively large he was.

"You may want to do something about that." Hope nodded to his hips as she pulled the Johnny down.

Ciaran grinned. "*You* may want to do something about this." As Hope sat up, Ciaran walked over and put her hand around him. "Ugh, alright. If I keep going, you'll never get fed. Food, anyway."

Hope laughed and shoved him toward the door. Ciaran stumbled for a second and then tucked his erection behind his waistband. Not much of an improvement, but it was something.

"Alright, love. What would you like to eat?" Ciaran put a hand on the doorknob, almost like an anchor.

"Sausage." Hope winked.

"You're killing me."

"Just wait."

Ciaran bit his lip and squeezed the handle of the door.

She really should behave. "Seriously, I'd eat anything, right now. Surprise me."

"I can do that. I'll pick out something amazing." His toothy smile was large on his face, and Hope warmed. Her skin burned and her heart pounded. He really did need to go now, before they got started again.

"Go. Quick."

"Okay, okay. I'm going."

Hope waved her hand, shooing him off. When the door was closed, and she was alone, she actually giggled.

Ciaran was gone for longer than expected. Apparently, she'd dozed off a little and woke up to the sound of the hinges creaking and the handle clicking back into place. The smell that wafted in made her mouth water.

"Oh, my Maker. That smells so fucking good." Hope sat and smiled at the massive amount of food Ciaran was bringing in.

"Sorry, that took me so long. I may have gotten a little carried away. Couldn't help myself." Ciaran sounded so happy about cooking. Not exactly a trait of the ruthless killer he could be. Hope didn't want to settle on that.

"You cook and do laundry. Are most humans like you?" Hope cocked an eyebrow.

"No. But, I was raised by my mam."

"Oh. That's not typical for humans?"

"Not always. Now eat."

As he set the tray down on the bed, Hope could see the scars on his knuckles. Ciaran's hands had been in hundreds of fights. He'd killed people; so had she. And yet, here they were playing house. But, Ciaran's kill at the brownstone, though definitely deserved, put them all in danger. It was careless.

"You still hungry?" Obviously, her face was giving her away.

"Yeah. I'm famished." The metal lidded food was like a fancy hotel.

"Good." Ciaran lifted the shiny dome and revealed what Hope believed to be the entire contents of his kitchen. The tray was large, but Ciaran had managed to cram the whole thing full of every breakfast option in the known universe.

There was wheat toast with butter and a jar of Nutella. An orange cut into intricate slices that zig-zagged with a cherry placed directly in the middle, a glass of what looked like cranberry juice, and that was just for starters. On a large plate was a huge helping of hash browns, an omelet the size of her head, and, of course, sausage. Patties not links.

"You're a patty guy, huh?"

"Hells, yeah. So much better." Ciaran grinned.

"I agree."

Hope picked up the large fork and napkin underneath the plate. She crossed her legs preschool style, which sort of hurt her thigh, and spread the napkin over her lap. Hope wanted to say something about the previous night, but now didn't seem like the time. Plus, her brain would operate better once she got some fuel in her tank. Ciaran sat down on the bed across from her.

As Hope ate, Ciaran watched her with a smile. Occasionally, she would offer him a bite, but he would just shake his head and say, "Not 'til You're full."

"You have to stop staring at me. It's weird." Hope raised her eyebrows and took another bite.

"Sorry, I just want to make sure You're okay."

"I'm fine. I ain't no wilting flower, Ciaran. I'm a demon. I can take care of myself. You just keep yourself safe, which will keep me safe." Hope didn't mean to let that last part slip out, and Ciaran frowned. "I'm sorry. That came out wrong."

"It's okay. I wanted to talk to you about yesterday, anyway." He took a deep breath and looked down at his hands.

Hope moved the tray of food to the floor and the silverware clanked loudly against the plate. She scooted closer to Ciaran and took his hands in hers.

"What is it?" Her voice was loud in the silence of the trauma room.

Ciaran didn't respond for a while and the soundless space weighed on both of them. Hope didn't want to push. This had something to do with what the dead snitch said, she was sure. The image of the M among his other scars flashed into Hope's mind, and she was unfortunately curious about what happened at the Inferno. She knew it was bad, but the vague things she'd heard from Ciaran only made her want to know more. It wasn't a flattering personality trait of hers, and she knew it.

Ciaran squeezed Hope's hands, and he finally looked at her. There were no words for the pain on his face. Her mouth fell open slightly, and she started to shake her head. He hadn't said anything. Maybe they could just forget it.

"You don't have to—"

"I really don't want to, but you're . . . risking your life. For me. You should know why it's not worth it."

She tried to rebut him, but he shook his head and waved away her words.

"Just let me get this out. All of it. No just the fights and killing, all of it." Ciaran gripped her hands so hard she could feel the bones in them squish.

Then, he got up and walked over to the corner of the small room. He faced the wall and pounded a fist against it. The sound was hollow, and Ciaran left his hand on the wall, still balled into a fist.

"This is easier. Okay?"

"Okay."

The room was silent again. Hope could see her fork starting to slide down the rim of her plate. It clattered noisily and settled with the handle stuck in a melted blob of cheese from her omelet.

"He knew. That prick who took us to the brownstone. He knew what the scar meant. I didn't realize it was still visible. When it was fresh, I had bloody Ms on my shirts for days. I wouldn't let anyone see. They'd know, too. Dimitri was the only person . . . and only 'cause he was the only one I'd let clean it.

"I really hoped after all the other scars, it wouldn't be so visible. But, I guess it's like my head. That never seems to forget about it, so of course, the scar's still there. Damn, Hope. I don't want you to know this, but you shouldn't do all this without knowing that I'm really not worth all this trouble.

"I'm not how I was. I'm not even mine, anymore. It just happened, too. I still can't think of a reason the bastard picked me. Guess, I'm lucky like that. He'd take me up to his box after the matches, especially if I won, and nearly beat me to death. I think a couple of times, I did. Die, I mean. He'd be standing across the way, all of a sudden, and the guard would be over me with paddles.

"That wouldn't be the worst of it. That other day, when I told you I have nightmares. God, I sound pathetic, but the thing is they feel real. I don't think I'm dreaming. I think I'm there, again, in the Inferno. It feels like he's down my throat all over again, makes me sick."

Ciaran started to pace back and forth. He was sweating and breathing like a runner mid-marathon. He was talking with his hands and ringing his fist like he was choking someone.

"I think the most fucked up things. It all starts spinning, and I remember the taste and the smell. I'm strong, Hope. After all the fighting, I'm deadly. How is it that I couldn't stop him? I should have. There's no excuse and now, all I can think about is how I want to kill him. Then, probably myself. I can't get the images to go away, and I'm just so tired of feeling so disgusting, so ruined, everything really.

"And then, you come along, and I actually want something again. Maybe, for the first time. But, how could some sick prick's fuck toy be the kind of man you deserve? Shit. I can't believe I said that. But, don't you see, now? Do you get it? I'm not a good man. I'm not a man at all. That's gone. It's been taken, and all I have left to offer is death. I can't even stand to be alone with myself. Why would anyone else want to hang around? I can't be with you. I let some guy fuck me, and either he's going to kill me, or I'm going to kill him. I just . . . Goddamn it, Hope. I let it happen. I just let . . . ugh. You can't . . . It's no . . ."

He was barely understandable through the sobs. Ciaran had walked up to her shaking his hands and head. Now, he was curled up in the corner, his knees to his face and rocking slightly. Hope tried to think what to say. She couldn't change what happened. Everything she'd feared about the *braednas* ceremony actually happened to Ciaran. She didn't know how he felt, and she couldn't tell him it got better. She didn't know that.

Marcus utterly destroyed Ciaran. He'd taken everything from him. Hope remembered the tender moments when they'd been together earlier, and to wrap her mind around the fact that Marcus used that same thing to torture and break Ciaran was nauseating. How could anyone do that? She'd seen evil in the world, hell, she made a living off of it, but her previous employer was by far and away the most depraved, foul man on the face of the earth.

Hope tried to move closer to Ciaran, but he was skittish like a wild animal. She moved slowly and quietly until she was sitting on the floor next to him. He shook his head and mumbled no to her. A tear slipped down her cheek. She tried to brush it away before Ciaran saw.

Hope couldn't have imagined something like what happened to Ciaran. *My* jabalv . . .

Hope lowered her voice and spoke as steady as she could, "Ciaran, you don't belong to him. You're yours. And furthermore, you're my *jabalv.*"

Ciaran looked up. He was frowning and shaking his head more aggressively.

"Remember, I told you about *omaeriku*? Well, I left something out. I can feel your pain, just yours. You're my *jabalv*, the one person in the entire world that can create that reaction," Ciaran stared into her eyes. "My clan believes when the world was new, all people were born with two heads, four arms, and four legs. I know, weird. Well, one day, the Maker decided the race had to be split so the Chakal could pass on their gifts to their children. *Shendara* split everyone in two. The males were given the gift to sense their own kind, and the females were given a reminder of the suffering their partners endured when they protected them. Only the other half of that particular female could ignite the bond. The other half of the original pair. The *jabalv.* The two halves would be whole. *Omaeriku*, the connection between twin souls.

"When I first met you, the bond was formed. . . . And man, did I not want anything to do with it. I'm not like that. But, I'm learning more and more that I didn't have a choice. It was always you. You were going to set off *omaeriku* and there was nothing I could do. You don't belong to him. Don't you see? You never have. You have always been mine. Look Ciaran, I can't change the past. I can't make it disappear. I wish I could. But, I can move forward. With you."

"But—"

"Do you want to? Do you want to try this?"

It was quiet for a long while.

"Yes."

"Okay, then."

Ciaran tried to smile but ended up just shaking his head and putting it back on his knees. Hope wrapped her arms around him. They stayed there all night, and Ciaran fell asleep with his head in Hope's lap.

FIFTEEN

This was the second time they'd fallen asleep on the floor. Ciaran liked the reason behind the first instance better. This morning Hope was leaned back against the wall with her arms hanging loosely at her sides. God, she must've been uncomfortable with his big head on her legs. Ciaran sat up and looked at her face. It was the same as always. Beautiful and strong, elegant and fierce, that was his Hope. *My Hope.*

She hadn't spoken to him in a different way after his breakdown. She looked at him the same, held him the same. Nothing was the same to him. He'd finally spilled about what happened at the Inferno. It was the first time any of that shit had made it out of his mouth. He had a bad case of verbal diarrhea. Nothing he could do about it now.

Hope looked so tired. Her brow furrowed like whatever dream she was having wasn't good. Ciaran knew how that felt. Then it occurred to him. He'd gone the whole night without one nightmare. For the first time since his escape, he slept without interruption.

She just might be right. Ciaran pushed Hope's bangs off her forehead and gave her a light kiss. Immediately, she relaxed, and a small smile spread across her lips. Hope said he was her *jabalv*, hers.

"I'll pull my shit together, somehow. I'll keep you safe," he whispered.

Ciaran shuffled on the floor so he could get at Hope's hospital johnny. He rolled the bottom up and inspected her leg. Alexander's amazing serum worked like a charm. Hope's gunshot wound was nothing more than a nasty looking bruise.

"Can't keep your hands off me, can you?" Hope was smiling down at him.

"Nope. Your leg looks good. Can't even tell you were shot."

"Care for a test drive?" She winked at him and opened her legs a little wider.

Like she just snapped her fingers, Ciaran was instantly hard. The reaction was just as fast and easy as when he first saw her. Could he still do this? After his confession, was he capable of being with her again? *Bound to her. Her other half. That seems a little too perfect.* Ciaran had never been particularly religious or spiritual. Hell, he'd always thought the world was just horrible and his luck sucked. To hear Hope say they were two halves of a whole was too good to be true. But, he'd seen it in action. He saw Hope experience his pain. Their connection to each other was a solid weight. Weirdest of all was the dream.

Every night, as he tried to feel like a man again, it was always her. It was always Hope in his dreams. The beautiful white streak in her hair, her curves, her strength. *Maybe it was real?*

"You think you're up for it? You lost a lot of blood."

"I can see that you're up for it. Now, please your woman." Hope grabbed his face and kissed him.

Hope's tongue darted in and out of his mouth, and Ciaran lost it. He wanted to show her he could still satisfy her, be there for her. That he wasn't broken. He wanted her desperately, more than just physically. Ciaran wanted to connect again, to be with Hope like they had in the beginning. And yes, he wanted sex with her. For hours. It felt like it had been years since they'd been alone together.

"Hope, ugh, we should go to my room." As Ciaran tried to talk, Hope kissed and licked his neck, moving lower and lower across his chest.

"Not so easy to think when someone is all over you, is it?" Hope clearly enjoyed teasing him, and dammit if he didn't fall for it every single time.

"You're gonna get it now, love." Ciaran's voice was a deep rumble and even to him, it sounded more animal than man.

"Mmm, bring it."

"Last chance. Say something, or you're mine to do with as I please for the next few hours. And know, I can't be gentle, not right now."

Hope laid back against the wall and lifted her arms over her head, crossing them at the wrist. The offer was clear thanks to the devilish grin on her face.

"I don't want this to sound weird, but this is important to me. Can you let me have total control over this?"

"Yes. I trust you. Plus, I had sweet before. Now I want to try rough." Hope bit her bottom lip.

"Uhh." Ciaran's pulse throbbed in his groin and had to focus on getting enough air in through his nose. "Alright, then. Rules."

"Rules?"

Ciaran smiled. "Total control, right?"

"Right." Hope cocked her head and gave him a sidelong glance.

For a moment, Ciaran was convinced she would change her mind, but then, Hope's eyelids softened, and her stare was all sex.

"Rules. If I ask you to do something, say, 'Yes, sir.' If I move you somewhere, hold that position, and last, if something is too much or hurts, you have to tell me. Got it?"

Hope tongued the silver ball that rested on the top of her full, bottom lip. "Yes, sir."

"Fuck." Ciaran groaned and faster than he knew he could move threw her down on the tiny bed.

The flimsy cot dipped and shook at the onslaught, and Hope bumped the IV bag, knocking it over. It burst open as it hit the floor and saline solution pooled under the bed. Ciaran shoved the metal tray out of his way, tipping it over. The supplies went flying, gloves and gauze and tape soaring every which way.

"Turn over." Ciaran practically growled.

"Yes, sir."

Hope slowly turned her back to him. She moved in sensuous curves, rocking her hips and displaying her arse. At this point, Ciaran was steel.

"Good girl. Bend down. On your elbows."

She bent over, bracing her weight on her forearms as instructed. The position made her hips come back and rub against his erection. Hope pressed into him in slow circles, and the tip of Ciaran's cock cried with anticipation.

As Ciaran untied Hope's gown, her skin was soft under his fingers. The white fabric slid off her shoulders revealing her amazing tattoos. They were more impressive every time he saw them. Ciaran feasted on her exquisite body and traveled the lines of her curves with his eyes. She was a work of erotic art, her breasts and arse the crowning jewels of a seductive masterpiece.

His pulse rushed through him, and the steady beat got faster and harder as it reached his erection. Images of sheathing himself deep inside Hope were intoxicating. The tension built to the point of explosion. Looking was light years away from enough. Ciaran pulled his shirt over his head and shucked off his pants. They were naked together.

Ciaran grabbed Hope by the hips making the hot core of her rub on his shaft. His hands groped her breasts, and the tight, rosy nubs at the tips hardened as he ran his thumb across them. He squeezed them hard, playing with the metal beads on either side.

Hope squealed and pushed back against his hips, exactly what he wanted. Ciaran squeezed again, harder, and Hope reared back, lifting herself to stand and landed in his arms, her back against his chest. She rested her head back on his shoulder, and the view of her naked body was breathtaking. The moans that escaped her as he continued to dominate her breasts were music to his ears. *Mine.*

"Say you want me." He needed to hear it. Ciaran slid a hand up Hope's neck and into her hair.

"I want you."

Ciaran gripped Hope's hair and yanked her head back. Now, he could whisper in her ear. Ciaran lowered his voice and brought his lips close enough to gently brush her skin. He gave a quick nibble on Hope's piercings.

"Say it properly."

Hope's response was a combination of barely audible words and breathy whimpers. "I . . . want you, sir."

"Good, love. You know I need this. I need you to let me have you. Yes?" Ciaran growled as he spoke, every inch of his flesh screaming for him to pounce, to take Hope now and fast. He wanted to savor the moment though. He wanted every minute to feel like years.

"Yes, sir. I'm yours. Always." Hope circled her hips again, egging on the orgasm that was already poised in his shaft. Hope was right, she was no wilting flower, and only total trust in him would let her relinquish control. It was . . . flattering and hot as hell.

"Mine."

Ciaran pulled Hope's head further back, the angle made her breasts push forward as she tried to breathe through her strained throat. Even though she was fighting to stand, Hope pressed herself into him and arch up with excitement. He wanted more of her, to make her exhausted from pleasure. Ciaran slid his hand down from her breast, across her stomach to her hips. Hope's skin prickled under his fingers, and she moaned louder.

Lust-fueled, Ciaran drove his fingers into her core. She jumped, shocked, but let him move in deeper and spread her legs further apart. Hope was on fire and decadently wet. He knew that he could make her orgasm in seconds, but he took his time, moving his hand in slow circles.

Hope gasped as the sensations took control, and Ciaran pulled her hair harder, creating a swirl of pain and pleasure. His blood boiled. Deep in his groin, the pressure skyrocketed to monumental proportions, and his cock ached for some attention.

"Do you want it, Hope?"

"Oh fuck, yes, sir." Hope's pleading voice raised as he pushed deeper inside her.

"Show me how bad." Ciaran used the fistful of hair to get Hope down to her knees. Without further direction, Hope faced him. Heaven was supposed to be perfect, ultimate bliss. Ciaran must have been there. The feeling of Hope's tongue playing along the sides and tip of his erection was undeniably fantastic.

Hope was perfect. She knew exactly how to push him to the edge. First, long slow strokes, and then, all of him was caressed by her mouth. First hard, then soft kisses, letting him move in and out, bringing him dangerously close.

"Ugh, fuck. Hope . . ." He needed to be inside her. Now.

Hope's breaths thundered, and Ciaran pulled her to her feet.

He spun her around and bent her over the fragile bed, pushing her head down to the white covers. "Don't move."

She was glistening and ready, but he wanted a quick taste. In a single motion, he tongued Hope's honeyed center. Her flesh was hot and sweet and begging for him. *Oh, lord.* Ciaran could barely think. Hope shuddered as his mouth and tongue made her positively weep with desire. She was aching for it as much as he was, and Ciaran was more than happy to tip them both over the edge.

He planted his weight on Hope's wrists, keeping her down as he thrust himself into her tight, warm core. As Ciaran moved in and out, Hope's hair bounced in waves across her back. Ciaran took a handful and pulled back once again. Hope screamed out as the new angle forced him deeper and began to rub on the sensitive spot deep within.

Each thrust hit the same wonderful place, and Hope orgasmed around him. The muscles tightened and coaxed his own explosion. Ciaran pumped his hips as hard and fast as he could, his erection sliding back and forth inside Hope and creating deliriously fabulous friction. He could feel himself about to lose it, and the tip of his cock tingled intensely. Any amount of control he might've had was completely gone.

Hope clawed at the bedding. "Ciaran . . . please . . ."

"I don't know. You came all those times without asking." Ciaran continued to pound into her.

"Fuck! Please . . ." Hope screamed out.

"Yes. Come for me." His last few words came out in grunts as Ciaran exploded.

They rode out an orgasm which seemed to last forever. The nearly unbearable bolts of sensations threw them out of reality, and as they climaxed, Hope and Ciaran bucked so hard the flimsy bed collapsed and fell to the floor.

For a moment, they both lay on the ground, having rolled off the broken heap of a bed, and tried to catch their breaths. As Ciaran's body temperature finally returned to normal, he realized they were lying in the spilled salt water from the IV.

"Oh, shit. You're soaked."

Hope's hair was dripping and sections of it stuck to her wet skin.

"Actually, it feels nice, but damn, Ciaran, you broke the bed," Hope sat up and leaned back on her hands. She started slipping immediately. "Fuck. You tore this room apart."

"Me? You certainly helped. The reason that IV fell over is 'cause you kicked it." Ciaran tried so hard to be serious, and Hope met his gaze. The next thing he knew they were laughing their arses off. "You're so beautiful. And damn, you really know how to please a guy."

"Ha! Why thank you. You're quite talented, yourself." Hope leaned in toward him and kissed him on the cheek. Ciaran laughed.

"What?" Hope raised her eyebrows.

"I just think it's funny that after the sex we just had, you kiss me on the cheek."

Hope smiled. "Well, you were sweet. Sweet gets kisses. Demanding gets ass."

"I like that formula. Why didn't we learn this in school?" Ciaran stood up and held out a hand. He helped Hope up and kissed her gently on the lips. "Well, love, time for a shower?"

"Oh, fuck, yes!"

Ciaran laughed and wrapped his arms around her. "We'll both need clothes. Here—"

He lifted up the hospital gown and watched as it dripped all over the place. "Okay, maybe not."

Hope hugged him close.

"Mad dash for my room?" he suggested.

"After you. Sir." Hope opened her arms up and gestured to the door. They both ran out as fast as they could, and Hope's laugh echoed through his home.

*

Ciaran let Hope finish getting changed and went to the kitchen to grab some breakfast. He padded up to the main one this time, seeing as he'd depleted the stock downstairs, and found Dimitri sitting at the breakfast table. Ciaran immediately regretted not putting on a shirt.

"Oh, hey, man. What's up?" Ciaran attempted casual, but the awkwardness hung around.

Dimitri was healed up, but he was also most likely still pissed. After all, Ciaran's rash decision to kill the lackey was what caused the shootout.

"Hey. Couldn't sleep. Apparently, you couldn't, either." Dimitri nodded at Ciaran's chest and smirked. Ciaran's back and pecs were covered in scratches. Needless to say, showers with Hope didn't consist solely of washing.

"Yeah, sorry for the visual TMI. How you feeling?" Ciaran sat down across from Dimitri. They both stared at their hands and tried not to breathe too loudly.

"Alright. So, what up with killing our lead?" Leave it to Dimitri to be blunt.

"He knew. And, I lost my shit."

"Can't do it again, bro."

"I know. I . . . I told Hope."

"No. Fucking. Way. Did you propose, too?" Dimitri smiled and put a hand under his chin like he was waiting for the next piece of juicy gossip. They both knew it was a big deal.

"Piss off. She's different, okay?" Ciaran shoved Dimitri's hand out from under his chin and made his head fall forward.

"Ahh, damn, boy. You got brimstone fever."

"Dimitri—"

"Brimstone fever!"

Ciaran punched him in the arm but had to laugh. "You're such a dick. Honestly, I really like her. I sound like a fucking sap, but I do."

"I know man." Dimitri exhaled loudly. "For what it's worth, she's one ballsy chick. Nice on the eyes, too." He pantomimed groping a pair of large breasts.

"For real, I will kill you."

Dimitri shook his head and rolled his eyes. "Love has given you a serious humor lobotomy."

Ciaran froze. Yeah, he was pretty sure he "somethinged" Hope, but even Dimitri could tell? So much for his poker face.

"I don't . . . I don't know what it is. Are we that obvious?"

"Yup."

"Well, shit." *But who did I think I was kidding? She makes me feel alive, and that's a huge change.*

Ciaran stood up and went to the fridge. The cool air was fucking amazing. He was pretty sure he was bright red from head to toe.

"Breakfast?"

"Yeah, man, get working in that kitchen! Fry me up some love!"

Ciaran picked up an oven mitt and threw it in Dimitri's face. "You don't shut it, and I'll be frying up your arse!"

"Did I miss something?" Hope came in through the doorway behind Ciaran. She was wearing her signature black leggings and a tight, black sweater. He could just eat her up.

"Just Dimitri being a royal arse."

"Oh, so nothing new, then?" Hope smiled at Dimitri and kissed Ciaran as she walked by to sit at the table.

Dimitri rolled his eyes. "Ha, ha. Very funny."

Dimitri leaned back and folded his hands behind his head. On the underside of his bicep, his black tattoo poked out. Ciaran forgot about it a lot. Considering Hope's tattoos, he wondered if it was a demon thing. Dimitri put his arms down when he saw Hope looking. He was so protective of his clan.

Hope took the hint and changed the subject. "You look better. Thanks, too, for getting me here. I heard you drove like a madman."

"You can thank Ciaran for that. If I could have gone faster, he would've made it happen."

Hope looked at Ciaran and may have blushed, but it was gone in a flash.

"I'm making some food, want some?"

"Yeah. Also, I was looking over some of the files in that box, and I think I have a lead." Ciaran realized that she held a stack of papers.

"When did you do that?" Ciaran set the cooking aside and went to the table.

Hope started to shuffle through the pages. "Right after the shower. I read fast."

"What did you find?" Ciaran leaned over, and Hope fanned out the papers over the entire table.

"Well, I think you were on to something. We can almost locate him by the properties he buys, but he buys so many we need to narrow it down. That's where the brownstone and what you've told me about Marcus come in handy. You said he has expensive taste, right?" Hope looked up at him, and Ciaran nodded.

"Yes."

"We grabbed the newest properties he acquired, within the last six months, and out of those, we can exclude some based on face value, alone. For instance, this one, an old packing plant, great resource, but Marcus wouldn't live there. And these," Hope spread out a bunch of forms like a deck of cards, "every single one is an office within a larger facility. Not a place he would live. These are acres of woodlands protected from development; these are trailer homes, and these are fake transactions conducted via a front company that goes right back to Marcus. Money laundering at its best."

"Wait, how do you know they're a front?" Dimitri beat Ciaran to the question.

"It's who paid me."

"Oh." They both nodded in unison.

"Anyway, the last five show promise. Here, this one is a pseudo-Victorian. Then, there's an old mansion from the 1950s, a country house designed to look like it's from the plantation era, a glass mansion-like thing, and a penthouse in one of the newest buildings in the city. He owns the top five floors."

The reports of the five properties sat in a line across the table. Marcus was living in one of them. There was no way to narrow it down further.

"Anyone else feel like we're going on a scavenger hunt?" Dimitri had a point.

"How—"

Ciaran's question was finished by Hope. "Are we going to get in and out? Yeah, I know. I've been thinking about it. One thing that's been bugging me is, well frankly, how we get away with murder. Now, I had people I used to clean up similar situations but seeing as they're his employees. I don't think they'll be too keen on helping."

"So, what are you saying?" Ciaran had a feeling this was about his less than tactful approach at the last safe house.

"We can't be messy. Nothing, and I mean nothing, left for the cops to find."

Both Hope and Dimitri stared at him. "Jesus. Yes. I get it."

"Sorry, but we can't afford a slip-up. Marcus can't know we're after him until it's too late to stop us," Hope grumbled.

"I know." Ciaran's balls felt like they'd been squished. He was a fucking liability. Goody.

Hope stared at the files, and Dimitri fiddled with his jeans. After all this time waiting for revenge, he needed to play it cool. The time had come to prove he could handle this.

"Okay. So how do we effectively sneak into the properties? As resident hit-woman, do you have any ideas?" Ciaran smiled at Hope. He really wanted her to stop making that face. *I'm not a child or a fucking dumb shit, talk to me.*

"Well, for these two properties, we can scout locations from the nearby buildings. Hopefully, the interiors will tell us enough. This one we'll have to walk through, since it's isolated, and the last two, unfortunately, a standard B and E."

"So, let's start with our recon houses. Take the easy ones out, first." Ciaran pulled the two files to himself.

"Agreed." Hope and Dimitri spoke at the same time.

Everyone stood up. Breakfast was off. They'd have to eat on the go. Thank god for protein bars. Hope and Ciaran went to his bedroom to grab supplies, and Dimitri said he'd meet them at the car.

The air was stiff in his room, and they were both too quiet. Ciaran went to his closet and pulled out a black duffle. Inside, many of the usual supplies were already loaded up. There were zip ties, plenty of ammo and guns, a small med kit, back up clothes and shoes, a hunting knife, rope, and a burner phone.

"Do you have binoculars?" Hope was pulling on her boots and her hair fell in front of her face. She was trying desperately to see what she was doing and not fall over.

"Yeah. You gonna make it there?" Ciaran chuckled.

"Longer than you if you continue to laugh at me." Hope shoved her foot down on the floor, forcing her boot on.

"We'll also need a remote listening headset." Hope pulled her hair back in a swoop and bound it into a ponytail.

"You're really all about the spy gear, aren't you?"

"I kill people for a living. I don't like to be spotted if I can avoid it."

"You must have to try very hard. You do stand out." Ciaran pulled one of his contraband SWAT vests out of the back of the closet. It'd been in the trunk of one of his jobs. *Bastard husbands getting their jollies off beating their wives like they were one of the criminals he dealt with.*

"I'm very sneaky, I'll have you know. Unless, of course, I'm experiencing pain for the first time."

"Sure," Ciaran dragged out the word. "Bad news, though, I don't have a remote listening thingy."

"Figured. My house is on the way. We can stop there and grab mine."

"You're taking me back to your place? Hot."

Hope walked over and for a split-second, Ciaran thought she was going to hug him or even give him a kiss. She tricked him, and instead, sauntered up and shoved him just enough for him to trip over his duffle. "Ready?"

"Yup." Ciaran stood back up and picked up the duffle. "You're gonna pay for that later, though."

"Promise?" Hope smiled.

"Damn you."

They walked to the car, and Ciaran had to force his eyes off Hope, so he didn't walk into something.

*

"I can't believe it." Hope knelt on the ground in front of her burnt house. Ciaran didn't know whether to change the subject or give her a hug. Hell, if it were Dimitri, he'd just make a joke.

"Hope—"

"Those fuckers! Do you know how much liquor I had in there?!" Apparently, Hope liked the humor approach, too.

"Think we can salvage any?" Dimitri kicked a piece of rubble and watched it bounce.

"No, unfortunately. However, I should be able to take the stuff from my closet."

"Not really that impressed with clothes, chica." Dimitri knelt down and continued to play with pieces of Hope's house.

Ciaran shoved him over and gave him the stink eye. The sting of the past creeped up as he remembered the last burnt building he saw.

Ciaran put a hand on Hope's shoulder. "This is 'cause of me."

"Don't worry about it. I failed a hit. He would've done it even if it weren't you." She put her hand on top of his and squeezed.

"So, I don't want to be harsh, but I don't think we have time to raid your closet. Besides, clothes wouldn't survive a fire like this."

"No, they wouldn't. But, that's not what I'm going for."

After a few minutes of digging through charred remains of a bar, some couches, and what was once a really beautiful TV, they found Hope's fire-safe.

"Got it." Hope put her finger to the biometric keypad. The door beeped and popped open.

"How exactly is that still working?" Ciaran liked technological advances as much as the next guy, but damn. Hope's safe made his stuff back home look like shit.

"Scratch and Dent fire-safe. It has two hours of fire protection at 1875 degrees. The biometric keypad was extra, but a girl has to protect her assets." Hope winked.

"Well, you've got to hook me up with your decorator."

As Hope dug around in what was clearly more of a secured storage facility than a closet, Dimitri kept an eye out for unwanted guests. Ciaran looked back at him to check in, but it seemed like whoever trashed Hope's place was long gone.

"Toss your stuff in the duffle. Someone's bound to notice the smoke." Ciaran held open the bag for her. His mind wandered a little, though, and he couldn't push out the thoughts of the Inferno.

"In his fifteenth bout in the ring . . . Laoch Dubh!"

Ciaran walked into the light and squinted. His cell was dark, and the fluorescence burned his eyes. The announcer grabbed his wrist and lifted his arm. The jerking motion killed, and the torn tendons in his wrist protested. The wraps he wore hid the raw, ripped flesh but stuck to the open wounds. Every time Ciaran clenched or went to punch, the woven material pulled on the scabs forming between his skin and the fabric. The chains in Marcus's office were really tearing his wrists up, and Ciaran was cutting over scars at this point.

"Ciaran? Ciaran, you home?" Hope waved her hand in front of his face.

"Sorry. We all set?" The worried look on her face burnt as bad as the old wounds. "I'm fine. Do you have everything?" *It's getting worse.*

"Yeah. My spy gear, as you call it, is all loaded up. To be honest though, I miss my clothes. I officially have two outfits left."

Ciaran's first days out of the Inferno he'd bought more clothes and shoes than he had in his life. Something about wearing the same clothes over and over was too much like being a prisoner again. He still kind of did though, black on black on black does not variety make. "We can get you more when this is over. We can even use some of Marcus's money if he still keeps a wad hidden in his safe."

"And how exactly are we going to get into his safe?" Hope smiled a dirty grin at him. How was she so good at flirting?

Ciaran sauntered up to her and took her hips. "He used the same code for everything. It's how I broke out. He seems too arrogant to change it. He can just kill me, after all."

Dimitri ran up to them, Romanov the Moment Killer.

"Company. We need to split. Now."

Ciaran and Hope whipped around to look at the road. Sure enough, cops were flying down the gravel.

"Shit. Out back here." Hope led the way behind a stand of bushes, out of view of the fuzz. They ran through the tree-heavy area.

As soon as they were covered by the shadows of branches, they doubled back toward the highway. Ciaran had packed the car up by the road, and he was damn glad he did. Hope ran around to the passenger side and Dimitri slid into the back. As the doors shut around him, Ciaran turned the ignition and sped down the asphalt like his arse was on fire.

The Crown still had some power in her and carried the trio safely to the next destination, the glass mansion.

"What kind of idiot lives in an all-glass house?" Dimitri peered through some binoculars. Ciaran smacked him on the back of the head and the binoculars whacked against his face.

"You know exactly who. Now, shut up. I'm trying to listen." Ciaran adjusted the buds in his ears. The stupid things were uncomfortable and kept falling out.

From inside the glass, Ciaran heard a big fucking nothing. If anyone was in there, they were dead. God, he was bored. Hope was quiet next to him and stared at the mansion like a wild cat hunting. She crouched near a piney bush and looked through a weird pair of glasses.

"What do those things do?" Ciaran whispered.

"They detect heat signatures. I can see if there's someone hiding or passed out or dead."

"Anything?"

"Maybe. Top floor. There's a warm patch, too hot for just a vent or something but it's not quite a normal body temp."

"Cat?"

"No. It's a bit big for a cat."

Ciaran looked through the binoculars again. He focused on the area Hope pointed out. There was a room up at the left corner. Inside was an ugly-arse couch that blocked most everything from view, but he could see a small black lump on the floor near it. It moved, and both Hope and Ciaran jumped.

"Movement." Hope's whisper was firm.

"Yeah. Black object by the couch." As Ciaran spoke, it moved again.

Now, both Hope and him could see that the black was, in fact, hair, short hair that was attached to a woman.

"Shit, that's a person. Why'd her temp be so low?" Ciaran had a feeling he already knew.

"'Cause , she's either badly hurt or dying."

"Fuck." Ciaran eyed the glass house. He didn't see security, but if they were going in, he had to be sure.

Ciaran reached into his pack and pulled out one of the Walther PPQs he'd packed. Ciaran lined up the front door.

"Are you fucking nuts?!" Dimitri grabbed his arm.

"It's the best way to draw out any security. We need to be sure before we run up to the door and get ourselves killed. I fucked up last time. Now, I want to be sure."

Ciaran popped off a couple shots and, not surprisingly, they hit the glass and ricocheted. *Bulletproof. Naturally.* The good news was no one came running.

"Alright. Let's go." Ciaran put the gun in his waistband.

Hope led the way, jogging to the front door. Ciaran followed with Dimitri bringing up the rear. He watched the line of trees at their back and covered the door while Ciaran and Hope screwed with the lock.

"It's a pin pad, and unfortunately, I don't have my auto key with me. Done lost it in a fire." Hope had pronounced it "fahr" and Ciaran laughed.

"Good thing I know the code." Ciaran leaned over to the door and swallowed hard. Accessing a memory of the Inferno, even a simple one, was like eating glass.

He'd spent months learning the code, and he'd use it against Marcus any chance he got. When he'd been at the hands of his old employer, waiting for his chance, he'd recited the numbers like a repetitive chant in his brain. Ciaran punched in two, four, seven, and three. The beeping of the keys filled his brain with sandpaper. A cold sweat dripped down his neck.

Hope's hand brushed his. It spoke volumes. If you were looking at her face, you wouldn't see the concerned support, you'd just see her usual, stoic expression. That spoke louder. She knew how he felt about being seen struggling, and she didn't draw any attention to it. God, fucking bless her, not that he thought god gave a shit.

The lock was beeping.

Hope nodded. "It worked. Open the door."

"Nice work, buddy." Dimitri slapped him on the shoulder. "Crack that bitch open."

He pushed open the door and shoved Dimitri inside. He followed with Hope and shut the door behind them. The inside was a little more mod than he thought it'd be, but everything looked like it had a five-figure price tag.

The couches and chairs were sleek, grey leather and every metal surface was a bright chrome. The metal beams that supported the house were black and stood out in hard lines. It seemed cold to him. There weren't any soft surfaces or colors. The industrial design didn't seem like Marcus's traditional décor. This was too "functional not frivolous."

"Hope, search down here for anything you think is relevant. Dimi—"

"Hope, search down here, what?" She interrupted him and glared with a hand on her hip.

"Please." Ciaran dragged the word out and pouted slightly.

"Oh, Maker. You're such a sap." Hope walked off, swaying her hips as she went. She must've known his eyes were fixed on her arse, and Ciaran shook his head to get his thoughts back in order.

"Dimitri—"

"Yeah, I know. You'll check the upper level, and I get the basement and other random shit. Why is it that I always get the fucking basement?" Dimitri rolled his eyes and walked toward the stairs. He was being a particularly large crab-arse, today.

"Hey! What's up, man?" Dimitri wasn't stopping and Ciaran asked again, "Seriously, fucker, what's up your arse?"

"Just have a bad feeling about all this, and I know you think I'm nuts when I say shit like that, so I was keeping it to myself."

Ciaran really wanted to lay into him for being such a snot, but he stopped. There was something about his tense shoulders, not to mention the person who'd yet to come investigate that made him believe Dimitri.

"Let's watch our backs, then. Yell if you need back up?"

"Yeah." Dimitri was surprised but didn't say anything else.

Ciaran turned and glared at the stairs. Even they were glass. They didn't have any risers either, and Ciaran was concerned they wouldn't hold his weight. As he went up, he realized that tactically speaking the glass was alright. It was bulletproof, so Marcus was okay there, and he could see pretty much everything inside the house from anywhere. *Clever.*

Ciaran studied the walls. Normally, Marcus hung disturbing Renaissance paintings of demons performing less than savory acts. Being glass, these walls couldn't have anything nailed to them. Nothing seemed right about this place, except the price tag and the overwhelming air of security.

The expanse of chrome and grey continued upstairs, and it finally hit Ciaran. *I'm such an idiot. How did I not see it, before?*

"Roger." Ciaran's deep voice echoed through the silent upper landing.

"Is he back?!" A quiet, raspy voice shot out from behind the leather couch on his right. The fact the person he saw through the binoculars was conscious, let alone speaking, was enough to make Ciaran's heart pound.

"Holy shit. You're alive." Ciaran approached the sofa.

"Stop! Don't come any closer!" she tried desperately to yell, but it came out in a crack.

"I'm here to help, and Roger isn't here." Ciaran took another step forward.

"Please." A small arm came out shaking. The woman held her hand up to keep him back. There was blood dripping off it.

"You're bleeding. I can help. I'm not gonna to hurt you. I don't work with Roger or Marcus. They, umm, sort of kidnapped me, too. I got away." Ciaran moved closer and closer as he spoke with both his hands up. It was like dealing with an injured animal.

The woman relaxed a little when they made eye contact. She searched him for something, a hidden malice, and wrapped her arms around herself. Ciaran could see, now, that she was bleeding because she'd been fighting against her binds. He knelt down and crawled toward her slowly. She wore a tattered, grey nightgown that was stained with blood and didn't cover much. The long t-shirt-like outfit must've been what she was wearing when she was taken.

Once Ciaran reached her, he examined her wrists. They weren't horrible, but the skin was definitely raw. He put his hand out tentatively, and when she didn't flinch, Ciaran scooted closer. The plate on the floor she was connected to was heavy duty. There was no way he was going to be able to free her without tools.

"I'm going to call my friends, okay?"

"Are they human, too?" She peered at him behind her short, black hair. It was matted, and she looked thinner than she should.

"Umm, no, but they won't hurt you. Dimitri is—Well, frankly, he's an arse, but he knows better. And Hope—"

"There's a woman. That would be okay." She perked up a little. Clearly, the example Roger set for the male species was just great.

"Yeah." Ciaran took her wrists and inspected the wounds more thoroughly. "So, what's your name? I'm Ciaran."

She was silent for a moment and stared at him oddly.

"What?"

"I've heard them speak of you. They do not like you."

"Ha! Can't say I'm surprised by that. The feeling is mutual." Ciaran smirked. He was in deeper shit than he thought.

"Miyu, my name is Miyu. Please, get me out of here." She held her wrists in front of Ciaran's face.

Ciaran turned toward the stairs and yelled, "Guys! Come up here, quick! And bring some tools!"

Ciaran couldn't understand why Miyu was locked up as Roger's prisoner. She wasn't from New York. Miyu looked Japanese and the slight accent fit. The circumstances of her arrival were most likely a result of Roger's meddling, but why'd he want her?

Ciaran saw Hope coming up the stairs at a jog, and Miyu tensed.

"So, what's the 911?" Hope stopped in her tracks when she saw Miyu. "She's alive?"

"Yes. Tools?"

Hope lowered her gun. "Dimitri's got them."

She knelt on the ground near him and for a moment she looked as terrified as Miyu. She leaned toward Ciaran and whispered, "Who's this?"

Ciaran sensed her tension.

"This is Roger's place. I knew something was off. Anyway, Miyu was his prisoner. We can't just leave her here." Ciaran expected a little resistance, but Hope just nodded.

Dimitri came pounding up the stairs. Miyu tensed again. He approached slowly when he saw her and handed Ciaran a toolbox. Dimitri raised an eyebrow.

"Just like the old days, huh?" He smirked, but Dimitri met Ciaran's eyes, and they both knew this was bad.

Inside the box were hammers, pliers, and what-do-you-know, bolt-cutters. As Ciaran got them in place to free Miyu, Hope and Dimitri were stiff as boards.

"You guys, okay?" Ciaran never would've thought they'd agree on anything.

Hope looked over at Dimitri, who nodded his head. "She's a demon."

Ciaran shook his head. "Okay . . ."

Miyu was practically cowering behind Ciaran, and she stared at the metal cuffs as he worked.

Hope shook her head. "It's not a surprise but . . ."

"But, what? Spit it out, already."

"Neither of us has been around anything like her. Frankly, we're a little nervous. She's . . . powerful." Hope stared at Miyu as she spoke.

Ciaran looked at Miyu. When she raised her eyes to his, they weren't denying what Hope said. They were confirming it. They thought she was dead with such a low body temp and yet here she was malnourished and injured, but very much alive.

"I mean, dude, why would Roger, Sir Tight-Ass, kidnap a demon? Not exactly his MO unless there's something he's hiding." Dimitri gestured at her with his thumb.

Miyu sat up more, and as Ciaran snapped open the chains, she rubbed her wrists.

"I understand your concern, but in all honesty, I just want to get out of here. Chakal, Drugha, I have no desire to stay in the city." Miyu looked at Hope, then Dimitri as she spoke.

"You don't have to leave on our account." Hope was shaking her head, but Ciaran couldn't stop staring at Dimitri. He looked like he'd been kicked in the gut.

Ciaran leaned in close to his friend's ear. "You cool?"

"Yeah, she's just . . . She is way fucking powerful."

"What do you mean?"

"Just forget it. We have more important shit to deal with."

Miyu was forcing a smile at Hope. "If you succeed in killing Roger and Marcus, then, maybe, I'll consider coming back. But, that is a very large maybe."

Fumbling like a baby deer, Miyu stood and leaned on the couch. "I do believe it has been a long time since I stood."

"Here. It's cold outside." Hope handed Miyu her jacket. Ciaran smiled.

That was her only coat.

"Thanks. Could you point me toward the road?"

"We can take you somewhere safe." Ciaran didn't want another demon dead because of Marcus.

"Really, it is alright. I prefer to be on my own."

"You sure?" Ciaran stood.

"Yes."

When Miyu was okay to walk, they left out the front door.

For a moment, they stared at the glass monstrosity in silence. He would be here, Marcus would set foot in this house, Roger, too, and they'd pour themselves a scotch and discuss how to kill him. Roger would be pissed about his lost prize, and Marcus would assure him that he'd get it out of that nuisance Ciaran.

Dimitri was the first to speak, naturally.

"Want to blow it up?" Dimitri smiled and held up a lighter.

"Does seem appropriate." Arson was kind of a tradition between Dentry properties and Ciaran.

Hope laughed, and the sound made Ciaran's nerves sing.

"Gimmie that." Ciaran took the lighter. "I'll be like eight minutes."

With that, he ran back to the mansion, a man on a very illegal mission. He went to the basement, first, no luck there. So, Ciaran went back upstairs and to the patio. There was a fancy-arse grill off to one side. It was built into a white brick surround. Near the bottom, there was an access door. Ciaran opened it up and viola, a propane tank.

"Ugh. Charcoal tastes better."

He took the tank. It read about three-quarters full. Behind the other side of the grill's doors was a replacement tank, and Ciaran took that, as well. He jogged back inside and straight to the kitchen.

There, Ciaran found a five-burner gas stove. He turned every knob but not enough to catch. Then, he went through every drawer and cupboard to find some kind of stable ignition source. The lighter wasn't going to cut it. There were metal strainers and cutlery, some weird slicer thing that looked like it could take your finger off, but no incendiary aides.

Ciaran went through the last drawer and found a laminated menu. Apparently, Roger would be having lamb with mint jelly and seasoned vegetables for dinner. There was a dessert listed Ciaran never heard of.

"Crem Broolee."

Near the back of the long drawer was a box with the word Hollowick on it. He opened up the magnetic lid and inside was a small but working torch.

"What the hell?"

Ciaran set one of the propane tanks on the kitchen's island in the center of the room. He unscrewed the valve just a touch and heard the satisfying hiss of gas escaping. Ciaran could smell the gas around him building, and he beat feet out of the kitchen.

He took the less full propane tank and set it in the middle of the hallway that led to the kitchen. Ciaran could smell more gas trickling down, so he quickly opened the front door enough to run through. He ran back to the tank and released the contents with another hiss. Ciaran scooted a catch-all table from the entryway near the tank and set the torch on top, pressing the auto-on button. A screw at the back let him control the flame, and he set it to half power. With everything in place, he hauled serious ass and slammed the door.

Outside, Dimitri and Hope leaned against his car and Miyu was curled into a ball on the ground.

"Duck!"

Just as Ciaran reached the car, where his friends were shielded from the blast, a massive boom rocked the ground. The mansion was instantly up in flames. They stared out over the hood of the Vic as the glass house melted and charred. Ciaran handed Dimitri the lighter.

"Didn't need it."

"What did you do?" Dimitri shrugged.

"Why's Roger got a torch in the kitchen?"

"It's for crème brûlée, babe." Hope smiled.

"Oh." He'd ask what that was later.

As the metal and glass heated to boiling, the oddest noise echoed in the once quiet valley. Debris fell from a black cloud of smoke above the remains. Hunks of books and what appeared to be a piece of the leather couch whacked against the hood of Ciaran's car. He just smiled.

"Fair's fair."

*

Ciaran stopped the car at the side of the road, and Miyu stepped out. She started off, but Ciaran just had to ask her something. He dashed over, leaving the car running. She still startled at his approach.

"Hey." Ciaran caught his breath. "How'd you know we were going to kill Marcus?"

"I'm not sure I understand you." Miyu was lying.

"At Roger's place, you said if we succeed in killing them, why did you believe that was what we were doing?"

"If what Roger said Marcus did to you is true, why else would you be there?" Miyu was so blunt about it. She turned and started walking away. "I won't say anything, but a word of advice. He is much more than what he seems. I'd hate to see you two separated because you underestimated him."

Ciaran was going to ask more, but he had a feeling Miyu wouldn't answer. She did hear Marcus and Roger talking; Ciaran believed that, but there was more. She seemed almost psychic. *More than what he seems . . . you two separated . . .* Miyu knew a lot more than she let on.

He jogged back to the car. The door squeaked loudly as he closed it and inside the air was warm. They needed to be gone. Ciaran drove off down the highway.

"So, where's the next house?"

Hope took out a map and opened it to the next circled intersection. "Closest is the Victorian. It's in that ritzy part of town by Crestview Drive and May Street, you know where the foundations of Endicott start, by West Corners?"

"That far out?"

"Unfortunately, yes, but the plantation is just past that. Okay, not really a halfway point, but we don't have a choice." Hope shrugged.

"We'll need gas, then. There's a station down the 76. We can take that, hop on the 13 for a bit and then, onto the 26."

"You know, if I'd realized most of my day would be in a car, I would've brought entertainment." Dimitri stretched out across the back and folded his hands behind his head.

"There's probably a book or two back there." Ciaran watched him in the rearview.

"I was thinking skin mags. Got any of those?"

"No." Ciaran shook his head, and Hope rolled her eyes.

SIXTEEN

When Ciaran pulled up the car, Hope looked at the dash. How had that only been an hour? Drives with Dimitri took like years. The pseudo-Victorian was one among many, stacked in a line on Crestview Drive, all imported from somewhere else to replace the original houses. They had brick walls of varying colors surrounding the front yards and metal plates at every entrance with the house numbers.

After Endwell and the surrounding area of Endicott had been abandoned, demon families got the pick of the litter. Apparently, they didn't know what was living next door. Hope shuddered at the thought of Marcus around children.

The house they wanted was a deep red color with black, metal bars fit into the architecture wherever possible. On the top corner of each floor were grisly looking gargoyles. They gave Hope the creeps.

"This more his style?" Hope asked.

Once she was able to break eye contact with the evil creatures, she looked over at Ciaran to see him swallow hard and squeeze his hands into fists.

"Yeah." His voice didn't so much come out of his mouth as fall out. He was transfixed on the house, and Hope saw little beads of sweat form at his temples.

"Hey. Ciaran." Hope snapped her fingers in front of his face. He shook his head and focused on her face.

"What? Oh, sorry. Yeah, this place looks much more like Marcus." Ciaran tried to play it off, but Hope was getting better at reading him, and she was pretty sure another memory had popped up.

"Are you ready to go in?" Hope kept her tone level.

"Yeah."

Ciaran shuffled toward the door, and Hope was glad Dimitri agreed to play lookout and keep his eyes peeled for cops. As she went inside with Ciaran, Hope turned around to nod at him. She'd never forget the look on Dimitri's face. He was standing with his back to the house and his head hung down. When he noticed her, he looked up for a half a second.

Dimitri looked older, so much older, and very tired.

It truly didn't occur to her that he might've suffered, too. Hope was so preoccupied with her own shit and of course, Ciaran, she forgot Dimitri was also a prisoner of the Inferno. Dimitri lowered his head as fast as he'd picked it up. Being around this house made him and Ciaran falter. *What had Marcus done?* Hope knew, of course, but she didn't understand.

As they breached the coat room, the air in the house smelled off. It was metallic and strong. Ciaran stopped just inside the main room and drew his gun.

"What is it?" she asked.

Ciaran waved Hope around to stand next to him at the edge of a large Oriental rug. It was deep red and looked heavy against the cream tile underneath.

Hope took in the layout of the massive room. The decor was so clichéd. It was exactly what you'd expect from the rich owner of a club named after a book about Hell. The walls were a dark gold with black trim and deep, blood red, accents everywhere. Red chairs, couches, curtains, rugs, red expensive shit was everywhere. And there were horrifying pieces of satanic art on the walls.

Renaissance work at its darkest hung in gilded frames. Images lined up in rows like a gallery, each with a gold plaque underneath crediting the artist. There was one from Dirck Bouts, another by William-Adolphe Bouguereau called "Dante and Virgil in Hell." *Fitting.* A painting by Giotto di Bondone made Hope stop. The plaque said it was part of a larger whole, but only hell was depicted here. The "King of Cannibals." Hope swallowed hard.

An enormous blue Satan sat perched on a man-eating dragon where part of a human hung out of its mouth. His feet crushed clusters of bodies and each outstretched hand held another corpse. Beneath his bulging stomach was the trapped form of a woman. All around him were damned mortals suffering tortures Marcus himself probably used. Flesh torn from their backs. Pain, so much pain.

Ciaran called out to her, breaking the painting's hold. A shiver crept up her spine and Hope hesitated before she continued her inspection. What else would she find?

Among all the furnishings and on tables were strange statues and devices. An iron maiden stood between the loveseat and couch. A terrifying contraption that stood on three legs and had a decorative screw on the top sat on the coffee table.

"What's that?" Hope looked at Ciaran.

"Pear of agony."

"What does it do?"

"You put it in an opening and turn the screw 'til the flesh tears." Ciaran moved his hands in demonstration.

"Oh."

Hope's eyes continued to travel around the space even as she told herself not to. In the far corner was another weird item made of wood. It was shaped like a chair sort of, but the "seat" was a large pyramid.

"And that?"

"Judas chair."

"Do I want to know what that one does?"

"No."

She'd been so distracted that when Hope finally saw a pair of shackles hanging from the ceiling in front of a huge staircase, she actually gasped. Ciaran moved next to her, and she saw the stain on the floor.

"Blood." Hope aimed at the stairs.

"Yeah, it looks old. Already coagulating."

Hope and Ciaran examined the brown-red pool.

"It's not that much. The person this belongs to wouldn't have died."

"Yeah, probably wrist wounds," Ciaran rubbed at his own wrists as he spoke.

Hope circled around and scanned the edges. "It's gravitational so that would make sense. Where's the owner, though?"

"I'll answer that with another question. Where do you think this goes?" Ciaran was at the side of the stairs, a hidden door had blended in with the crown molding.

"Now, how did you find that?" Hope smiled and furrowed her brow.

Ciaran shrugged. "I fell on it."

As Ciaran pushed open the door, the cold air that rushed out stole any warmth that lingered in the room. The stale, rancid stench that oozed out made them both cough. It was so much stronger now that the secret door was open.

"Fuck me. I changed my mind. That person's definitely dead."

Hope put her gun back in her belt and covered her face. She tried to breathe through her mouth in shallow, steady puffs.

"Here." Ciaran handed Hope a small napkin to tie around her face.

Ciaran was already wearing one and looked like a robber from a cartoon but at this point, it was a necessity. Hope tied the soft fabric around her nose to protect her from the stink.

"Thanks. You know, for napkins these are pretty nice."

"Remember who we're dealing with?" Ciaran stood just ahead of a breakfront that held expensive china and evidently napkins.

"But napkins? I mean, they're napkins. Who cares?"

"Marcus, apparently. Let's go. I want to know what's down there and then leave. I don't like having to . . . Well, you know."

"Yeah." Hope turned to the hidden room. "Deep breath, sexy."

Hope sucked in a lungful of air and held it as she got closer to the hidden chamber. Ciaran walked behind her and put a hand on the small of her back. He didn't seem to think anything of it, but Hope was very aware of the gesture. PDA was not done in her clan. And still, she relaxed slightly.

Hope reached into the darkness, feeling along the wall for a light switch. She groped the cool, cement and came up with a big, fat nothing.

"There's probably a pull cord in the middle." Ciaran's voice was loud behind her, and Hope jumped.

Hope smacked the arm closet to her and knew it was a good hit when her own arm burned. "Jesus, warn a girl or something."

"Sorry. Light?" Ciaran pushed her a little further into the room.

"How the fuck did I end up going first?!"

Hope tried to side-step Ciaran to push him past when her foot slid out from under her. She started to fall backward and scrambled to grab something in the pitch-black. A pull cord just like Ciaran said was waiting, and Hope gripped, but it wouldn't hold her weight. Thankfully, Ciaran's arm snaked around her waist.

"Thank Maker."

The light flicked on as Ciaran halted her momentum. She smiled up and let go of the thin cord.

"I almost cracked my . . . What is it?"

Ciaran didn't respond. He just slowly helped Hope stand and backed up until he was flush against the far wall. Furrowing her brow, Hope shook her head and tried to walk to him. Ciaran pointed behind her.

And there it was. A little pile of what used to be a person on the floor. The remains were decaying quickly, thanks to the cool, wet air of the basement, but Hope could tell it was a boy, a teenager.

As her eyes traveled across the body, Hope heard Ciaran gag. The boy was curled up into a ball with skeletal arms wrapped around his frail body. He was naked, extremely malnourished, and long lines were carved into the skin of his back, crisscrossing whip scars similar to Ciaran's.

The boy's skin was a striking blue that must've been beautiful. The old blood they'd seen was indeed from wrist wounds, and as Hope walked around to the front of the body, she saw the raw flesh behind shackles. He was so skinny, too skinny. His skin hung from him, and there was a pit where a full belly should've been. She saw even more whip lashes across the boy's chest and Marcus had sliced him below his waist. *Monster.*

Hope held bile down as she almost retched. *Where's Ciaran?* Against the far wall he sat with his knees in his face. She knelt in front of him, blocking the carnage.

"We need to go. Ciaran, come on. Let's go." Hope struggled to get him to his feet. Ciaran's eyes were wide, and he wouldn't blink or look away, tears threatening at the corners.

"He's so small . . . so small . . ."

"I know. I know, baby. Please, we need to go." Hope's voice started to crack, and her eyes prickled and blurred.

Something snapped inside her. Hope wanted the tears to fall. She was sad, really, horribly sad that a demon kid was dead. Images of the *braednas* temple and Ciaran's back swam in her brain. Flicking pictures of flesh ripping under a whip, a bright blue fading to grayed denim.

"Hope, we can't let him . . ."

"We won't. He won't get away with this. I promise you." Hope held Ciaran's face in her hands. Her blood rushed and her throat ached, and her lungs struggled to take in the impossibly thick air.

"We won't, but we need to go. He could come back. And . . . and we need to report this."

Ciaran nodded and finally blinked. As they both got to their feet, everything around her crushed down. A mother of another clan was mourning her son, the way she wished she mourned for her own mother. And, whatever Marcus had done could've been done to Ciaran, to other boys, other demons.

Before she'd even met Ciaran, Hope could've lost him.

Why hadn't she seen it? Marcus had hidden this part of himself so craftily behind tailored suits and eloquent speech. She'd signed on to do as he asked without questioning him.

The paintings up the stairs of demons and the devil double imposed themselves over the images of the boy behind her: Satan devouring and violating and flaying the tiny forms. Hope could see Marcus Dentry's eyes smiling from the face of Lucifer. He'd never stop this, and a cell couldn't contain his evil. There was only one option, and at that moment, Hope understood why Ciaran had killed the man who mentioned the M.

The air in the main room was amazing. It cleaned the musty death from her lungs. Hope ripped off the napkin protecting her face and threw it to the floor; the stenches had trapped themselves between the tight fibers. Ciaran was behind her, closing the door and wiping the handle with his own napkin.

"No fingerprints."

"Right. I'm not a fan of theirs, but you think they'll do something about this?" Hope was skeptical the Newborn City Police Department would be much help.

"I know someone who will." Ciaran pulled out his cell. "Hold on, okay?"

"Sure."

The smell of the room under their feet stuck to her. Tossing the napkin did nothing to help. It was in her hair, her flesh, her clothes. Hope pulled her hair back into a ponytail and took off her sweater. She held the garment by the neck. She'd toss it as soon as possible.

"Detective Anderson, please." Ciaran didn't sound like himself, his voice a rough edge.

After a brief hold he said, "Hey, Lucas, got a sitch you may want to check out."

Ciaran put the phone on speaker.

"Hey, Ciaran. Why is it that you never call to say hi? There's always some emergency."

"Sorry, but this one's pretty bad. 1309 Crestview Drive. Bring a crew."

"Damn, buddy, that's out there. It'll be a sec before we can get out there. You don't need to stay, as always."

"Lucas, one more thing. It's a demon, probably nineteen or twenty and male. May want to warn your guys."

The line was silent for a while, the tension almost tangible.

"That's so young. Fuck. Alright, I'll handle this myself."

"Thanks. We'll get out of here."

"Keep that buddy of yours out of trouble."

Ciaran winked at Hope gently. "I'll do my best."

"Later."

"You, too."

Ciaran hung up and stuffed the phone back in his jeans. He walked over to Hope and took her whole torso in his arms. For a second, they just stood there, but soon they remembered where they were and the pressing need to evacuate.

"I . . ." Ciaran shook his head.

Hope turned to leave and pulled Ciaran along with her. They held hands as they walked out.

"I am with you?" Ciaran said.

"You are."

Dimitri stood with his back to the house. He was so still, like one of the frozen images inside the Victorian. The sun was setting and something metal in his hand reflected the light. It looked like a dog tag or a med bracelet, but as soon as she was close, he put it away.

"Anderson's coming."

Ciaran walked over to Dimitri, and they clapped arms, pounding each other on the back like they hadn't seen each other in years. It was strange to watch, but more than that, Hope was a little envious. Ciaran mentioned that Dimitri was the only person he'd trusted in a long time, and Hope didn't have that. She never clicked with anyone from her clan, no one ever did. They all kept to themselves. The intimacy she'd shared with Ciaran was very much the first, both in a sexual way and as a friend. And he had a family, a mother who didn't leave him. Okay, this line of thought was getting her nowhere.

She walked over to Ciaran and mimicked his gesture from earlier. With a hand on his back, she entered the conversation.

"A kid? Seriously, will that fuck stop at nothing?" Dimitri was seething, a strange "power" emanating from his hands. Ciaran didn't notice, and Hope assumed the only reason she did was because she was a demon.

"You know he won't. He's gonna find another and another. He can't stop and neither can I."

"Well, fearless leader, where to next?" Dimitri slapped him on the arm and faked a salute.

"No calling me that." Ciaran rolled his eyes, but Hope couldn't help smiling.

Ciaran shook his head but the laugh he was trying to hold back came out anyway. The tension was breaking, and it needed to. None of them would survive this if they held onto the gore.

"It's your new title, get used to it." The little Russian was starting to grow on her, sort of like a parasite fish on a shark.

"If you don't want it, I'll certainly lead you idiots. Plantation?"

They both stared at Hope in awe for a moment. She smiled and walked over to the driver side of the car.

"Keys?"

Ciaran fumbled in his pocket, barely managing to toss her the keys. She slid into the car and turned the ignition. As Dimitri and Ciaran got inside, Hope adjusted all the mirrors and the chair. Dimitri assumed his position, asleep in the back in a matter of moments, and Ciaran sat down next to her.

"So, this is a mutiny?" Ciaran sounded a bit lighter.

"You can call me Captain."

"You're gonna pay for that." His eyes took on a devious cast, and he cocked a crooked grin.

"Am I, now?" Hope teased Ciaran's lips with hers.

"Keep it in your pants, sluts. I'm still awake back here."

Hope sighed and sat back in her seat. Ciaran apologized with a shrug and a smile. She wanted some time alone to reconnect with him. They were alive, and Hope wanted to focus both of them on that.

*

After stealing a few weapons at the empty plantation, the ride back to Ciaran's house was awkward. No one, not even Dimitri, said a word. Apparently, the guys weren't a fan of theft, and Ciaran was noticeably upset. When they finally reached Ciaran's massive house, everybody just filed into their rooms and retired for the rest of the night.

"As the grave" barely described the silence. It wasn't like him, at least as far as she knew. It was weird and wrong, but she didn't know what to say. Instead, she just sat on the end of his bed and watched him.

Ciaran went to his closet and opened the doors. Whenever they changed together, he always turned his back the other way, but now, it was as if he wanted her to look.

The swirl inside her head was frustrating, to say the least. The shirtless view made her skin tingle, but the pain and anger in him made her nauseated and guilty. Guilt was definitely among the emotions she could live without.

The clang of Ciaran's belted pants hitting the floor smashed into her. He was gorgeous, and she couldn't seem to remind her body that he was pissed at her and it wasn't happening. The silence made her skin itch. Just as Hope went to say something, Ciaran turned to face her. His masculine glory was something she usually couldn't pull her eyes away from, but now, Hope wanted to stare at the floor. It wasn't happening, however; the weight of his presence forced her eyes up.

"It occurs to me that you really know only half of the emotions and sensations out there. you've seen the light, but you've never really felt the dark. You get them both. Would you go back to feeling nothing?"

"I don't think so, but truthfully, this is overwhelming." Hope was drowning inside herself. Her heartbeat sped up and a light sweat broke out on her forehead. The nausea was stronger, too. All the sensations combining to form something new. Hope wanted to curl into herself and go to sleep.

"I just want to go to bed. Morning will be better." Hope pushed her shoes off and crawled under the covers, pulling the blanket over her head.

But Ciaran whipped the blanket off. "That's not gonna work for me. You can't run, trust me I've tried."

There was the faintest smile on his face, but Ciaran wasn't happy.

"I'm not. I'm just tired. We both need to rest." Hope sat up and met his stare.

"Alright."

Ciaran embraced her. A pang in her chest ached. Hope still thought about all the things that could go wrong, all the ways these new emotions could hurt her and Ciaran.

"Why don't you get more comfortable? Sleeping in jeans is rarely fun."

Hope took off her pants and returned to the bed next to Ciaran. His skin was warm against hers, and she felt a bit calmer. He stroked her hair, and his breath moved the strands at the top of her head. With her cheek against his chest, Hope heard his heart pump blood steadily. Hope thought of the boy they'd found.

"How are you still alive, still functioning, after everything he did?" she asked.

"I'm stubborn."

"Ciaran, I'm serious."

"I know. And a large part of it was being stubborn. I couldn't let him win. I couldn't let him get away with what he'd done. To me. To the others."

"This is so not what I expected, but I guess that's just how it goes when you've never felt anything before. And you've been taught to fear it."

"I don't think I like your clan very much. You'd think they would want to teach you about what could very well happen."

Hope laughed. "They're more like ostriches. They stick their heads in the ground. Maybe, that's why there aren't that many of us."

"Ha, no wonder you didn't fit in." Ciaran squeezed her. "I like this, learning about you."

"It's like I'm learning it, too. Looking back without a hold on my feelings is fucking trippy."

"I can imagine. Sort of."

The room fell silent, and Hope assumed they'd both traveled into their minds. She couldn't stop thinking about her father's words and the *braednas* ceremony; the past images blocked everything out. Hope wanted to talk about it and yet . . . *How can I feel two contradictory things at the same time? How do people deal with this crap?* The questions would go unanswered for now because the desire to sleep overpowered her.

*

"Damn that window! It's only six fucking a.m.!" Dimitri's voice boomed from the upstairs and woke both Hope and Ciaran.

Hope stretched out, taking up the whole bed, and pressed herself up against Ciaran's hips. At first there'd been an unconscious desire for space, but now, Hope enjoyed the hiss she elicited from him as she rubbed her ass on his erection.

"You always seem to have such good dreams in the morning." She rolled over and faced his smile.

"Not really my choice. It always happens."

"Always?"

"Well, mostly, yeah, guys relax when sleeping, then morning wood." He gestured to himself, and Hope laughed.

"Really? You've got to be kidding?"

"No. You really don't know much about the birds and the bees, do you?"

"The what?"

Ciaran pulled her tight to him. "Never mind."

"You could always educate me." Hope wrapped her hand around his shaft and squeezed gently. Ciaran moaned loudly, swiveling his hips so he could move in and out of her hand. She loved watching the pinch between his brows like he was concentrating hard.

"Ugh, I don't think you need any schooling in that particular subject."

Hope watched proudly as Ciaran's eyes rolled back, and he moved quicker in and out of her palm.

"Tell me what feels best. How else am I supposed to know?" Hope let go and smirked.

"You—Damn, Hope. Something tells me you're good at reading people's reactions. Just watch. I won't be able to hide how good something feels." Ciaran put her hand back, made her grip tightly, stroking up and down. His eyes closed, and Hope teased his lips with nibbles and licks.

As Ciaran's tongue darted in and out of her mouth, Hope knew he wanted inside her. The motions between their mouths mimicked the thrusting of their hips. Hope broke the kiss slowly and pushed Ciaran back against the headboard. His muscles were taut, and his erection was straining his boxers. She moved on top of him and slid down so her mouth hovered over the tip of him.

He shucked his underwear in seconds.

Back in position, Hope licked her lips and gently touched the tip of her tongue to his glistening skin. With her hands on his hips keeping her steady, Ciaran shuddered. She traced his blunt head in long, wet strokes. The small hole at the end shimmered with excitement. It was crying; it wanted more so badly. The salty taste was familiar now, and Hope knew it meant she was doing something right.

Ciaran's hands gripped the sheets until his knuckles went white. When she let him all the way inside her mouth, he gasped and gripped the fabric even more tightly. Hope changed positions and let her arm hold her weight. With her other hand free, she stroked his shaft as she suckled at the tip in dragging pulls.

"Fuuuck." The gravely sound of Ciaran's voice was exaggerated.

Hope positively beamed. At this point, she could've asked him to make dinner for her every day in a pink apron, and he would've said yes.

"Good?" Hope stopped, making Ciaran shoot up and grab the back of her neck.

"Yes. Don't stop."

The grip on her neck was enough to make her skin burn, but Ciaran could've forced her head down if he wanted. The fact that he was trying to maintain control was hot as hell. It made Hope want some payback, to push him to the brink over and over like he'd done to her.

When he laid back down, Hope started again. She took her time, dragging out each stroke, each lick, to torture him with pleasure. She wanted to make him moan, to show him how much she wanted him. He was so soft yet hard, smooth but deliciously ribbed.

She watched and listened, taking cues from his body's reactions. When she took in all of him, Ciaran bucked. In between those thrusts, Hope dragged her tongue up the base to play at the tip. Ciaran moaned and cursed. With a spark of ingenuity, Hope caressed the heavy weight beneath his shaft. Each time she sucked, Ciaran gasped.

He was getting close and Hope enjoyed listening to his breath rocket in and out of him. Ciaran's grip on the sheets moved to her hair, his fingers knotting themselves in the thick waves and creating tiny tendrils of pain that made her hungrier for his release.

"I'm really close, Hope. You should—"

She answered by devouring him and groping the tightening, ever sensitive skin beneath his erection. Ciaran got so hard with no choice but to give in.

She stroked his shaft in rough, fast circles to tip him over that edge, and Ciaran did give in. His hips pumped, and he roared out as the orgasm rocketed out. She didn't stop until he was still and smiling. The look on his face was priceless. Stretching out beside him, Hope collapsed and echoed his smile.

"Holy fucking mother of god. You are amazing. Just . . .wow." His voice was breathy and rough.

"Why, thank you. I do pride myself on being a fast learner."

"Well, gold stars." Ciaran rolled on to his side. "I feel a little guilty, though. You didn't really get anything out of that."

His smirk made her heart pound. She'd have to check for bruises on her knees, she'd fallen for him so hard.

"You could return the favor." Hope winked at Ciaran, and he immediately leapt on top of her, lifting her hands over her head.

"I suppose I could." Keeping a grip on her wrists with one hand, Ciaran reached down her stomach. His fingers were fierce as they teased her core and soon that wasn't enough for either of them.

Ciaran made circles inside her. She was slick under his fingers and moaned with each dexterous swirl. Hope wanted desperately to squirm, but Ciaran held her in place, watching her with hungry eyes. As she started tipping over that cliff like Ciaran had, the circles inside her changed. Ciaran found a spot that was nothing short of magic. Ciaran stroked her gently at first, but when she fought against his hold, Ciaran pressed into her with animalistic ferocity.

The sensations were so intense Hope thought she might pass out. She was about to explode when there was a magnificent tingling. Ciaran's motions coaxed the feeling to mind-blowing proportions, and Hope cried out as she orgasmed.

"Fuck. That was intense." Hope had trouble speaking through her breaths.

"And quick, you were pretty built up, huh?" Ciaran flopped down next to her, making her bounce.

"Yes, extremely."

"Job well done, I'd say."

Hope shoved him, and he slid off the mattress and landed flat on his naked ass.

"Whoops."

Hope barely had the strength to help Ciaran back up. The orgasm had been more like a long, dirty marathon than a quick release. *How am I supposed to walk now?*

"Well, as Dimitri pointed out about an hour ago, it's early. Why don't we relax for a while? We can both regain our strength and then get breakfast."

"You read my mind." Hope shifted over and opened her arms up to Ciaran.

He smiled and fell into them. They squeezed a tight hug and then lay next to each other with their eyes closed.

SEVENTEEN

A penthouse, naturally. Ciaran was less than surprised that Marcus had a five-floor section of a skyscraper among his assets. The thing was steel, chrome, and expensive. Donald fucking Trump would be shown the door at this place. *And fuck the both of them.*

"Subtle is not in his repertoire, is it?" Hope zipped up the black, leather jacket she'd insisted on buying. It looked damn good and made regretting the purchase near impossible.

"'Bout as much as yours." Ciaran winked at her.

"What can I say? I like to make my presence known. When the time is right, of course."

"Of course."

Dimitri ran over from the maintenance entrance. At first glance, Ciaran wouldn't have recognized him. Wearing a baseball cap and a shirt with the building logo wasn't his normal style.

"We're clear. Elevator's on hold."

Ciaran had to hand it to the guy, sneaking in as a member of the outsourced cleaning crew was brilliant and chatting up one of the other employees and making friendly, even better. He'd gone in and out of the building multiple times now, and no one seemed to care.

"Let's go." Ciaran gestured to the door.

They ran over and rode the service elevator to the top floor. No one had access to the floor without a clearance key and there'd definitely be security. So, as they traveled up, Ciaran got his gun ready.

He nodded to Hope, and she set her duffle down and dug around inside. Then, with Dimitri elbowing him in the back because he was changing, Ciaran flicked the elevator off hold. A pair of Walther PPQs fit perfectly in his waistband. Hope slipped two into holsters on her thighs and put a pair of Springfield XD-S .9 mms in her shoulder harness. She was like a kid in a candy shop when she saw them among the loot from Marcus's "industrial storage."

He couldn't blame her. These were apparently Hope's go-to for a mission with an ambidextrous magazine release so that she could use both hands. Seeing her in action was impressive, if a bit frightening, and emotion-light Hope was probably downright terrifying.

Ciaran regretted every life he'd taken at the Inferno and after. Hope didn't even remember all the lives she'd ended. Right now, it didn't matter really. It was a helpful skill, and they had a job to do.

Dressed in his own set of leathers and a black shirt, Dimitri joined the gun party. He leaned over Ciaran's shoulder and grabbed two SIGs from the bag, another nice choice.

"Now, I'm feeling like we didn't bring enough heat. I don't like that we only have one way in and out," Dimitri said.

Ciaran didn't disagree. "Yeah. I know, it's a shit sitch, but we have to make it work. This very well could be the place, and that bastard's not getting away."

"This might help with that." Hope pulled out a small, metal canister from the now very empty duffle.

It was a stout cylinder with a button-like piece on top. As Ciaran looked closer at the device, he saw a clear tube wrapped around the top of the can.

"Is that what I think it is?"

Hope smiled. "Don't worry, it's not mustard gas or anything."

Dimitri clapped her on the shoulder. "Damn girl, you're crazy."

"What is it, then?" Ciaran adjusted the guns at his belt.

"It's tear gas. It's not going to kill anyone."

"Okay, positions?"

Ciaran ran through the plan in his head. The tear gas would definitely help. They'd have some cover as they opened the doors and came out into the main hall. Thank god for those records they found, or they'd be going in completely blind. As it was, blueprints only told them the layout, not who was in it.

"Ready." Hope had her first set of guns in her hands.

"This is gonna suck. But, hey, let's go!" Dimitri pretended to shoot his "pistolas" in the air and earned himself an elbow to the ribs via Hope.

Ciaran held his PPQs tight and prepared to open the doors. He flicked the switch for an emergency stop on the elevator and power was cut to the moving box. Ciaran shoved the doors apart, and when there was enough space to stick a head through, Ciaran stopped pulling. Hope carefully leaned out of the elevator.

"One down the hall, south end, two shadows on the east wall, and I can hear talking. Male, most likely hired guns, considering they're talking about who gets the late shift." Hope came back inside the elevator. "Think the master bedroom is east past the help."

"Let's take out the solo flyer at the south end. Don't want someone waiting behind us. Hope, would you oblige?" Ciaran made like Vana White at the door, a gleaming smile exaggerated on his face.

"She gets to have all the fun." Dimitri leaned against the rear wall and folded his arms.

Hope just smiled and nodded. Slipping through the doors, her leather tight against her pale skin, Hope looked like a black mamba stalking unsuspecting prey.

When she was clear of the doors, Ciaran watched from the gap. Her black clothing concealed her from the man she'd seen who stood with his back to her in the dark hallway. Hope's soundless approach seemed to drag on for years but came to an abrupt end.

The glint that bounced off Hope's knife seemed so bright it might give her away, but she cleanly slid it through the man's throat. The patter of blood hitting the floor was the only sound. There was no scream and no flop from the body. She was certainly a pro.

Ciaran walked quickly toward her when she signaled for help carrying the dead weight to the elevator. They pulled the body inside and dropped it at Dimitri's feet.

"Aww, Christmas came early this year." Dimitri stepped over the corpse and stood alongside Ciaran.

Hope brought up the rear this time, and they approached the hired men to the east. Ciaran got in earshot and heard their ridiculous conversation.

"Dude, I'm not dealing with him!"

"You're a fucking pussy. Why you 'fraid of some dick in glasses?"

"He gives me the creeps, k? I mean, Dentry's a fucked-up guy with all his sex shit, but that other guy, ugh. Have you seen him eat?"

"Fuck off, Randy. Just do the fucking job."

Ciaran walked to the end of the hall with Hope while Dimitri waited behind. He nodded, and Ciaran pressed his ear to the door where the men patrolled.

"Ready?" He looked to Hope.

"Yup." She unwrapped the clear tubing from around the can.

It was about three feet long when she was finished. As Ciaran listened to the continued argument between the men, Hope looked up at him and Dimitri, the length of tube stuffed under the door.

"Now's a good time to put on those fancy masks I brought." Hope lifted a hand and waited for Ciaran to hand her one.

He absolutely hated wearing the mask. The inside smelled like arse, and it made him slightly claustrophobic. He adjusted it on his face, but it wasn't working.

"Would you stop that?" Hope raised her eyebrows at him.

"It's uncomfortable."

"It's not meant to be comfortable. It's meant to keep you from breathing this shit in."

Ciaran put his arms down with a huff. "Fine."

Hope balanced on her toes, a hand ready above the top of the grenade. "Okay, they're not going to stay in there. It takes about thirty seconds to fill the room and then, they're going to come running out crying. Should be easy enough to knock them out when they pass us. Ready?"

"Ready." Ciaran positioned himself to strike the head of the closest exiting mercenary.

Hope released the gas and a soft hiss sounded. The can did its thing, and within a few moments they heard the yelling and scrambling of two men trying desperately to get out. Hope jumped up and took a few steps back. As soon as she was clear of the door, the men came running out. Ciaran hit one of them on the head with his gun, and Hope stuck a foot out, tripping the other.

The man fell forward and smashed his head on the tile. Dimitri landed a blow to the back of his head and the three of them smiled.

"That went better than I thought it would." Dimitri's voice was muffled by the mask.

Hope opened the windows in the now empty living room. The remaining smoke slowly bled out and after a few minutes, the room was clear. They took off their masks and tossed them on the low-slung couch.

"They're definitely out. Also, it smelled like rubber-coated ass in there." Dimitri shoved a thumb at the gas masks.

"Old supplies." Hope shoved the masks back in the duffel.

"Where'd you get 'em, anyway?" Ciaran went through the unconscious men's pockets.

"Cop was selling some old shit for some extra cash."

"Is that legal?"

"When you're a cop, it is."

Ciaran shook his head. He found some phones, a wad of cash, and smokes on each man, nothing helpful. The phones were burners, and they'd be dead after a day with no way to charge them. He moved on to examine the living room.

There was a short-fur rug, off-white and not cheap. An array of tables flanked every piece of furniture, and the caramel-colored leather couch was pushed up against the back wall. All in all, it screamed pretentious. There were even maps and endless volumes of hardbound books on the Middle and Dark Ages. Only a handful of lamps lit the space. Bookshelves were also built into the walls, a bar sat near the windows, and there was a door to an adjoining room.

The glasses on the bar looked recently used. The crystal containers of brandy and wine were half full or less. The "oil lamp" on the bar, which was actually electric, cast a glow through the translucent liquid, making maroon and brown swirls dance across the pale carpet.

Knowing about Marcus's tendency to hide things in plain sight, Ciaran looked through books. Big mistake. The assortment was limited to the study of medieval torture and some of the most depraved authors, the Marquis de Sade, who he quoted regularly, *Perfume* by Patrick Suskind. Ciaran stepped back and had the profound desire to shower.

His lunch rebelled and his forehead moistened. The room was just so damn quiet, and now that the excitement had faded, only the rank stench of Marcus dripped from the room. Ciaran looked to Hope. She was just as tense.

"What's up?" He walked over, taking out his gun.

"I can hear breathing in the next room. Something's . . . off."

"It's a demon. I feel it, too. Old. Strong. Definitely not Marcus." Dimitri stood to Hope's left and raised his SIG.

The adjoining door led to the master bedroom.

Hope took out her pistol and nodded. "After you, hun."

"Gee, thanks."

No need to beat around the bush at this point. They'd taken out the security, time to face the music. Ciaran's pulse echoed in his ears and his palms sweat. *No Marcus. So, what are you?*

He swung the door to the "main show" open. The air that flowed out must've come off a glacier. It was black inside and his eyes struggled to dilate fast enough. Ciaran held up his gun anyway.

"Guys, can you see anything?"

Who knew, maybe their demon retinas processed low-light better. Obviously, their ears worked better. Ciaran looked back at them but before he could hear an answer, he was knocked on his ass, hard. His head met the floor, and he thought he saw a torso dripping entrails fly out the window. *Oh, yeah, concussion.*

Ciaran wobbled up to a stand, grabbing his head. Everything he saw was vaguely grainy and reddish.

"What the fuck was that?!" Hope's voice was a loud reminder of reality.

"I don't know! Fuck me, Ciaran's hurt." Dimitri must've been close because that demon's mug was up in his face in two seconds flat. "Hey, buddy. You okay?"

Ciaran was pretty damn sure he said, "Yeah, of course." But what he heard sounded like "Meh, off borse." *I sound like a fucking drunk.* Hope was suddenly behind him.

"I think he has a concussion. At least it feels like he does. I'm not a fan of this sensation." She was moping about his headache.

"Neat trick." Dimitri smiled.

Ciaran started to see straight again, the tunnel of black around his vision fading to reveal a very bright light bulb fixed to the wall, which he could see really well from the floor.

"I'm fine. But damn. Never been knocked over like that. Umm, by the way . . . did you guys see a, well, a torso fly out the window?"

"I saw it, too." Hope rubbed her head, and Dimitri agreed with a short nod.

"Oh, thank god. I thought I'd majorly damaged my brain. What was that?"

"Fuck if I know. And that worries me." Dimitri stared off into the bedroom. *The bedroom.*

Ciaran pulled up on the doorframe and swung himself in. The bed where the "thing" had been was empty. A tiny blood spot on the floor and broken glass were the only things left. Whatever it was, it took Marcus somewhere he couldn't be attacked.

Ciaran had been a few feet from Marcus, and he was gone, again.

"Dammit!"

The wall that had been holding back the monstrous, drooling figure made of hatred and a taste for blood was blown to smithereens. Ciaran half expected to see smoke billowing around his face. His stomach churned like a fucking witch's cauldron, and Ciaran realized both Hope and Dimitri were silent.

"Did you see him?"

"A piece of wall swiveled. Secret door, like a haunted mansion or something? He used stairs to go down." Dimitri grumbled.

"And you guys just let him go!"

"Don't fucking start, Ciaran. We tried to stop him, but he was too close to the exit, and it locked after he went through." Hope pointed at him and, shit, if looks could kill.

But why? Why were they always one step behind? Ciaran paced back and forth in his heavy boots. *Fuck it all.*

Ciaran's brain turned up the jackhammer routine when he caught movement to his left. Someone stood in the shadows at the end of the hall. The moon peeked out from behind a cloud, and Ciaran could see light reflect off a pair of small, round glasses.

"Roger."

Before he could register what else had shown in the moonlight, Ciaran ran toward Roger. He leapt at him, desperate to tear into his flesh and hear his limbs crack. If he wasn't so fucking pissed, he might've noticed the .45.

Ciaran was on the floor before he even felt the bullet punch a hole in his leg. The burn grabbed his attention and the image of dissecting a frog's thigh in middle school popped up. He was sick to his stomach.

Three more shots sounded off around him in quick succession. Dimitri fired at Roger, but moving targets were tricky bastards, and he only connected with the wall. Ciaran looked for Hope, but hands pulled on his wrists and dragged him backward.

The next few moments were like a choppy phone call with shit reception. Going in and out of consciousness had its benefits though. Every time he passed out, he got a vacation from the world-class pain lighting up his leg. The trip down what he assumed was the hall was pretty smooth, but as unconsciousness tried to make him its permanent bitch, the floor underneath him disappeared.

It was quickly replaced by another one. *Did Hope drop me?* Ciaran needed to let his eyeballs settle in his skull if he wanted to find out.

"Did we get to the elevator? Definitely thinking hospital."

"I was thinking morgue." The voice was deep and polished like a pair of Italian loafers, and 100% not Hope's.

Ciaran tried to focus his eyes, but the lights going on and off raised the difficulty level to Hell mode. The distorted image of a grey, wool blazer over a burgundy vest burned into his optic nerve. *Fuck.*

"Finally, I was wondering when you would realize I wasn't that little tart. You all really have made quite the mess."

Roger's constant condescending always drove Ciaran crazy.

"Why take me? Why not just leave me to die?" Ciaran tried to move, sit up, roll on his side, anything, but an expensive shoe pushed him down.

"What, and deprive Mr. Dentry of his favorite toy? No, no, I aim to serve. Moreover, I might be hungry after he's finished with you."

Ciaran must not have heard right. No way Roger wanted to eat him. Cannibalism seemed too messy for that guy. And then he noticed his arms were heavy and cold. Not good, he was losing a lot of blood. Damn him. If he would've just been patient. He pushed down on his femoral artery, but if Hope and Dimitri didn't find him soon, Roger would be right about the morgue. Where was he, anyway?

The metal floor was a bed of nails and when he was able to look down, he saw it was diamond plate sheets. *That wasn't in the service elevator. There's another one?* The trip down seemed much longer. And aside from the constant pressure on his chest, the room could've been empty. Mr. van Stratton was completely silent.

Ciaran pictured him as a long, thin reaper waiting to devour his soul. Okay, he was being a little morbid, but time was not his buddy right now. Banging and creaking of old steel echoed as the elevator came to a halt. As the doors slid open, Ciaran saw a grate blocking access. Roger opened things up, and it was way too loud.

"End of the line, Mr. O'Connor. I am glad we had this base renovated. It's so much more useful now, don't you agree?"

Ciaran absolutely could not put up a fight. He had to maintain pressure on his wound and passing out was a definite no-no. Roger dragged him by one arm and against the resistance of Ciaran's planted feet. Bastard that he was, Roger kept pulling. At this rate, Ciaran's shoulder would dislocate.

He'd lost this fight and should focus on stopping the bleeding. The room was dark, and Ciaran could only make out cube shapes scattered about, probably boxes, and a long rectangle that was probably a table.

Roger tossed him on the cold metal like he was a bag of feathers. It was nice against his arms and face. He'd gone from cold to hot in a flash.

"You are quite inept, aren't you? To let yourself be captured and wounded because you barreled at me like a moronic bull. Tsk, tsk."

Ciaran wanted to argue, but Roger was right. Bull was nice considering the jackass he'd been. If something happened to either Hope or Dimitri, he'd never forgive himself. He wasn't going to last much longer, however, and wouldn't have to feel bad for long.

"Now, before I must take my leave so you can entertain Mr. Dentry, tell me something if you would. Those demons you came with? I remember your friend, who I'll also have soon, but whoever is the female you brought with you so foolishly?"

Ciaran stayed quiet. Hadn't they met already? Though, he was a personal assistant and couldn't be expected to remember her. The swirl of thoughts literally hurt, and Ciaran tapped out. His brain was too furious at him for whacking it against the inside of his skull multiple times.

Roger, not being a patient man, just scoffed. "I have other ways of learning her identity. Of course, if you won't be of any help, I shall just have to say goodbye and turn you over to Mr. Dentry. She is worth quite a bit to me in her current state, and I would be prepared to reward you."

Ciaran glared at him.

"No? Very well then."

Ciaran drifted in and out. Roger's words were audible, but they didn't mean anything anymore. Something about Hope, current stake, no, wait, plate. God, help him, he just wanted to go home. He'd fucked up so royally; he knew it, and couldn't he just go to sleep, now?

The sound of metal banging echoed all around him, making his teeth vibrate painfully. A bright light practically burned out his eyes. Was he dying? He'd heard in church as a kid that you saw a bright light and felt a sense of peace. He didn't feel particularly peaceful. In fact, he was pissed and cold and his leg hurt. So, not dying, unless he was going somewhere unpleasant.

"Back up, fuck face!" Dimitri was so weird. He always came up with such funny names for people. Ciaran remembered how he'd gotten him through nights deep in the Inferno. *What a good . . . demon, yeah . . .*

Ciaran didn't know what was coming and going. He was an imitation battery that was totally drained. The numbness in his fingers tingled like ants were crawling on him. There was a clicking noise close to his head.

"Ciaran! Ciaran, don't pass out! Fuck, his teeth are chattering." Hope's hands on his face were very warm. God, he was sleepy.

"Ciaran!" Hope shouted at him, but he couldn't respond. She pushed on his leg or maybe an elephant crushed him. The hot jolt of pain woke him up.

"Ahh, fuck." Thick, tendrils of fire coursed around and through his muscle. Ciaran got the strength to sit up and looked around the room. They were alone, no Roger, just Hope and Dimitri.

"I, ugh, fuck." The surge of energy was wearing off.

He watched the room get smaller and smaller as the edges of his vision turned fuzzy and deep red, like staring at the sun with his eyes closed.

"Zip it, bud. We're taking you home," Dimitri ordered.

Ciaran wanted to fight so he could apologize, but it was like Dimitri's words were a magick spell. He passed right the fuck out.

EIGHTEEN

The beep of the monitor was loud in Hope's ears. Thank Maker, Gallo had come as quickly as he did. And that Dimitri had gotten them into that locked room. The sight still reverberated in her head.

Dimitri just touched the handle and in a brilliant flash of energy it melted in his hand and the remaining door was a pile of rubble at his feet. The display was insane. Hope had heard of demons with such remarkable abilities but thought it was her clan's version of an urban legend.

When he'd unleashed his abilities, his eyes turned solid black and his hands glowed blue. He seemed colder, harsher, even . . . cruel. She wouldn't have been surprised if he'd tried to peel Roger's skin off his bones.

And it just got more bizarre. Dimitri wouldn't help her carry him. In fact, he wouldn't really touch anything. Hope assumed it was because he'd poof whatever he touched. The glow in his palms had taken a while to recede, and he hadn't touched jack shit until it was completely gone. He hadn't spoken, either.

Ciaran almost bled-out in the car, but thankfully, Hope had packed a med kit and was eventually able to slow the bleeding. He was unconscious the entire drive and mumbled incoherently in his forced sleep. Hope was covered in his blood. Her hands, her clothes, even her face. But Ciaran was stable, and her new clothes smelled like Bounce.

Ciaran had just snapped, like the idiot he was, and then Hope noticed the pain in his leg. In all the commotion, they'd lost him to that prick.

The pain. She'd been able to use it to find Ciaran, his wound an excruciating LoJack.

With Dimitri running the show, she'd been a glorified dowsing rod. He practically had to shove her along too, since the closer she got to Ciaran, the more her thigh throbbed. She could barely think, let alone fight, and it pissed her off. The whole thing was a shit show.

"He should wake up soon." Gallo's voice made her jump.

"Oh, great. Thank you."

The room went silent apart from the beeping and breathing.

"Are you alright? You seem off." His gentle concern was both comforting and annoying.

"Long night."

"Apparently. I don't want to put my nose where it doesn't belong, but . . . whatever you guys are doing, be careful. I don't like to see you guys injured all the time. I would just come over for a beer if you miss seeing me. Plus, at least from the outside, it seems like this situation could get out of hand fast, and those are very hard to reattach."

"Ha, well, it should be over soon."

Gallo nodded, obviously not convinced, and packed up his supplies. He explained to call him if needed and that he'd be back tomorrow to check on Ciaran.

He would wake up soon. And just what exactly was she supposed to say?

Hope sat there, dragging her fingers up and down the raised sections of her chair's arms. The cushion squeaked every time she moved and that was quite a lot, thanks to her anxious position switching. *Wake up soon, my ass.*

She closed her eyes and leaned back. Ciaran had been so reckless, and now she was panicking about whether he was okay. How could someone you cared about drive you so crazy? Even when she'd left her clan, Hope was never that reckless. He had a score to settle, sure, but . . . *Ugh.*

Controlling emotions had always been her bread and butter, easy as pie. Now? Ha. What fucking use were all these feelings, anyhow? They didn't make her a better fighter, or navigator, or tactician. As she weeded through the mental garbage that consumed her brain, Hope was left with a rather unsettling question. *To bond or not to bond?*

It was the only major decision she'd had to make in, well, ever. The responsible, feeling adult she was not, and she wasn't always enjoying this change. Hope wanted to scream but given her current surroundings, she decided not to. She wanted to kick the damn chair she sat in and wake up Ciaran's stupid ass and beat the shit out of him for almost dying on her.

The sheets rustled, and Hope looked over to see Ciaran attempting to sit up.

"Want some help?"

He looked up and smiled, flopping back down on the bed with a sigh. With his eyes closed, he said, "I thought you were asleep."

"Nope."

"Well, I see that now."

Hope stood up, her back cracking loudly, and walked to the med bed. She was starting to get used to this room, the whole house, really. It was weird. She helped Ciaran scoot back, and they both hissed as his leg kicked up a jolt of nerve lighting. They'd gotten him mostly upright, so it would have to do.

"Thanks." He paused for a second. "That doesn't really cover it. I'm sorry . . . for everything."

"I know you are." Hope stared down at her hands. Unknowingly, she'd reached out and taken his.

"I really fucked up."

"Yeah."

"I don't know how to move past it. I keep thinking I have it under control and then, I see Roger, and I totally lose it."

Hope couldn't think of anything new to say. She'd already told him everything she thought he needed to hear. It wasn't making a difference. "Keep trying."

"Yeah."

It got very quiet, and Ciaran squeezed her fingers. His thigh burned and his lower back hurt. There was a mild headache from dehydration too. It all weighed down on her, pressing against her skull like a vice.

Ciaran broke the silence. "Was Alex here?"

"Yes, he sewed you up. He'll be back tomorrow." Hope tried to perk up a little.

"Did he say I could walk?"

"A little, why?"

"I need to pee."

They both chuckled. She looked up at him and his eyes said volumes. He was trying, but it'd be a long process. *How long though?*

"I can get you there, but then you're on your own."

"Deal."

The trip to the bathroom was horrific. She almost dropped him twice, and it had to be one of the longest piss breaks of all time. Hope got Ciaran back to the bed, and he looked immensely pleased with himself.

"Damn, that felt good, but now I'm exhausted. Yet another bonus prize of a gunshot wound."

Hope smirked. "Wouldn't have happened if you kept your cool."

"Am I gonna live this down, anytime soon?"

"Nope."

"Fair enough."

"You just . . . It's frustrating. Not to mention, actually painful for me, too."

"I know. I'm very sorry." Ciaran gave her hand a squeeze.

"Look, don't take this the wrong way, but I'm going to go lay down. I wanted to make sure you were okay, but I learned something at the penthouse. If I'm farther away from you, I don't feel your pain as much. And without the aid of morphine, sleeping last night was near impossible."

Ciaran looked like he'd been shot again. The guilt almost hurt as bad as his leg. This was so fucking hard. She just wanted a nap, why should he make her feel bad about it?

"Okay. No, really, you should go. You need sleep, too." He shook his head and patted her hand. Damn him for being so nice about it. *Why is this so complicated? I never had to approve naps when I was alone. Damnit.*

"You sure? I don't want you to be mad or something. Just tell me if you don't want me to go."

"Really, it's fine. I want you to sleep, and if you can get away from the pain a little, then please do."

He seemed okay enough, so Hope just nodded and smiled. She leaned down to give him a hug. Their mystical bond tugged at her, and she bit her lip while he couldn't see.

"Call me or text if you need anything." Hope patted the phone on the small table when she stood up.

"I will. Now go before I force you to rub me feet."

"Gross. I'll check on you in a few hours, okay?"

"Okay."

The door was cold and heavy in her hand. It closed quietly behind her, and she walked the two flights up to the attic like her feet were made of lead. The metal steps echoed around her in the open hall on the first floor. She prayed Dimitri would be nowhere in earshot. The attic had a TV and watching something pointless to distract herself sounded perfect.

She'd found it when Gallo had been working on Ciaran. Hope had to get away from the pain. The room was clean and cozy too. There was a bed tucked into the corner, and the walls were wood and unfinished. An angled window let in light from outside. Hope could flick on the boob tube and enjoy the flashing images. She switched it on, wishing for the resolution of her old television.

It only got basic cable, but Hope found a *Die Hard* marathon. Bruce was learning who had broken into the building and captured the hostages. Hope remembered the first time she'd seen the movie. How she thought it would've been easier to just bomb Hans Gruber, hostages or not.

She got comfortable, wrapping herself in a quilt. Being cold was becoming one of her least favorite sensations. Focusing on the screen, Hope watched things explode, Bruce crawl through an air duct, pull broken glass out of his feet, and completely flip his shit when he realized Mr. Gruber had his wife. Well, ex-wife.

Hope didn't get that bit when she was younger, or BC as she was now referring to it. Before Ciaran. She thought it was stupid to risk yourself for some woman, but now . . . Hope could actually see herself doing the same. Talk about scary. She swallowed hard.

Is that what she was expected to do, risk everything, even die? Hope had no desire to die, and she was a little pissed that she was supposed to be okay with it.

"Why doesn't he just stop getting shot?!" Hope yelled at the TV.

It was by far the weirdest shit she'd ever done. Venting to an electronic device, contemplating her death, feeling sorry for a fictional character, flying between angry to sad to missing Ciaran even though he was down fucking stairs, and then all the way back to angry again. Hope was going insane.

Suddenly, she was hyperventilating, and it was a million degrees. Everything looked like it was underwater, and her nose plugged up. She was crying. No, actually, she was bawling. It was uncontrollable. She sat there on the antique bed and became a demon waterfall. It must have gone on for twenty minutes, and then stopped. Most of her just calmed down, except for her stomach which was beyond empty. Dear Maker, Hope wanted a steak.

"What the hell was that? I have no control over these useless emotions."

Hope took a few deep breaths and stretched. Somehow, crying made her head and back ache. When she stood up, the room spun. *Man alive. Guess I'm hungrier than I thought.* The first few steps to the door were less than stellar, and Hope had to hang on to nearby furniture.

Thankfully, the kitchen seemed to appear magickally before her. The gleaming, silver refrigerator a beacon of delicious glory, and something smelled amazing. Was it the golden loaf of bread waiting expectantly on the counter or the Granny Smiths in the bowl next to it? Both?

"A hunk of cheese would make this."

Hope opened the fridge and dug in the dairy drawer. She found extra sharp cheddar and Havarti, so she took both. She sliced big chunks of each block, grabbed a couple of apples, and used a giant serrated knife to cut up the bread. Hope plopped it all on a large plate from under the sink and covered it with a cloth. She was so damn excited to eat, she almost didn't bring anything to Ciaran. But, her brain remembered that he hadn't eaten, either, and it really would be the "right" thing to do.

As she walked to the med suite, Hope decided the layout of the house was all wrong. There should be bathrooms every ten feet. *I've got to pee like a German racehorse.* Her full bladder squeezed with every step and at some point, she'd dropped a piece of bread on the floor. *Fuck it.*

Ciaran was awake when Hope got there.

"Hey, hungry?"

"I was just about to call you." Ciaran smiled and set his phone back down.

"Well, ask and you shall receive. I brought bread, apples, cheese, and the overwhelming desire to urinate."

"Ha. How about you go, then, and I'll set up the food?"

Hope agreed. "You know it was never like this when I couldn't feel. I just sort of went when I figured I should. This sucks donkey nuts."

Ciaran laughed, and she set the food down on the bed. It seemed like forever before she finished, and she got woozy again when she stood up off the toilet.

When she came out, the food was laid out enticingly on the table, which Ciaran had moved between the bed and the extra chair. Hope sat down and folded her legs under her on the flimsy seat. She looked down at his leg and stared at the bandage.

"It doesn't seem bad. Is it bugging you?"

"Oh, no. I was just thinking."

Truth, she was thinking. About how reckless he was and how he almost got himself killed and how it was mostly her fault. If she'd never gone to his place, if she'd never met him, none of this would've happened.

"Are you gonna eat?" Ciaran had started and looked so very happy to have food.

He was such an idiot, but apparently, she brought that out in him.

Before her, he'd never run off half-cocked to kill an old boss. But who knew? Maybe he had. She didn't know. She didn't know *him*.

At once, the food didn't look so great, but she had to eat. Hope put a couple pieces of cheese in her mouth but couldn't swallow right away. The flavor just melted onto her tongue. The taste didn't seem right.

Leave him.

Hope almost choked on the cheese. Did she really just think that? Some part of her knew it made sense. Ciaran wouldn't risk himself for her anymore. She wouldn't have to feel all this pain. It'd be so much easier. But there'd be no him, either. None of this team stuff. No asking for permission. No backup, no partner. *Fuck it all.*

Hope finally swallowed. She could take care of Marcus and be gone in a matter of days.

Making a decision seemed to settle her stomach. If she worked really hard to convince herself it was the right one, which took longer than it should, she could eat.

When all of the fuel was consumed, Ciaran laid back. His color was back, and she had to admit that his leg felt better, too. That Gallo was a miracle worker. *I'm distracting myself. Damn, it was almost working. But I'm really no good for him.*

"I needed that. I feel like a million bucks. In fact, I think I can make it to my own bed."

"Okay. Let's rest there for the night. In the morning . . . we can talk about what to do next."

Hope forced a smile. Ciaran should have a good night's rest, at least. He wouldn't see the benefit of her absence right away. Hope couldn't deny that or the fact that she was thrilled to be returning to the land of non-feeling. It'd just be so much easier, and easier was good. Right? She wouldn't feel, wouldn't have to compromise. She liked to lead, and now, she could again. But then, he smiled at her.

A goofy, satisfied grin. The one he wore after sex and apparently, after food. He was so beautiful. He was so infuriating. Every inch of her was more alive when he was around. It sang with energy and . . . fragility, too much fragility. *If he could just listen to me and let me take care of this. Yeah, not gonna happen.* Ciaran was too proud, too stubborn, and too angry.

How were they supposed to be "meant for each other?" It was too difficult. The reality was she'd been right. It was just chemical. *Then, why does it hurt so badly?* Hope dismissed the thought. After all, she was still in the grips of *omaeriku*. She would end it in the morning. It was better for both of them.

*

The night came soon enough, and after helping Ciaran to his bed, the two of them decided to go to sleep. Only one of them was successful at that.

The silence made Hope's thoughts loud and unrelenting as a jackhammer. She knew she wouldn't sleep, but she didn't expect the upset stomach. It churned and churned until she was so nauseated she had to walk around. Upon a successful breaching of the bed, Hope went out into the hall and headed for, well, she didn't really know.

The house was so quiet as she paced. Her legs got tired from the numerous circles. Maybe it would be enough to get her to sleep? Even if she was still nauseated and so bloated she looked like a cow.

But her brain still churned. Their connection was a liability for both of them, and she would protect them both by getting gone. She'd promised his sleeping figure it was for the best.

Hope repeated the mantra over and over. *Safer, stronger, safer, stronger.* As she crawled back into the warm bed, it was her last conscious thought. Sleep finally claimed her, Ciaran's hand on her arm.

*

The nausea was back with a vengeance. This time the more she moved, the worse it got. She couldn't decide if she was hot or cold either. Hope kicked the blankets off, only to start shivering moments later. Her abdomen was swollen, the pressure making the band of her panties too painful to stand. She reached a hand down to hold the elastic away from her, and though her body liked that, it didn't agree with the movement. She barely made it to the bathroom.

The good news was once she puked, she felt way better. In fact, now, she was hungry. Dear Maker, her stomach pissed her off. Hope straightened and walked to the sink. She swished around a mouthful of water. With a quick glance in the mirror to fix her smeared mascara and pull her hair up into a ponytail, Hope went back out to the bedroom.

Somehow, Ciaran managed to sleep through the whole thing. He was *so* helpful. Hope went to the smaller kitchen on the lower level. She didn't want to risk seeing Dimitri.

As Hope dug through the cupboards, she heard nothing above her. No sounds of the asshat making fried liver in squid gravy. *Ugh, so gross. Come to think of it, though, I haven't seen him since we got back. Not my problem.*

Hope found some Bisquick in the pantry that wasn't quite expired and there was a bottle of Aunt Jemima's in the fridge. With a frying pan, some butter, and the batter ready, Hope cooked up a stack of flapjacks. Unfortunately, as she watched the third pancake turn golden in the pan, Hope couldn't bring herself to be hungry.

The smell wasn't it. The perfect circles of yellow fluffing in the pan looked beautiful, but all Hope wanted to do was scream. She wished she'd never taken the hit. Hope flicked off the stove, put the ingredients back in their respective places, and threw out the pancakes. It was like she'd never been there—clean and empty and quiet.

Hope looked at her shaking hands and sighed. She'd never cared about food or got sick to her stomach or cried. This was all happening because of Ciaran and her curse of a legacy. He pushed his face right into her life and changed everything. *Damn him. Damn myself.*

Hope was about to boil over. She needed to leave before it got any harder. The mantra repeated again. *Safer, stronger, safer, stronger.*

The room was still dark, and Hope assumed Ciaran was still asleep. Hope stuffed the few clothes she had inside a duffle on top of some guns; she'd need those, too. After all, Marcus wasn't going to shoot himself. As she slipped on her shoes and zipped up her bag, Hope looked back at Ciaran.

His back was to her, and she thought of the scars. He'd be safer, he had to be. Hope's eyes began to burn, and her heart drilled in loud, hard pumps. A tear slid out. Hope quickly wiped it off her cheek and took a shuddering breath.

"I hope you understand this. I'll take care of Marcus, just take care of you. It's what I'll be doing. I . . . I knew I'd be bad for you. I'm . . . this wasn't going to work. It couldn't. . .. Bye."

The sound of her voice barely broke the air.

Hope closed the door behind her and jogged up the stairs. She walked to the rear of the house where the large kitchen was. She'd need food eventually. Hope noticed it was untouched. Dimitri never did cook. Considering that according to him, only a crazy person gets between him and his breakfast, she assumed he was sleeping.

Hope put the duffle on the counter and began to toss a few apples inside.

"You weren't gonna say anything."

Hope froze, and her stomach hit the floor. Ciaran's voice ripped into her chest. She couldn't believe he was up. This was exactly what she was trying to avoid.

"Just go back downstairs. This is the right thing to do." Hope zipped up the duffle and slung it over her shoulder. She had to get out.

"Hope, you can't—"

She had to face Ciaran; the exit was right behind him. "Actually, I can. Look, this is better for both of us. It was fun, sure, but who are we kidding? I don't do relationships."

Hope started for the entryway, but Ciaran didn't budge. She shoved past him and nearly made it out.

"You wanted this. Why are you running away? I felt it. I felt how much you cared. Don't say you don't do relationships just 'cause you never have." Ciaran's eyes were begging for something, but she just couldn't.

"I . . . I'm sorry, but no. I didn't feel anything. I liked the sex, but that's all it was, sex. Don't read into this. You barely know me."

"I know your feeling for the first time, and it scares the hell out of you. I know this bond isn't something you can shrug off. I know you're stronger than me, and I know it makes me feel better, like I can do this. I know this is more real than anything either of us has ever known or expected or prepared for."

"Well, apparently, I don't do real, either. I'm leaving."

Ciaran was quiet for a moment, but he clenched his fists.

"You're such a fucking liar." Ciaran glared at Hope. His dark brows pinched together in a nasty scowl, and Hope forced herself to swallow.

"Ciaran, fuck off. I know myself better than you do. This can't work."

Hope tried to push past him again, but Ciaran grabbed her shoulders. The pain in her arms was nothing compared to her chest. He was too close, and Hope couldn't breathe.

"No. Don't you dare. You're not running from me. No more quitting. You say you never back down from a fight. You say you always get your target, but make you push for something real, something good, and you run like a coward. You don't have to act so strong. You don't have to do everything alone. Not everyone will leave you."

His fingers dug into the flesh of her biceps. Hope's eyes burned.

"Let go of me, Ciaran. We're done. I'm not quitting because there was nothing here that I felt attached to. You're wrong about me, about you. Clinging to me like a pathetic lovesick child. I don't need your bullshit, telling me I'm not living, and you know I want this. What a joke. I've got everything I need right here." Hope pointed to her chest. "I'm more than enough. I don't need some fucking savior to make me feel whole. You do.

You need a fucking army to lift all your baggage, and I'm sick of it. Pawn your problems off on someone else. I'm done."

Hope threw Ciaran off her, and he fell into the door behind him. Hope could feel the round edges of the handle stab her in the back, but it was nothing compared to the look on Ciaran's face. She turned back to the rest of the house and left through the main door.

Hope all but ran to her car, nestled in with Ciaran's Vic and Dimitri's old beater. For a second, she wanted to turn and see if Ciaran would chase after her, but the cold sweat returned on the back of her neck and her heartbeat echoed in her ears.

Hope forced back the desire to sob and let a feeling of numbness crawl up her spine. It was an old habit, pretending, faking, and she would do it again. Sensations would dull. And numbness was her drug of choice. Pain and fear could be ideas again.

The duffle bit into her shoulder and her back burned. *Ignore it.* As Hope got past the cars, there was a sharp pain in her side and knuckles. Ciaran's pain. *Ignore it.*

Hope kept going, and the sensations did dull. She couldn't take her car; people would recognize it, so she just kept walking. In her head, Hope counted. When she reached five hundred, she could barely feel anything.

Hope found a small car at the side of the road and broke the window. After she hotwired it, she sped down the highway going north. Sensations dulled even further.

"Safe. Alone. No ties. No people. No things."

Hope repeated it over and over as she watched the yellow centerline of the highway pass under her car. *No people, no things, no people, no things, no things, no . . . thing . . . nothing.*

NINETEEN

The burn in his back started to fade, but it was replaced with a burn in his chest. His stomach acid churned, and Ciaran paced the kitchen floor. Hope had just left. What the hell was he supposed to do?

He was about to start after her, but he heard Dimitri come out of the room he'd been using. Ciaran needed a second opinion. *Kiss her, beg her to stay, yell at her. It's a tossup.* But he needed her back. So fucking what if she was convinced this wouldn't work. He'd change her mind.

Loud footfalls approached the room, and Ciaran was actually glad, for once, that Dimitri was sticking his Russian nose in his business. He hobbled as he circled the kitchen, his spine did not like the door right now. Dimitri was walking slower than ever, and Ciaran leaned back against the sink.

"She felt that. Damn her. Ugh, fuckitall, I care about you, Hope." Ciaran wiped his hands over his face and then ran them through his hair. "Dude, I need your help, bad. I know I'm whipped, but I gotta get her back."

Ciaran walked toward the hall since Dimitri was a fucking snail today. When he looked up from the floor, Ciaran stopped in his tracks.

"I think you will need to find someone else to help. Mr. Romanov is indisposed at the moment."

Marcus. Ciaran cursed under his breath. He breathed shallow. His muscles tensed. It was like he'd been punched in the gut and the face, simultaneously.

When he saw blood on Marcus's sleeve, Ciaran could barely keep his tone level.

"What did you do?"

"To Mr. Romanov? Do not fret, love. I will be having so much more fun with you. Ciaran, my boy, you have been quite the thorn in my side, as of late. Tsk, tsk, you know what they say. Naughty boys must be punished."

Marcus smiled, and Ciaran forced down the nausea. It wasn't the first time he'd heard that.

"How'd you find this place?"

"You know that bullet my assistant shot into your leg? It was equipped with a tracer. It really is the best way to hunt and track an animal." Marcus chuckled. "Now, where did my assassin go? I really must have a discussion with her about performance."

Ciaran folded his arms over his chest. "Long gone. You scared her away."

"That simply is not possible. Our little demon is not that smart. Besides, why would a woman who cannot feel pain be scared of me? Silly boy, you really cannot lie to me."

Everything about him made Ciaran's skin crawl. But Marcus didn't know things had changed for Hope, and he wasn't going to.

"Do you see her? I don't. She's not really a team player. She probably just cut her losses and bolted."

"She will have to be tomorrow's problem. For now," Marcus put a hand in his pocket, "I will deal with you."

Before Ciaran could dart out of the way, two sharp claws bit into the flesh on his side, shocking him. He couldn't control his muscles and fell to the ground. The waves of electricity bit through him and sent every nerve in his body into overdrive. His eyes forced shut, and Ciaran writhed on the floor. He struggled to look up as the shocks stopped. He saw black loafers close to his face. One planted on his ribs while the other shoved his cheek to the side.

"Well, are you not an eager bootlicker?" Marcus's voice was too loud, and apparently, Ciaran was drooling.

Ciaran spat on Marcus's shoes and saw blood land on the polished leather. Biting his tongue was another delightful side effect of being electrocuted. Marcus kicked him in the ribs and pulled on the trigger again. The shock restarted for an agonizing ten seconds, and Ciaran passed out.

*

The dripping noise was both a godsend and a curse. It gave Ciaran something to think about, but the repetition was maddening. He needed the distraction though; the ever-present pain was getting to him. Ever since he woke up,

Ciaran wished to pass back out. The metal cuffs that held him down on the table dug into his wrists and ankles; the table itself was raw and splintered, and of course, there was the rope around his neck that kept him down.

The light above flickered, and the plastic casing was yellowed. *Definitely not his digs.* Ciaran let his head fall to the side and started seeing glowing, red dots. The edges were orange and in the center was a green smudge. As seconds passed, Ciaran knew they would soon disappear. Except they didn't. Instead of slowly fading, the dots swam and spun.

They morphed into a long, curved line. Slowly it developed features: arms, legs, a torso. A face pushed out of the center and smiled. It had sweet, full lips, penetrating eyes, and waves of hair bursting out around it. *Hope.* Ciaran tried to sit up, but the rope put a stop to that.

She danced in front of him and reached out. Ciaran wanted to go to her. She shouldn't be here. It wasn't safe.

Hope's glowing form spun and leapt around the room until it suddenly changed. In a blink, Hope was bound. Her arms tied behind her back; her legs tied together. Her eyes pleaded for help, for release. She couldn't scream or speak. Just like him, she was trapped in Marcus's basement. Ciaran struggled against the cuffs and yelled for her, the pounding in his head ringing like unwelcome church bells.

He tried to break free, to reach her, but there was no freedom from the metal chains that held him down. Ciaran's throat was raw inside and out, and his eyes too dry to produce tears. Ciaran slipped back into darkness.

This time, when he woke up, the dripping had stopped. Ciaran was still chained down to the rough table, and scabs had formed on his wrists and ankles from fighting the cuffs. He eyed the room and found Marcus standing at the foot of the table.

"—listening, are you?"

Ciaran cleared his throat. "Sorry, what?"

Marcus crossed the space to him in two strides and backhanded Ciaran across the face. He took a deep breath and exhaled slowly before he spoke again. "I said, you are not even listening to me, are you? It is quite rude to 'zone out' when someone is speaking to you."

"Hate to burst your bubble, but I don't give a shit. Especially, since you're, in fact, torturing me. Talk about bad manners."

That earned him another slap, and this one drew blood. Marcus licked it off his fingers and walked a few steps away. Across the room, he'd set up another table with an array of heinous tools. Ciaran tried not to look, but like anyone else, he had to. That's why it was there, a form of mental warfare to spice things up.

Laid out in glistening horror were knives, pliers, a deep, red candle, a long whip with tiny, bladed tails, and a set of golden brass-knuckles. The worst thing he saw, however, was a small, brown jar getting warm above a candle. Marcus opened the ceramic lid and dipped a blade into the pinkish cream.

"That's it?" Ciaran faked a scoff. "I'd have thought you would have more medieval devices."

Marcus laughed. "So, it *was* you who broke into my Victorian. I did go back for my belongings. However, those are antiques. I would not want to depreciate their value by use."

As soon as the jar was open, the fowl, herbal smell of the Yohimbe flooded the room. Ciaran gagged, so he tried to breathe through his mouth and escape the smell. He had to close his eyes. Ciaran couldn't bring himself to stare Marcus down. It was happening again, and he silently begged for death. *I can't give him the satisfaction; I can't die easy.*

Marcus rubbed the scorching knife and cream on his skin. Ciaran held back a scream, but his body still reacted to the salve. He couldn't fight the change in his groin. The Yohimbe increased and drew blood flow.

While he tortured the most sensitive part of Ciaran, Marcus was deathly quiet. Everything was a blur of hot wax, whips across his torso, slices with knives on his legs, and nauseating manipulations done by teeth and hands. Ciaran fought to keep himself together, wishing to any god that might be out there that he could force himself to pass out. Marcus wouldn't let that stand. Every time Ciaran got close, Marcus lashed at him, the pain bringing him back around.

The exhaustion combined with the pain to create a swirling delirium where his brain tricked and toyed with him. Marcus controlled everything. Ciaran was just a marionette responding to the puppeteer's controls, and it only got worse.

Marcus caressed him. It made Ciaran think of Hope, of their time together. The feel of her warm skin beneath his fingers, the slick fusion of their bodies; it all danced in front of him, and it was all a lie. Ciaran wanted thick, brown waves cascading around him, not this ashy blond.

Ciaran couldn't hold back the scream. His body was a traitor. All it knew were sensations, not the origin of them. Marcus just laughed.

The ideas of Hope were ripped away and replaced with awful truth. She wasn't there. Ciaran was alone with Marcus Dentry, a toy in his control. When reality became even too much for his drugged body to ignore, Marcus started in with the pain again. Between each stroke of the whip, Ciaran saw Hope's face. He had to make it through this without giving in. Even if Ciaran was worthless to her now, at least he could protect her. *Keep her safe.*

"Where is the demon?"

Ciaran stayed silent. Marcus put on brass knuckles, and they glinted in the light. He cleared his throat and held his hands behind his back.

"Must we do this the hard way?"

Ciaran gave him nothing.

"Very well."

Marcus landed a blow to Ciaran's left eye. The socket nearly broke and the swirling black of unconsciousness stung him behind both eyes. This wouldn't be enough to make him talk. Ciaran prepared for the pain of shattering bones. He wouldn't say anything.

"Where. Is. The. Demon." Each word was punctuated by a jab to the gut, the final blow landing back on his eye.

It throbbed, the soft organ battered. Would he be able to see out of it again? Not that his life expectancy stretched much farther than a few more hours. He was losing blood from the slashes on his thighs and the whip wounds, the punches Marcus landed on each injury increasing the blood loss. Ciaran's lower ribs were probably broken, and it got harder and harder to breathe. He'd pass out soon.

Marcus held a candle flame to the inside of Ciaran's thigh. He shot up as much as he could and gasped as air returned to his lungs. The oxygen only made his senses wake up, and the burn was excruciating. The smell of burnt flesh wafted around him. Those nerves in his leg would never feel again.

"You are not going to fall asleep on me, are you? No, no, that will not do. But my, you are the muscular one. Have not been neglecting your exercise, have you?"

Ciaran's breath was ragged, and his good eye was wide in his face. He didn't know how much more he could take. God, he didn't want to die like this, but this madman couldn't get his hands on Hope. Unfortunately, Marcus seemed to see his life fading and switched to a softer, if more malicious, form of torture. *Dimitri, please find me.*

He thought of how he'd found Marcus, his hands bloody and coming from his best friend's room. Dimitri couldn't be dead, not because of his sorry arse. Ciaran gritted his jaw. Everything was Ciaran's fault. He was the reason Marcus had come; the reason Hope would be a bigger target now. If he ever got out of even one of the cuffs, Ciaran would snap Marcus's neck. At least then, he'd die happy.

Marcus stopped what he was doing. The grime and filth the prick left on Ciaran were seeping into his core, and the open wounds at his pelvis. Marcus walked back to the table. Ciaran just stared at the ceiling, but out of the corner of his working eye, he saw Marcus pick up a different knife. Marcus tossed it between his hands, breathing on it and wiping it on his shirt.

"You will not tell me anything about her?"

Marcus stroked his chin, then crossed his arms over the Armani button down and huffed. "You show such devotion to her. Can you not see that is all I wanted from you? Why choose a filthy, demon whore when a true, remarkable specimen lies before you?"

Ciaran honestly never thought about what Marcus wanted from the situation. The only thing he'd ever asked himself, over and over again, was why him? Ciaran never understood why, out of all the people trapped in the Inferno, Marcus Dentry, ultimate fuck-bag of all fuck-bags, had chosen him as his personal plaything.

"Ciaran, you look as though you have a question. By all means, ask away. I would never lie to you." He smiled and leaned in close to Ciaran's face.

Damn him, but Ciaran had to know.

Marcus laid his head on his arms and stared at Ciaran. Talking was exhausting, and Ciaran reached for the words. Marcus waited, and then proceeded to torture Ciaran's betraying body part, likely out of boredom.

"Why me?" Ciaran's voice was a raspy whisper.

"Speak up, Ciaran."

"Why me?" He growled out the words.

Marcus walked back to the table. He eyed the large blade in his hand and shook his head. His hands glided over the utensils and finally stopped on something small that Ciaran couldn't see. Then he came back and laid the tiny blade on Ciaran's stomach.

The room hung in silence.

In one smooth motion, Marcus picked up the knife and carved an M above Ciaran's groin between his hips. The cut bled in a slow stream, and Ciaran held his breath behind gritted teeth.

"Because you are mine."

Marcus flicked the end of the dagger up as he finished his etching. He smiled, touched his tongue to the bloody metal, and licked up the liquid, swallowing what he'd taken from Ciaran.

*

Marcus had cut on him for hours when he finally forced himself to stop. Either that or kill Ciaran on the first day. Then, he went up a staircase to "wash up for dinner."

Before he left, Marcus cleaned the slashes in Ciaran's flesh, applied searing antiseptic, and more of the Yohimbe cream to keep him unwillingly ready. Ciaran tried to break his binds, to escape, but the leather straps were too well made.

He was alone.

Behind the herbal stench was the distinct wet smell of old concrete and mold. Ciaran tried to focus his good eye in the dim light and inspect his surroundings. He could see the table and behind that a rough rock wall. *Underground, under a house.* The ceiling was made from beams of thick wood and spacers.

The construction was professional but old. He was most likely in another Victorian. Ciaran couldn't see the floor, but by the soundless steps Marcus had taken, he assumed it was dirt. And then he got dizzy.

He closed his good eye and filled his lungs. Behind his lids, Hope appeared. She was lying beneath him, and his hands were around her throat. Her eyes pleaded with him for air and still, he wouldn't release her.

Ciaran snapped his eye open.

He would never hurt Hope. The memory of a similar sight punched out his air. *No, that was different. Hope enjoyed it.* But how far would he have gone? Was he a monster just like Marcus? Ciaran screamed a breathy, strangled howl.

Ciaran slammed his head down on the wood. He couldn't think of Hope while he was like this. But she was driving away, flying down the highway. She'd be far away from him. *Safely away from me.*

He pinched his eyes shut and then opened one wide. Ciaran needed to examine his wounds. Depending on how serious they were, escape would be either extremely difficult or impossible. He struggled to take an inventory of his slashes and burns with one working eye. It wasn't good.

Ciaran was mangled. The slices on his arms weren't bad, three out of ten at most, but the gashes got worse as they neared his groin. Five or six out of ten. The M between his hip bones was really only a four but it felt like a million.

He looked at the burn on his leg. It was FUBAR. Ciaran was lucky Marcus cleaned it or he'd have died from infection. Although that eventuality still lingered. Marcus may not have killed him today, but he would, once he was done with him.

Boots thudded on the stairs. Ciaran considered faking unconsciousness, but Marcus would just find a way to wake him up.

"There now, so much better." Marcus had changed into a new, clean suit. It was dark blue, and he wore a bright red tie. Ciaran thought about spitting on it.

"Going out?" He didn't like the sound of his haggard voice.

"No, no. I would never leave an evening just peaking in excitement." Marcus walked to Ciaran's head. "There is so much more to be done."

He stroked Ciaran's hair. He tried to pull away, but the rope held him in place. He tried to face the other direction, but Marcus grabbed Ciaran's hair and pulled him back.

"No, bad dog."

A hard slap landed on Ciaran's nose. He snapped his teeth at Marcus's hands, might as well act the part. The grip on Ciaran's bangs stayed firm.

"Hungry?" Marcus threw Ciaran's head down, his skull hitting the wood.

"No particularly."

"Of course, you are. Strapping, young man such as yourself, you must have quite the appetite." Marcus went to the other table and reached beneath it. He pulled out a bottle of red wine and two goblets. The glasses were the same as in the safe house, one a twisted devil's face and the other a squid-faced demon.

"Ahh, it is such a good vintage. I always have a bottle on hand. I purchased every single one. Yes, that is correct. I own every last, magnificent bottle of Del Diablo. No one in the world, except for me, has been able to taste it. I track wine, and I knew this one would be something worth tasting. Oh, how I was pleased. The manufacturer had already bottled his harvest for the season, and I made him sell it all to me. Admittedly, he was a little disappointed that I would be his only customer, but I persuaded him to see things my way. And would you like to know why?"

Marcus uncorked the wine and poured some into each cup.

"'Cause You're an obsessive fuck?"

Marcus walked over to Ciaran's side and poured some of the wine onto his groin. Ciaran hissed as it worked its way into the healing M and down his scorched thigh.

"Now, now, you must maintain good manners, Ciaran. Although, you are not entirely wrong. I do feel a bit of a compulsion to own all my favorite things. I am not indiscriminate, however. All these items have a theme." Marcus paused to sip. "Ahh. I will give you another try to answer correctly. Can you tell me what the theme is?"

Ciaran attempted a shrug, but his bound wrists made the gesture ineffective. "Fuck if I know."

More wine poured on him, followed by a swift backhand.

"Disappointing." Marcus swirled the wine around in his cup, the one with the face of a devil, and sighed.

"Dante," Ciaran said it under his breath.

"What was that?" Marcus leaned down.

"I said, Dante. Your theme. Dante, the Inferno, the paintings, the face on the cup, you seem to be fascinated with the devil." Ciaran spoke as loudly as he could and Marcus flinched.

"That earns you a drink."

Marcus grabbed Ciaran's mouth and forced it open. He poured half the glass down his throat. Ciaran gagged, and it splashed all over his face. The wine stung as it hit his eyes and went into his nose. Marcus chuckled and walked back to the table. Some of the alcohol pooled in Ciaran's ears.

"Perhaps liquids are not your forte." Marcus set the cups down. "You were correct, however. I do have an appreciation for the Light Bringer. Can you blame me?" Marcus turned around in a fluid motion and stared at Ciaran.

He didn't answer. Ciaran knew this would be quite the speech, and he'd rather have it over with. Marcus leaned back on the table and crossed his arms over his chest.

Ciaran didn't know which was worse, the physical torture that pushed him to the brink of death or the endless prattling of Marcus's ridiculous speeches. His pain was at war with the disgust and rage swirling around in his head, and Ciaran could see that Marcus was pleased. It'd be so much easier if Marcus was just a brute, but the fucker had to be an educated sociopath.

Marcus began pontificating, speaking about his past fascinations and the enormity of his detailed research into the first Fallen. The prick loved the sound of his own voice almost as much as he enjoyed cutting on people.

"The majesty of his form and works is utterly impressive. To refuse to bow to the corrupted, inferior beings as the other angels did: He is remarkable. He used the demons as they should be used and fraught the failing humans' lives with endless, exquisite punishments in line with their crimes. You probably view him as evil, yes?"

Again, Ciaran said nothing.

"Yes, of course, you do. Like most, you are wrong, incredibly so. How is he evil for wanting to be free? He was supposed to accept humans and their filthy demon cousins as beautiful gifts, instead of the failed experiments they are. It is deplorable. Christians have it all wrong. Lucifer is not the brother of the demons; he is their ruler, their master. He uses them to serve his own purposes. I only hope that he sees my own works as the great homage I intend them to be. That he allows me to join his dark kingdom. To worship him and torment the lower souls for him."

Ciaran's resolve was failing. The prick was insane, and the words were out of his mouth before his rational side could stop him. "I'm sure you'd be welcomed to hell as his new bitch. He'd put you at the other end, screwing a twisted fuck. Too bad he doesn't exist."

Ciaran gritted his jaw and shook his head slightly. *Why did I say that?* He could see the change in Marcus's eyes. The cool calm faded to a deep fury.

"You will be convinced soon enough that the Dark Prince is real. Do I recall you saying you were hungry? I believe I do." The words were flat and emotionless.

Marcus's hands went to his belt and unfastened the buckle. Ciaran swallowed hard. He'd been such an idiot, letting his temper get the best of him. Ciaran knew what was coming next. His heart beat so hard inside his chest Ciaran was sure it would explode and burning nausea crept up the back of his throat. Right on cue, Marcus reached into a small wooden box and pulled out a small, metal device.

As Marcus approached him, Ciaran tried to hold his mouth shut, but Marcus forced open his jaws and wedged the device between his teeth. The bars held his lips apart, and the metal bit into his gums making his jaw ache. Ciaran started to drool and tried to will himself to pass out.

"Time for dinner."

Ciaran tried to choke himself on the rope around his neck, and the pain in his throat melted away. The world swam around him, and suddenly

Ciaran was drunk. In his mind, Ciaran went someplace else. He could stay there and wait for it to be over.

Marcus set upon him like a rabid animal, the ferocity enough to choke. Ciaran didn't even try to breathe and the ache from his jaw and throat barely registered through the near unconscious fog.

As the moments dragged on, Ciaran thought over and over, *Hope is safe. Hope is safe.* The sweet smile she smiled only for him, the artwork all over her gleaming skin, the pure white lock of hair amidst all the deep brown waves, she'd be safe.

Tears threatened to escape Ciaran's eyes. The frenzy continued, and Ciaran could feel Marcus's nails dig into his scalp. *Hope is safe. Hope is safe. Stay safe.*

The only reward for Ciaran's determination was the fact that Marcus was a short-lived participant. When it was over, Ciaran gasped involuntarily. His throat was raw, he continued to drool, and his eyes watered relentlessly. Ciaran's gag reflex was tested, and he silently begged to die.

When he could finally bring himself to swallow, Ciaran nearly threw up. Marcus walked to the table, zipped up, and reached for one of the brass knuckles. *Please, kill me.*

One hard punch to the face and Ciaran was out.

*

Ciaran woke up in a different position. He'd been flipped over onto his stomach and his head was strapped down to the table.

"Wakey, wakey."

Marcus stood before him with the black whip in his hands. The tails dangled from his fingers and made little clinking noises as the knives at the ends bumped into each other. Marcus wore only his white shirt now, sleeves rolled up to his elbows. *Hope is safe. Hope is safe.*

"Where is the demon?"

"Not this again."

Marcus slashed the whip across his back.

"Where?!"

Ciaran grunted as the bladed ends tore his flesh, but he didn't say anything. *Hope is safe.*

"Tell me! Stop protecting that whore!"

Five more slashes ripped open Ciaran's skin, and he could feel the blood flow in hot streams down his sides.

He didn't speak.

Marcus might just let Ciaran die before he got any information. Ciaran bit his teeth together and tightened his jaw as the pain seared his back like white-hot nails forcing his flesh apart.

"I am going to find her. Then, I am going to make you watch as I tear her open with my blade; long, slow strips of skin that I will peel off her bones. She will bleed to death, and it will all be because of you. If you would have had the decency to die when told, she would not have doomed herself."

Marcus must've used all his strength this time. When the whip came down, Ciaran had to scream. The knives cut into him, and Ciaran could have sworn they gouged his bones. Blood flung off the whip in thick droplets that fell on Marcus's pristine white shirt. His tormentor breathed in ragged gasps. Ciaran could bleed out. Marcus would have to stop if he didn't want Ciaran dead.

Ciaran waited for unconsciousness. He'd won this round.

TWENTY

Hope couldn't feel anything extra. She ached from sitting in a car all day, but every sensation belonged to her body. Unfortunately, unrelenting nausea was one of them.

It'd been hours, but still, her stomach churned. The sun was dropping low, and the orange glow made her eyes sting. She'd passed the border into Canada, it seemed like a safe bet. Gods, she was lightheaded, probably because she couldn't bring herself to eat. Of all the sensations she'd discovered, nausea was by far the most agonizing.

The lights on the highway were blinding. It was like every other driver on the road had their high beams on. The air in the car was tight and stuffy too, so Hope cracked a window. The rush of cool mist was amazing but driving in the rain sucked. The wipers could barely keep up. As droplets landed on her shoulder, Hope shivered. With a sigh, she rolled the window back up and immediately, the car was too hot again.

The glass started to fog up like her body was a furnace. Hope cracked the passenger side window and for a moment achieved a level of comfort. As the sun dipped down behind the line of trees, the headlights from the oncoming cars got brighter. Hope was half tempted to flash her lights to see if they really had forgotten to turn their high beams down.

Her headlights hit the space just in front of her car and started wobbling. The cars on the other side of the road disappeared into a tunnel of shadow. Hope clenched the wheel, shaking her head. The world's strange liquid movements didn't stop, and she poured sweat. The road was checked with black and gray spots. It was like a TV with bad reception. She had to pull over.

With the stolen car safely at the shoulder, Hope dug in the duffle bag for one of the apples. She forced herself to swallow the juicy chunks and tried not to gag at the sweet smell. Hope had to wait for the food to stay down before braving another piece. The spots in her vision cleared after the apple. Yeah, *low blood sugar.*

After another apple, Hope was impossibly tired. She reclined the chair and settled back. It wasn't comfortable, but her exhaustion was stronger than her desire to change positions. Dreams filled her sleep almost immediately, and Hope saw images of red smears dancing and mingling in the air. A deep red, the color of blood, swooped and spun in great spirals, while another smear of deep burgundy dashed quickly back and forth in straight angles.

As they met, the colors burst into a new hue. A brilliant, bright purple, the color of fresh orchids, shot forth. It swooped in circles and jutted in straight lines. Then, the images changed, all the smears of color pulled together and spun into a tight ball where they hardened into stone. Great cracks formed in the ball. The dark grey orb began to fall, faster and faster until trails of fire scorched the air behind it.

The ball shot through the rock and concrete and metal like they were tissue paper. When it seemed it had fallen thousands of miles, the stone crashed into a clear glass and shattered. The pieces exploded, billions of tiny particles flying out at the speed of light and slicing her skin. The blast targeted distinct parts of her body, her eye, her back, her groin, her inner thigh, seeking them out like a bullet.

Then, everything fell silent. Her injured parts died, and her heart thudded deep in her chest. One thud and then nothing. Whatever powered the ethereal body she occupied in this strange place at the bottom of the world couldn't or wouldn't go on. It just stopped. There was nothing but cold blackness and silence.

The sun beat down on her face and Hope wiped sweat from her forehead. She sat her chair back up, and Hope's stomach gurgled. The abstract, vague, and yet purposeful images still clung on behind her eyelids.

She wasn't faint anymore, but her intestines still protested every movement. She felt like an old lady too, all frail bones, and shaky knuckles. As she started the car and took off, Hope rubbed her eyes. She got a nose full of the car's cherry air freshener and gagged. *Nope.* Hope chucked the foul thing out the window, the sound of rushing cars like a metal concert in her skull.

"What's not messed up with me?"

Hope considered the fact that she might be sick, but how? Both Ciaran and Dimitri were healthy, at least as far as she could tell. Hope looked at herself in the rearview and frowned. Paler than normal, bags under her eyes that looked green and purple and brown. Yup, wouldn't be winning a beauty contest today. And she felt like shit.

What was she supposed to do if she was sick? Where would she go? Hospitals in this part of Canada were still human only.

The car rumbled beneath her. Where could she go? But as a car zoomed by her window, Hope noticed a green travel sign with three major cities on it.

"You've got to be kidding me."

Somehow, in her delirium, Hope had managed to find the highway she knew best. She was minutes from the turnoff for the abandoned road that led to her clan's land.

Hope cursed and punched the steering wheel. But, not being an idiot was a point of pride with her, and Hope knew she'd have to be if she didn't take the opportunity. She didn't know what was wrong with her.

"Damn it."

Against all the odds, Hope was getting a family reunion. Would her father still be alive? Would they even recognize her? *Maker, a drink would be nice right now.*

Hope was nauseated the entire trip, and it only got worse when she hit the driveway. Nothing had changed. The trailers, the people who hung around in their stained tank tops on lawn chairs, the sneers. It was exactly the same.

Hope got glares as soon as anyone saw her. She thought of her mother, of the pain she caused.

Eyes scanned her when she got out of the car. Fingers pointed at weapons still attached to her hips. Gravel crunched under her feet, screaming at her like a chainsaw carving a tree. Hope practically ran to her father's trailer, and the sight made her stomach drop to her feet. It looked so much worse than when she'd left, patched metal littering the sides.

Hope knocked and heard the floor creak inside.

"Comingah." Her father's voice yelled a croak.

When she opened the door and his eyes met hers, her *padru* backed up gasping. Hope followed him in and shut things up behind her.

"Maker! What are you doing here?" Pleased didn't exactly describe his reaction.

"Hello, *padru*. I hope you are well." Hope hated pleasantries but belittling herself would hopefully lessen his anger.

"Go. You didn't want to be here. Why come back? Go." His English was chopped, and his voice was a thin wisp.

"I need your help. I'm sick, I think. You're the only one I could think of who might know what to do. The Chakal have doctors, and right now, I need one." Hope walked toward him, and he flinched. "*Shendara*, father! I'm not here to start a fight. I need your fucking help!"

Hope collapsed to the old linoleum floor. She was hyperventilating, and the excitement made her stomach shrink and threaten to spill its contents. She tried to breathe through the churning in her gut. It made her eyes water. She rubbed the tops of her thighs with the heels of her hands.

Her father was gravely quiet. He stared at her like she was a specimen in a lab. When she was able to stand again, he looked at her quizzically like she was faking. *Seriously?*

"Father."

He crossed his arms over his chest and said, "Tell me your symptoms."

Hope sighed and pulled out a flimsy, metal chair from the kitchen table. She took a few breaths so she wouldn't give her father an impromptu shower.

"I'm nauseated and hot and weak. I've never felt any of it before, and now, all I want to do is sleep and throw up and sleep some more."

He gripped his chin, eventually sitting across from her and taking her pulse. "You are feeling these things?"

The question should've been so innocent. Her father would never let her live down the fact that she'd succumbed to *omaeriku*.

"Yes. That's not the important part. I'm sick and I need to fix it."

He gripped her wrist. "Mmm, your pulse is fast. Have you been sleeping?"

Her *padru* seemed completely unmoved by her statements. As if she weren't actually there. *Shendara*, she hated this place. "Yes, sometimes when I don't want to."

"Migraines?"

"What?" She'd never been sick. Didn't he remember?

"Headache? Lights and sounds too much?"

"Yes."

"You have *Wanyabas* time before you go, yes?"

"Yes . . ."

"Need blood sample. Need to check the blood."

Her father went to his bedroom and came out with a medical kit. He sat down at the table with her and had her put the inside of her elbow at his disposal.

"Too many things. Could be this, could be that. We will take blood and be sure."

Before the word okay could escape her lips, her father stuck the needle into the fattest of her blue-looking veins. The pain was only a quick sting, but she wanted to cry for some reason. Her father filled a small vial with her blood and stoppered it. He stood, motioning for her to follow. Stepping outside, a number of Chakal watched them as they went to the medic trailer.

Inside, the surfaces looked sterile and clean. They'd obviously spent any money they made from selling goods to improve the doctor's office. A man came out of the back and smiled at her father. His eyes fell on her. The brief conversation that took place between him and her *padru*, entirely in Chakalian, confessed that she was indeed his awful daughter and here because she'd gotten herself sick.

The doctor took the blood sample and disappeared into the back room. Hope sat in a small chair and waited.

Moments dragged on, and Hope couldn't keep her legs still. How the doc was even getting results was beyond her. Had they finally gotten the internet? She would've asked but thought it best to say as little as possible.

Finally, he came out and beckoned for her father. They spoke quickly, too quiet for Hope to hear, and then her father nodded and came back to her chair. "Okay, we are finished. Come back to the trailer. We have to get you settled."

"What?"

"Enough, you come with me, now."

Her father walked out and back to his home. Her instincts screamed to tell him to fuck off and leave, but if she needed some kind of treatment, this was the only place she'd get it.

She met him inside. "So? What's wrong with me?"

He wasn't paying attention to her. His voice was a low rasp as he rattled off instructions into the phone. From what Hope could hear, someone was supposed to come over and pack up her things. Her *padru* hung up and went to the back, coming out with a duffle.

"Put your things in here. You will stay with Elena 'til it is over."

"Wait, what? No. Why am I staying with anyone? What's going on?"

"You go on too much. You know a female's place. This is what is done. The *waekyana* must be isolated until the *braednas* has finished." Her father tossed her the duffle. "For your things. You will stay with Elena 'til done. Then, you can go as all the others have."

The burn crawling up the back of her throat nearly choked her. Her father was waiting for her to do something. Hope recognized *braednas* but couldn't place *waekyana*. What was going on with her?

"Father, I don't understand. What is wrong with me?"

"Not wrong. You have finally fulfilled your duty. You will provide the clan with a *yanyas*."

Hope fell to her knees, and the pain from hitting the linoleum floor barely registered.

She threw up at her father's feet, and a wave of heat rippled over her, making her shake. Hope knelt there on her hands and knees, gasping for air.

"What?" Her voice barely escaped her gritted teeth.

"You've made such a mess. Clean up, and we will go."

Hope looked at him and saw her *padru* cross over to the sink, wet a paper towel, and drop it in front of her. Hope wiped away the small pile of bile and crumpled the paper towel into a ball. Her father pulled her to her feet and shoved her to the basin. She threw the towel away in the garbage can underneath and rinsed out her mouth.

"Hurry now. Need to get to Elena."

Hope remembered where she'd heard the name. Elena was the midwife.

"I can't. This can't . . ."

"You will. You will do right for your clan. You have betrayed us enough. I will stand for no more." Some of the meat was back in her father's voice, and Hope could feel his cold glare on her back.

She faced him. "Betrayed you?"

Who said that? It certainly wasn't her. It couldn't be her; the voice was too quiet and small.

"Speak no more, *whonadana*. For *Shiahla's* sake, you use no *impraenata*. You instead take up with some *olanyala* and bring forth a mongrel. The *yanyas* will be ours, and we will raise a good child with no influence of the *madru*. While you are *waekyana* with *yanyas*, we will suffer your presence. Once it has arrived, you will be cast out again as a *radackla*."

Hope couldn't breathe or swallow. She was trapped in a limbo where she couldn't do anything with her lungs or vocal cords or tongue. Everything went dry, and she seriously contemplated a fifth of whiskey. She couldn't do that, though, could she? Dear *Shendara*, what happened? *Pregnant . . . I'm pregnant. . . .*

Her father's words hit her. Hope had been with an *olanyala*. An outsider impregnated her. She knew only one person who she'd slept with, Ciaran.

"I don't understand, you said it was impossible to be impregnated by a human!"

"A human! It is so much worse. A half-breed."

"You said it wasn't possible!"

He said nothing. It was all the answer she needed. Hope's hand went to her abdomen. All of this was too much, too fast. She'd just left Ciaran not even two days ago. Hope shook her head and turned back to the sink, hanging her head.

With her eyes closed, Hope tried not to be sick again. *This is a dream.* She'd wake up in her apartment about to carry out the hit on Ciaran. She couldn't be pregnant. Hope could *not* be a *madru*. As soon as the word entered her head, Hope thought of her own mother. She'd cut her off, they all did, and Hope did. She was taught to isolate herself. No connections, no *omaeriku*.

Yeah, that worked out. She'd still met Ciaran, and even though she'd fought against it with all her strength, they were bound. But she'd cut and run, drawn her line in the sand and turned her back on him. *To protect him. I protected us both. Ugh, I protected myself.*

Something in her chest cracked. Hope couldn't tell if it was real. It seemed like she couldn't feel anything. Right now, she wasn't even nauseated. Hope felt nothing. She was empty.

"You must nourish the *yanyas*."

Her father was talking to her and then, leading her out of the trailer. The wind came in gusts across her face, and she had to blink away tears. And then Hope was inside another trailer, Elena's home, the birthing center.

Elena took Hope to a dimly lit room near the back of her red-walled trailer. She told her to eat, placed some stale bread in Hope's hand, and stayed to watch her chew. Once the slice was gone, Elena forced a glass of ginger water down Hope's throat. She took the empty container that was somehow in Hope's hand and nodded. Elena laid her down in a bed, blew out the lanterns, and told Hope to sleep. So, she did.

*

Something dripped in the corner. The beat was relentless. Hope sat up, throwing the sticky sheet off her and stared around the room. As she looked around, the dripping sound evaporated.

"You are awake." Elena's harsh voice cut through Hope like a razor. The day before had, in fact, happened.

"Fuck. You scared me." She rubbed the sleep out of her eyes.

"Come. You eat now. No more language." With a swish of a curtain, Elena disappeared behind a layer of darkness. Her English was worse than Hope's father's.

Hope pulled aside a thick drape that hid the unwelcome sun. Light streamed in like water through a destroyed damn. *Pregnant.*

Hope walked over to a dresser she hadn't seen the night before. The mirror showed her reflection from head to knees. She turned sideways and looked at her profile, examining her stomach. What would the baby be like? There had never been a Chakal-human hybrid. Even the words sounding strange.

The Chakal weren't purebred demons, but they never mated with humans. She couldn't imagine how the child would suffer if raised by her clan. *My child.* Hope sighed and raked her hands through her hair.

And Maker, she was disgusting, all sweaty and needed a shower. Hope found a change of clothes in the shallow drawers. The loose-fitting men's t-shirt and black leggings were one of several. There was no underwear. Once she'd changed, Hope left through the curtain. Elena was waiting at a small table with a plate of eggs and bread, more of the bread she'd eaten last night. Hope put a hand over her mouth and shook her head.

"I don't think I'm up for that."

"Fine. Tea, then." Elena scurried to the kitchen and poured a cup of green tea. She set it down with a slam and walked over to the counter, folding her arms.

"You don't want me here."

Elena scoffed. "Not all so lucky. Some of us no have child. No *omaeriku.*"

Hope bit her tongue. Someone actually wanted this.

"You actually want *omaeriku*?"

Elena froze. She hadn't meant to say that, and her wide eyes were afraid. "I shouldn't . . . I sorry."

Hope shook her head. "Please, don't. Just tell me the truth."

Elena came and sat across from her.

"I don't know good words in English, say best I can."

"Alright." The tea burnt Hope's tongue.

"*Araj*, pain, we know is bad, very bad. Other feelings, hot, cold, hungry, wet, we know nothing. We only see with eyes, only live with bodies."

"I don't—"

Elena gestured around her. "Want more than this. Live, eat, sleep, die."

Hope stared at the surface of her tea, the light green lake in her cup. "I did, too. It's why I left. Now . . ."

At that, Elena left again, and Hope was alone.

The inside of the trailer was small and red, very red. All over the walls were women in various stages of motherhood, pregnancy, birthing, holding the new *yanyas*. Not an image of pain in sight. Hope remembered being told the cost of creating a life. She'd had pain, and there was more to look forward to.

As Hope ran to the room at the back, she was almost sick, but breathed herself through it. Everything around her seemed to move too fast and Hope just stood there for what seemed like years.

Then the pounding of her heart became the pounding of feet, and harsh voices at her door.

"Hope!"

Dimitri burst in and grabbed her arm.

"Let her be, demon!" Her father was behind him.

Hope's jaw fell. Dimitri wore the same clothes from when she'd seen him last, and dried blood matted down his hair on one side.

"What are you doing here?!" Hope's eyes couldn't get wider.

"I used some old contacts. Found the Chakal lands." He was out of breath. "Ciaran's been taken."

Hope's heart fell through the floor, and Dimitri stared at her expectantly. "Marcus?"

"Yes."

Everything in the room dropped away. Marcus had Ciaran.

"How?" Hope's voice was flat.

"I don't know. He knew where the house was." Dimitri scanned the room, "What the fuck is going on?"

"Demon, go! Not for you here!" her father yelled.

Hope looked down at her stomach, the round curve she'd thought was bloating, bulging through the leggings.

Her father stepped between them. Hope couldn't speak.

"Hope, seriously. I need your help. You can find him."

Hope's *padru* looked over his shoulder at her. "Explain."

"My *jabalv*, he's been kidnapped."

"Not of our concern is human matter, not for us." He turned back to Dimitri. "You go, now."

"Father, *padru*, he is my *jabalv*. Shouldn't I protect him?"

Without looking at her, he said, "No protect. Must stay here."

Something pulled deep inside her. It was strong, and it demanded she leave, immediately. Hope looked down again at the small bump of life. She put her hand there and noticed something, a connection.

"No."

"Daughter?"

"You've already said that I'm a *radackla*, a traitor. Well, so be it. I won't sit by. I thought I could . . . But I was wrong, so very fucking wrong. I would've never come here if I didn't think I was dying. And you didn't even help me. This was such a mistake. This is one *madru* who will not be separated from her *yanyas*. Goodbye, Father."

Hope grabbed the duffle that sat atop the old dresser and pushed past her father, pulling Dimitri along.

She took a last look at the images on the walls. What had she been thinking? Hope shook her head. Apparently, the pregnancy symptoms had robbed her of judgment. Her heart pounded, and she remembered the last words Ciaran said to her. *Not everyone will leave you.* Hope reached inside to that connection with her unborn child. *I guess not.*

She ushered Dimitri outside the trailer and ran to the car waiting in the driveway. The POS was still running.

Hope stared over the roof of the car at her father. "Let's go."

*

Ciaran's kitchen was a disaster. There was blood on the ground and the back lock had been picked.

"Tell me what happened," Hope said.

"The night we got back, after Gallo left, I passed out. I heard my window open, so naturally, I went to check who was so desperate to see me. I woke up in my room, bleeding from my forehead, and you were both gone. I didn't know where else to look for you, so I figured I'd start with your family. How does this help?"

Hope sighed and put her head in her hands as she plopped down in one of the kitchen chairs.

"It's helpful because we know that someone faster than you learned our location. Marcus is human, so he must've had help. They must've tracked us, but we didn't see anyone that night." Hope was nauseated again and she took slow, deep breaths.

Dimitri nodded and then snuck a glance at her growing tummy. Hope had been avoiding any discussion about it, but it appeared that had come to an end.

"What?! Just, what?!" Hope tried not to smell the metallic scent of the blood.

"Sorry but come on. You're . . ." Dimitri sat across from her.

"Just say it."

Dimitri swallowed and couldn't meet her eyes. "Pregnant."

"Yes."

"And this is a new development?"

"Ugh, yes! I only just found out." Hope laid her head on the table.

"It's just that, weren't you like *way* smaller a week ago?"

Hope spoke without raising her head. "Women of my clan have a short gestational period."

"What?"

"We're not pregnant for long. Just like two months or so. Give or take a few days."

"Oh."

Hope looked up at him.

He said, "See, that info is helpful. 'Cause you like, look really bloated or something."

"Gee, thanks." Hope's head felt strange, and everything was wavy. "Fuck! I hate this." Hope stomped a foot down. "We have to find him. I have to . . ." Her voice evaporated.

"You have to what?"

"Apologize to him. We fought, before I-I left." Hope sagged.

"What do you mean?" Dimitri's voice was hard.

Hope didn't think she could handle one more person yelling at her, but if she really wanted to make this work, she needed the support of the best friend.

"I panicked. I've never felt anything before, and I'm not being metaphorical. I've never felt any sensation before I met Ciaran. It's part of female Chakals abilities. Then, fucking ***omaeriku*** happened, and I feel everything. Pain, heat, pressure, hunger, and I can feel Ciaran's pain, too.

Yup, another gift of the Chakal. Fuckers. And it was too much. So, I thought it would be safer and easier if I weren't around. I broke him down and I left. I wish I hadn't, but I don't know. I guess this is what regret feels like. When you can't physically feel, I think it messes with your emotions. I went to my clan. I thought they would help. They told me I was pregnant, and then you showed up."

Hope was standing now, and she finally let herself take a deep breath. Dimitri stared at her with wide eyes and brows up to his hairline.

"Okay . . ." Dimitri nodded. "So . . .wow. Damn, I'm trying to follow everything you just said."

Hope let Dimitri digest his fiber-heavy meal of words, and she sat back down. He watched her for a few moments. He tented his fingers and squinted at her. "So, I need to be clear about one thing."

"Okay," Hope said it quietly.

"Do you care about him enough to really do this?"

Hope breathed hard and swallowed. She stared at the house around her. She thought about the baby, the pain, pleasure, compromising, and tough conversations. She could still run. If she wanted.

Or she could stay.

She could hurt in every way possible. She could take responsibility for herself and for a tiny, new person. She *could* stay.

"I do."

"Good."

"You're okay with this?" Hope expected a bit of resistance.

"Hard to argue with a crying, pregnant demon."

"Oh, fuck." Apparently, her face had sprung a leak, and Hope tried to mop up the mess with her sleeve.

Dimitri laughed, and she punched him in the arm.

"I can still kick your ass." She looked at her tummy. "For now, anyway."

"Yes, you can. But don't, alright? I think you two should give it a go. I, umm, think he would want this, too."

Hope opened her mouth to question, but Dimitri shook his head. She couldn't help but chuckle a bit at everything. She'd gone from ruthless killer to sap in the space of a week. "I'm embarrassed, now. Also not a feeling I enjoy."

"Ever notice how that word actually sounds like, umm, bare-assed. Weirdly accurate."

Hope really laughed this time, and Dimitri took her elbow as she stood up and he said, "You look kind of good this way. And don't tell Ciaran I said that. He'll kill me."

"Ha! He's gonna kill me, first. I can't imagine he liked what I said."

"He'll get over it. Just show him your boobs. But, we need to find him first. Any ideas?"

"Yes, actually." Amidst all the nausea and hormones, Hope determined the only way Marcus had the opportunity to get a tracer on them. "We need to go down to the emergency suite."

"What am I looking for?" Dimitri pulled the metal tray back to its standing position. "And why does this place look like a bomb went off?"

"Marcus probably came down here looking for the same thing. We need to find the dish that has Ciaran's bullet in it."

It was in the corner, pushed up against the wall. Hope sat down on the bed with it in her lap, waiting for things to stop spinning.

"Don't puke on me, okay?" Dimitri held his hands up in front of her like it could stop the Linda Blair.

"I'm not. Get me a screwdriver and a pair of pliers."

"Okay. I guess I'll be right back."

Dimitri returned with the tools, and Hope took the pliers to hold the bullet still. It still had some blood on it.

"Roll that tray over here, would ya?"

Dimitri obliged, and Hope braced the nose of the bullet against the lip of the tray. Hope took the screwdriver and placed the flat tip in place with one hand and held the pliers in the other. She needed more hands.

"Hold the pliers. Please."

With her now free hand, Hope grabbed the metal spreader that lay on the floor, its head nice and flat.

"Just hold that steady." Hope remained focused on the screwdriver's round end.

Hope hit the tool with the spreader as hard as she could. The metal clanged near their faces. After two more attempts, the jacket popped off and the bullet's interior was a mess of wires.

"What the hell?" Dimitri released the pliers.

"Tracer round, more high-tech than usual. We can get an IP address."

"You can do that?"

"Well, no. Got any contacts?" Hope smiled.

"Sure, just 'cause I have a few, suddenly, I'm in with the mob or some shit."

"Dimitri."

"Okay, okay. We need to be fast. He isn't out at night."

"Seriously?" Hope giggled slightly.

"He's an Icarus."

"A what?"

"A demon who gets their power from the sun. They refuse to be awake when it's not up."

"Okay then." Hope shoved off the bed and they left.

Dimitri drove to quite possibly the worst part of Newborn City. Trash covered the streets, homeless sat in cardboard homes, and demon prostitutes were a staple on every corner. But hell, she'd become an assassin to escape her past. Was sleeping with people any worse? *Mommy, what do you do for work? Oh, honey, I kill people. Yeah, that's gonna be fun.*

"Hey! Hope!" Dimitri waved his hands in her face. The car had stopped facing a dirty, brick building.

"Sorry. Thinking."

"Well, we're here. Are you okay to fight?"

"Will I need to?"

"I don't think so, but frankly, bad shit seems attracted to you."

Hope met Dimitri in front of the building's metal door and put an arm around his neck.

"What can I say? I attract trouble," Hope squeezed, and Dimitri grabbed at the choke hold, "but I can handle it."

Hope released him, and Dimitri stumbled.

"Clearly." He rubbed his neck. "Now, Leo is kinda weird. He'll clam up fast if we push him too hard, okay?"

"I'll only step in if needed."

"Fair enough."

The door was more rust than steel, and it squeaked so loudly the rats in the alley stopped what they were doing. Once inside, the smell was overwhelming. It was so sweet, and Hope put a hand over her mouth. Among the various wires hanging from the ceiling, baskets of circuit boards, and industrial remnants of the acrylic factory, were orange slices, hundreds of them. Hope gagged.

"Oranges? Really?"

"Ever heard of an oriole?"

"The bird?"

"Yeah. The Icarus is a sort of bird shifter with a few specific traits. The bird likes oranges. It's all he eats. Well, and some insects."

Hope breathed through her mouth. "Gross."

"Don't tell him that," Dimitri went toward a door labeled 'office.'

Hope followed but still held her nose. Her sense of smell was in overdrive, and it all made her sick to her stomach. The office was messier than the front. Strange contraptions, dismantled computers, and at least twenty monitors decorated the room.

"Leo! Where are you!?" Dimitri shouted, turning in circles.

A blinding light engulfed the room and a man's figure was silhouetted against the glow. He descended with his arms held out wide, his black wings tipped orange.

"He's also one of the most arrogant bastards I've ever met," Dimitri whispered.

"Goody."

Once Leo landed, the light show ended. However, if that weren't enough, he was also shirtless and his long, golden hair draped over his shoulders. He still hadn't put his arms down as he walked to Dimitri.

"Old friend! What up!? Brought me a new project to distract me from this boring-ass city?"

He certainly didn't talk like the angel he pictured himself as.

"Actually, yes. Hope?" Dimitri took the tracer round, and Hope was glad to keep her distance. Leo smelled like the sickly, sweet citrus he survived on.

"You could've at least made it challenging." Leo took the device and folded in his wings. He walked to a desk with a three-monitor setup and a wooden stool.

"So, what do you want? Manufacturer, duplication specs, how to do it better?" Leo turned the tracer around between his fingers.

"The IP address of the origination signal. I want to know where it's sending the GPS data." Hope spoke from a distance. Her breakfast actually stayed down this morning, and she wasn't losing it now.

"Child's play." Leo dug around through the device with tweezers like he was digging for buried treasure.

He pulled out a tiny circuit board, and he put on magnifying spectacles. His eyes blew up behind them, and Hope stifled a laugh. A cord and some sort of adaptor connected it to his computer.

Leo's fingers flew across his computer, and a DOS screen pulled up the chip's data.

"Okay, owner's listed as one Dante Alighieri, dumb. IP address here and address is blank, of course." He leaned back, his wings rustling.

"What? There has to be something."

"It's encrypted." Leo's eyes were closed.

"Can you decrypt it?" Hope moved closer out of frustration and immediately regretted it.

"Duh. Who is this chick?" Leo pointed at her but spoke to Dimitri.

"This is Hope, and I'm sure she didn't mean anything by it." Dimitri took a deep breath. "Look, Ciaran's in trouble, and this could help him."

Hope paced with her hands on her hips.

"Well, no need to fear. Leo is here! Just let my program do its thing." Leo folded his hands behind his head and the orange smell got stronger.

Hope coughed and held her stomach.

"If she yacks, she's cleaning it up." Leo looked horrified by her queasy stomach.

Hope was about to go over to Leo and punch him so hard the stink would fall off when Dimitri stepped in front of her.

"This some Inferno bullshit?" Leo peeked up from his computer.

Hope raised her eyebrows at him. "How could you tell?"

"His fucking name says Dante Alighieri." Leo rolled his eyes. "That's the author of the fucking book."

Hope had the distinct impression that Leo didn't like her, and she didn't really care.

Dimitri took a step back and regarded his smelly associate. "Well?"

"Yeah, got an addy for you. Come on, who do you think you're talking to?"

Leo showed the address on a map, zoomed to the house, and Hope could see a black Mercedes parked in its drive.

"That's his car." Hope stumbled.

Hope knew that car; she'd ridden in it.

"Hope, we got him." Dimitri walked in front of her, face right up in hers.

"Yeah . . ." She was overwhelmingly tired and sick. "Maybe, a trip to the bathroom is in order." She needed fresh air.

As she left, Hope heard the blood in her ears and her stomach churned. She was definitely going to be sick. She burst through the metal door and ran to a giant, leafy bush. Hope heaved, and the contents of her stomach became the contents of the shrub. Dimitri was through the door and behind her moments later.

"You okay?" Dimitri stood behind her.

"No." Hope's tears flowed harder. "I can't do this. I'm constantly sick to my stomach. I'm tired and achy, and I'm fucking crying, crying! I can't handle anything. Smells are like ten billion times stronger, and I just want one mother fucking day where I eat my breakfast and it stays down!"

"Tough."

Hope's mouth dropped. "Excuse me?"

"You don't have a choice, right now. I know you feel like shit, but welcome to life. Most of us have to deal with pain all the time. So, woman up." He cocked a crooked smile. "I've had some experience with sucky gifts. We can't change it, and no I'm not going to tell you what it is. Don't ask. Now, take a deep breath and let's go."

Dimitri walked to the car and got in the driver seat. Hope wiped her face, took the recommended deep breath, and followed him in.

*

Hope watched as the streets flew by and the car made its way to the outskirts further west. Dense forest framed the highway. No one ever bothered keeping the woods back. As a spark of nausea bloomed, she forced herself to breathe it away. It was working pretty well until a slash of hot pain ripped through her back. Hope yelped.

"What?! Are you okay?!" Dimitri swerved.

"I don't know. There's pain. It hit my back like a knife. I . . . I don't think it's mine."

"Not following."

"I think it's Ciaran's. We're getting close."

"Not really. We're still twenty minutes out."

"Then, how—" Another slash. Hope grabbed her back and her stomach at the same time, "Son of a bitch!"

She looked down at her stomach, a human would look this big in their second trimester. Something moved inside her and Hope gasped.

She.

The thought came like breathing. The baby felt her father's pain, and Hope could feel her child's. Their gifts were connected, amplified by each other. But how? There hadn't been any *omaeriku* for her baby, but her *yanyas* was also part-human, and that combination of DNA had never been seen. Somehow, it had created a miraculously powerful, little . . . girl.

"Hope, you're freaking me out." Dimitri glanced back and forth between her and the road. "What's going down, chica?"

"It's her. It's the baby. She's amplifying my abilities. We're going the right way."

"Okay . . ." Dimitri nodded slowly. "How long?"

"Not far. Just keep going straight."

The trees flew past them in blurs of green, the melting images created pine-oak hybrids, and Hope was wracked with stabs of pain each minute. They were getting closer.

The twenty minutes passed, and the sensations intensified and pulled her to the left. The baby felt it too. *This is so fucking weird.* Hope swallowed. *Help me. Help me find him. Focus on Ciaran.*

"Left." Hope pointed and a rocky driveway appeared.

Dimitri practically slammed on the brakes and swerved to make the turn.

Gravel crunched under the tires of the old Crown Vic as they parked. The trees were thick and dark green. They were further north than they should be. There was a deep chill in the air, and the sun seemed far away. Had they crossed the border?

Hope saw no signs of life. No birds sang, no bugs buzzed, no wild creatures scurried. There was nothing.

"Something feels off." Hope cocked one of the pistols and held it at her side as they got out of the car.

"I know," Dimitri took a pair of handguns, "but what more can we do? We know he's in there." He checked the ammo, tucked a dagger in his boot, and locked up the car.

Hope nodded. "Keep low and follow me."

They crept along the forest floor, sticking to the shadows. Hope had to focus her breathing, each step making Ciaran's pain more unbearable.

When the Victorian came into view, Hope stopped short. The house was all black. The shutters, the drapes behind the glass, the shingles, siding, doors, and even the wood porch, like it had been dip-dyed in tar. It was . . . horrifying. Dead and rotten.

"What the fuck?" Hope whispered.

"He has a dramatic streak."

Marcus had overlaid pieces of Gothic architecture. This should've been a family's home, but there were hideous gargoyle-like creatures perched near the door and wrought iron filigree scrolled along all the edges. *Dramatic is an understatement.*

Hope surveyed the house. The only way for them to remain covered by the trees was to go in by the bushes under a second story window. Dimitri looked over, and Hope gestured to the site. He nodded.

Using the banister and the thick railing, Hope hoisted herself up to reach the bottom of the window frame. She used all her strength to pull up, and tumbled inside, rolling with the momentum quietly and protecting her stomach. Dimitri crawled in after her.

She opened the door to a hall, and her senses were flooded, like a motor she seized up. An herbal smell hung thick in the air, and Ciaran's pain was completely unfiltered. Hope fell to her knees.

"Hope. Hope, get up." Dimitri was firm and quiet.

"I can't. . . . It's too much." Hope squeezed her eyes shut and gripped the carpet. Below her, Ciaran was right below her. "Ahh, Dimitri." Hope couldn't help the volume. It burned horribly.

"Come on, Hope. Pull it together. You can feel how much he needs us." Dimitri's eyes were desperate pleas.

Hope met his stare, and the baby squirmed inside her.

"Okay, okay." She stood up and focused on her daughter.

Dimitri put a hand under her elbow to steady her, and they made their way down the hallway. The house held more red, more horrid sculptures, more depraved demons raping their human slaves in gilded frames.

Muffled grunts and screams leaked through the floorboards. Ciaran's strangled cries burned Hope's ears like acid.

Hope and Dimitri stepped onto the main floor. They hadn't seen anybody, but then something shot out at them, and they were electrocuted. They collapsed, shaking with pain. Hope watched shoes approach, and the pain stopped. Roger van Statton, second in command, loomed over them with a wicked grin.

"Motion detectors. Honestly, you didn't see that coming?"

Hope clenched her teeth. She'd been stupid, distracted, and Dimitri was unconscious. He took a lot more than Hope. She tried to pull the clamp out, but Roger kicked her hand.

"Patience. Mr. Dentry is on his way."

As if on cue, Marcus came up from the basement, shirtless and smiling.

"Sir, our guests have arrived. What would you like to do with them?" Roger polished his glasses on a handkerchief.

"Take Mr. Romanov to one of the cells. He will fetch a pretty penny and her?" Marcus put a boot on her throat. "This whore dies. I put so much time and work into training you, and how do you repay me? You steal things that do not belong to you."

Hope couldn't breathe. She clawed at Marcus's fancy shoes. Roger tapped him on the shoulder.

"Sir, may I suggest, otherwise. This one has something I want." Roger looked at Hope's stomach like a hungry hyena.

"What could this *thing* have that's worth her life?" Marcus pushed her face to the side using the toe of his Gucci's.

"She carries something that could be of great use to me."

"Ugh, fine. You finally have a toy to replace that Miyu, but you will let me use her, first. She needs to see who really owns Ciaran. Is that understood?"

"Of course, sir." Roger slunk away.

You'll regret keeping me alive.

Marcus grabbed her by both arms and lifted her off the ground. The pain of his grip was nothing compared to what she felt coming from Ciaran.

"First, however, something tells me that you will be easier to maneuver if you are . . ."

Hope assumed the next word was 'unconscious' seeing as Marcus raised his arm over her head and struck her. Hope bit her tongue on impact.

TWENTY-ONE

The web of points and cracks and edges in the rough, granite wall pushed into Ciaran's bad eye. Instead of the somewhat more comfortable lying position on the table, he was bolted to the wall, the granite cutting into his flesh. Ciaran was pressed to it face first, his wrists cuffed high over his head. His legs were stretched apart with his ankles chained to the rock.

The unfinished stone found each of his wounds and because of how he was chained, Ciaran couldn't help but lean into the abrasive surface. The granite spikes stuck into his skin like tiny nails with the fierce desire to slowly punch their way through his body, popping out the other side like flowers in the spring. Ciaran could feel them dig into his swollen eye, his elbows, his raw chest, his hip bones, the inside of his knees, and especially his groin. That hurt more than anything.

Ciaran tried to look down with his good eye. He could see his feet. They were dirty from the floor and leftover wax and blood and other fluids that had dripped down from between his thighs. He started to adjust in his chains to take some of the pressure off his wrists, but his choices were all bad. He'd either cut off blood flow to his hands or shift his weight onto tired, chained legs. He alternated between the two. Ciaran promised Marcus he wouldn't die easy, but god, he was exhausted.

Marcus. Ciaran's shoulders ached so badly it was difficult to move. The process of adjusting took at least five minutes or maybe five years? His perception of time was distorted, and he couldn't make heads or tails of how long anything took. *Heads or tails, such a weird phrase.* Why was he thinking about coins or words or the origin of such words? Etymology, his brain told him. The word for the study of word origins is etymology. *Fuck myself to hell and back, already.*

"Awake, I see." Marcus had slithered up behind him.

Even as malnourished as he was, Ciaran found the strength to tense up and hold his body tight. Images of the previous torture crept up his spine and made Ciaran grit his teeth. He shut his good eye, and Marcus came around to his side.

"No use playing possum. I know my good boy is awake. How are you doing this fine day?" Marcus rubbed his hand across Ciaran's hair, petting him, and then poked each of his bruises with a stout finger.

Ciaran jerked despite himself. Marcus chuckled at his small victories. He reached between Ciaran's legs and prodded the burn on his thigh. Ciaran yelped and grunted. Marcus continuing to laugh.

"Yes, I am doing quite well. Thank you for asking," Marcus went around to Ciaran's back and gripped a handful of hair. He pulled back and strained Ciaran's sore neck.

"Today will be very special, my boy." Marcus leaned in close. "I have decided to extend my hospitality. Up until this point, I have had all the fun. My, you are quite filthy, are you not? I can fix that."

Marcus released Ciaran's head and focused on the wax covering his groin, pushing Ciaran's hips away from the wall and forcing his weight onto his wrists and ankles. Marcus used his nails to pick off the hardened remnants of candle drippings. The skin under the wax pulled as it separated from his skin, and Ciaran winced as the pain rippled through him.

The last pull was long and slow. Ciaran could feel as each tiny centimeter of wax left his skin taking with it bits of hair and flesh. Marcus laughed, again, that damn self-satisfied laugh that made Ciaran want to rip his own ears off. Marcus slapped him, slapped the now raw and bloody flesh, then switched from his front to Ciaran's back and the slashes there began to bleed again.

As the bastard went to work once more on the fresh injuries from the wax, little flecks of blood splashed onto the wall in front of Ciaran and onto Marcus's shirt. It stung horribly when Marcus reached lower and manipulated him.

Ciaran tried to think of anything else. The same image from the previous onslaught came to him. Hope was safe, driving away in a car, a nice brown car, with her hair billowing around her from the open window.

Ciaran had to force himself to stop. He couldn't think of her when someone was using him like this. But then Ciaran's mind conjured up images of his kills deep in the belly of the Inferno. He saw Ireland. He saw Marcus's past torment blend into his current assault. Ciaran's stomach twisted, and he forced back a gag.

Marcus paused to shove Ciaran's face into the granite wall; the battered eye burned and throbbed. He fought back, but Ciaran's strength had diminished, not eating for however long. His legs began to shake, and he couldn't pull his head back.

"Cannot find the strength, can you?" Marcus released his grip. "Good. This should be easy for me. I want to try a little exercise."

Marcus backed up, and Ciaran tensed. It wasn't the first time he'd heard the words. Ciaran shivered. Marcus walked to the table of tools, and Ciaran caught a whiff of the horrid cream. He swallowed hard.

"You have been quite resilient to every attempt I have made to get you to reveal that demon whore's location. Not one slip up." Marcus saturated Ciaran in the Yohimbe. "You must still believe that she is special, powerful. You are, of course, wrong."

Ciaran tried to block out his voice. Hell, even focusing on the pain was better. Ciaran's head lulled to the side. The weakness made him furious. He'd gone without food and lost so much blood.

"You are not paying attention again!" Marcus slashed him with the whip.

The ripping sensation forced Ciaran back to reality. He grunted, and the force of the strike pushed him into the sharp wall.

"Did it occur to you that I'm suffering from blood loss and focusing on your grating voice is not my greatest concern?"

Marcus released the whip again, this time hitting high on Ciaran's back by his neck.

"Try harder." Marcus set down the whip and began pontificating again.

"I believe I have been going about this the wrong way." Marcus had been mostly out of his line of sight but now he leaned back against the smooth section of wall to Ciaran's left.

The bastard talked with his hands as he unbuttoned his shirt three holes down and rolled up his sleeves. *Time for the dirty work.*

"Obviously, you are physically broken, but you are not, however, compliant." Marcus unzipped his pants but did not remove them.

Ciaran closed his eyes on reflex. The mantra started in his head again and his muscles twitched with anticipation. *Safe. Sound. Safe. Sound.*

"So, what say we try something more . . ." Marcus moved behind Ciaran and whispered close to his ear, "personal."

Ciaran wouldn't let himself scream. It was happening, again. And again, there was nothing he could do about it. He stared at the floor, and a tear slid out the corner of his battered eye. *Don't come back. No, Hope. No . . . hope. . .*

*

Ciaran couldn't tell how long he was out. He had dreamed Marcus had devoured the bits of him, gnashing on his bones. The space between his brain swirled, and the itch of Marcus's laugh burned.

He'd seen Marcus smile with Ciaran's flesh between his teeth, and a strange, white ball floated in the center of his cleanly picked ribcage. The ball of light was faded, weak. Marcus, who'd somehow grown fangs and claws, skin covered in the dead chunks of Ciaran, saw the light trying to survive. Marcus flopped off his chair like a bloated fish and slithered to the remains. He picked around inside the carcass, nibbling bits of Ciaran's lungs and liver. Marcus even popped a testicle into his mouth like a gumdrop and sighed contentedly.

The small ball of grey-white light flickered. Marcus flicked the remains of Ciaran's heart out of the way and examined the orb, turning it back and forth between his claws. A look of realization had passed over his filthy features and half his mouth rose in a grin.

He took the ball to his table of tools, and set the shining, twitchy light on a metal plate. With a huge hammer, covered in chains and dried blood, Marcus smashed the little light, and it burst into a thousand pieces. They slowly burnt out like embers falling to the ground. Ciaran was now wholly and truly dead.

But when Ciaran blinked, he was still naked and covered in filth, lying unchained on the floor. In his entire life, he had never wanted a shower so badly. Ciaran tried to change positions, but it hurt too much to sit. His side ached from lying on the hard cement. Without many options, Ciaran settled for lying on his stomach. He wouldn't stay like that when Marcus came down again. Ciaran squeezed his fists and eyes shut.

Relieving the pressure from his side felt amazing, but he noticed the rest of the damage. His back was so raw most of the nerves were dead, his eye was completely swollen shut, and it throbbed with every heartbeat. Even Ciaran's feet ached from standing.

Ciaran turned his head away from the stairs. He immediately regretted the decision. The offensive, granite wall standing in front of his good eye was an unnecessary reminder that laughed at him. There were stains dripping from its surface.

Ciaran struggled to sit up and move away, but nausea gripped his stomach with iron hands. The heave of his stomach almost broke his ribs and the taste of bile filled his mouth. There was nothing to come out.

He was drenched in sweat and crying when it finally stopped. Ciaran was too weak to care about anything, and the realization passed through him like air from a freezer. On his hands and knees, Ciaran crawled to the darkest corner of the room. The longer he was awake, the more his senses picked up things he wanted to ignore. The acrid musk of male sweat, the sour stench of Marcus's excretions.

He would die down there, but not for a very long time.

Ciaran didn't want anyone to find him. He wanted nothingness. The lyrics of an old song trickled through his mind. . . . Something from the time before her. Her name was even in them. Oceans and destiny. Disappearing under the tide. *The Great Below.*

In fashion with the torture, Ciaran could still picture her. He couldn't bring himself to even think her name, but her face burned his retinas. She hated him; she had left him for good reason. Ciaran vaguely remembered being mad at her. It didn't seem important anymore. . . . *Would she come? No. Don't.*

Ciaran coughed. He hadn't spoken for a long time. His throat was raw and dry. Searching the room for water, he found nothing. Then, it occurred to him, the table of tools was just above his head.

Ciaran shook so hard he could barely stand, but he made it.

He could kill himself with a dagger, right here and now. He would be done with it. It was gone, however. The majority of the items were awkward or too large to hide from Dentry. The small, metal rod that lay near the edge, however, was something. It would have to do. Ciaran fumbled for the rod, his depth perception was awful. As soon as the device was in his hand, Ciaran collapsed onto the floor. His arse bones, not to mention his arse itself, hit the concrete and the tender area stung. . . .

The floor above him creaked, sending clouds of tan dust into the damp air. He was coming back. . . .

The thought was quickly followed by the slamming of shoes on the stairs.

Ciaran did his best to cover himself and conceal the metal stick. He placed the rod between his thigh and calf, squeezing it in place. He kept his eyes on the floor and prayed that Marcus just wanted to beat him.

"No, it's not Marcus." Roger stood over him, and his shadow was elongated from the single light behind him. The blackness ate up Roger's form, and the temperature around him dropped.

"Your demon friend." Roger crossed his arms over his chest. "What is his race?"

"Haven't we . . ." Ciaran's voice was a raspy crackle of consonants, "done this before?"

Roger bent at the knees and sunk down, balancing himself on the balls of his feet. "Mr. O'Connor, you understand that you *will* die here. Yes?"

Ciaran nodded with a glare.

"Mr. Dentry will drag it out as long as possible. He will make sure you suffer for days, weeks if he can, before he lets you expire. I, on the other hand, am willing to end your painful existence quickly."

Roger stood back up and turned to the table. He let his fingers run across the metal supplies.

"Tell me what race he falls under, and I shall end all of this. I can also assure you that Mr. Romanov won't suffer. If, however, I must figure it out myself, I cannot guarantee that arrangement. This is a one-time offer."

Ciaran went with the truth. "I don't know."

"Surely you—"

"No. I never asked." Ciaran let his head fall back on the wall.

"Suit yourself." Roger headed toward the stairs and paused with his hand on the railing. "This didn't save her. You understand that, don't you? You've just given him a new obsession, and you know how he treats his obsessions."

The slap of his Italian loafers lingered long after Roger had left. Ciaran shook harder as he thought of the car and the girl driving it.

He could see her hair blowing, the tires spinning as the sun set slowly. A cloud passed over her sun, and her face was cast in shadow. The car disintegrated, falling away to reveal a cement floor. She was naked, bleeding, and cold. She was here.

He blinked and it was gone.

Ciaran burst out into one gasping sob. He squeezed the contraband weapon so hard his hand shook, and his knuckles threatened to stab out through the skin. Ciaran didn't plan on living long after his next visit from Marcus.

But Marcus would die before he did.

When the ground shifted above him and sent more particles of dust raining down, Ciaran tried not to move and saved all the strength he had left for Marcus. Ciaran heard his blood in his ears, noticed the pulse in his demolished eye. Vision was still a skill he was having trouble with, so Ciaran squinted.

Suddenly, he was in a cold sweat, feverish when another delusion claimed him.

Before him, standing in a pool of rotting blood, Ciaran could see Lucifer laughing at him. His face was distorted, but his eyes were clearly Marcus's. Massive ram horns spilled out of his forehead and curled back. He had a gaping mouth of tiny, sharp teeth, all of them yellow and decayed. Lucifer—Marcus —was large and had stubby goat-legs.

He chewed on a beautiful woman with silver-streaked hair.

Ciaran's heart crunched. When she was nothing more than a blood stain, Marcus, in the form of his idol Lucifer, beat his massive wings, but he was frozen in her blood.

Ciaran recognized the scene from Dante's *Inferno* and it snapped him back to his body. The tale was so old, but Ciaran got the impression it was written about Marcus. The levels each a layer of the crimes he was guilty of: wrath, violence, lust, greed. There would be no tragic hero in this tale though, no purgatory, no paradise. No redemption for a fallen warrior, only two murderers killing each other.

What will happen after? Ciaran heard the voice of his thoughts so loudly in his head. He had thought so little in such a long time. He dreamed, had delusions, but he hadn't talked with himself. The answer was, of course, very simple. Marcus would either kill him, or Ciaran would kill Marcus and then himself. Somehow.

The idea seemed pleasant. Ciaran was so tired, so fucking exhausted, unconsciousness in any form sounded amazing, but most definitely, a permanent one. Right now, he was in Marcus Dentry's basement and under his thumb again, his escape meaning absolutely nothing, and death seemed like a fitting reprieve.

Ciaran thought of the people in the world and imagined them looking into the mirror with disgust. Humans, demons, whatever, they were all messed up creatures: all an experiment gone wrong. Cells had divided one too many times, and instead of all this amazing brain power being good for the world, they were a plague that ravaged and consumed everything in their path.

The blackness of the world *was* the world. It was a sick and dying organism that would soon be burnt out by the sun, but not soon enough. All the little pieces, all the people, knew they had to go during those times they looked in the mirror and saw nothing. They saw only a void that pulled in horror and filth and disease and pain.

They saw the truth. We'd all thought it, and then shied away, but it was the truth. We are pitiful excuses for life. If you'd believed that you were ugly, you were right. If you believed you were stupid and useless, you were right.

Ciaran wished to be rid of the disgusting mass that was his existence, and all he had to do was wait. *We die to make room, and it has to be that way,* 'cause *we are a fuck-up that needs to be wiped clean so a new fuck-up can take our place.*

The sound of the basement door opening echoed. This was Ciaran's chance.

He gripped the small, metal rod and balanced on his knees. Ciaran couldn't let himself get too excited, however. There was one final outcome for today, and he needed to prepare for that.

The dark figure that came down the stairs walked with a swagger, and the smile on his face was pure avarice. Mr. Marcus Dentry could smile all he wanted, Ciaran was going to kill him or die, both of which would piss him off. That made Ciaran slightly happy.

"Good afternoon. How is my pet doing?" Marcus stood just past arm's reach with his hands in his pockets.

He nodded at Marcus in response. Ciaran was afraid if he spoke, he wouldn't be able to hold back the anger boiling inside.

"Good." Marcus turned to grab a pair of cuffs off the table. "I thought we would continue our experiment."

This was his chance.

With a hard shove, Ciaran released the energy he'd stored in his legs. He ran to Marcus as fast as his stiff legs could carry him, raising the rod over his head and leveling it at Marcus's temple. The metal gleamed, and Ciaran focused on driving the blunt end of the device directly between Marcus's hairline and his eye.

He moved four steps when he stumbled. The ground under his feet seemed to move further away, and Ciaran fell at Marcus. He was louder than planned, and Marcus turned as Ciaran's bare feet hit the cement. He'd pictured the metal rod smashing into Marcus's temple, then bashing the rod as many times as it took into his head to kill the bastard. That did not happen.

As Marcus turned and grabbed for Ciaran's wrist, the angle of the rod changed. Now, the pointed end was facing upward, and the last of Ciaran's strength abandoned him. Marcus gripped Ciaran's wrist, and in a desperate attempt to inflict any damage, Ciaran stopped fighting. The skinny end of the rod shot up and smashed the bottom edge of Marcus's jaw. He bit his lip in the process and a drop of bright, red blood dripped onto his fine, Italian suit.

As soon as Ciaran released the tension in his arm, the rest of his body decided to join in. Marcus glared down at him, kicking Ciaran and slamming his body into the dirty concrete. He kicked and kicked until Ciaran spat blood.

"You fucking whore!" Marcus leaned down and pulled Ciaran up by the hair. "This cost five-thousand dollars!"

Leave it to Marcus to own five-thousand-dollar suits.

Ciaran grabbed at Marcus's grip on his hair. It did nothing to stop him from shoving Ciaran's face into the granite wall. The spikes bit his flesh with tiny, rock teeth. The pain was disorienting, and Marcus had his arms and legs bolted to the wall in seconds. Ciaran was helpless against the binds and the lashing that was sure to come.

Marcus went straight to the longest whip. The strikes were gargantuan blows that nearly split him in half. The end of the whip had tiny metal balls sewn into them. They punched him and stole his breath.

"You, pathetic waste."

Slash.

"You were mine."

Slash.

"How dare you betray me?!"

Slash. Slash.

Ciaran could barely breathe and blood poured from his reopened wounds. When would he just die?

"You will never know the amazing things I could have given you!"

Marcus hit the back of his legs and Ciaran jerked forward into the wall. The force made the skin on Ciaran's face split open.

"You will never know anything ever again."

Marcus would throw out his shoulder if he kept whipping Ciaran with no focus. After a moment, he seemed to realize that. The strokes became slower but much more accurate. Each blow landed in the same spot as the last. Each blow made his ribs ache and forced Ciaran to cough out air.

Time seemed to slow, and the blows, the lashes, were years long. The spaces between eternities of white-hot needles were blinks, mere heartbeats. Ciaran wasn't standing anymore but hanging from numb hands. The gasps he tried to take burned. When he did exhale, he coughed blood. Ciaran choked on it.

"That's right, Laoch Dubh."

Marcus struck him between the legs.

"You wish that you had been more accepting, now!"

The sting in his balls sang and he gagged. He was flipping channels between unconsciousness and the dreaded clarity of pain.

Dentry grabbed a stout club.

The attacks were like getting hit by a truck. Marcus assaulted his ribs and legs. Ciaran could feel the bones bruise and imagined his skin darkening to a black-purple. He coughed out more blood, and his chest was heavy. Soon, Ciaran would be dead.

The sweet black nothingness hung over his head, and Ciaran saw stars in it. The Gaelic words of his mother filled his head. *Briseadh agus brú ar do chnámha!* A breaking and crushing of your bones!

"Sir," Roger stood on the stairs, "we have guests."

The beating stopped, and Ciaran fell into the granite wall, barely noticing the spiky texture.

"Who?"

Marcus turned and glared at his second. Ciaran watched, somehow still conscious.

"The other targets." Roger raised a brow and walked back upstairs.

Marcus's eyes gleamed with evil glee. He tossed the club aside and drew even closer to Ciaran. Gripping his naked, tender flesh, he squeezed, and Ciaran managed to bellow in agony.

"This is going to be so much fun." Marcus twisted his hand, causing a bit more pain, and then left.

Something inside Ciaran felt more awake suddenly, powered by dread. When he heard the commotion above him and the familiar scream, Ciaran's stomach fell through the earth.

Hope.

TWENTY-TWO

Whatever pressed against her back was cold and sharp. At first, Hope thought it was a bed of nails but realized she was standing, chained by her wrists and ankles. They hurt terribly, more than they should for only a few moments in chains. As consciousness slowly floated to the surface, everything hit her.

The shock would've been enough to steal Hope's breath, but the heavy, throbbing ache in her ribs sealed the deal. She knew her torso would hurt from the kicks she received, but this was vastly more intense. It was like she'd been beaten for hours, and just as the thought occurred, Hope remembered where she was.

As she jumped awake against a granite wall, the chains rattled. The room was dark, and her surroundings came into focus slowly. Hope could make out two tables, a set of stairs, and some tall, upright figure just in front of her.

"Finally." Hope recognized that voice. "You know, Ms. Turner, it is quite rude to keep people waiting."

The back of a man's hand struck her cheek and made Hope bite the inside of her lip. Her eyes burned, and she spit blood onto the floor.

"And chaining a person to the wall is what?" Hope glared at him. Even in the shadows, Marcus Dentry's eyes stuck out in the dark like a rat's.

Marcus said nothing but turned to the table that faced her vertically. He pulled a cord above it and light exploded into the room. Hope had to blink several times before the red and green dots left her eyes. It was definitely a basement, and on the table to her left, malicious metal tools gleamed.

Hope swallowed. Marcus stood at the other table, and she was afraid to look. But she had to.

Ciaran was bolted to the table. Hope's mouth fell open, and no matter how she tried to hold them back, tears rained from her eyes. *No, no, no, no, no . . .*

He seemed to bleed from everywhere. So many cuts and bruises and slashes, and he was barely breathing and filthy. Worse, Ciaran seemed so much smaller, thinner, even after a few short days. Hope was nauseated and furious, and she felt all of Ciaran's pain. She couldn't stop sobbing. She'd traveled light years to get to him. He was so close, just a few feet away, and he was dying.

Hope fought against the binds, screaming at Marcus in guttural shrieks. Ciaran barely moved. She yanked and jumped and twisted to break free, but it did nothing. *Shendara curse Marcus! Fucking hell! Damn it! This can't be happening. I can't lose him.* She needed to reach him.

"Ciaran."

He roused at the sound of her voice.

"Hope . . ." Ciaran rumbled a dry crack of noise that cut her heart like a dull blade.

Hope cried harder, hot, angry tears that left tracks down her face. The sound of the rattling chains was ceaseless because she wouldn't stop fighting them. She pulled them harder, and mortar dusted slightly around her.

"Let him go, you son of a bitch!"

Marcus laughed. "If you think I will ever listen to a disgusting demon whore, you are sorely mistaken."

Marcus walked to the table of implements and picked up a club.

"You," Marcus came back to slap her, "have taken something that does not belong to you."

Dentry walked over to Ciaran and raised the club up over his bruised ribs.

"Don't, please, don't do this," she begged.

"This is mine." He struck Ciaran's ribs and she yelped with him.

"What is this, now?" Marcus repeated the action. They both hollered. He looked back and forth between them.

"Stop this you piece of shit!" Hope screamed.

"You do not feel pain." Another strike. "What happened?"

It got harder to lift her head, so Marcus pulled her up by her hair. She just glared at him. When he shook her head, Hope spit in his face, and he struck her again.

"This is truly remarkable. I thought I would just have to beat you for my own pleasure but now, you feel it, you feel his. How?"

Hope said nothing.

"No matter. It appears I can kill two birds with one stone." Marcus left her to hang from the chains.

He struck Ciaran with the club over and over, laughing as they both flinched. Ciaran's consciousness was a miracle and a curse. Hope didn't know how long she could last and didn't have any clue what effect this would have on the baby.

"You fucking son of a bitch! Get away from him, you fucking prick!"

Spit flew out of her mouth as Hope continued to struggle against the chains. She was a fuming engine of fury, and Marcus would die in her hands. Ciaran was in pain everywhere, but behind it was a powerful exhaustion that made his eyes burn and his headache. Hope knew he was hanging on by a thread. *I won't lose you. I won't lose you, damn it!*

"This is quite fun. I wonder how sensitive this new gift really is." Marcus placed the club back on the table.

"Where to start this little experiment?"

He ran his hands over the various tools.

"Ahh, this should do nicely." Marcus picked up a nasty looking spur, the tines especially sharp.

When he pressed the small, metal wheel into Ciaran's flesh, the sensation didn't register, at first. There was a faint prickling, but it went in and out of her range. Ciaran would jerk and crack unwanted smiles. It must have tickled, and Hope couldn't feel that. Marcus pressed harder using his pointed finger to grind the tiny teeth into Ciaran's flesh. Hope felt it bite Ciaran's skin like so many bugs feasting. It made her grind her teeth and squirm.

"Fascinating."

Marcus went back over to his torture devices. He picked up something that looked homemade, a custom designed implement of heinous perfection. The metal contraption looked like a tiny rake with extendable teeth.

"Do you have to own the same body part to feel it suffering?"

Marcus dragged the barbs across Ciaran's most sensitive skin. They both gasped and hollered.

"Apparently, not." Marcus walked to her, studying her face. "Tell me, what is that like? What does it feel like on your end?"

Hope struggled to glare at him. Damn him, damn Marcus Dentry to the blackest of hells.

"Well?"

"Just pain, you sick fuck."

Hope knew she would pay for it, but it kept the bastard's attention on her, instead of Ciaran. Marcus slapped her and then quickly landed a punch on the opposite cheek. Panic raked across her as Hope realized he could've struck her stomach. She couldn't show her concern. This had to stop, soon. If Marcus started to pay more attention, he would see she was distinctly rounded.

Ciaran was nearly unconscious, and when Hope strained, she could see his torso darkening. His ribs were definitely broken, and his skin was turning purple and yellow with contusions.

"Ciaran . . ." Hope stared at his face. She wanted to see his eyes flutter open, even for just a second.

"Stop that." Marcus punched her in the face again, circling around them like a vulture. "I really do not understand what he sees in you. Perhaps a closer look is in order."

Marcus procured a knife from the table. As he came up to her and paid more attention, his eyes widened when they fell on her stomach.

"What is this, now?"

He lifted the hem of her tank and placed the blade against the soft cotton. He wasn't careful with the dagger, and as he cut the shirt in half the knife nicked her sternum. Hope hissed in a breath, the burn from the cut at odds with the cold air around her. In a quick set of flashes, Marcus cut off her bra. With Hope naked from the waist up, Marcus inspected her like a critical art patron, smiling at her breasts.

"Put on a little weight? I honestly did not believe you could become pregnant. Does Ciaran know you have been sleeping around?"

Marcus grabbed her throat and squeezed. Hope fought against his hand for oxygen.

Between gritted teeth, Hope struggled to speak. "It's his, moron."

Marcus's eyes went wide, and the whites seemed to expand. Veins in his forehead and neck stood out in stark lines. His brows narrowed, and he squeezed tighter on her neck.

"You slut. He is mine. Mine! After I am finished with him, I am going to gut you and watch as that abomination dies, taking you along with it."

The last of his words were whispered in her ear, and Hope fought against the rising bile in her throat.

"No." Ciaran sounded like an eighty-year-old, croaking as he fought his binds.

His skin was a hollow, greyish white. He needed a hospital and food. Somehow, Hope had to break out of these fucking cuffs and get to Gallo.

"What?" Marcus's voice was utter disgust as he dragged his blade under her collarbone, "I see nothing worth any amount of devotion or kindness. I am so disappointed in your performance and allegiance, Ciaran. Do you know what I do with tools that no longer serve me? I dispose of them."

Marcus walked to Ciaran, and time slowed to a crawl. She watched as Marcus took off his belt and sauntered behind the table where Ciaran lay. Hope thought she screamed, but her ears weren't working. She struggled with the chains, jumping and yanking, and still, she heard nothing. Marcus wrapped the belt around Ciaran's neck and pulled it tight. His eyes popped wide, his face turning red.

Then something dusted onto her knuckles and forearms. After days of a large man fighting against them, and now her, the chains were loosening. Hope pulled harder, practically leaping in place. The metal cuffs dug into her wrists, and she bled. She wasn't moving fast enough. Even as time felt slowed, she was slower. The crushing pain of Marcus's belt kept Hope from taking deep breaths, so she had to force air into her lung with tiny gasps.

Ciaran was slipping, and Hope heard the last conversation they had echoing in her head.

"I don't do relationships."

"I am sorry, but no. I liked the sex but that's all it was. . . ."

"Ciaran, fuck off!"

"I'm done. . . ."

Hope dripped angry tears on the floor. She'd just been scared, but the fear of losing Ciaran was like acid. It crawled over and under her skin, black bile that threatened to consume her and leave nothing behind. Hope's baby kicked deep inside her womb. *I can't lose you.*

The belt made squeezing, leather noises. Ciaran's throat was trying, but the pressure was unfathomable, Marcus's grip crunching the cartilage of his throat. Hope saw the mad glint in Dentry's eyes as he murdered her *jabalv.* Still, she fought against the chains.

But it was too late.

When the pain reached gargantuan proportions, Ciaran jerked, and a final puff of air fled his mouth. Hope felt nothing. Absolutely nothing, not the chains, not him, not her stomach, Hope was completely numb.

The scream Hope released made all the sound return. Marcus looked over and smiled. She wasn't sure if it was the adrenaline, the fury, or the weak mortar, but Hope tore her arms free of the walls. With the table within reach, Hope grabbed the keys for the shackles and unlocked her legs. She stepped free of the wall, staring at Marcus. He was frozen in place, eyes as wide as saucers.

Hope walked to him and felt nothing. The room wasn't long, and it only took her a few strides to reach Marcus. His human shock was no match for her speed. In one clean motion, Hope snapped his neck, grabbing his head and twisting it the wrong way, the crack echoing in the concrete room. His body fell to the floor, wearing its head backward.

The adrenaline was gone as fast as it came, and Hope slumped to the floor. On her hands and knees, Hope scrambled over to Ciaran. She pulled him down from the table as gently as she could and knelt next to his head, putting her hands on his face.

"No, no, no . . ."

Tears fell onto his face. Hope was lost in her head. She had no idea where to go or how to go. She shook her head.

Hope put her lips on his, tilting his head back. *Basic CPR. Start there.* Hope watched Ciaran's chest and saw it rise with her effort. She compressed over his heart, pumping his blood for him.

"Open your eyes."

More pounding and breathing for Ciaran.

"Open your eyes."

Two. Breaths. More. Compressions.

"Open your eyes, Ciaran. Please, Damn it. Open your eyes."

Breaths. Compressions. Tears.

Hope made a fist over his heart. *Pound. Pound. Pound.* She felt nothing.

"Open your eyes!"

Hope was screaming and sobbing. The halves of her shirt hung open and the wound on her chest dripped a stream of blood. She would've ripped out her heart and given it to him if it would've helped.

"Open your eyes!"

The orderly compressions were gone, and Hope beat furiously on Ciaran's chest.

"Damn you! Open your eyes!"

Hope pounded and put her forehead to his. "Open your eyes. Please . . . I love you. Come back."

Ciaran gasped.

Hope was about to hit him again when she realized he'd moved. She saw his eyes struggle to open and look at her.

"Ciaran!"

He took ragged gasps as his face turned from blue to pink. Hope sobbed all the harder as the pain from Ciaran returned to her body. She held his face in her hands, her forehead pressed to his.

"Ho . . . ope . . ." Ciaran tried to say her name, his breathing raspy.

"Shh, we have to get you out of here."

A look of fear blazed across Ciaran's eyes, and they darted around the room.

"He's dead."

Ciaran stared at her in shock, and slowly shook his head.

"I'm going to try to get you up." Hope pushed her hand under one of his arms and began to lift him to his feet.

They both gasped, and Hope dropped to a knee as the pain from his ribs and back kicked into them like a gunshot.

"I—"

"What did I say? Save your strength. We're going to Gallo."

Ciaran looked around the room again.

"It's okay. He's really dead." Hope ached everywhere and absolutely loved it. "Don't ever do that to me again."

Ciaran nodded just before he passed out.

Hope got Ciaran upstairs. Apparently, Roger was long gone. He either saw the scene or had other plans. He would be tomorrow's problem. Hope leaned Ciaran against a couch on the floor.

"Just hang on. I have to get Dimitri." She kissed him, and he moaned in pain. "Ow. Sorry. I'll be as fast as I can."

She dashed back to the basement and searched for a second door. Hope found it and kicked it in. The room was pitch-black, and she groped in the darkness for the switch.

"Hope?" Dimitri's hands were chained far apart, and he was sitting on a dirty floor.

"Hey. Are you okay?" She went over to his hand with the key she'd stolen from the torture table.

"Am I okay? What the hell happened?" Hope released his hands, and Dimitri rubbed his wrists. "I just woke up."

"Marcus is dead."

"Ciaran?"

"He's alright, for now. We need to get him to Gallo, fast." Hope helped Dimitri to his feet.

"Hope, what happened?"

"Not now, we need to go."

Dimitri didn't argue. They ran up the stairs and got Ciaran into the car.

Everything moved at light speed, making up for the slow down earlier. They flew down the road, Dimitri behind the wheel, and Hope with Ciaran's head in her lap. He could barely remain conscious, fading in and out. She stroked the side of his face. Hope wanted to hold him closer, but her swollen belly took up too many inches.

His breathing was labored. The wounds on his back were dried, but filthy. They had to be disinfected. His whole body did really. Hope stared down at his face. How long had they been in the car, years or minutes?

Ciaran started shaking. Hope tried to rub his arms, but he wouldn't stop.

"Shit. Dimitri the shock's getting worse." At her words, the car punched forward. "Did you get a hold of Gallo?"

"No. Here, try him again." Dimitri tossed her his phone.

Hope caught it and punched in the number Dimitri yelled back to her. The ring in her ears went on forever, and then the phone went to a generic voicemail. Hope hung up and called again. After three times, the line picked up.

"Ugh. Hello?" Hope forgot it was the middle of the night.

"Gallo. It's Hope. Ciaran is badly hurt. We need you to meet us at the house, now." Hope listened to him shuffle around on the other end. "I'm not sure . . . he's going to make it. I already had to perform CPR." Her voice barely broke through the receiver.

"You did well. Now, I'll stay on the line with you to coach you through this." She heard him close a door. "What are his injuries?"

"He stopped breathing. Marcus strangled him with his belt." She fought back the urge to cry. "I think his ribs are broken. Marcus beat him with a club. He's been down there for days."

Gallo was quiet, and Dimitri looked back at her in the rearview mirror. His face was drawn into a grim mask.

"Anything else?"

"He's covered in cuts and slashes."

"Are any of the cuts bleeding?" A car started on Gallo's end.

"Not really. He's really cold."

"That's common. Do you have anything to wrap him in?"

Hope looked around the POS car. On the floor was an emergency kit. *How have we never seen this before?* There were flares, a seatbelt cutter, an orange safety triangle, and low and behold a silver blanket. Hope pulled it to her and wrapped it tightly around Ciaran. The blanket was like plastic and rustled loudly.

"Done."

"Good. Now, you said he injured his ribs?"

"Yes."

"Okay. This is going to be hard, but I need you to gently feel them to see if any of them are angled into the lungs."

Hope touched his chest with her fingertips. Internally, she couldn't feel anything that indicated a punctured lung.

"I don't think so. His back is worse."

"Where exactly? Be as specific as you can."

"Over his kidneys and on his side under the ribs."

"Damn. He may have lacerated his spleen. Tell Dimitri to bring him straight to the med suite and try not to move him too much."

"Okay." Hope squeezed Ciaran's hand. He was completely unconscious now. "Stay with me. Don't die, dammit."

She leaned in close and kissed his forehead. They got to Ciaran's house a bit later; years later, months later, she didn't really know. Ciaran didn't get any better, but he didn't get noticeably worse. Hope saw Gallo waiting outside the door wearing scrubs and holding a large bag.

"I got him, Hope. Open the doors for us, okay?" Gallo took Ciaran from her and nodded at the door. Hope could barely step away, wanting to carry him herself, but she did and all but ran for the door.

The trip to the med suite was a blur of doors and orders from Gallo. They burst into the quiet space like an invading army. Gallo and Dimitri put Ciaran on the hospital bed, and Hope rolled over the metal tray.

"Thank you." Gallo opened his bag. "Dimitri take this IV bag and hook it up. Hope, take these scissors and cut four pieces of tape."

They both complied, immediately. Hope didn't even know Dimitri knew how to hook up an IV. When she looked at it, she could see the famous, red serum.

"That's . . .?" Hope asked.

"Yes, more of the serum. This is a highly concentrated form." Gallo had washed and gloved his hands. He took the tape from Hope and gestured for Dimitri to roll the bag of serum over to Ciaran's side.

After swabbing the back of Ciaran's hand with iodine, Gallo inserted the thin needle into Ciaran's bright-blue vein. The red miracle pumped into him, and a bit of color came back into his cheeks, but not enough. "Alright, Hope I need you to help me roll him, gently. Just get him up on his side so I can see his back."

Hope tried to be as gentle as she could. Gallo leaned in and inspected the cuts and whip marks. He swabbed the lacerations and gouges with more sterilizer. Ciaran hissed unconsciously. Gallo instructed Hope to lay him back down and looked up and down the rest of Ciaran's gashes, nodding to himself.

"None bleeding, good,"

"What about his spleen?" Hope barely managed to get her mouth working.

"Let's take a look." Gallo went over to one of the walls and pulled on a drawer handle. Instead of a single cupboard opening, an entire piece of the wall revealed an X-ray camera, at least that what she assumed it was.

"Don't tell anyone, but I may have procured the camera under less than legal circumstances." He was trying to break the tension.

"I won't."

"Good." Gallo unlocked the breaks on the bed. "Dimitri, Hope, you'll have to leave while I run it. There's only one protective vest."

Dimitri had to drag Hope out of the room, and frankly, she didn't actually remember leaving. One minute she was in the room, the next she was in the hall. Dimitri and Hope were both leaned back onto the wall. The air was thick with awkward silence.

"You okay?" Dimitri said.

"Not really. You?"

"Not really."

They stared at the floor and waited. Every single time Hope closed her eyes, she could see Ciaran lying dead on the basement floor, and every noise she heard from inside the med suite made her stand up and look at the door. Squeezing her hands into fists, Marcus's neck snapped between her hands. Hope stifled a gag and pinched her lips together.

"You killed him." Dimitri moved in front of her.

"What?"

"Marcus."

"Oh . . . yeah. I snapped his neck."

"Good." Dimitri smiled a tiny, cocked grin, but it slipped away.

"He can't—" But Hope couldn't finish.

The door opened and Gallo came out. His forehead was misty, and he was breathing like he just sprinted.

"You can come back in."

Hope followed Gallo and the pit of her stomach clenched. Ciaran's bed had been moved back into place but there appeared to be blood on his mouth.

"What the hell!?" Hope ran to Ciaran's side. He looked better, surprisingly better.

"He'll be okay. I'm sorry I had to keep you waiting so long, but I needed to make sure he didn't have any internal bleeding. The concentrated serum worked, and I didn't have to open him up. The spleen looked good under the X-ray."

"Really?"

"Really. I do have a few questions, though."

Hope couldn't stand anymore, and she fell into a chair which had somehow materialized behind her.

"What happened?" Gallo's voice brought her eyes up, "The damage to his . . . Well, it's extensive. Someone seriously injured him."

"I don't really know. He was missing a few days. Marcus had . . ." Hope trailed off and looked down at Ciaran's hand.

"Okay. This is a salve I made from the serum and a combination of some herbs. I need you to apply it daily. Also, we should apply some now, do you want to . . ." Gallo looked over to Dimitri.

"I'll go." Dimitri left, the door closing quietly behind him.

Gallo took Hope's hand and guided her to the sink. She scrubbed her fingers and palms till they were red.

"Okay, that's enough, Hope. Put these on."

Gallo handed her gloves and then the container of serum. They each took a place at Ciaran's side, and Hope stared at his face. Ciaran looked better, but he was still unconscious. And even with his eyes closed, he looked tired, beaten.

"I don't think—"

"I really think it will go better for him if it's you. He is out, but he can sense your presence."

Gallo rolled down the blanket which covered him, and Hope teared up. Ciaran's skin was mangled and raw. She could feel the slow ache and knew this would hurt immensely. Her hands shook the entire application.

When it was over, they were both sweating, Ciaran's a nasty, sick glow, and Hope's a steady mist on her forehead. Gallo packed everything up and checked Ciaran's vitals and supply of serum. Then, with no small amount of effort, he forced her out and took her into the larger room down the hall.

"Hope?" Gallo waved a hand in front of her face.

They were in a different room, now. They'd just come in, right? It was like Hope's brain was powered by a very tired hamster with a broken wheel. Her eyelids were heavy, and she was sluggish. Was Gallo talking?

"What?"

"I said I should check you out, too."

"Me?"

Hope had entirely forgotten about her chest. The wound was small, though, and the bleeding had stopped a long time ago. She supposed it would have to get cleaned but Gallo seemed so worried about it. It was just a cut.

"I'm fine. I don't—"

"Aside from the obvious bruises and the laceration on your chest, I think you need to tell me about that." He looked down at her stomach.

"Oh."

"Are you . . .?"

"Yes."

Gallo placed his black medical bag on another rolling metal tray. Ciaran must have a bunch of these, she thought. Hope couldn't remember him grabbing the bag or sitting down in the chair. She looked around her. Hope struggled to swallow.

"Hey, you okay there?"

Gallo turned around to face her and wore a stethoscope.

"Yeah. What are you—?"

"I just want to have a listen, okay?"

Hope nodded. Gallo seemed to be interrupting her a lot, but she didn't have the energy to care.

"You didn't seem this big a couple of days ago when I saw you." Gallo was asking the question without asking it.

"I know. I'm only like a week along. Do I look huge?" Hope was sure she did.

"No, not at all. Sure, bigger than most would, at this point, but not like your full term or anything."

Gallo made her take a few deep breaths and listened to her heart. He checked her pulse, grabbed a cuff from his bag and checked her blood pressure, he even took her temperature. "Thanks. Are you sure?"

"Yes, you look like you're entering your second trimester, but I'm assuming you don't have the same gestational period, considering."

"No, about two months."

"Wow, that's fast. To me, anyway."

"I sort of forgot about . . ." Hope started to shake. With all the activity and drama, she'd totally forgotten about herself. *I'm gonna be a great mom.* At that, she started to cry.

"*Shendara,* dammit! I can't fucking stop." Hope tried to mop up her face with her sleeve.

"It's the hormones. And with this kind of progression, probably a lot of them." Gallo pulled a tissue out of his bag and handed it to her.

"What don't you have in there?"

"An ultrasound. Which I would suggest you get. However, everything sounds good. Your blood pressure is a bit high, understandably, but I would avoid stress from now on. Let me just listen one more time and then I'll stop prodding at you."

Gallo put the head of the stethoscope on her little, rounded belly. He concentrated hard.

"Can you even hear anything?" Hope had never been to a doctor before.

"Yes of course." Gallo held the round end in place and handed her the earpieces. "Listen."

Hope tried to hear something through them. At first, all she could hear was her own breathing and the sounds of her blood in her ears, but then the faintest *whoomph* noise registered. "What was that?"

"Movement."

Hope's eyes widened, and damn her revealing face, but she just couldn't wipe away the grin. The father of the child in question was still healing, and she had no idea how she was supposed to help him, but here she was smiling about a little noise.

"Hope." Dimitri called over from the now open door. "What's happening?"

She thought about Ciaran's naked form lying underneath the flimsy blanket with his eyes closed tight. Eventually, he'd wake up, and she would have to tell him. *I think I'd rather eat glass.*

"He's stable. I just wanted to check on her and . . ." Gallo answered Dimitri, and they both looked at her.

She handed the stethoscope back and stood up. "I'm good, right?"

"Yeah, I would like you to come down to the free clinic where I can perform an ultrasound. But yes, everything sounds fine."

Hope put a hand on the flesh holding her daughter. She would go in, of course, but if she was honest with herself, she was a little worried what he would see.

"You don't have to go now but after things settle down a bit." He apparently read some of the apprehension in her face. "I'll leave you guys for now. Do you mind if I use one of the guest rooms? I don't want to go far."

"No, go ahead, man," Dimitri answered as they walked out of the larger room, and Hope stood in front of Ciaran's door.

Gallo smiled and left. Dimitri stood behind Hope, and the hall went quiet.

The sound of breathing filled the space. Hope opened the door finally and stepped inside. She pulled a chair over to the side of the bed and watched as Ciaran's eyes darted left and right behind his closed lids. This happened before, and Ciaran had barely survived. What would happen now?

"He didn't have you before."

Hope looked to Dimitri. "How did you know what I was thinking?"

"Because I was thinking it, too." Dimitri brought his eyes to her, and they burned. "I remember it. I was there through the whole thing. I hope it's different."

Dimitri nodded to her. "I'm going to go rest. Having your arms stretched out and listening to torture is really exhausting." He winked and Hope shook her head. "Will you be okay?"

"I don't know. We'll see."

Dimitri left her alone in the room. Hope pushed the chair closer to the bed so that the edges of both were touching. She brushed a bit of Ciaran's bangs out of his face. His color did look better and the sunken qualities of his eyes and stomach seemed to be lessening. *That serum is a miracle.* She laid her head down near his hand, which she held.

How many more times could she do this? How many times would he let her? She'd almost forgotten how they left things. Could he look at her the same after all that? Did she deserve it?

Ciaran was warm against her. Hope knew he would wake up soon enough, and they would have to . . . talk. She turned her head on the bed to look down at her stomach. As if on cue, her daughter kicked hard. She closed her eyes and tried to rest. All three of them would need it.

TWENTY-THREE

How could he have slept here? Marcus would be coming any second, and Ciaran didn't relish the idea of how he'd wake him. He was so warm here. That was wrong. He shouldn't be warm, but as Ciaran felt more and more awake, it was the only description that fit; groggy, sore, but warm. Ciaran noticed something round beneath his hand and movement beneath that. Ciaran jerked up.

Ciaran realized where he was. The room was white and clean and smelled like soap. He was in the med suite. But how? His pulse rocketed. Ciaran couldn't be back; it wasn't possible. A memory of Hope's face over his rushed to the surface. Frantically, he searched the room for her. His eyes couldn't focus right away, and then he remembered his hand. When he looked down and squinted, Hope slept soundly beside him.

"No." Ciaran lifted his hand quickly. He was back. How could he face her? How had she even found him? Panic tightened Ciaran's throat and made his heart try to escape his chest. His movements woke her.

"You're awake." She struggled to sit up, her eyes half closed, and she was so quiet.

Ciaran couldn't remember a time Hope spoke quietly. He never thought you could miss something that annoyed you, but he did now.

She shuffled herself around, a blanket tucked around her, and propped herself up on her elbows. "Do you remember how you got here?"

Ciaran shook his head. "No. I don't even remember you finding me."

The room was quiet, really fucking quiet. He couldn't think of anything to say. *What the hell sounds good in a situation like this? Hell, are there even situations like this?* There was one thing he was curious about, though. How did Hope get to him?

"How . . ." His voice was scratchy, and he had to clear his throat like five times. "How did you find me?"

Hope had been preoccupying herself with staring at the floor and fiddling with the blanket. When she looked up at him, he almost didn't recognize her. She seemed different. Her skin was flushed, and she almost looked . . . scared.

"That's a long story. Short answer? Dimitri helped."

"That is short."

And the silence was back. Dear god was there a more awkward moment in the world than this one? Hope stifled a shiver, and it made Ciaran's chest ache.

"I'm surprised you came."

There it was. He said it. He was surprised that she'd come. She'd no reason to.

"I know. Would you rather it not be me?"

"Sort of."

Hope's eyes went wide and then dropped again to the floor.

"Just that, I'd rather you not have seen me like that. It hurts deeply that you saw, that you had to be the one to take care of me. I would've rather it be . . . Well, no one. I, umm— don't want to talk about it."

"Okay."

Ciaran tried to blink away the moment, but each second his eyes were closed, he saw Marcus, felt Marcus. He swallowed down the rising bile and shifted higher in the bed to sit up. "Is Dimitri okay?"

Hope gave him a gentle smile. "Yeah, he's in his room resting. He was really great. Got us here in that crap car like lightning."

"That sounds like him. And you?" Ciaran gave her a once over. Her skin seemed a bit pale.

"I'm fine. Glad that you're okay." She squeezed the blanket in between her fists. "I, umm. . ."

"What?"

"You really . . . scared me. I thought you were gone. Actually, for a second you were."

"I don't remember."

Ciaran may not have a memory of that, but the previous events wouldn't fade. His pulse shot up. He had to blink to get the thoughts to recede back into the darkness.

"How are you feeling?"

"Fine," Ciaran lied.

"I mean, really?"

"Ha, caught me." Ciaran thought about a response and shrugged. "I'm tired and sore and angry, but I'm not dead. So, I guess there's that."

"Well, maybe, you should rest. I can leave you alone for a bit."

"I . . . I guess I wouldn't mind having a second to just lay here."

Ciaran watched as Hope nodded and knew she was faking her understanding. She wanted him to want her to stay. And it wasn't that he hated her and wanted her gone forever; it was just complicated. A moment to think about shit might help.

Hope went to get up, and then suddenly stopped like she'd laid an egg or something.

"What it is?"

"I . . ." She was frozen, her arms poised on the chair.

"Hope, really, one of us has to be good at talking, and it's not gonna to be me."

As she stared at the floor, Hope stood up, the blanket falling to the ground. Ciaran almost passed out. There was a round lump under her shirt. But how? It'd only been a few days. Hadn't it?

It took him a few heartbeats to form words, and Hope just stood there, waiting.

"What? How?"

"Well, we . . . you know. . . and then I . . ." Hope pointed to her stomach and pinched her lips together, her brow furrowing deep over her eyes.

"But how's that—"

"Possible? To be honest, I didn't think it was. I know it's fast. Chakals don't stay. . . Well, it just goes faster for us."

"I just, but you, I can't . . ."

Hope stepped toward him, and Ciaran shook his head. As she got close, he pushed farther away on the bed until he'd mistakenly provided her with enough room to sit. He kept shaking his head.

She tried to touch him, and Ciaran flinched. Oh god, he was sobbing and didn't care. He could barely breathe. How could he have let this happen? How could he have doomed a child to his parentage? He gripped his hair, closing his eyes tightly.

"Ciaran." Hope put her hands on his. "Ciaran, stop. It's okay."

"How the fuck is it okay? I may as well be dead for all the good I'll do as a father!"

Ciaran wouldn't talk about what happened, ever, but his mouth seemed to disagree. The damage was just too great to contain. "You need to go back to your clan."

"What?" She pulled her hands away.

"They'll know how to treat you there." Ciaran squeezed his hands into fists.

"I can't." Hope lowered her eyes to the mattress.

"What do you mean, you can't? You have to. You shouldn't stay with me." Ciaran knew Hope would do just fine on her own.

"Well, I can't go back. They won't let me. I've been shunned by them. They won't have anything to do with us." Hope put a hand on her stomach as she said *us*.

"Why?" Ciaran shook his head.

"Because of this." She gestured again, and Ciaran could see her knuckles were scabbed. "Part human. It's strictly forbidden in my clan. No interbreeding. The fact that I was supposed to carry on my father's genes made it worse. I had to leave."

"You tried to go back?" Ciaran had taken her clan from her.

"I did. They treated me like furniture. I wasn't a fan."

"I'm sorry. You could've gone back there, been safe, if it weren't for me."

"If I wouldn't have passed out on the drive, I wouldn't have gone there. Trust me. This has nothing to do with you. Don't let their backwoods thinking make you feel guilty."

"Even if I didn't, I would still have plenty of material to work with."

"Ciaran—"

"Just don't." Ciaran fell back on the bed and covered his face with his hands. "Do you have any idea how fucked up this is? I should never have slept with you. I was an idiot to risk it. No matter what you said. Obviously, it didn't mean anything. Here you are, infected with the tar I gave you."

Hope's eyes pinched in anger. "Ciaran—"

"Let me finish. This can't work, just like you said, and the last thing I want is to hurt you but ruining two lives is worse. I can't get out of this hole. Maybe before, but not now. Not after a second time. And it was so much worse. I'm so much worse."

Ciaran could feel the spin start inside his head. It came fast and hard.

He would shatter into a million pieces and kill two people with the shrapnel. He wanted to stand up, to walk around, but under the thin film of the blanket, he was naked. He couldn't stand to see himself.

"You're the same to me." Hope had such pity in her eyes it made Ciaran want to throw up. He turned away, pulling the blanket along like a tail.

"How can you even think that?!" Ciaran shook his head and pounded a fist down on the mattress. "Wait."

Ciaran hung his head down. He couldn't believe he was going to ask, to reveal the truth, but he had to make her see. Hope had to understand that he wasn't that man, anymore, a man at all, for that matter. There was no repairing his broken pieces now, no making it whole. Things were missing, some in the basement, some so smashed they'd turned to ash, whatever reflection was once cast, would never be seen again. His broken pieces were good for nothing and no one.

"What is it?" Her voice was steady.

"What did you feel? From me in Marcus's basement?"

"I felt your pain."

Ciaran turned around and stared straight into Hope's eyes. "Be specific."

"Why?"

"Do it."

Hope was quiet for a moment, her eyes pooling with tears. "I felt you get whipped. I felt you get beaten with a club until your ribs broke. I *felt* you die, choked to death."

There was no hiding her anger, but he had a point to make.

"Before then. What did you feel when you were close to me but not there?" he asked.

"More pain, Ciaran. More strokes of the flail."

"That's all?"

"It was enough."

"Not to understand. You only feel pain. Nothing else comes through to you. You can't understand the other sensations that can break a person." Ciaran looked away and gripped the sheets until his knuckles turned white.

"What are you talking about?"

"I wouldn't tell him. Where you were. He tried every type of pain he could imagine but still, I wouldn't tell him." Ciaran swallowed down bile. This would make her see.

"He beat on me, poured hot wax on me, cut me, but still nothing. If it'd ended there, if he'd let me die, but no. Said he had an experiment to try. Said it needed to be personal. He used my mouth before, but he knew it hadn't worked. There wasn't any sound from me, though. I didn't tell him, but my body gave in. Do you see now? You felt half of what happened. You didn't feel my own body betray me and give him what he wanted!"

Ciaran screamed, shaking Hope by the shoulders. "Do you fucking get it, now?! You need to leave!"

He couldn't breathe through the sobs. He shook Hope, trying to burn the truth into her. It was too much for his weak body and his heart pounded. The room was blurry to his leaking eyes, and he was hyperventilating.

It was all out now, and there was no joy in the clean slate. All he could think, all he could feel, was the burning of his flesh at his defiler's touch. He wanted to black out, to pull the plug on the relentless procession of graphic clips that ran behind his eyelids. The pit of Ciaran's stomach clenched, and he leaned over to puke bile onto the floor.

Hope placed a hand on his back so gently he could barely feel the pressure. "No."

Her hand stayed, and she pulled his face around to look at her. Her deep brown eyes were all tears. Ciaran tried to pull his face back, but she put both hands on either side of his head, wiping a thumb across his lips.

"*Mieklana*. I am so sorry. I'm so sorry for everything I said before and for taking so long to find you. I'm sorry I wasn't there, that I wasn't ready for this, and that I ran," She let the tears fall down her cheeks. "I've never felt anything before, and I got . . . scared and I ran. I'm so, so sorry."

"I don't know how to get to you. You're so far away. There's only darkness. I don't know how to get out. I don't know where you've gone, or where I've gone. I just . . ." Ciaran didn't recognize his own voice, it was small and slight like a child's, and Hope was practically in his lap. He could barely look at her face, but he didn't want to look away, either. He hurt everywhere, and the sign of their union was unavoidable, but he was so far away from them.

"We can do this, together. I do believe that, but I'm gonna need you here. This, all of it, is brand new to me. I don't know what to say that will fix everything and make it all better somehow. I do know that I won't spend one more day without you." Hope shook her head, the stubborn burn of her eyes and the grip on his head kept him still. "So much of this is my fault, too, but we're not going to solve anything dwelling on the past."

She slumped against him lightly, and Ciaran tensed. He was rigid, as she rested her head on his chest. He couldn't bring himself to hold her. *How am I supposed to do this?*

"She takes so much out of me."

Ciaran froze, his eyes wide, staring at the wall behind Hope. "What?"

Hope lifted her head, and a small smile sat crooked on her face.

"She." Hope put his hand on her stomach.

There was a large thrust under her warm skin. The child was alive, moving. "I have a daughter."

"You do. We do." She put her hand on top of his.

Ciaran hadn't been a part of a family in so long. "I don't know if I can do this."

"Try. Please."

Ciaran thought of the life inside Hope and looked at her face, it seemed so different than before. They were both different people, Hope stronger, him . . . broken. *Can I do this?* "Okay."

Hope moved closer to him. The pressure of her presence made Ciaran squeeze down on his spine. He was fucking skittish around the mother of his child.

"Damn it, Hope. This is so hard." Ciaran pulled away from her slightly.

She frowned.

"Fuck, I'm sorry. I just see it in my head when you touch me." Ciaran shook his head as his eyes involuntarily closed.

"Look at me," she said and Ciaran locked eyes with her. "I love you."

Ciaran's mouth dropped open. He never thought she'd say that.

"Hope . . ." He dropped his head to her chest and breathed her in. The smell of her was like nothing else. It was just Hope. *Just Hope.*

Ciaran heard her heart beating in his ear and the air flowing in and out of her lungs. He couldn't stop shaking. "It's like I'm still there, and this is the dream. It happened. I would see you and think I was out, and I'd wake up down there. He still has his claws in me."

"Marcus Dentry cannot hurt you, anymore. He's dead."

Ciaran sat back and looked at Hope with wide eyes. "You shouldn't have to clean up my messes, but thanks."

"He threatened someone I loved, nearly killed you. I'd do it again." Hope leaned in to hug him, and Ciaran was stiff.

"I wish this was easier. I can't stand this. I want to only think of you."

"Focus on me. Keep your eyes open and see that it's me."

Hope leaned back into him, making herself small in his arms. Ciaran saw her silver streak spread out across her back. It was her. It was truly his Hope.

"I thought I was dead. I was alright with it. But if I . . . I can have you again. . . ."

"You have me. I'm not going anywhere." Hope put her hands on his face. They were soft and gentle. She leaned close and kissed his forehead. She smelled clean and fresh, like rain. *Just Hope.*

"I love you, Hope. I love you. I love you. I love you."

Ciaran fell into her arms and laid his head above her belly. Deep into the sleeping home of his daughter, he whispered it again.

*

A month and a handful of days had passed, and Hope's belly grew more and more round with each morning. Ciaran got healthier and stronger and was even able to pick up his routine of sparring with Dimitri in the mornings. The nights after he'd returned were horrible. Terrible dreams of the pain and humiliation haunted Ciaran. Each time, Hope had been patient with him, as he remembered where he was. He'd go down to the gym and punch his way through the night until he was level, and she'd always be waiting, an understanding presence he could feel holding him up, but a black smudge still hung over him.

Ciaran could hug Hope, hold his hand over their moving daughter, on a rare occasion, let Hope rest her hand on his back, but nothing more. Each time he tried, the images of his torture came rushing forward to grip his throat like a vice.

They both knew it had to change. They loved each other, and yes, he still wanted her, but there had to be action. Ciaran never thought about how important sex was, but earlier in the relationship, it had helped them to connect and made him feel capable again. They needed that now more than ever.

So, he went to their bedroom with a strange, perfect solution. He just had to be strong enough to go through with it. Ciaran told Hope to meet him down there after she'd finished eating. He'd learned not to get between a pregnant woman and her food.

So, he waited.

Ciaran stared at the rope he held in his hands as he sat on the end of the California king. He tried to adjust in his jeans. It wasn't helping, and Ciaran knew it was because he was a nervous fucking wreck.

The yellow glow from the lamp made the blues in their room look dark and ominous like he was going to have sex in a horror movie. *Ah, fuck. I didn't need that image.*

Hope walked into the dark room.

"Hey, sorry. I ended up having to pee. Of course." She sat next to him smiling. "What's up?"

Hope was so beautiful. Even carrying their child, she'd never lost the devious gleam in her eyes and her body changed in the best ways; it was strong and healthy.

"I think I know how to fix, well, us."

"I wasn't aware there was something wrong."

"It's not like that. You helped me recover from the basement but there's still something holding me back from you. Something keeping me from . . . being with you."

Hope looked down at the floor. "I know, but there's no rush. If I made you feel—"

"I made me feel it. Being around you does the same thing to me it always has. I do want you. There's just a wall of anxiety that blocks me, but I do think we can get past it."

Ciaran turned to face Hope, and she looked down at his hands. "Is that what the ropes are for? Not sure the baby will appreciate restricted blood flow."

"They're for me." Ciaran's heart thundered in his ears. He couldn't make eye contact with Hope.

"Ciaran." Her concern bit.

"Hear me out." He brought his gaze to hers. "I want this. I want to feel you again, feel alive again. It's my head. I need to convince it that I'm with you, without letting myself run. I have to push past this. All at once. No pussyfooting."

Hope furrowed her brow. He could see her work it out in her head.

"Well, if you're sure. I want to help. I do. I just don't want to do something that will make it worse. But I have always wanted to take control for a change." Hope smiled at him sincerely.

Ciaran tried to smile back. The thing was he was terrified. Ciaran absolutely did *not* want to relinquish control, but that was the point. He was safe with Hope, and he had to force his unconscious to see that.

"Sorry. I was trying to break the tension."

"I know." Ciaran handed the bonds to Hope and stripped.

He hadn't been naked in front of her since the day she brought him back. He had to take his clothes off fast before he let the thought surface fully. Behind him, Ciaran heard Hope make a small noise. He turned around and saw her fighting back tears.

"Damn hormones."

"Is it that bad?" Ciaran had also never looked down.

"No. You look okay. It's there sure but not horrible. Really."

Ciaran swallowed and finally looked down for the first time since it happened. He was covered in scars, but if he was honest with himself Hope was right. Instead of a jagged buildup of tissue, Ciaran saw smooth, pink lines. He knew the serum Gallo used had saved that part of him, and he was more than glad. *Enough thinking.*

"I want you to . . . tie me up." The words were shaky.

Ciaran walked back to the bed and sat near the head behind Hope.

She had to turn to face him. "Ciaran. This feels wrong. You're stiff as a plank and not in a good way."

"Hope, please. I literally don't know how else to make myself stay put."

"I won't force you to do this." She blinked fast to whisk away tears.

"You're not."

Ciaran got up on his knees and put his hands on her face. He kept his eyes open but didn't hesitate. Ciaran pressed his lips to Hope's. It was their first real kiss in over a month. She was warm and clean. The velvet of her skin opening to accept his tongue. God, the feel of her. As Hope returned the kiss, and the old pull between them strengthened. Her hands went to his back and Ciaran held back a flinch. Hope leaned back breaking their contact.

She put her hands on his arms. "Better?"

"Yes. Don't stop, though."

She didn't and Ciaran let her trace her fingers around the curves of his muscles. They were hot and hungry, but she stayed slow.

Hope brought her lips to him in another kiss. As she straddled his lap, the swirling waves of her hair fell over his arms. She paused momentarily to lift her black nightgown over her head. Her pale skin glimmered in the soft light, and Ciaran traced her intricate tattoos with his eyes. She still left him in awe. He took in her bare flesh and realized how close they were to joining, she hovered inches above him.

His head spun with conflicting feelings. He was desperate to push his hips forward and lock himself inside Hope, but the memory of being an unwilling receiver crept up his spine. He shook despite himself.

"I—"

"Shh." Hope leaned him back to lie on the bed using kisses to distract him. A circle of rope formed against his wrist. Ciaran held Hope's eyes, and another circle formed over his other wrist.

With his arms secured above his head, the panic started to set in. Hope must've seen it because she planted another gentle kiss on his lips. She moved down his chest with them, landing on each scar. As she did, a brief flare of remembered pain shot through his brain, but the gentle caresses calmed his nerves. Even still, when she reached his groin, he tensed. She didn't stop there but the movement drew Ciaran's attention to himself. He was pleasantly surprised to see that he was, in fact, aroused by her touch.

"Hope." He didn't want her attention. He needed to remind himself who he was with.

A ring of rope now circled each ankle, and Ciaran couldn't move. The panic hit hard, now, and Ciaran pulled against the binds at his wrists. Hope straddled him, putting her hands above his heart.

"It's me." She kissed his mouth, then each nipple. Now, his heart beat fast for another reason.

Hope left enough slack in the ropes for Ciaran to sit more than lay, so he lifted himself closer to her. The bit of freedom made a world of difference. He did have control over this. Hope would do whatever he asked. He trusted her.

The thoughts in his head changed. Ciaran wanted more of Hope, and it started to be more powerful than the other emotions he experienced.

The feeling of Hope's fingers exploring his skin made Ciaran tingle. Everything about Hope and the room and the feelings were different than that other place. It was warm, not frigid, he was in a soft bed, and the look in Hope's eyes held only a love for him that Ciaran couldn't believe he'd earned.

Hope pressed Ciaran back down to the bed and lowered herself closer to joining him. Ciaran's hips jerked forward, and when he saw her glistening, he lost any remaining apprehension. The woman he loved, with a heart he thought was lost, long ago, was finally leading him out of the dark.

"Now. Before I tear free from these." The words came out in a growl.

Hope lowered down. At that moment, they were utterly connected, physically through their contact and the growing life of their child, and through their decision to persevere together.

They both rode out the emotions contained in the space, and suddenly, Ciaran no longer felt like a stranger living a life he almost remembered. The connection he thought he'd lost for good was back. He had his Hope back, and he was even getting himself back. They came hard and quick, but the moment between them would last far beyond that night.

Hope untied Ciaran, and he lay in her arms, a sprinkling of tears landing on her chest. "I thought I'd lost you, lost myself."

"You didn't."

"I guess not." Ciaran smiled against her skin and smelled the sweet, indescribable essence that was his Hope. "Thank you."

"That's what a . . . Well, it's what I'm here for."

"What was that?" Ciaran looked up at her, worried.

"Oh, no, I'm fine. I just . . . I don't know what to call my role in your life. For the Chakal, it's *jabalv*. The person who initiated the bond. But for you . . . what are you supposed to call me?"

"How about wife?"

Hope shot up and looked down in awe. "Did you just ask me to marry you?"

"I guess I did. That should have been more romantic, huh?" Ciaran bit his lower lip.

"Frankly, I'm just surprised you asked. I never thought . . . Wow."

"Is that a yes?"

She smiled so big Ciaran was convinced her cheeks would ache for days. "Yes!" She shook her head and pulled him into an embrace. "No dress."

Ciaran pulled back to give a classic puppy dog face.

"Ha! Fine. But no white, I hate white."

"Agreed."

TWENTY-FOUR

Ciona's little body squirmed incessantly. Dressing her was not a task for the weak. Neither was her birth for that matter. The grunts she made when Hope pulled the shirt over her small head were positively her father. Hope laughed. At this point, only a few months past the eventful day, Hope was just glad that her daughter seemed happy. Being burdened with the ability to feel pain, from her father and from Hope's own body, was certainly confusing to the baby. Ciaran had to be extra careful when in the room with her, but thankfully, now that she wasn't in the womb, the distance she could sense pain over was significantly reduced.

Hope sighed. If only that had been the worst part. She could remember the daily battle to get Ciaran to touch her. He was so frightened he might cause her pain or drop her, but the worst was the fact that Ciaran still felt like he didn't deserve a family. He tried to hide it from her, but it didn't work. Hope had gone into labor and then suddenly, she was here. Ciaran was so skittish it had made Hope want to scream. Their daughter had even gone without a name for a while because Hope refused to give her one without her father's input. But then, it happened.

One day when Hope had just about reached the end of her rope, she needed a break and handed Ciona to her father. Through his protests, the little beauty had looked up at his face, touched his hand, and said, "Dada." Ciaran was putty in that girl's hands ever since. Hope could remember the exact moment and smiled.

"Did she just?" Ciaran's face was white with shock.

"She did. And I'm not even mad that I wasn't her first word." Hope began to tear up.

"First! Holy shit."

"Ciaran, really, she just started talking, don't teach her shit or any curses for that matter."

"Sorry." He stared down at their daughter, who had so much of her father in her, and a smile crept across his face.

The baby chirped and giggled at him.

"Yeah, that's me. I'm your dada. Sorry about the rotten luck."

The girl just continued to smile and then reached out her arms in a big open V. Ciaran's face stilled, and he stared down quizzically. He brought her closer and her little hands grabbed each cheek and squeezed. The tiniest hug he'd ever received. Ciaran gasped a crying laugh, and Hope did the same. A tear fell onto her forehead, and Ciaran wiped it away with his thumb.

"Can we call her Ciona?"

"What?" Hope had assumed she'd be Baby forever.

"It was my mother's name."

Hope tingled with goosebumps and her tears flowed even more. She tried to wipe them away as quickly as she could, but Ciaran pulled her close and held her tight.

"Of course. I love it."

Ciona it was, and with their daughter named and cuddled between their bodies, she smiled and squirmed happily.

As if on cue, Ciona babbled something loudly as she almost rolled herself off the changing table. Hope sat her up, and the little grin on her face was all trouble.

"A bit like your mom, I see."

She gurgled a reply. Life would be so much easier when she could talk. Well, sort of. As the little stinker continued to wriggle about, Hope looked down at her shirt. Spit up, milk, sweat, some of her own food. Yeah, she needed to change. She set Ciona down inside the Pack 'n Play Dimitri bought them.

"Let Mommy change, huh?" Hope used a soothing tone in an attempt to stop the forthcoming wail.

She stepped into her closet, removing the horrendously dirty pajamas.

"Aye, please let her change."

Hope jumped. She smiled to herself and turned to face Ciaran who stood in the closet doorway. She leaned on one leg and let her arm fall to her side. His eyes glanced up and down her naked form, and Hope ate it up.

"It's not wise to sneak up on a demon, you know?"

"I'm willing to take the risk for this one."

As Hope walked to him, Ciaran pulled his shirt over his head. The flex of his muscles made her hot and hungry.

"You know, I'm supposed to be working out right now."

"I thought I'd help with that." Ciaran scooped her up and caressed her breast with his free hand. His grip was hard and his kisses animal. Hope gasped through her smile.

"Ugh." Ciaran slid a hand to the very slick part of her. "Bathroom."

Ciaran carried her to the cool room so they wouldn't wake their now sleeping child. He set her down on the counter and pulled his running shorts down. Hope barely had a chance to admire Ciaran's impressive erection before it was sheathed deep inside her. The mirror that hung on the wall to the side of them acted as a playback for their performance.

She watched Ciaran thundering into her. He met her stare in the mirror and smirked.

"Staring at me arse, I see."

"Always. It looks good when you move in and out of me."

Ciaran thrust harder. "Does it, now?"

They continued in a fierce rhythm until they both came in an unbridled wave. Ciaran set her legs down and pulled her in for a kiss.

"I'm going to hop in the shower. I don't want to be known as the *stinky*, crazy guy."

"Ciaran, you're not crazy. And if I remember correctly, even your therapist thinks that."

"She has to be nice; I'm paying her."

"Ugh, well, I'm sure Dr. Reynolds appreciates the shower, just don't be late."

"I'm good. My appointment's not for another hour. Now, if you'll excuse me."

Ciaran practically strutted as he got in the shower, and Hope smacked his ass. Just as the shower came on, Ciona began crying.

"And apparently, I'm going to heat up a bottle." Hope shook her head and grabbed her robe.

"Would you distract her 'til I'm out? I want to feed her."

"Sure." Hope blew an unseen but heard kiss and went to take the wailing, little stinker upstairs.

Epilogue

So much time had gone by, and still, there was no new information. Aside from the fact that Marcus was dead, there wasn't much to be grateful for. Dimitri was tracking yet another lead, and it wasn't looking good. He wanted a break, but Roger wasn't going to kill himself, and whatever that weird-ass demon was up to was still a mystery. In the kitchen, Dimitri could concentrate without the stuffy air of the study, but he'd have to go back there eventually. Hope came in and found him studying attacks at the breakfast table. He nodded when she went to the fridge but then put his head back down.

"Hi, Dimitri. How are you?" She was sarcastic as always.

"Hi, Hope," Dimitri put the papers aside, "I'm distracted. The attacks are getting worse."

"I know, but you need to give yourself a break. The point of moving in here was to pool our resources, not have you be strapped all the time." Hope plugged in the bottle warmer.

Ciona must be hungry, again. Honestly, Dimitri didn't know how Hope did it. He was so awkward with the baby.

She set Ciona down in her highchair, and Dimitri quickly avoided eye contact by glancing at the night lit grass outside. The trees and bushes were dark silhouettes against a lighter, navy sky. As his head turned, Dimitri caught sight of a pair of red eyes.

"What the . . ."

As soon as he blinked, they were gone. Dimitri shook his head. *Okay, maybe a bit sleep deprived.*

Hope looked over, confused. "Did you say something?"

"Nope."

"Okay. I'm serious, though. You need to rest. You look terrible."

"Gee, thanks. I'm fine." Dimitri thought about the eyes. "Actually, it might not be a bad idea. Ciaran go to his thing?"

"To therapy? Yes. You can say it, you know. It's not a bad word."

"I know. I'm just living in a constant state of fear that you're going to talk me into going."

Dimitri cocked a grin, and Hope dashed over to the bottle, probably to stop it from getting too hot.

"You helped me convince him. And it's helping. It could help you, too." Hope looked back over her shoulder and smiled. "You don't seem as bad, though, for good reason. But I'm sure if you ever did want to talk, Ciaran could get you in. Or you could just talk to him. He's becoming rather insightful. It's annoying."

Dimitri laughed, but he knew he'd never go. Hope didn't know what was going on in his head, not even Ciaran did, and he wanted to keep it that way.

"We're going upstairs. You should at least get a few hours of sleep," Hope said.

"Yeah, okay."

Dimitri left his papers spread out on the table and followed Hope up the long staircase. They separated at the top, and he walked to his room, flopping down on his mattress. He kicked off his shoes and took off his shirt. *Just a few hours.* As he rolled over onto his stomach, Dimitri could have sworn he saw the red eyes outside his second story window. Wow, he really did need sleep.

ABOUT THE AUTHOR

After graduating from college, I got right to work with my professional writing degree. I spent many years growing my skills with SEO content marketing while always finding time for my creative writing passion.

Now, I live in the sweltering inferno of Las Vegas and spend much of my time working as a freelance content writer for companies like CBR. When not hard at work, I typically wrangle alligators, otherwise known as my kids, and "nerd out" about Dungeons and Dragons.

Writing brings me nothing but joy, and I'm excited to share my love of words with you.

And don't worry, Book Two, Burn the Bone, is coming…

Follow me on Facebook, Twitter, Instagram, & TikTok as @rejohnsonauthor. Or on Tumbler as @theguildedtypewriter. If you leave a review or make anything to do with the book, which would be absolutely fantastic, be sure to tag me! I love interacting with my followers and sharing everything you guys do.

Want More of Newborn City?
Join the Demon Club on **Patreon**
Like **R.E. Johnson** on **Facebook**
Sign up for my **newsletter**
Rejohnsonbooks.com

CPSIA information can be obtained
at www.ICGtesting.com
Printed in the USA
LVHW091109221022
731316LV00009B/623